Michael, Waiting

Helen Inkster

Best wishes
H Inkster.
(Mo)

authorHOUSE

AuthorHouse™ UK
1663 Liberty Drive
Bloomington, IN 47403 USA
www.authorhouse.co.uk
Phone: UK TFN: 0800 0148641 (Toll Free inside the UK)
UK Local: 02036 956322 (+44 20 3695 6322 from outside the UK)

© 2021 Helen Inkster. All rights reserved.

No part of this book may be reproduced, stored in a retrieval system, or transmitted by any means without the written permission of the author.

Published by AuthorHouse 07/30/2021

ISBN: 978-1-6655-9184-3 (sc)
ISBN: 978-1-6655-9183-6 (hc)
ISBN: 978-1-6655-9192-8 (e)

Print information available on the last page.

Any people depicted in stock imagery provided by Getty Images are models, and such images are being used for illustrative purposes only.
Certain stock imagery © Getty Images.

This book is printed on acid-free paper.

Because of the dynamic nature of the Internet, any web addresses or links contained in this book may have changed since publication and may no longer be valid. The views expressed in this work are solely those of the author and do not necessarily reflect the views of the publisher, and the publisher hereby disclaims any responsibility for them.

"People were created to be loved. Things were created to be used. The reason the world is in chaos is because things are being loved and people are being used."

Introduction

This story is set in Scotland's capital city in a small, exclusive restaurant attended to by Michael, the acting head waiter, whilst his colleague recovers from illness. It is fortuitous that Michael is given this chance, as being a head waiter is one of his life's ambitions. However, his ambition is being hampered by him being still in the throes of grief and loneliness. His mother died the previous year, leaving this forty-year-old man completely alone in the world, having grown up with only her for company. He has no friends and very little in the way of hobbies. He likes to run to his work, and that is usually a six miles round trip. We follow Michael through trials and tribulations as he takes hold of his life, turning it around and creating new friends—and not without some drama and a few surprises. Pick up this book and enjoy his successes and sympathize with his failures as you absorb the story that is.

Chapter 1

Michael had opened the front door and left it ajar to let in the morning air. The cleaning lady was furiously hoovering the carpet, and the dust motes danced in the shafts of sunlight streaming into the front of the restaurant. Michael hummed a tune as he carefully polished the cutlery before moving on to the glasses. The sunshine gave everyone a sense of well-being, as the sun was not a frequent visitor to this part of the world.

A sunny day in Edinburgh is something to be thankful for, as the city is not best known for sunshine and cloudless skies. It is better known for the castle, the palace, and the old stone-built tenements rising to six levels, plus the rain and mist. Somehow it didn't seem to matter about the dreich weather. The city was so wonderfully full of places to go. However, it was the start of June, and the warmth of the approaching summer was beginning.

The tasks he was performing were very much routine. He was able to allow his mind to travel back into time and relive the sunny days he spent with his mother growing up in the outskirts of the city, being able to find places to go to enjoy the good weather. He remembered the days when he would run up and down the grassy steps in Comiston Park. He looked forward to a trip by bus to the zoo to watch the famous penguin walk. Allowed out and about from their pond, the colony of penguins would walk round the paths.

When his mother took the plunge and learned to drive, she bought a small car, and its arrival took them further afield. Michael enjoyed the weekend trips to North Berwick, a seaside town a few miles from

Edinburgh. His first trip across the Forth Road Bridge took them into Fife, making for an exciting day.

Sadly, his mother had died a year and a half ago, and the ache of grief and loneliness he experienced was still very much part of his thoughts. Although it was over a year since his mother was cremated, he was still wrapped up in grief. Having no siblings or father, he found himself quite alone. He was aware, however, that he was now beginning to remember the happier times rather than the dark place he had been in. Fortunately, he was of a stoic disposition, strong enough to park his feelings whilst carrying out his work responsibilities. He did start to be concerned that his work was possibly being affected and that he might lose any opportunity to be promoted should he just function and not excel. He needed very much to carve a life for himself and find ways of socializing and perhaps make friends. He could not countenance making his workplace the central place of his life; he needed more.

His workplace was a small, exclusive establishment owned by Olivia Black and normally assisted by her head waiter, James. Unfortunately, James was ill and for the time being unable to carry out his duties. Michael was head waiter and front of house manager, temporarily. The restaurant was buried in the heart of an upmarket part of the capital. It was surprisingly busy, given its location. Tucked away in the centre of Morningside, the Dhugall was able to keep the tables filled. The diners would start arriving in the early evening, taking advantage of a pre-theatre menu.

A short stroll along the road to the cinema or a few steps in the other direction took one to the theatre. Rarely would one be able to walk into the restaurant and find an empty table. It was a comfortable and nicely decorated establishment that could serve around forty diners.

Once the early theatre diners left for the various venues, Michael and his team would work at high speed to restore the restaurant to its normal pristine appearance, ready for phase two and the later diners.

Many years before, the restaurant had been a dwelling. However, a creative conversion in the lower ground floor, which was extremely well done, together with the serving of some of the best Scottish food in the area, assured its success. The decor was subtle, with full-length velvet drapes and paintings by local artists on the walls. On shelves were ornaments from Edinburgh's history and some interesting ceramics by a local potter. The restaurant had been named after Dougal Black, its founder. His son, the second Dougal Black, had taken up the reins when his father died. "Dhugall" is a Gaelic spelling of the proprietor's name and means *dark stranger*.

Sadly, Dougal junior passed away a couple of years ago, leaving his wife, Olivia, to carry on. After much thought and professional advice, Olivia decided to keep the restaurant going. Dhugall and Olivia had not been able to have children. As an intelligent woman, when it was obvious there would be no babies, Olivia decided to work alongside her husband. Olivia was responsible and involved with the administration of Dhugall. Her husband managed the front of the house. Together they made a formidable team.

Olivia missed him greatly. At first the early throes of grief had almost forced her to sell up and retire. She was now completely alone, mirroring Michael's life of being an only child and having no relatives to speak of. Without her few close friends and the restaurant, she doubted she would have been able to carry on. Having Michael as her head waiter was a help to both of them, as their grief mirrored each other's and a great understanding flowed between them.

Being still relatively fit and active, and having just had her sixtieth birthday, Olivia felt she needed something to occupy her mind and challenge her. She then decided she would run the restaurant for three years and see how it went. If at any time she thought she was not keeping up the standard, she would sell. In the meantime, she had Michael and his team to keep the plates spinning. She knew she had to bring Michael up to speed to place him in a position to be her number one. Sworn to secrecy, only she was aware that James would not be returning to his head waiter role.

She was sure she could make it work. More than anyone, she understood Michael's mindset and was as gentle with him as she could be. They had worked together for ten years now and had become good friends. Olivia did not know what she would do without him, and Michael, too, felt that the friendship helped him through the dark days of bereavement. She could not bear the thought of letting Michael go. The waiter and friend Michael Whittaker, an extremely talented front of house manager—apart from his chronic shyness, which was something he managed to put to one side—was an excellent employee. Olivia hoped that giving Michael the top job would give him confidence and help with his feelings regarding the death of his mother.

During her husband's mantle, she had seen areas that could improve the ambience and was now ready to contemplate making the subtle changes she felt would improve the atmosphere and attract the younger set. Acutely aware her clientele was an older crowd, Olivia felt she needed to attract the thirty-to-forty-group. Realizing the changing eating habits, and the public being notoriously fickle, she researched other restaurants by once a week spending an evening with a friend while enjoying the menu of a competitor in another part of the city.

This kept her apprised of current trends. She was able then to keep the chef informed, which enabled him to keep up to date without changing the essence of her establishment. Olivia had retained the staff her husband had brought on board. It was very much a matter of "If it's not broken, don't fix it."

Olivia left the front of house management to her acting head waiter; Michael was filling in, and Olivia was watching. She did not involve herself in the daily waiting, clearing tables, and serving drinks and dinners. Instead she managed the administration side of the restaurant, which, the Dhugall not being a large establishment, left her with time to spare. She would come in most days, check that all was well, and disappear to her local bridge club or golf course.

Olivia was sure Michael had hopes of the head waiter job. He had mentioned a long time ago his ambitions, and Olivia was keen to help make them come true. However, his shyness and lack of worldly knowledge were stumbling blocks.

Michael's interaction with customers was very special. It was as though he stepped onto a stage and performed. Olivia wondered whether his performances would be enough. Michael, being forty, felt it was time to fulfil his long-held ambition—but not at the cost of a colleague being superseded by illness. He couldn't even begin to contemplate looking for another job, as he was not confident enough in his abilities to embark on a change.

With each passing year, Michael's skill had improved. He was so popular with some of the regular clients that they would ask for Michael to attend to them. He was tall, reaching six feet, and was now slim and muscular owing to his habit of donning sports clothes and shoes to run to and from work, some three miles there downhill and three miles back uphill. His once ginger hair had darkened down to a warm mahogany, and together with his blue eyes, he struck a handsome figure. Occasionally he would drift back to the memory of those days when he ate more than he should, and his now slim figure was so different from that of the overweight teenager he once was. The gym at the college had inspired him to lose weight. Now, not having time to exercise at a gym, he chose to run the six miles a day to and from his workplace.

He was uncomfortable with strangers in his private life, having been an only child, and was not encouraged to socialize much. When Michael was about three, his mother became pregnant for the second time. His father, according to his mother, left the family; and even when the pregnancy terminated too soon, he did not return. He apparently could not face the responsibility of children, and the miscarriage did not change that. Michael grew up having only Mother for company, a situation both he and, especially, his mother enjoyed.

He did not remember his father and had no contact with him. His mother expressed a reluctance to explain any further. Michael grew up believing that not everyone had a father.

His mother, Jean, reverted to her maiden name of Whittaker and changed Michael's to match. He grew up never knowing his father's name or the status of his existence.

Michael developed glandular fever in the early years of his high school, and the six-month absence did nothing to advance his scholastic abilities. Not being able or encouraged to catch up, he shut down mentally and left school as soon as he could. He had nothing to stay for. School was very unpleasant for him. His peers mocked his ginger hair and chubby appearance; the girls were particularly merciless.

He had performed reasonably well in his early years, but the bullying and teasing were too much for him. It had been such a horrible experience that by the time he was into his teens he just wanted to leave school. He would, when it got particularly bad, avoid school and wander round the links and the meadows. He would spend his dinner money on a fry up of chips and a bridie, or even a pie. He would come to regret it as he got older and more than a little rotund.

As he grew, Michael liked to prepare food and cook. Once he was quite competent, he would serve a meal to his mother, usually on a Saturday evening once his mother returned from her weekly visit to a friend, Angela, who had been her bridesmaid all those years ago.

Although he had little experience of eating out, he and his mother would usually go out to eat once a month and on birthdays. When they did, he took every opportunity to watch how the waiters went about their jobs.

Michael was fast approaching his sixteenth birthday, and it was time for him to decide on which way his future would lie. He was adamant he would not be staying at school a moment longer than he had to. He and his mother had many arguments about this decision, and this was probably the only time they fell out. His mother brought the local paper one day and showed her sulking son the advertisement for a technical college which specialized in catering qualifications, as it had become obvious that was the direction the young man wanted to take. However, to his chagrin, this was achievable only with the requisite number of ordinary grade certificates. Michael was furious. He would not go back to school. His mother pointed out that the required certificates could be studied for at the college. "That would mean I was exchanging one school for another," wailed Michael. After much discussion, Michael eventually realized he was beaten, and an application form was duly completed and sent off to the college.

The technical college, west of Edinburgh, offered sixteen-year-olds school certificate tuition, and for a small grant and his fees paid, Michael was offered a place studying for his O grade subjects. It was altogether a better environment for Michael, and he flourished. He passed the five exams needed for inclusion in a catering course and was taught the skills needed to work in a restaurant. He was drawn to serving tables and enjoyed the modules where the tutor would take him through the procedures. Four years later, at the age of twenty, Michael was ready to participate in a working environment. With his new certificates, and skills to match, he stepped out into the world to start work in a large restaurant in the position of trainee waiter, which the college had helped him find. He became ambitious for the first time in his life. He would be a head waiter in an up-market restaurant one day.

Chapter 2

Aware in his subconscious of a rising hubbub in the room, he roused himself back into the present. He smiled as he realized that during his flight back into the past, he had finished his polishing and had set the tables, all by rote, and his team were arriving to take on board what the evening would bring.

His habit, as the evening got under way, would be to stand in the shadows close to the door of the kitchen, observing the patrons entering and being shown to their tables by Michael's team. There were usually two waiters and Michael in a session. This meant that the team had to pull together to maintain the level of service the visitors to the restaurant expected. There was a high proportion of regular diners.

Michael allowed his team to deal with the diners arriving; however, when one of his special clients arrived with their guests, he would step forward and deal with the seating arrangement himself.

He was on edge tonight. It was the first Friday of the month, and a party of four ladies who frequented the restaurant every month were due to arrive soon. As far as he knew, this party did not go to the theatre, but rather more of a reunion with good food and a hefty helping of the much-feted house wine. One of the four in particular could be offensive, and he did not enjoy their visit one little bit.

He had served their table faithfully and skillfully for approximately ten years. Occasionally they would not appear, their standing arrangement having been cancelled. This usually meant holidays and sometimes a change of venue. Michael was always surprised at the regular visits, especially as almost every visit brought a complaint.

In that time, he had been mocked, teased, shouted at, and made miserable by those women. As he stood waiting, he scanned the restaurant, making sure the tables were set correctly and in order. The reservation diary had been checked to ensure the seating plans were correct.

As the early evening had just swung into action with diners arriving, tables were not yet ready for clearing. These early diners would mostly go up the road to the theatre or the cinema. He wondered what particular performance was on this evening. He seldom had time to read the local newspaper; far less to go to the cinema or theatre. *Who would accompany me?* he thought. Again the loneliness washed over him, which made him think back to earlier, when he realized he was going to have to make a new life. He pushed the thoughts to the back of his mind and was able to take stock and gird his loins for the evening ahead.

A disturbance at the front door brought Michael out of the shadows. The party of four ladies had arrived, along with the accompanying laughter and squeals. He suspected they had started the evening off in one of the local pubs. There were four steps down into the restaurant, and to his shame, he wondered whether they would make it down the stairs in their high heels. However, tonight they were shown to their table all in one piece.

A waiter was summoned, coats removed and placed in the hanging space, and menus distributed. Michael would see to the taking of the orders for both food and drink, as although these ladies had not reached the level of status some of the patrons had, they were nevertheless regular customers and he had decided long ago they were to be treated well. As they were difficult to deal with, the responsibility was his alone.

The drinks order was taken, although he could probably have guessed the order without asking, such creatures of habit they were: a bottle of Prosecco as a pre-meal appetizer, followed by one red wine and one white wine. A debate followed as to which wine they would have, and as usual Monica was hell-bent on the best of house, forgetting rather selfishly that the other ladies were on a much tighter budget. A compromise was reached, and a bottle of Rioja and a bottle of Pinot Grigio duly chosen.

The four ladies had all been to school together, and although they were reaching their forties, they continued to meet every month for food and a night out. The pretty Anna was a paralegal in a prestigious firm of lawyers, the bad-tempered Monica was a personal assistant to the CEO in a downtown electronics company. Dorothy was a nurse and was now reaching the top of her career. She deserved it, being gentle, kind, and patient. Lastly, Pamela was flighty and not very conscientious. She had gone through various jobs, the current one as a croupier in the newly opened casino in Corstorphine. Although she pretended she was happy, she did feel she had lowered the tone.

Michael could have predicted their choices. Three of them would order the specials, but the fourth, most difficult to deal with, ordered a sautéed chicken caprese with a red pepper pesto sauce—one of the most expensive items on the menu. She requested the sauce be extra spicy. That was not unusual. Monica, the lady in question, was, like her companions, in her early forties and single. In Monica's case, her husband had left her for his secretary a little over a year prior. Still bitter, she was permanently in ill humour, and the thought of the divorce still to come did nothing to improve her temper.

She was, however, independently wealthy, as she had both the house up until recently inhabited by her and her husband and a rather large amount of cash in the bank left to her by her now deceased parents. Her soon to be ex-husband had decided to make a play for the house, and this did rankle. The house had been in her family for three generations, and she felt that he should have no claim on the house. He had already had the lion's share from the sale of the property they had jointly owned prior to the death of her remaining parent five years before.

At the time, her soon-to-be ex-husband had agreed not to lay claim to the house or the bank account. Monica had realized by this time that her husband had what was kindly described as a "wandering eye", and she was well aware of his penchant for playing while away from home. Monica had guessed their days as a couple were severely limited, hence the reason to make safe her inheritance.

Embittered by the feeling of being abandoned, she shopped in the best boutiques and stores, becoming more difficult as the weeks and months went on. When quizzed about the timing of any future divorce, Monica would snarl and reply, "Over my dead body." She had not confided in her friends regarding the fight she was up against with the division of assets and was not willing to share, as the ladies were not really close friends and Monica was not the confiding sort.

The others, however, were more placid and looked forward to enjoying their girly night out. The option to exclude Monica had occurred to them, but no one had the courage, and it seemed they were always making excuses for their bad-tempered friend. Michael glided over to take their order. They had chosen the much less flamboyant hunter's chicken and fish pie for two. Monica however, had selected the grilled salmon with a white sauce. To be fair to Monica, the bills were settled individually.

The wine was duly presented, and the cork popped. Michael did the honours, and glasses were poured. The ladies loved their "fizzy". Not being able to afford the real thing, Prosecco was a good substitute for bubbly. The food would be delivered once the fizz had been consumed. During this time, the four had a small aperitif delivered, sometimes known as an amuse-bouche. They had all chosen the prawn cocktail as a starter, a firm favourite.

It didn't take long for Monica's bad-tempered voice and waving fork to signal Michael to attend to her. Inwardly shuddering and wondering what could be wrong tonight, he walked over to hear what she had to say. Her behaviour never changed. Every month she would kick off, and she was just the sort of woman that provoked real annoyance in Michael.

She had decided that the Prosecco had lost its sparkle. It was flat, she complained. Although it could be seen at a glance this was not the case, Michael returned the bottle to the kitchen and delivered a fresh one.

It didn't take long for the replacement bottle be consumed, and the food duly arrived. Just as he thought peace had broken out, he heard Monica's harsh tones once again. At a level everyone in the establishment could hear, she summoned him to the table.

The problem appeared to be that the spicy pesto sauce was too bland, not spicy, and it was to be represented in a more agreeable fashion, immediately! Michael heaved one of his famous inward sighs as he reassured the patron it would be attended to, before marching back to the kitchen.

The other three ladies tried to pretend they weren't there as Monica, in her shouty voice, told her friends in no uncertain terms that the sauce should have been medium bordering on hot but was mild bordering on horrible. Covert glances were shared amongst the ladies; yet again, Monica's mortifying behaviour had caused their acute embarrassment.

What was not known to the others was that Monica had received a particularly uncomfortable communication from her ex-husband, which had put her in a foul mood; and rather unfairly, Michael was the target of her vitriol—never mind spoiling a much-loved meal out.

Alfredo, the chef, was mortified. He had renamed himself Alfredo to give himself some credibility when he began working in kitchens. He thought having an Italian name would accomplish this. However, as he was really Thomas McLeod from Portobello, with an accent to match, it didn't quite have the impact he had hoped.

However, he was the consummate professional, and an excellent chef to boot. He redid his dish, as the spicy sauce was an integral part of it. Michael returned to the table to be greeted with "About time, too." With a courtly bow, he delivered the replacement meal and retired to his corner.

So far, the team had been really pulling together. Friday was as always very busy, but they all worked like clockwork, and so far all was well, apart from the hiccup from the ladies' table. But it was too good to last.

The shrill sound of his name heralded another complaint from Monica, who was again trying to attract his attention. With a sinking feeling, he went over to find out what could possibly be wrong on this, the third, summons. Monica, her face set in a frown, her half-moon specs perched at the end of her nose, was complaining very loudly that the sauce was still too bland. Michael could feel the anger rising. Normally a placid person with a slow fuse, he was able to tolerate most situations. This was not one of these times.

At that moment, his trip to the kitchen was interrupted by the arrival of another of his special customers with a party for a table of eight. Michael knew he would be busy with this table, as they were always given the best of attention. That was the attraction of this small, exclusive restaurant. Patrons knew they would always get excellent service, a large wine menu, and an extensive first-class choice of food.

In a quandary as to whom he should deal with first, he hurriedly took the discarded food back to the kitchen. To his delight, when he returned to see to the new client's needs, one of the team was busy taking coats, straightening cutlery, and taking drink orders. A sigh of relief emitted from his lips as he went to their table to greet them. He would thank his colleague later.

This table of diners is usually booked in for a Saturday, but he remembered it was a special occasion—a birthday or anniversary; he couldn't quite remember. He checked the booking before he served them. It appeared to be a special birthday celebration, and he suddenly remembered the delivery of a cake bearing the number sixty that was safely tucked away in the kitchen, awaiting the birthday chorus and the ceremonious cutting of the cake. Michael made a note to himself to track down the sgian dubh normally brought out on such occasions

The one saving grace with these clients was that, although the best of service and food was a requirement, they were not demanding and were a good meal in nice surroundings. The restaurant was a nice, relaxing establishment. Ancient Hunting Stewart tartan curtains were hung at every window. The tables were topped with snow-white tablecloths and linen napkins. The cutlery was polished, and the glasses sparkled. The chairs had matching tartan upholstery, and there were scenes from Edinburgh hung on the walls. A bit of discussion occurred when a gift of a painting of the new Queensferry Crossing arrived, and it was yet to be hung. Some quarters felt it was too modern, and that decision was still to be made. With the anticipation that things could go badly, the utter unfairness of it all caught him unawares as he marched back to face Alfredo, his temper well and truly up. This surprised his team, as Michael usually had a very slow fuse. Grumbling, Alfredo prepared another plate, adding an extra spoonful of hot chilli at Michael's suggestion. The meal was delivered fairly swiftly, and Michael carried on with his duties.

The table of VIPs were starting to get their food served, and just as Michael was beginning to relax, he heard the dreaded *"Michael!"* By now he was beginning to suspect that the awful Monica had realized there was a table of customers getting VIP treatment and it wasn't hers. Michael was so sure of this he started to burn. His slow fuse was lit. Over to the table he went again, his sympathetic face on once more. Michael, if nothing else, was in control.

"How can I help you?" he asked.

"This food is so weak there is no way you can call it spicy pesto. I have a good mind to report you to Trading Standards," said Monica in a loud voice.

By now the patrons were all looking and listening, and Michael was furious his lovely restaurant was having a bad time. This time without the smile, he snatched away the plate and marched to the kitchen. The chef and his team had never seen Michael in such a state. He was so furious he wasn't thinking straight. He took a portion of the pesto sauce and put it in a bowl, emptied the jar of paprika into the sauce, and gave it a good stir before plating the food.

He marched back out, placed it on the table in front of Monica, and stalked off.

As she took a mouthful, she was conscious of the attention she was getting from the other diners at neighbouring tables. She took a second mouthful and was becoming aware of the heat permeating her mouth. She gulped down a large mouthful of wine and reached for the next forkful. She was aware she was the centre of attention—and not in a good way, as she could hear the sniggers and suppressed laughter. Now Monica was in a temper, and she tried not to show that her mouth was on fire. She threw her napkin onto the table, got up, retrieved her coat and bag, refusing help from the staff, and marched out. Michael got a long-held wish when she tripped going up the stairs.

The silence in the room was deafening. It lasted a few minutes, and once Monica was safely out of the restaurant, the hubbub started and conversations continued. Michael was still very angry and had not thought through any repercussions. He continued to attend to the customers, including the table of only three. The ladies quickly finished their meal and asked for the bill. Michael duly obliged, omitting Monica's meal. As the ladies departed in muted tones and said goodnight, the atmosphere started to lighten.

Michael was now very upset. It was obvious the behaviour of just one diner had strongly affected those eating, and he didn't know how to change this. He carried out his duties as well as he could and tried to make sure all of the customers were enjoying their meals in spite of the incident. He made short work of the clearing, possessing a talent rarely seen. He was able to load his tray in such a fashion he could clear a whole table in one go. He was not comfortable with full plates and glasses so he kept his balancing act for the empty plates and glasses. His forearm and bicep on his right arm were very muscular because of the weight he was constantly carrying around,

It seemed a long time until closing time, but it came eventually. Michael then made his way home feeling that this had been the worst night in living memory.

Chapter 3

Michael had cooled down by now and became desperately concerned that he would lose his job. He came into work full of trepidation. Not being of a nature to hide from his mistakes, he sought out Olivia immediately and duly confessed. Although she had been a good and fair boss, he was fully expecting a barracking and possibly the loss of his job.

Olivia, much to his surprise, thought the whole thing was very amusing and said she wished she had thought of it first. She had come across Monica's bad behaviour herself and reiterated yet again that she was not sorry to see her go, thinking there was no way she would be back. What Michael was not aware of was that Olivia had known already. A couple of the team had been laughing about it, and Olivia had demanded to hear the whole story. She could be heard chuckling all the way up the stairs.

Michael slowly walked downstairs, and to his great surprise (and secret delight), his Friday night colleagues gave him a round of applause. Feeling slightly bemused, Michael set about his tasks and started to look forward to Monday, as he had a few days off during the upcoming quiet spell. It was just before the tourist season and the famous Edinburgh Festival started; Olivia felt all the staff should get some time off before the onset of the summer buzz.

Michael had heard the new Borders Railway had reopened and had decided to take the train to Hawick and visit the Minto Hills, an organization named Visit Scotland in Jedburgh had, on his request, sent him a map of the routes around Minto, Denholm, and Hawick. They had thoughtfully sent him a bed and breakfast guide, and he decided to spend a few days in the area doing a spot of rambling and sightseeing. He confirmed he could book his tickets over the phone and collect them in the morning, and he had the foresight to book his accommodation in advance. He had been attracted to the bed and breakfast chosen because it was homely, with home-cooked food and real coal fires. It was a wonderful few days exploring and climbing. The weather was kind, and he had a marvelous time.

All too soon, it was time to get back to work. As it was the start of summer and the weather had warmed up, he donned his running gear, and his thoughts turned to the previous Friday. He wondered whether there had been any repercussions. Although Olivia had come down on his side, Michael was afraid that business may have taken a knock.

When the restaurant had been refurbished, the owners had thoughtfully built in a toilet and shower upstairs, as well as a small lounge area, some lockers, and Olivia's office. It gave the staff some comfort while on their breaks. One of the staff suggested a computer be installed, but Michael didn't give much support for this. Being a bit of a technophobe, he couldn't see the value in it. They would have to work harder if they were going to change his mind. However, the refurbishment did mean that Michael could freshen up in the shower when he ran to work.

On arriving at work, after his shower and change of clothes, he made a beeline for the diary. He quickly took in which regulars were booked in and which other reservations had been made.

Happily, he surmised that the Monica incident had not done any real harm. He casually flicked through the remaining pages of the month, spotting one familiar name after another until he came to the first Friday. The ladies' reservation had a line through it. It being a standing reservation, he checked the next month and the next ... no ladies' reservations. He had fully expected Monica would not come back, but the other ladies were well behaved, and Michael felt a keen sense of loss.

Chapter 4

Michael climbed the stairs to let Olivia know he was back and ready to go. She proceeded to give him a briefing of what had been happening. She was secretly pleased to see him. He had been missed, and she was more than happy to turn the front of the house back over to him. He was surprised that she had not mentioned the cancelled booking. He confessed that he had noticed the missing reservations, but Olivia was completely unfazed. She had been unhappy with their behaviour for quite some time, and it was only at his suggestion that the booking stood. Apparently Pamela had telephoned on Monday, cancelling their arrangement.

Michael shrugged his shoulders and started his preparations for the evening ahead. Checking the tables with the diary to make sure the booked tables were dressed properly, he placed reserved signs on the appropriate tables. The evening went well, and with a sigh of relief, Michael locked up the restaurant for the night and he and the team finished the clean-up.

The days and weeks meandered along, and all too soon it was the first Friday again. Michael, checking the reservations, noticed there were still a few tables available. This was unusual for a Friday, and for a moment he thought the nonsense with the four ladies had adversely affected the trade. Then he remembered that it was only eleven o'clock and telephone bookings would start to come in, as clients familiar with the procedures knew to phone after twelve, when Dhugall opened for business. Sure enough, the phone started around noon, and before long the tables were full, apart from the table for four.

The table usually frequented by the ladies remained unreserved. The day wore on and merged into evening, and the patrons began arriving to take up their reservations.

Michael was kept busy and had little time to think as he dealt with the clientele in his usual deferential fashion and with a quiet efficiency which had become his trademark. When it was time to close up, Michael went through the routine of cashing up and making sure the tables were all cleared. The kitchen staff were deftly dealing with the debris that accompanies a busy restaurant. As he glanced round, he spotted that the ladies' table had not been occupied all evening. He sadly reflected on how he had partially caused this rift, and as it was so against his nature, he felt remorse and not a little sad. He would just have to fill the table.

The days crept past and into months, the capital would welcome the influx of visitors enjoying the varied entertainment of the festival during August and September. Michael always felt it would be nice to go to some of the events, but when the city was busy, so was he.

The festival came and went, with life going on as before. With summer fading into autumn and the temperatures dropping, he put his running gear away for the winter as he started using the bus to get to work. Michael loved summer, and as autumn brought its own beauty with the changing leaves, he felt sad—especially as the time since his mother's death had now stretched to two years. Michael lived in a modest two-bedroom house which he had shared with his mother until her death. Now he had it all to himself.

He had never married nor sought to be involved in a relationship, primarily because he had been comfortable just being looked after by his mother, was reticent in making friends, and had difficulties making conversation due to the bad memories of his school days and the horror of the merciless teasing. He was particularly uncomfortable conversing with females. In the restaurant, he could hide behind his professionalism.

Because of the hurt he still felt at the way the girls in his school had treated him, he had poor expectations of finding a person to share his life with. Nevertheless, he felt very alone. He had no siblings, and his mother, also an only child, had left him without family when her fatal heart attack took her from him. She had only been sixty-four.

Chapter 5

Michael's mother had been a young bride and pregnant when she married Michael's father; she had only been nineteen. She gave birth to a boy and named him Michael, after his dad. She left college to care for her son, as childminding and nurseries were not prevalent in those days and it was normal to be a stay-at-home mum. It did mean she was unable to continue with further education, but his dad continued with university. Times were hard for the new parents living on a student grant and the various part-time jobs Michael senior could squeeze into his busy schedule. Jean, however, was in seventh heaven bringing up her new little son. Her life revolved around young Michael, and she had little to no inclination to change it.

With his wife obsessed with the baby and the constant demands for money to pay bills, Michael senior left his wife and child, as he said he could not cope with family life. Jean was devastated. How would she manage? This was her primary concern; she wasn't particularly perturbed that Michael had left. The baby took up all of her time. Her remaining parent had recently died and were not available for support. She had, however, left a modest two-bedroom terraced villa to Jean, her only child, which had been paid off a few years back when her father died and left an insurance policy of some considerable amount.

Life was difficult, but young Michael and his mother managed to get by, and when Michael started to earn a wage, life became easier. He had no inclination to move out of his childhood home. He was quite happy to be looked after, to be fed, and to have his laundry taken care of. It was an arrangement they both were comfortable with. Now that he was without his mother, he felt her absence keenly and was having great trouble coping with the loss.

The restaurant was quite different during the day. The kitchens were running at full tilt preparing for the evening, but they offered light lunches from noon until 2.00 p.m. As the premises were open for the preparatory work, it was common sense to offer food at the same time. The young sous chef was given the responsibility of making soup and preparing sandwiches, as most of the trade was pushed for time, being office workers around Morningside and Bruntsfield.

One day as Michael was polishing cutlery and folding napkins, he took a phone call asking to reserve a table for the evening.

It was unusual because it was a table for one. The caller gave his name as MacGregor. Michael confirmed the booking and terminated the call. He looked around the tables thoughtfully. *Where would be the best location for Mr. MacGregor?* Some restaurants can make a singleton uncomfortable, and Michael did not wish to be party to that. He chose a corner table so the diner could have his back to the wall whilst still being able to see what was happening in the room. The booking was for 9.00 p.m., which was quite late but not unusually so. Nevertheless, Michael was curious.

The evening trade started to appear and slowly the tables filled up. Michael was taking care of the diners and carrying out his duties with the restaurant becoming busy. The murmur of voices heard throughout the dining area was music to his ears indicating happy people eating, drinking, and conversing with friends.

Before he realized it, the time was nine o'clock and his table for one was waiting to be seated. One of his team got to him first, and the booking process had automatically logged the table number. He saw a tall man with grey hair, and inwardly Michael thought he was probably older than he looked. Michael had the feeling he had seen him before but couldn't recollect where or when. As the young waiter carried on serving Mr. MacGregor, Michael returned to his vantage spot and continued surveying the room, making sure all was in order.

The restaurant started emptying around ten thirty, and last to leave was his table for one. He took the opportunity to enquire about his dining experience and was delighted to hear that Mr. MacGregor had enjoyed himself immensely and would be returning. Happy that there was another satisfied customer, Michael finished his duties certain in the knowledge that it had been another successful evening, contributing to the popularity of the restaurant.

He took what he thought was a routine call heralding a booking for the Friday, a table for three at six o'clock, pre-theatre time. Upon asking the name for the booking, he was surprised to hear a name from the near past. As he terminated the call, his mind was going over what had been said. He flicked back through the bookings diary and found the same name on the booking for four on every first Friday of the month, the last one being the fateful evening when it all went horribly wrong.

Michael shook his head. *A coincidence*, he mused. Still, he was rather looking forward to seeing whether his guess was correct. Firstly, it wasn't the first Friday of the month, and the table was for three, not four. If it was indeed the famous four now down to three, who was missing? Michael took an educated guess.

The various scenarios meandered through his consciousness. Finally, it was Friday, and promptly at six p.m., Pamela, Dorothy, and Anna arrived. Not surprisingly, Monica was the missing fourth. It was an absolute pleasure for Michael to serve the ladies. They behaved beautifully. They were having a great time. Laughter and enthusiastic conversation made the evening go with a swing. Finally, Dorothy, apparently having been appointed unofficial spokesperson, apologized for their companion's bad behaviour on their previous visit. Michael demurred, indicating it was forgotten; but no, Dorothy was going to explain.

Naturally, Monica was not coming back, and Dorothy confessed that the quartet had been patronizing another restaurant, which was why they had not booked for the first Friday of the month, being otherwise engaged. But now they had decided that with or, preferably, without Monica, they would be resuming their Friday night date. Michael was quietly ecstatic. He fervently hoped they would persuade Monica to stay away. Dorothy indicated also, without being too disloyal, that Monica's behaviour had not improved.

The ladies left thanking Michael for his attendance and remarking that they were off to the cinema in Morningside Road. They bustled out all chatty and happy, so different to their lost visit. "See you in two weeks!" they chorused. A generous tip was found on their vacated table. Michael went home happy.

Chapter 6

Michael had recently been aware of a change in his attitude. The death of his mother had affected him badly. He was coming to terms with her being gone forever. While he missed her dreadfully, the searing pain of grief seemed to have abated, replaced more and more with a quiet acceptance. Coming back to an empty house still gave him a jolt. *It's a good job I learned to cook*, he thought, but the vagaries of the washing machine still gave him a few fraught moments.

Although his career was very satisfying, he really started to think he should get out more. Some of his shifts gave him until 5.00 p.m. before he had to be on duty. Surely he could be doing something which would bring him into contact with human beings other than those he served—maybe on an equal footing for a change. He was reading the newspaper, and just for fun he looked at the advertising to see whether there were any activities he could join. He read the classified section and two adverts attracted his attention. The two advertised activities were poles apart but strangely attractive.

The first one was a call for new members at the local golf club, and to further tempt members in, the joining fee, a not inconsiderable amount of money, was being waived for the next six weeks. Michael pondered. He had never played golf before, but he was strangely drawn to the idea. He would meet new people, and there would, he was sure, be a social life he could participate in. Naturally he would need lessons and playing partners, and the call for members came just as summer was sliding into autumn and the weather was starting to deteriorate. It would also be expensive.

This was a consideration Michael put to one side. He had not been a spender, and he had a fair few pounds in the bank plus funds from an insurance policy, not yet touched, paid after his mother's demise. She had also left a considerable sum of money. Perhaps this was the thing to do. He would visit the golf course on his next day off and find out more about taking up golf. He smiled at the thought. He considered himself quite fit and agile. He thought to himself, *"How hard can it be?"*

Chapter 7

Michael's mother had left, as part of her possessions, a car—a small runabout which was kept in a lock-up along the street. Latterly she had not driven, and Michael had no use for it. Living in the city gives rare occasions in which one can drive and get parked. Only when one drives out of town is it more pleasant. However, owing to Michael's inertia after his bereavement, the small car had not been sold. So when his late start, which was Thursday this week, came around, he happily managed to start the car in spite of its long sojourn being static. He headed off to the outskirts and parked in the car park marked "visitors' parking". He was at the golf club. On telephoning the club earlier in the week and being put through to the club captain, he had been instructed to be at the club by 10.00 a.m. in a manner that bore the truth of the captain's military background.

It was an impressive building, and from what he could see, the course was tidy and well maintained. *Good start*, he thought. *I wonder whom I should see to answer my question?* On walking into the clubhouse, he quickly sourced the bar/lounge. Thinking, quite rightly, it would be the perfect place to start, as it seemed to be the only place there were people about, he strode purposefully to the bar, looking much more confident than he felt.

He felt like a gunslinger in the O.K. Corral. The silence was deafening. Heads turned and stared. Michael began to have second thoughts and was about to turn on his heel and escape when, from the assembled company, a stout, short, ruddy-complexioned man in tweeds (naturally) came towards him with a welcoming smile and outstretched hand.

Upon greeting Michael, the man announced himself as William Gladstone, the club captain. William recalled from their telephone conversation that Michael had expressed an interest in joining the club.

Biting the bullet, Michael explained he had seen the advertisement for new members and decided to visit and find out more about what was on offer.

Michael at this stage did not mention that he was looking to make new friends. He thought it would sound a bit needy. His total inability to hit a golf ball, never mind the total absence of golfing gear—indeed including clubs—also went without being mentioned.

What Michael did not know was that he was exactly what they wanted—a customer for the professional shop and, with a bit of luck, maybe lessons—fresh blood, as some say. William said he was delighted to help and asked Michael to follow him to the office, where they could talk privately.

William sensed that Michael was out of his comfort zone. Although Michael had attempted a show of nonchalance, the club captain had been around the block a few times and felt a private conversation was more appropriate. If the conversation went well, he would consider taking Michael back to the bar and introducing him to the club stalwarts. He may have been all bluster on the outside, but the club captain was, underneath it all, a kindly, intelligent man.

Michael explained what he was trying to accomplish. He tried to adopt a confident tone and a comfortable demeanour, but memories of his school days flooded back. He shook himself to forget that particular trauma. But he did explain he had not played the sport before. William, completely unperturbed, said that if the terms were suitable and if Michael wanted to pursue golf membership, he would take him down and introduce him to the club professional and see about lessons. William also hinted that the club professional was doing a special offer on lessons because of the darker nights and the Scottish winter weather.

Michael listened carefully to the conditions of membership and the costs involved. He was reassured that when he was ready to tackle the course, there would be playing partners aplenty. Also, once a week members turned up at a certain time and foursomes would be made for them.

The captain also indicated that for a beginner this was the best possible time to learn, as he could have his lessons and practise on the range, and when spring arrived, he may well be ready for a game or two. He also mentioned Michael would need to have a conversation with the secretary of the club, as he was the man for the financial side. Michael was to phone

Michael, Waiting

and make an appointment. He gave Michael a couple of leaflets pointing out the phone number. The captain explained apologetically that the secretary was not available today.

Michael thanked him for his kindness and requested time to think about it, but he asked whether, while he was here, he could speak to the professional if he was free, thinking that he should have all the costs before he made an appointment. William nodded enthusiastically. "Good idea," he boomed. "When you are finished with Mark—he's the pro—come back up to the bar, and we can socialize with the old worthies, giving you a feel for the atmosphere. The men in the lounge are usually here every day, so best you get to know them." Michael agreed, and together they trouped downstairs to the shop where Mark held residence.

William introduced the two men and headed back to the bar, where, he explained, a pint was waiting. "Hopefully we will see you upstairs when you are done," the helpful captain barked.

Michael took to Mark straight away. He was a young professional golfer with an engaging manner. He made Michael feel comfortable. Not many strangers had that effect on him, so feeling more at ease than he thought he would, he explained to Mark what he was looking for and told him that at this stage he was gathering information. Mark indicated that he had a half set of clubs, second-hand, owned by a member who had since given up playing, which would be a good start. Reasonably priced, it would enable Michael to learn and practise; and if he felt inclined, he could add to the set, as the manufacturer was well known and still in production. Mark then explained the cost of lessons. More and more, Michael was experiencing an enthusiasm hitherto unknown for him; but as a frugal person, he was dismayed at the mounting costs.

Michael asked to go home and think about it, do his sums, and get back to him. Mark thought this was a sensible idea, and as the two men shook hands, Mark hoped he would see Michael soon, and they parted company.

His first reaction was to sneak out of the club and jump into his car, but sensibly he went to the bar, as he felt William would make a better friend than an enemy. He was welcomed in, and a drink was offered. Michael had serious qualms about alcohol and driving, so he insisted on an orange juice.

Concerned that he might offend the members, he explained he had to work later and alcohol was not permitted. The boys seemed satisfied with his explanation and started to introduce themselves.

By the time he had drunk his orange, his head was buzzing. He would never remember the names, and he just wanted out and to get back to the peace and quiet of his empty house.

Chapter 8

Once he got his head on straight, Michael still had a couple of hours before he had to get ready for work. He felt this would be a good time to speak to the book club, his other choice from the notifications he had seen. The number he called was answered by a soft highland voice, but Michael was shocked; he had not expected a woman to answer the phone. He hadn't considered it. As he stuttered out the reason for his call, he was starting to get cold feet and was trying desperately to get out of the situation. However, he was not ready for Elizabeth's tenacity. Before he could protest, he was set up with a date and time to present himself along with his first book. He was to read as much of it as he could manage, Elizabeth had picked up on his awkward shifts and had told him to be prepared to discuss what he had read. She even managed to prise his telephone number out of him. The call terminated, and Michael threw himself onto the sofa and in horrified silence wondered what he could do to get out of this.

Michael was not the most assertive of men, and the idea he would have to interact with the female of the species filled him with terror.

He then mulled over his day. A horrible thought crept in. What if there were no males in the book club? As procrastination was another of his foibles, he decided to wait and see, and he headed off to the local library to see whether he could procure the dreaded book, all the while doing the golf club sums to see whether this would be worth it.

As he ambled down the road to the library, he gave himself a sound talking to. So what if there is a female presence at the book club. I serve ladies at the restaurant. How can this be different? Then he thought about the change in his quality of life he held in his grasp.

It was probably one of his busiest days off he'd had for a while, and as he presented himself for work, his head was buzzing. He had managed to find the book he needed, so there would be no late-night TV for him. He would have to start reading. Although he felt under duress, Michael was an honourable man and had agreed with the book club that he would attend the meeting the following Monday, so attend he would.

One of the first things Michael always did when he turned up for work—after his shower, of course—was to check the booking diary to see what he was up against. Thursday evenings were not as busy as the rest of the week. Michael had always thought late-night shopping had something to do with it. However, it was a fairly big turnout, and Michael knew he was going to be busy. With all thoughts of golf and books pushed to the back of his mind, he set to work.

He noticed the MacGregor entry for 9.00 p.m. It had been a few weeks since Mr. MacGregor had expressed delight at his food, departing with a promise of returning. He had requested the same table.

The evening went well, and on the stroke of nine Mr. MacGregor presented himself to be shown to his pre-booked table. Michael got to him first. He took his coat and escorted him to the table. Mr. MacGregor expressed delight at his request for the same table having been honoured.

He was a pleasant, quiet, and unassuming man, and Michael could not shake off the feeling they had met before … but when?

Mr. MacGregor asked Michael for his advice on the evening specials and ordered a bottle of red wine. Michael gave Mr. MacGregor a few minutes before approaching the table to take the order.

Heading for the kitchen with the food order, he thought to himself what a lovely, well-mannered gentleman his diner was. He was delighted to see him returning. Once more his client ordered from the special menu and chose a full-bodied Rioja to go with his paella. The restaurant had decided to hold a themed evening, with a certain part of the menu having a selection of food from around the world, and Mr. MacGregor had decided to go with the Spanish theme.

Michael carried on with his duties, and most of the patrons were ready to go by 10.30 or 11.00 p.m. Although his diner had arrived at a rather late hour, he finished sharply on the dot of 10.30 p.m. The clean-up involved table clearing, with everyone pulling together to be able to go home as soon as possible. Michael jumped into action to deliver the bill for his mysterious guest an return with his coat. Once more, Mr. MacGregor was profuse in his thanks and praise, and he left a generous tip.

The first Friday in October came around fast, and it was the ladies' night to take up their booking. Michael was not experiencing the usual dread he used to feel. It was the three well-behaved ladies. Michael relaxed at the thought and set about his preparations for the evening ahead. On the stroke of six,

the ladies arrived, and Michael crossed the room to attend to them. He realized very quickly there was something amiss. Where was the chatty laughter from the last visit? The cause was soon apparent. There were not three ladies but four. Monica was a member of the party. It was surprising how the mood changed with her presence.

Michael's professionalism came to the fore, and he quickly reset the table to accommodate the extra place, took their coats, and distributed the menus. He took the opportunity to go through to the kitchen and warn Alfredo that they could be in for a bumpy ride. The chef's expletive was certainly more Portobello than Mediterranean.

Michael glided over to the table and, with a fixed smile, proceeded to take their order. The ladies were very quiet, as was Monica. He dared to hope that she might behave. Their usual Prosecco was opened and poured, and the food ordered with no changes. It was straight off the menu. Michael was perplexed. It was like a different party.

He shrugged and carried on about his duties. The busy Friday night left him with lots to do. Not a sound came from the ladies' table except for the murmur of conversation. Eventually the bill was called for, and the ladies made tracks to go. Money was sorted out, and coats were fetched. The others left, leaving Monica still sitting at the table, alone. Reluctantly, Michael cleared the table. Out of preference, he would have had one of his team do the table, but he was not a coward and did the deed himself.

When he came back from taking the plates to the kitchen, he was astonished to see Monica still sitting at the table, which was now topped with just a fresh white damask tablecloth. Michael went over and asked whether there was something he could do for her. Did she need a taxi? Where had her friends gone?

Monica took a deep breath and started to talk. She was still at the table because she wanted a word with Michael, she announced. She started to tell him what had transpired after she left the restaurant that last time. "I want to apologize for my extremely bad behaviour on my last visit," she explained, "and I want to let you understand that it won't happen again. I was aware that my friends were visiting your restaurant and they had not included me in the invitation. I was told in no uncertain terms my behaviour was inexcusable and under no circumstances would they allow me to join them. Even an apology would not do, but I am here tonight to make an apology. I am so very sorry, Michael! I won't even excuse myself by trying to explain I was having a difficult day. That should not have even come into it. I am leaving now, and you will no doubt be delighted I won't be back. My friends will"

Michael only just managed to keep himself from allowing his jaw to drop and gazing at her, open-mouthed. But he maintained his dignity. With lightning speed with his first words, he accepted her apology and—unwisely, he thought afterwards—told her she was welcome to come back.

She nodded, thanked him for his generosity, and left the restaurant with Michael trying to process what had just happened.

Michael finished clearing up and, leaving the restaurant in good order, made his way home. His head was full of the day's happenings. The Monica incident crowded out his other thoughts, and he had difficulty in bringing his head back to the decisions he had to make.

He waited until he got home and settled. He poured himself a decent shot of his Highland Park whisky, a gift from Olivia. Sitting down and sipping slowly, he pondered on what was, for him, a really busy day. *Is this how other people lived their lives?* he wondered.

He brought his daydream back to the present and mulled over the golf club facts and figures. He pulled the leaflets and pricings out of his well-worn jacket and started checking the figures. A complete technophobe, he used pen, paper, and the calculator he had used in college.

Firstly he considered what to do about golf. Was he perhaps a little old to be starting? Then, remembering the members he met, he changed his mind and thought, "Am I too young for this?" He mentally totted up the costs involved: the start-up costs and then the ongoing costs. It was quite a tidy sum. The book club was an easier choice. There appeared to be no costs involved apart from bringing something to eat with coffee. He decided he would attend and perhaps give it maybe four weeks as a trial. The lady who was president of the club held the meeting in her home in Comiston, which was just a short walk from his house.

Then he thought about the confrontation with Monica, the biggest surprise of them all. As she had indicated she would not be back to the restaurant, Michael felt a little relieved that the stress of her visits was not an issue, and his worrying thoughts of her causing trouble soon dissipated.

He retired to bed with his book and read the first chapter. It was a complicated plot, and Michael found his attention wandering. He decided that after the day's happenings, the complicated storyline was not relaxing him after all. He decided to try to sleep, and he drifted off thinking he would have to make notes regarding the book. And so he slept, forgetting his loneliness for the first time.

Friday came, and with it came the usual bustle of a busy night. The festival was over, but still the attendees came to eat and enjoy the atmosphere. During his afternoon break, Michael, having written down on the back of an order pad, of all things, the costings of the golf club membership, read over his arithmetic. Although the total seemed large indeed, he was a man who did not spend money foolishly, and he did have money in the bank—more than enough to cover this expense. Surprisingly, he made the split-second decision to become a member. He will visit the club again tomorrow. As it would be a Saturday, he felt he would have opportunities to speak to those in charge. William, the club captain, had told him he would have to negotiate his membership with the club secretary, and he was usually in the club on a Saturday. The phone call was made, and the appointment confirmed for 9.00 a.m. The secretary explained he was on the tee for 10.00 a.m.

Michael rose earlier than usual. His shift didn't start until 5.00 p.m., as the lunchtime trade was very quiet at the weekend, most of the diners having the weekend off. He would normally use that time to lie and then do chores, but not this morning, as he rose early and dressed carefully, hoping to create a good impression. As he glanced at the mirror to confirm he passed muster, he realized that as he rarely went anywhere, his casual clothes looked somewhat jaded. *Hmm*, thought Michael, *I think I will have to do some shopping.*

When he got to the clubhouse just before 9.00 a.m., to his astonishment he found the place packed with golfers on their way out and those having breakfast. His heart sank. He thought, *This is the wrong day. Shows just how little I know about golf.* However, to his delight, William spotted him from across the lounge area and bustled over to see what he could do.

His late start was explained, and the 9.00 a.m. meeting revealed. Though he had been hoping he could meet with the secretary and set up a membership, he realized that it was a busy day and asked when would be a better time to call in. "Nonsense," said William. The club secretary, Andrew, would be skulking in his office and reading the paper, having had a bacon sandwich delivered. Andrew usually tried to avoid members in case they had grievances to share with him. William went on. "I'll just escort you up to his office, and you can take it from there." Before Michael could argue, William added, "And don't be put off by his manner. He is a man of few words and can be a bit dry."

William ushered Michael up the stairs and made introductions before vanishing back to his drink. He never played on the weekend, leaving the spaces for those who couldn't manage a weekday.

About an hour later (Andrew was, if nothing else, thorough) he had to get to the tee. Michael descended the stairs and went into the lounge. He caught William's eye and was waved over.

The captain was sitting at a table with three other golfers. They looked as though they had known each other forever. "Well," boomed William, "are you a member now?"

"I'm afraid not," said Michael sadly. "Why not?" asked William.

Michael explained that it was a requirement of joining that he be recommended by two existing members. "I don't know anyone," he remarked sadly.

"I know that," exclaimed William, "I just didn't think it was important. Give me your nomination form." William proceeded to complete his name in one space and, turning to his friends, requested a volunteer to do the honours. "You seem like a nice chap," said William. "I'm sure you won't cause any trouble. But just for the record, what do you do for a living? Where do you live? Are you married?"

Michael answered all their questions, his mood lightening as he spoke.

They all raised their glasses and welcomed Michael to the club. "Best you pop upstairs and give Andrew your forms," instructed William.

Michael, Waiting

"I can't do that," explained Michael. "Andrew left to go on the tee. I don't expect he will be back anytime soon." He told his new friends and sponsors he would call back at a time when Andrew was not on the course. He bade them farewell and headed for the door, only to bump into Andrew. He asked the times when he might return and deliver his membership forms. Andrew explained that his partner had left a message that he could not make the 10.00 a.m. slot and they had been rescheduled for 2.00 p.m.

Brandishing the form, he told Andrew he had the nominations required. Andrew looked at the signatures and, peering over his glasses, said, "Why am I not surprised?" Michael left the secretary's office half an hour later, clutching what seemed a vast amount of paperwork. He was considerably lighter in the pocket but was now a fully paid-up member of the golf course. He was delighted, too, because the membership cost less than he had expected, as the usual time for renewal was April and he had only the pro rata costs at this time.

Now he was off to the professional's shop to arrange lessons, after bidding farewell to his new-found "friends", thanking them profusely. Fortunately

Michael had the foresight to bring his shift patterns with him, hoping to fit in with the times available. Michael decided that he would book ten lessons to begin with. Now that he had committed himself financially, he was prepared to commit himself physically and mentally. This would take him into the winter, and as suggested, he would visit the indoor driving range next to the course. Lessons duly booked, Michael went to his car and drove the short distance home. Feeling pleased with himself, he prepared his lunch and made ready to start work later that day. He wondered just when he was going to have time to read the book!

Chapter 9

His next day he started at five was the following Monday, and it was time to fulfil his promise to attend the book club. The book was *Five Red Herrings*, a mystery written by well-known author Dorothy L. Sayers. Michael had never heard of her, but she had died some time ago, and he made up his mind he would try to find out more about her.

He had read a couple of chapters and taken a few notes. He was nervous about appearing stupid, knowing that his academic prowess was limited. However, he did like the book and thought it may be a bit of fun. He girded his loins and took off down the hill to Elizabeth's home and rang the bell. He was ushered in and greeted with animated voices, all of which seemed to be talking at once. Happily, he detected masculine tones and immediately felt better. *Not* all *women, thankfully*, he thought to himself.

Elizabeth escorted him into the lounge, where a group of about ten people sat in chairs, settees, and at the dining table. He quickly spotted that although the majority of the company were female, there were three men. Elizabeth introduced the gathering one by one with a short description of their interests and where they lived. Elizabeth explained that some month's other members took turns at being hosts, but she hastened to add that it was not mandatory. As Elizabeth went from one member to another, Michael froze. The member he was being introduced to was none other than Monica. She had previously been looking down, scanning her notes, and he had not seen her. There was no doubt, however, that she had seen him first.

He nearly bolted. Then he very quickly decided she would not chase him away. If he were to discontinue attendance, it would be on his terms and not hers. They nodded to one another, and Michael found a seat, happily, across the room from Monica. He didn't contribute much. This being his first time, he wanted to reconnoitre.

At the end of the meeting, as everyone got up to leave, Monica came up to him and indicated that it was nice to see him again. Michael murmured his thanks and headed off home to get ready for his shift. Walking back up the hill, always the more difficult way, he contemplated the pros and cons of the book club. He had hoped it would be a method of being introduced to books and writers to give him ideas about what he would enjoy reading. The club was organized differently. He was expected to discuss his impressions of what he was reading, and the book choice was not his.

It was obvious some of the members, having been members for some considerable time, enjoyed the sounds of their own voices and, given the opportunity, would lecture on and on, ad infinitum. Michael was not sure this was an activity he would enjoy, and the presence of Monica did little to make him any more enthusiastic. Still, he would give it some thought, and as Elizabeth was the hostess again next month, he felt obliged to go. It was a decision to be taken another time.

As Michael got home plotting lunch, his mobile rang. This was a rare occurrence. Since his mother had died, he'd had little use for the phone and was contemplating doing without. He had not taken the offending article to the meeting, but it was merrily playing "Fleur de Lys" on his coffee table.

He picked it up and examined the call to see whether he should answer it. There had been some recent calls from marketing companies, and he tended not to answer those. However, in the display, Olivia's name appeared. The phone stopped ringing and, to his dismay, indicated that he had five missed calls, all of which were from Olivia, his boss. *Oh no*, he thought. *There must be a crisis at the restaurant.*

He immediately called back. His effusive apologies were cut short. Olivia had decided to hold a staff meeting at 3.00 p.m. but wanted to speak to Michael alone prior to the meeting. She asked how long it would take him to get into work. Calculating swiftly in his head, he suggested he could be there around two. Olivia seemed satisfied with this and terminated the call. He was left listening to the dialling tone, as Olivia had hung up. Michael switched off the call and, full of thought, made his lunch, got changed, and caught the bus to take him into town. He would not have time for his customary run. On the bus, his mind went into overdrive. *What on earth could this be about? Surely not downsizing the staff. The appointment of a permanent head waiter?*

Michael felt crushing disappointment. He was going to be passed over for promotion and was being prepared for a new head waiter. Michael wasn't known for his optimism. He arrived at the restaurant full of doom and presented himself to Olivia and get the matter over. He began thinking he may have to look for another position, and he didn't feel up to working under a newcomer, especially if he was going to have to train him or her in the intricacies of the establishment.

Trying desperately to maintain a poker face, Michael met up with Olivia. Firstly, she apologized for breaking into his downtime. She understood how precious it was, but the meeting was necessary, and as the senior member of staff she felt it was only right he be informed of what was happening before the rest of the staff. Michael's heart sank. It was looking more and more as if he were either being passed over or, worse, losing his position.

Then Olivia delivered a not-so-surprising piece of news. James, the head waiter, currently on long term sick leave, was not getting better, and the up-to-date position was that he had decided to declare himself unfit for work and resign from the restaurant. What wasn't generally known, which Olivia had promised James she would keep to herself, was that he was, in fact, terminally ill and was unlikely to survive past Christmas.

Although James was Michael's mentor and had trained him for the past ten years, outside of work they did not form a friendship other than a strictly professional one. Michael did not know the nature of the illness and, being the reclusive type, had avoided seeking him out. Michael waited for what would come next.

Olivia made a surprising statement. She told Michael she was not replacing James yet. She wanted the right person for the job, so she asked Michael to prepare a report on how he saw the future of the restaurant, including any changes he would make and altogether see if his vision matches hers. Michael was dismayed. He knew he would have difficulty in preparing such a document, given his lack of formal education, but he realized he had to overcome his fears if he wanted to remain in post.

The staff meeting, Olivia stated, was called to look at the menus and decide what would be the special dishes for the autumn–winter season. Olivia changed the menus every spring and autumn to reflect the changes in temperature. Olivia's way of thinking was that there was no call for a thick broth in the height of the summer.

Slightly mesmerized by the meeting, Michael slowly made his way downstairs to round up those members of staff who would be responsible for preparing, cooking, and delivering the new menu. It was a noisy affair, each member of staff wanting his or her ideas to be considered.

Michael was unusually silent. Although neither had his contract been terminated nor had a newcomer been appointed over his head, the enormity of the task was not lost on him. He realized he was being asked to put a business plan together, and he didn't know where to start. He knew no one who could help either.

The one fortunate matter was that Olivia was heading off for a month-long cruise and he didn't have to produce the plan for at least six weeks. He knew, of course, he could not put this to one side. This was no "I'll think about it tomorrow" scenario, and he decided that he would have to take notes every day to analyse what was working and, more importantly, what was not.

As he signed on for his shift, a thought popped into his head that it was no more "business as usual". Michael wanted this promotion so badly he could taste it. Maybe it was time to act like a head waiter and prove he was the right man for the job. Olivia had assured him, at the very least, that the temporary waiter drafted in on busy nights would continue to assist Michael so his daily workload would not get worse.

The days passed, and Michael had never been busier. Firstly, and the most important task, was to create a business plan; then he had a book to read, and tomorrow was his first golf lesson. He was beginning to think he had bitten off more than he could chew. Perhaps the book club was a step too far, and the attendance of Monica was not helping him to keep going. There was more to think about. It was still a week to the next meeting—plenty of time to make decisions.

Chapter 10

It was time for Michael to sample his decision regarding playing golf—"learning to play golf", rather, was the more accurate description. The next morning, he arrived at the golf course and parked his car in the members' car park, which gave him a little glow of satisfaction. He was a member of a club with people who seemed to be quite friendly. He presented himself at the professional shop, ready to start his first lesson.

As the small matter of clubs had not yet been discussed, Mark had placed a couple of clubs out for his use. Mark explained that they would start with a 3 wood and move on to a 5 iron. Michael looked at the young pro blankly. He could have been speaking a foreign language, such was Michael's knowledge of the game. They headed out to the practice field complete with clubs and a bucket of golf balls. Mark teed up a ball and demonstrated how to swing the club, followed by hitting the ball.

The comment "How difficult can it be?" came back to haunt him as strike after strike could be described as best as a "fresh air shot"—a kindly way to describe a shot with the club head totally missing the ball. After about ten humiliating minutes, Michael finally hit the ball and was surprised, given the amount of effort he had put into the swing, that the ball moved only about five feet. *Have I made a huge mistake?* thought Michael.

Mark took a different approach and proceeded to work entirely on his swing, ignoring balls. By the end of the lesson, Michael was exhausted but grudgingly felt he was starting to get the hang of it. In a moment of glory, he managed to send the last ball straight down the middle, as golfers often say, and it travelled for over one hundred yards, according to Mark. Michael felt maybe this was going to be okay after all.

Michael went home feeling as if he had achieved something. He happily considered when he would become proficient. His imagination took him to the pretty course, and he looked forward to the day he would make a good fist of a full round. He was looking forward to making new friends—something that had eluded him growing up.

On arriving home after making himself a coffee, he picked up the book club's recommendation and started to read. The book was hard going, and he wasn't enjoying it much.

He had decided that the work plan Olivia had asked for was going to take up his spare time. He would be unable to keep to his book club obligations and had decided to leave the group. He would think again after Christmas and certainly after he had submitted his business plan to Olivia for her approval. It was all too much too soon. He had gone from being alone and missing his mother dreadfully to having so much to do he didn't have time to indulge in grief.

He arrived at the book club. He thought he would get there early and get the opportunity to discuss his current situation and decision to leave the club before the members arrived, but to his horror, along with his host Elizabeth, Monica was already in place. Nothing else for it, he confessed to Elizabeth in earshot of Monica, and his embarrassment was acute. Elizabeth, making sympathetic murmurs that his work had to come first and she would be delighted if he reconsidered and presented himself back in the new year.

The rest of the members had started arriving, and rather than leaving as planned, he decided to take part in the meeting one last time. He had already decided it would be for the last time. He had no intention of returning in the new year, and his second attendance only confirmed that this activity was not sitting well on his to-do list.

When the meeting closed, Elizabeth let the members know Michael would not be returning for the near future due to work pressures, and as they all said their goodbyes, Monica came up to him and expressed sympathy. Being the garrulous sort, she felt compelled to ask what was so difficult for him. Reluctantly, he explained about the possible promotion and the business plan he had been asked to produce. Monica demanded an explanation as to why this was a problem, and Michael, by now pink with embarrassment, explained his problem. They were alone in the room,

Elizabeth showing out her guests, when Monica made an astonishing suggestion. "As a PA to the CEO," she said by way of credentials, "I would like to help you. Call it compensation for the way I have treated you in the past. Will you let me help you put together your plan? You give me your ideas, and I will present them for you in a professional plan, hopefully creating a good impression."

Michael started to refuse, saying he couldn't possibly put her to so much trouble. "It's not trouble," she argued, "it is a favour for a friend, and the restaurant needs you—and in a more senior position. Let me do this for you. Give me your ideas, and I will make a document to be proud of. When is your next morning off?"

Michael, feeling he had boxed himself into a corner with no escape, murmured, "Thursday."

"Then Thursday it is, in the reading room at the library," finished Monica with a determined look in her eye. "Ten o'clock now, and don't be late," she instructed as she swept out of the door. At the last minute, over her shoulder she reminded him to bring his notes, and she left with a flourish.

"What was that all about?" asked Elizabeth. Michael admitted the offer and explained he knew her as a client at his restaurant. Elizabeth was delighted. "It will give her something else to focus on," she said. "Monica has been so wrapped up in her divorce she has not made good company. Her boss has given her compassionate leave to sort out her problems, but he won't wait forever. You are doing her a favour, Michael." Elizabeth then showed Michael out, reiterating the invite to return to the club when it was more convenient.

Michael got home and started preparing lunch and getting organized for work. He was dumbstruck. Had he just dreamt this whole conversation?

Going to meet Monica at the library was the first step. If she was there, it would prove she was serious. He faced the situation with a mixture of trepidation and elation. But Monica? Of all people, she would be the last person he would think of as helpful. However, she was most persuasive, insistent almost, and she did appear to have the skills. Maybe for once Michael could do well not to look a gift horse in the mouth. Thursday was going to be interesting.

Tuesday arrived, and Michael, not on shift until 3.00 p.m., had arranged another meeting with Mark. As he had no clubs as yet, he was tempted to walk. It was only about a mile, and it would save the hassle of retrieving his car from the lock up. He got himself in the appropriate clothing—polo shirt. slacks and a V-neck sweater—all of which he now had in his wardrobe, courtesy of the gents' outfitters in George Street. Michael set off to meet the golf professional. As he walked briskly along the street, he began to muse about the life-changing decisions he was making.

The promotion was top of his list, and he was apprehensive about what would happen when he met up with Monica. He had spent some time (when he had it) going over his notes and putting them in some sort of order. *Why?* he thought. *Why should I be trying to impress this woman when she has been the source of misery to me? Is this a way she could make amends?*

Chapter 11

Parking the thoughts of his meeting with Monica in a couple of days, he briskly walked to the club. He had decided to take a block of ten lessons before deciding one way or another.

Mark was serving a customer who was trying to decide which club to select. *This could take a while*, thought Michael. As he browsed around the tiny shop, he wondered how Mark could make a profit with such little stock. Then it occurred to him he should maybe take advantage of the second-hand clubs that had been mentioned on his first visit. Judging by the prices on the brand-new stock, Michael realized it would be a wise purchase. But not just yet; he wanted to make sure he could hit a ball today!

Minutes later, the customer, who turned out to be a senior member, asked to try out a club on the practice area. Agreeing to this request, Mark rolled out Sellotape and stuck it on the face of the club. Michael was curious. *Why did he do that?* he mused. The member thanked him. Mark then explained he was starting a lesson and would not be free for an hour should he wish to complete the transaction. The member explained he was due on the tee in twenty minutes, whereupon Mark agreed that if the club was satisfactory, he could remove the tape and take it with his other clubs to play his round. If not, he was just to leave it next to the counter.

Michael, listening to the conversation (he wasn't eavesdropping; it was a small room), was impressed at the level of trust, and his estimation of the club went a notch higher. Off they went to the practice ground, and the success of Michael's progress increased. After hitting a good many balls properly, Michael started to feel some enthusiasm and was effusive in his thanks.

The young pro was a good and patient teacher. By now Michael was striking the ball well, if not a great distance, with both the 3 wood and the 5 iron. Ten minutes before the end of the lesson, Mark indicated to Michael to return to the clubhouse and the shop. Mark was going to take Michael through the different situations meriting the change of club size. When the lesson was over, Michael went home to make lunch and get ready for work, thinking he had made a good choice. His natural athleticism was a help to his progression, and he decided he would drive to his next lesson and arrange for a set of clubs all to himself.

He had thought about it long and hard and soon realized that having his own clubs, firstly he would get used to them, and secondly he could visit the driving range and practise. He began to feel a strange sense of elation with the way his life was shaping up. Maybe his mother was still looking after him.

It had started to rain by the time Michael was ready to leave for work, so he decided to go by bus. Arriving at the restaurant early, he had time to check the diary. Taking it with him, he managed to purloin a cup of coffee from Alfredo, who was grumbling as usual, and retired to the upstairs lounge and staffroom. Looking for any more information he could use for the business plan, he noticed that Mr. MacGregor had booked in for a table at his usual time of 9.00 p.m. Looking back through the diary, it appeared that his visits were always mid-week with no real pattern other than a couple of months between visits. There was still no companion; the table was for one.

Michael started his work thinking about Mr. MacGregor, and his imaginative mind started mulling over what the story behind it all could be. As the restaurant got busier, all thought of his customer flew out of the window, and before he knew it, he was welcoming Mr. MacGregor, seating him at his favourite table, and presenting the menu. His order off the daily special menu was hunter's chicken washed down with a couple of glasses of house Pinot Grigio.

When the time came, Michael cleared Mr. MacGregor's table, offered coffee, and made all the usual pleasantries: "Did you enjoy your meal?... Was everything okay for you?... Would you like a coffee?" All the while, he was hoping for some sort of indication of what Mr. MacGregor was like as a person. Michael was intrigued.

This tall, quiet, and unassuming man was keeping himself to

himself. Usually the patrons would gossip and give out information about themselves, which, if Michael had to operate in that manner, would make him shudder.

As he arranged the coffee for Mr. MacGregor, Michael added a small nip of Drambuie to the tray. It was a practice usually associated with upper-class hotels in Europe and, with Olivia's blessing, was passed on to certain customers frequenting the restaurant. If Mr. MacGregor was surprised at the gesture, he didn't show it, but on his way out he stopped and thanked Michael for a very pleasant evening. Michael was very impressed with his demeanour and looked forward to meeting and serving the mysterious Mr. MacGregor again.

Michael's alarm clock woke him at 8.00 a.m. on Thursday morning. After silencing the beast, he blinked a few times, wondering why on earth the clock had gone off this early. Then he remembered.

His stomach did a somersault as he realized it was Thursday, his day off, hence the surprise of the alarm jangling in his ear. He was meeting Monica to go over his business plan. Not wanting to be late, he quickly shaved and showered.

He felt like a girl on her first date as he dragged garment after garment out of his wardrobe, trying to decide what to wear. He laughed at his reflection in his mirror and selected a pair of navy trousers and a polo-necked sweater, smiling all the while about his thinking that what he wore was important.

He had to be at the library by 10:00 a.m, and not wanting to arrive hot and bothered, he decided to go by bus. It was a fair distance, and even with Edinburgh traffic he figured it would take him at least half an hour on the bus, but he decided to make it forty-five minutes, just in case.

After breakfast, not having made much of it as his nerves had killed his appetite, he searched the house for something appropriate to put his paperwork in. To his chagrin, all he could come up with was a plastic supermarket bag. A bag for life it was called, and Michael strangely found this funny as he grinned all the way to the bus stop. Unaware of his smiling face, he was conscious of people he hardly knew saying good morning or smiling back. *Odd*, he thought while boarding the bus that would take him to Fountainbridge Public Library. He was mystified as to the reactions of his fellow travellers, not realizing he was still smiling.

Michael, Waiting

On arriving early, to his delight, he found the reading room. To pass the time, he availed himself of the daily newspapers and started to read. Concentrating on a particularly interesting article, he failed to notice the arrival of Monica until she stood by his chair and made herself known.

Stuttering apologies as he stood up and greeted her, Monica waved them away and seated herself at a small table set for two, beckoning him to sit opposite.

With embarrassment, he emptied the paperwork out of the plastic bag he was so ashamed of and looked at Monica with trepidation. He had a vision of her saying that she couldn't make anything out of it and that this would be disastrous. Michael did not know how to take it forward. However, to his delight, Monica swept the paperwork into a neat bundle and proceeded to go through his workings page by page.

About an hour later—Michael, if he had been inclined to bite his nails, would have been down to his wrists by now—Monica spoke for the first time. "Michael, this plan is excellent, and I am sure, on the strength of it and your exemplary performance in the restaurant, it will indicate how well you are suited for the position." Michael visibly collapsed with relief.

He had not realized just how tense he had been or just how important this was to him. "However," continued Monica, never one known for her tact, "it needs to be tidied up. I will take it away with me and work on it, and we can meet up at your convenience. When's your day off next week?"

Michael had swung from pleasure to disappointment and back to pleasure. "It's the same as this week—Thursday," answered Michael.

Same time, same place," stated Monica, who was not known for her sparkling conversation. She then swept majestically out of the door, having filed the paperwork in her capacious handbag. *Didn't manage to fall down the steps*, thought Michael, somewhat unkindly. He was feeling just a trifle shell-shocked.

Although it was not his day off, that being reserved for Monica, his meeting with Mark on Tuesday morning came around again. *The weeks are going in fast*, thought Michael. *It will be Christmas before we know it.* He made a mental note to discuss it with Alfredo when he got to work. *It will be time to sort out Christmas menus and start the very understated advertising for the Christmas specials.* They didn't open on Christmas Day as a rule. Olivia had thought that so many of the bigger establishments were open, and at exorbitant prices, usually having put on some sort of entertainment. Michael thought that they could offer an alternative and vowed to set up a plan for Christmas Day that would not lower the tone of the restaurant. *I can include it in my business plan*, he thought happily.

Chapter 12

Mark greeted him like a long-lost friend when Michael arrived at the Club and began by announcing that today they would be going out in the buggy and driving round the course. It was a parkland course with few inclines. As they motored round, Mark was struck by the green fairways and manicured greens.

"How do you keep the course in such good order?" asked Michael, not having experienced a walk round the fairways and greens of a golf course before. Mark explained all about the ground staff and the rules and etiquette of the course as they were travelling round.

"Of course the buggies are for rent and usually made available for the more elderly players. Visiting parties, too, usually book the buggies, but indeed they may be rented by anyone," the young pro explained. "A man of your fitness would probably walk round. It takes about three hours to play the full eighteen holes."

It had taken very little time to traverse the course, familiar excitement was growing in Michael. Back on the practice area for the remainder of his lesson, he casually mentioned that if the second-hand clubs were available, he would be interested in a look with a view to buying. At the end of the lesson, Mark demonstrated the clubs and told Michael the half set would be sufficient for now but to look to upgrade as he got better at the game and started to take part in competitions. Mark took him through all of the clubs, explaining their purposes, and finished off by towing Michael out of the shop and back to the practice area.

Michael was tall, but happily so had been the previous owner, and the clubs were perfect in length. The deal was done and the money exchanged. Michael now felt a big commitment, and although he had only parted with one hundred pounds plus another ten for a large bag of 'lake balls,' it was enough to seal his enthusiasm and impatience in getting started. Proudly stowing his new possessions, he drove home to once again get ready for work.

Tuesday evenings were not busy like the weekends, and it was a good time for two of the three other waiters in the team to have days off. Michael had to step into the breach, and his shift started with the polishing of the cutlery and setting of the tables, with Michael not forgetting to place the reserved signs on the appropriate tables.

He noticed that whoever had taken one of today's bookings had pencilled "anniversary" next to a couple who had been before but quite some time ago. Michael made a mental note to deal with them personally. He took great pride in returning guests. The restaurant was popular for special occasions like anniversary celebrations, having the sort of intimate atmosphere that couples favoured. They didn't encourage birthday parties, as the eating area was small and party poppers were frowned upon.

It transpired that the anniversary couple were celebrating forty years together, and as Michael went through the ordering of food and drink, he made sure the guests were taken care of. Before the meal and wine arrived, Michael presented the couple with a complimentary bottle of Champagne, as forty years was just a bit special.

A pang of jealousy got Michael as he never had any anniversaries to celebrate, never mind forty of them. However, he put it to one side and enjoyed the moment when the couple popped the cork.

Wednesday came and went, and all too soon Michael found himself on the bus taking him to Fountainbridge and Monica. He had finished reasonably early the night before and had time when he got home to draft up his ideas for Christmas to gauge Monica's reaction.

As a customer, she was the obvious choice; and as she was not one to hold back, she would give an honest and truthful answer. Michael considered this ruefully as he remembered with horror some of the remarks she had made after her meal was delivered.

Although he was some ten minutes early when he reached the reading room, Monica was already there. Michael was secretly horrified. Gentlemanly behaviour, according to his late mum, demanded the male arrive first and not keep a lady waiting. Michael squashed that thought, thinking that

Monica had not yet displayed ladylike tendencies, so he let himself off the hook on that one. Besides, he was still early. He joined her with an apology for keeping her waiting, to which Monica replied that her bus had been early.

He sat at the table, looking at her expectantly. Monica had in front of her what looked like an A4 booklet. She slid it over to him. He looked with total surprise at a booklet with a white cover held together with brass split pins and a square panel on the front headed "Business Plan by Michael Whittaker." He was astounded. He had not been expecting such a professional presentation.

All he could think to say was, "How did you know my name?" Monica laughingly explained she had telephoned the restaurant and one of the waiters had told her. She confirmed she had already known his first name was Michael.

Reading through the pages, although he recognized the content, he could not believe how good it looked. He couldn't thank her enough.

While Michael was totally effusive in his praise and thanks, Monica cut him off to indicate how much she had enjoyed doing it, hoping that his boss would take on board the suggestions, which Monica had indicated she approved of. Feeling as though he was taking advantage, he did two things that later led him to wonder what had given him the courage to do them. He first of all asked whether Monica would put his Christmas thoughts into some sort of manageable order and asked whether he could thank her by taking her to lunch.

Monica responded in a very Monica-like way and said it was the least he could do! Michael was taken by surprise, and as Monica burst into laughter, he smiled and realized she was making a joke. Without asking for an address, he asked which part of town suited her, as he would not be taking her to his place of work; that would be a step too far. Monica indicated somewhere in Morningside would suit.

Michael thought for about ten seconds before suggesting the Canny Man's on Morningside Road. This quirky restaurant was famous for the artefacts crowding the walls and the many shelves around the nooks and crannies of the restaurant. It had always been a favourite for Michael, and he welcomed any opportunity to revisit. As it had been some time since he had visited, he was excited to get the chance to go back. To his delight, Monica told him it was a favourite of hers and said she would be delighted. They arranged for 1.00 p.m. the following Thursday, with Monica promising to bring his Christmas ideas typed up for him. After he thanked her one more time, they parted company and went for their respective transport.

Travelling back to Mortonhall, Michael tried to put some order into his head. He was totally astonished at what he had done. Not only had he invited a woman out to lunch, but the woman had accepted. Notwithstanding the acceptance, the lunch date was Monica, the woman who had made his life a misery every first Friday of the month until he took his revenge. How could life's happenings turn around in such a short time? He was really confused and totally spaced out by it. He remembered those occasions when Monica had been at her worst. But she did deserve a lunch after the magnificent job she did on his business plan.

Having spent most of his adult life starting with catering college and then moving on to working in eating establishments, culminating in the one he worked in now, he had not really experienced the administrative side of life. He had, of course, learned how to use a word processor to enable him to make menus, but those were simple documents. Nowadays that was Olivia's forte, and by no means was he in a hurry to change that. The business plan looked so professional, and any misgivings he had on his part melted like snow off a dyke at the thought of treating this woman to lunch.

It was the first Friday of October, and Michael checked the diary. Sure enough, the ladies were booked in, but he noticed with a small pang that the table was booked for three. Monica, true to her word, would not be part of the party.

Chapter 13

As he set their table, placing the reserved notice, he wondered whether the other three knew what had transpired over the last week.

The party of three ladies turned up on time, as they usually did. Michael went through the well-practised routine, which saw the party seated, menus distributed, and drinks orders given.

He had noticed a change in his dealings with customers. He felt more confident and made conversation with the regular diners. Thinking about the change, Michael decided that this had come about as a result of the lifestyle changes he had made, and he was really looking forward to Olivia's return next week so he could show his plans for the restaurant. Next week could be a very interesting week indeed.

The weekend passed very quickly, and as usual, Michael was on duty. Monday was to be the book club day; however, Michael had prearranged to come into the restaurant in the morning to meet with Olivia and report the activities and, more importantly, how busy it had been during her absence.

Also, he had not made any progress with the book he was required to read, having had to return it to the library. It wasn't a difficult decision to skip the meeting. Besides, he had told them he wouldn't be back. He had given the matter of not returning to the book club some thought. It was a decision he regretted, and he had decided to go back, just not today. Tomorrow was his golf lesson, and he was looking forward to that.

He had made up his mind that he would head to the Braids and spend a couple of hours on the driving range on Wednesday before starting his work.

Michael announced his arrival at the restaurant via the internal phone, and Olivia asked him to come up and see her. Looking bronzed and fit,

Olivia smiled and motioned Michael to sit down. She had made coffee, and the tray was in front of him. "Pour us a cup and let's get started," she said.

Over the next hour, Michael, referring to the notes he had made, gave her a full and comprehensive report on how the restaurant had fared in her absence. Michael handed her the bank deposit slips, as he had been banking the takings on her behalf. This was not his normal routine, but during Olivia's absence it would have been foolish not to secure the cash. Olivia thanked Michael and congratulated him on a job well done.

The moment he had been apprehensive about—no, actually dreading—arrived with Olivia asking Michael whether he had made any progress on his views of the future and the direction he saw the restaurant going in. All of a sudden, he felt very vulnerable. His whole future depended on the next hour or so. He excused himself to retrieve the business plan from the staffroom. He didn't want to bring a supermarket bag into the meeting. He had done that once, and he hadn't liked it. He made a mental note that perhaps the purchase of a lightweight briefcase might be a useful addition to his meagre possessions.

On his return, he placed the file prepared by Monica in front of Olivia. Olivia stared at the document, not hiding her surprise at the professional presentation. She flicked through the pages silently, absorbing nothing but seeing all. Eventually Olivia looked at Michael, who held her gaze, and quietly and with wonder said what was probably an understatement. "You really want this, Michael, don't you?" She hadn't realized just how important this was to Michael.

She pulled herself together and said, "You have obviously put a great deal of work into this, and it merits proper consideration. Can we reconvene on Wednesday for a proper discussion?"

Michael didn't know whether to be pleased or not. *Giving my proposal more consideration must be good news*, he thought while agreeing to meet on Wednesday around eleven. Michael could still make it to the driving range. He would just have to start early.

Back downstairs and into the daily tasks requiring his attention, Michael did not have time to consider all that Olivia had said. He did mull over the comment she made about really wanting the job, and he felt justified to have made the effort. When he met Monica for lunch as a thank you, he would be sure to make it clear that, win or lose, he was grateful for her input.

He had been so engrossed in his meeting that he hadn't checked the diary. He gave himself a telling-off for not fulfilling his duties, so he was taken by surprise by the nine o'clock arrival of the gentleman known as Mr. MacGregor.

Quickly pulling himself together, he directed Mr. MacGregor to his favourite table, which was, thankfully, free. With menus produced and drinks orders taken, Michael carried on with the eternal clearing, polishing, and generally making sure everything was up to standard.

Chapter 14

As Mr. MacGregor paid and prepared to leave, he leaned towards Michael and very softly said to him, "I was very sorry to hear about your mother passing." As Michael stuttered his thanks, thoroughly taken aback, Mr. MacGregor left the building, leaving Michael practically open-mouthed. It took a while before Michael fully understood the situation, or so he thought. The first thing he considered was how Mr. MacGregor could have known about the loss, and then he realized that Mr. MacGregor must have known her.

This was a strange thought. Michael had not seen his mother socialize apart from meeting an old school friend for a meal on a regular basis. Maybe he was a neighbour, but it was a puzzle. Michael and his mother were very close, and other people did not feature largely in their social sphere. Michael remembered, to his embarrassment, the fuss he caused when the lady from next door arrived to baby-sit during those times when his mother did go out to meet Angela.

He was still mulling over the bolt from the blue of the evening before as he arrived at the club for his fourth lesson. He proudly carried his clubs to the professional shop, as he was determined to practise with his own clubs so he could get used to them.

Of course, the first few strikes went all over the practice grounds, but slowly he adjusted to the weight and length of the club. Before long he was striking the ball consistently, the flight going well. Michael now started enjoying himself, and as the lesson finished, he thanked Mark and headed off thinking he would get more practice at the driving range tomorrow. Mark had told him the practice area was free to be used whenever he wanted. Michael felt he wasn't quite ready for that. Besides, walking up, down, right, and left retrieving balls was no fun when he could get a bucket of balls and not have to collect them.

Nothing exciting happened in the restaurant today, thought Michael. *Thank goodness.* Although he felt he was dealing with life's complications better than usual and that his confidence was improving, another conversation like the previous night's would have given him a fit of the wobbles. He was now focusing his thoughts on tomorrow and the meeting with Olivia. Monica had thoughtfully provided a photocopy of the plan to allow him to study it at length and be ready for questions.

Michael gazed at Olivia as she turned the pages of his plan. She had been unexpectedly quiet throughout the short time he had been sitting across the desk. She looked up and caught Michael's gaze.

She smiled, her eyes twinkled, and Michael's hopes began to rise when suddenly e, Olivia said, "Would you like to be my head waiter and be in charge of the front of house?"

Trying to remain cool, calm, and collected, Michael countered with "Would there be any change in my terms and conditions?"

Olivia threw her head back laughing, and Michael thought that he had blown his chances until "Of course, Michael. You will get a substantial pay rise, an extra week's holiday, and the opportunity to help select your deputy." She pushed a document towards him. "Take this home and read it. All the information is there for you."

"In that case," said Michael, "I accept."

Michael spent the next half hour going over his business plan, and to his immense satisfaction, it really did mirror Olivia's hopes, dreams, and aspirations. In some cases, she preferred Michael's strategy, which was more workable than her own. "You know, Michael, I was not sure that you would be up to the responsibility and was reluctant to promote you. However, since I have returned from my holiday, I have noticed a more confident and approachable you. The plan clinched it. Michael, I am delighted you are going to be my right-hand man. Congratulations."

In a daze, Michael slowly descended the stairs. What had just happened was beyond his wildest dreams, and his lifelong ambition to be head waiter was coming to fruition. He knew he had to maintain the standards and possibly improve on them, but Olivia had been insistent she would not interfere downstairs, though if there were to be any major changes, she would be looking for at least a run-through with him.

They agreed on a weekly meeting—especially at first, while Michael settled into his new role. After shaking hands, he excused himself and returned to work.

Michael mulled all of this over as he cleaned glasses and cutlery. Checking the diary for reservations to set the place settings, he was taken aback when he discovered Olivia had followed him downstairs and was addressing the assembled company, intimating the change of management status for Michael. Although a very introverted man, he nevertheless was well liked, and a round of applause erupted. Blushing furiously, Michael thanked the staff, but Olivia whispered in his ear, "Michael, remember you are in charge now. Polishing cutlery and glasses are not your jobs any more. Learn to delegate." She practically hissed the words, and then she turned and went back to her office—or sanctuary, as she liked to call it.

Michael was stunned but quickly realized that Olivia was merely reminding him that his status had changed and he had to revise his actions accordingly. Tony, the young waiter who had been deputizing while Michael had been acting up, was duly summoned, and Michael explained that his duties would be changing slightly for the next few weeks. He was to ensure the cutlery and glasses were sparkling.

Tony looked somewhat annoyed. It would appear he was unhappy with the situation. More than once Michael had chided him gently when he wasn't putting full attention to his responsibilities. He had been mentioned as a possible deputy, but Michael had indicated he might not come up to scratch and had asked whether he could have time to observe him—maybe a month. Olivia had no problem with this, as she, too, had thought he was a bit of a slacker. *He was good enough to keep on*, thought Michael, *but not up to the mark to deputize for me.* Michael had planned a holiday in January, but nothing was booked yet. He considered he may have to postpone. The restaurant came first.

Thursday dawned. This was the most frightening thing he had had to do in his adult life—taking a lady to lunch. If she had been less of a dragon, it might have been easier, but with her sharp tongue, he knew it may not be a pleasant experience. Girding his loins, he headed to the bus stop. Ordinarily he would have walked, but on an occasion like this, he

Michael, Waiting

did not want to create a bad impression by arriving windswept and a trifle sweaty with the exertion.

To his delight, the pub was quiet, and having reserved in advance, he was shown to his table to wait the arrival of his lunch guest. Happily, he had arrived ahead of her; he was ten minutes early! He had brought the local paper to occupy himself while he waited.

At 1:00 p.m. on the dot, Monica arrived and joined Michael at the table. After they had exchanged greetings, Michael passed the menu to Monica, as he had already decided, and asked what she would like to drink. Monica indicated she would love a white wine, and being a bit of an expert, Michael ordered a bottle of a middle-of-the-road Sauvignon Blanc. Monica, having stuck to the house wine at the restaurant, was impressed. Not since her husband had left had she been in a situation to drink a good wine.

Monica adopted a conspiratorial stance as she leant forward to ask Michael how his business plan and the meeting with his boss over. Michael, blushing furiously, was able to confirm his newly appointed status. With a muted applause, Monica offered her congratulations and ordered a bottle of bubbly to celebrate, for which she insisted on paying.

Monica looked at the menu but very quickly closed it again. Like Michael, she was familiar with the menu and had only checked to make sure her choice was still listed.

Meanwhile, the wine had arrived and been opened and poured into sparkling clean glasses. Michael went to the bar and, after Monica chose the same items as he, ordered the famous smorgasbord with salmon and prawns. *Seems we have similar tastes in food*, he thought. He requested the lunch not to be served until the champagne had been dispensed with, which surprisingly took a relatively short time.

Much to Michael's surprise, the lunch was going well. Monica had a keen but dry sense of humour and kept him entertained, sometimes laughing out loud at the exploits in which she had been involved. Many of the anecdotes highlighted a self-deprecating demeanour, which surprised Michael. Her attitude whilst eating in the restaurant had on all occasions portrayed her as a somewhat arrogant know-it-all.

Michael, to his surprise, was enjoying lunch in good

company—something he had not done for as long as he could remember, excepting the odd birthday meal with his mother.

All too soon, the meal was over, the wine drunk. There came the realization that they had been sitting, eating, drinking, and conversing for more than two hours. Beginning to feel he had overstayed his welcome, Michael arranged to settle the bill. Just as he was about to help Monica out of her chair and into her coat, she extracted a file from her oversized bag. Handing it to Michael, she informed him she had arranged his Christmas ideas into a file to show to his employer. "I hope it works for you," she said, and she thanked him for lunch.

Monica waved away his thanks and told him how much she had enjoyed lunch; however, she also had a favour to ask. Michael was wondering what he could possibly do to help this woman when she started to explain. "The company I work for hosts a Christmas ball for their employees for services rendered. It is a free meal and bar. As it is a ball, we are expected to bring a partner. I have two choices. I can stay home and have my colleagues feel sorry for me having no partner—as you know, my husband sloped off with his secretary—or I can ask you to be my plus-one for the occasion."

Michael was first surprised and then horrified. The very thought made him feel weak at the knees. He thought long and hard, and as the silence lengthened, Michael digested what he had been asked to do.

Trying not to put his feelings first, he remembered that this lonely and difficult woman had done so much for him, and he could not, in all honesty, let her down. A glimmer of an idea came to him, and he invited Monica to sit down and offered her another drink while they discussed the request.

Michael ordered two gin and tonics and explained that his first reaction had been to refuse, but mindful of the favour that had been done for him, he was happy to hear more about what was required. He admitted that formal occasions were an anathema to him, having not been anywhere grand in his life, and the last time he had attended a dance it was his school leaving dance, and that had been a nightmare.

Monica, while listening to Michael's story, felt a rush of guilt. Michael, from the first meeting, had not recognized her or her companions. They were part of the gang who had made Michael's life a misery at school. She contemplated making a confession but mentally shook her head. *I will keep that information for a more appropriate time, if that ever happens*, she thought. She outlined the basic requirements and answered all his questions. With the semantics over, Monica then explained the dress code, the venue, and the transportation arrangements.

As Monica listened to Michael's scanty description of his social life, or lack of it, Monica remained silent, digesting the information gleaned from this proud, shy man. Metaphorically holding her breath, she waited for his decision. A second drink had been ordered, and it was nearing five o'clock when suddenly Michael spoke up and agreed to be the partner for the ball. Monica let out a sigh of relief. It had been an embarrassment to admit to her work colleagues that her husband had left her for a younger model, Michael's decision was a huge relief to her. She would enjoy not explaining Michael's status to these women at her workplace.

Monica suggested that they meet up in three weeks, the week before the ball, to discuss last-minute arrangements. They would meet for lunch at the Canny Man's, but this time Monica insisted she would treat him. She also wanted to pay for the formal attire hire, but Michael insisted he would provide his outfit.

The pub had a reputation of providing a free buffet at five, and as the two had consumed a rather large quantity of alcohol, they decided to have a few nibbles off the buffet before heading home. They felt it was too good to miss as they sampled the different items on display.

Chapter 15

Walking home, the earlier rain having stopped, Michael pondered on this surprising turn of events. He could not believe what he had let himself in for. His first priority was to arrange cover for the evening, which was a busy one in the restaurant. Tony was likely to be out of sorts, as he would have to work harder than usual—something he had an aversion to. Then he had to arrange the hire of a suit. He was sure there was a dress suit hire shop further up the road on his way home.

He came out of the shop slightly bemused. In his slightly inebriated state, the salesman had no difficulty in persuading Michael into hiring full highland dress. When told it was the tartan of Clan MacGregor, he smiled to himself thinking about the dinner guest who occasionally frequented the restaurant. He would enjoy telling him this little anecdote. Then he remembered the last conversation he had with Mr. MacGregor and decided to have the conversation to clear up the mystery.

Arriving home having had quite enough to drink for the day, Michael made himself a pot of tea. He thought it would be a good idea to read the book club book, as the hard work aided and abetted by Monica regarding his vision for the restaurant was finished with. He scoured the lounge, wondering where he had put it, until the memory flooded back. He had returned it to the library. Switching on the television, he surfed channels to find something to watch. He left the news on, and the next thing he knew, the gin and tonics had taken hold. He was still in his armchair at 3.30 a.m. He staggered up to bed vowing to avoid daytime drinking in the future.

As the weekend came and went, he managed to retrieve the library book from the library, but he had no time to read any of the content. Thinking he had better shelve the Book club this week, Michael laughed

Michael, Waiting

softly as he realized his own joke and headed off to the driving range. It was a pleasant day, if a little cold, and as he proudly stowed his new clubs in the boot of the car, he ruminated on how life was changing. He was changing as well, and as his confidence grew, he felt a little burst of happiness.

Chapter 16

The restaurant was as busy as usual and as Michael eased into his new role, he felt a great sense of achievement. Tony was still acting up but not making a decent fist of it and Michael vowed to deal with the problem after the Christmas festivities were behind them. The decision to open on Christmas Day had not been taken lightly and Olivia had sought the approval of all the staff affected before publishing a Christmas Day menu along with a festive menu on the two weeks running up to Christmas.

In his new role, Michael was aware of all eyes on him, and although he was popular with his colleagues, Tony, for one reason or another, disliked Michael and looked for opportunities to undermine him. Not being very smart, Tony did not realize he was being watched and assessed, and every now and then Michael would have a conversation to persuade Tony to act in a more positive way. This did nothing to allay Tony's sense of unfairness, and Michael was getting exasperated.

He decided to ask for a meeting with his boss firstly to arrange his time off and secondly because Michael was fast beginning to realize that Tony was not proving to be a good fit. Michael desperately needed Olivia's advice, as he was beginning to cloud the atmosphere of the restaurant.

Michael's upcoming social engagement and Christmas bought Tony more time. However, Michael requested to bring in one of the reserve waiters on a shift pattern not worked by Tony. It would be a try-before-you-buy scenario, and Olivia was more than happy to accede to the request. She suggested Peter, who was in his early fifties and had proved to be very efficient and charming to the guests.

Both Michael and Olivia agreed. Peter was very experienced and kept his hand in being on a staff agency's books. Michael felt this would work well and, after obtaining his number, used Olivia's phone to call Peter and offer him, for the foreseeable future, the weekend shifts. Peter was delighted to have steady income and agreed to the offer with enthusiasm. He contacted the agency and removed himself from availability on the days Michael had offered him.

With Peter agreeing to start on Thursday, Michael went back to the restaurant to continue his duties safe in the knowledge he had an understudy for now. Going downstairs, he realized there was a bit of an atmosphere. No one would meet his eyes. Michael quizzed the staff as to the problem and immediately noticed Tony was missing.

The story unfolded. Tony had noticed he was on full shift to cover Michael's absence during the ball and had not taken it well. He had been rude to the clients at the table he was serving, and the clients had left their food, thrown money on the table, and left the building. One of the other young waiters had remonstrated with Tony, who was now out the back, smoking furiously and sulking.

Michael's first reaction was to give Tony the sack on the spot, but unsure of legal protocol, he decided to run it past Olivia even before he spoke to Tony. He'd be damned if he was going out the back to drag Tony in for a dressing down.

Olivia listened carefully to what Michael reported, and like Michael, she wanted him dismissed on the spot. However, he was entitled to a warning according to industrial law. In this case, the quiet words Michael had given Tony were sufficient to warrant a verbal warning. Whilst Tony was giving his version of events, Olivia indicated she would draw up a first written warning and it would be handed to Tony today. Michael was instructed to inform him of that as the interview terminated.

With a heavy heart, he went back downstairs to find an even blacker atmosphere which was palpable throughout the restaurant. Tony, back from his smoke but not his sulk, was having a massive tantrum. Angry at the lack of support from his workmates, he was pulling tablecloths off the tables, scattering cutlery to the four winds. Maybe he had designs on a new career as a conjurer. After his conversation he would have with a furious Michael, a new job was going to be a necessity.

Michael turned on his heel, mounted the stairs with a heavy tread and walked back into Olivia's office without knocking. If Olivia was surprised, she didn't show it. Michael was usually so deferential; this behaviour was out of character, so Olivia leant back in her chair, all ears. She was seeing a stronger Michael, and it pleased her greatly.

"Tony has gone too far. At this moment, he is pulling tablecloths off tables, scattering cutlery plates—you name it. The restaurant is like a bomb site. Make that letter an instant dismissal letter on the grounds of gross misconduct. I will be in the staffroom with Tony when you are ready."

He almost barked that at Olivia. She was too surprised to do anything other than acquiesce.

Michael marched down the stairs and ordered Tony to the staffroom. Tony looked as if he were going to refuse with an arrogant "you can't tell me what to do" attitude, but one look at Michael's face and he changed his mind, heading up to the staffroom as told. Michael shut the door and turned to his employee, who seemed to be calming down.

"Well," said Michael, "I want an explanation for your disgraceful conduct." Tony started whining about shift patterns, how Michael was always the one getting favours, and so on. Michael shook his head. "Tony," he said, "you are the laziest, most inefficient waiter I have ever had the misfortune to meet. I do not want a repeat of this behaviour."

"I am sorry," stuttered Tony. "It won't happen again."

"No, it won't," said Michael. "You won't get the opportunity. Your contract with this establishment is at an end. You are fired." On cue, Olivia came in and handed the letter to Tony.

Realizing the futility of arguing, Tony asked when he would have to leave.

"If you get downstairs and help clear the mess you have made, you will be paid for one week, and you will work that week and carry out your duties in an orderly fashion," Olivia said. "You will not pick fights with anyone, and you will be polite and courteous to everyone—co-workers and especially clients. Will that suit?" Tony agreed and was sent down to start the clear-up.

Fortunately, the restaurant was between lunch and dinner, and with all hands-on deck, order was restored on time. Not trusting Tony to fulfil his contract, Michael called Peter and asked him to come into work as soon as possible to discuss the shift patterns. Michael explained the situation and requested that especially on the Saturday of the ball, Peter would be

Michael, Waiting

necessary. Peter was between jobs, and he had no work lined up for the rest of the week and could start tomorrow. Michael had decided to have Peter shadow Tony in the hope it would keep the restaurant working smoothly.

With all of that out of the way, Michael went back downstairs to see how the clear-up was going and assess the damage. It had obviously looked worse than it was because the tables were mostly reset and the broken crockery cleared. The breakage count turned out to be two side plates, a cup, and a saucer. The sugar bowl was upside down, but the contents—sugar lumps—were already cleared up. The sound of the Hoover jarred Michael's nerves, and after telling Olivia, he slipped out the door for a walk round the block to settle his shattered nerves and get some fresh air.

On arriving back some twenty minutes later, and after checking all was well in the restaurant, Michael climbed the stairs to Olivia's office, this time knocking. He hadn't had a chance to explain amidst all the fuss with Tony that he had arranged cover for the Saturday three weeks hence as he had a social function. Agreeing immediately, Olivia was tempted to quiz him as to the nature of the social occasion, but remembering his shyness and knowing better, she told him that was perfectly fine. Michael then went on to ask for permission to advertise for another member of staff. Olivia agreed this would be a good idea but felt it should be on a part-time basis with a view to extra hours. With a cheeky grin, she remarked it would be nice to have a lady in the place. Michael gave her an old-fashioned look as he turned and left the office.

As she was left to her own devices and the drama was over, Olivia began to think about Michael. Firstly, his confidence was growing almost daily. He was incredibly efficient at his job. He seemed to get the best out of his staff, but most intriguing of all, where was he going socially on a Saturday night, and how had he produced the business plan? *One day all will be revealed*, Olivia thought optimistically.

Chapter 17

Mark, the young golf professional, had given Michael five lessons now, and Mark could see him progressing well. Naturally slim and fit, he found the golf swing relatively easy to master. He was still guilty of the occasional air shot and also shafting his ball into trees and bushes. Bunkers were part and parcel of every golfer's game, and Michael was proving to be rather adept at pitching out of the many bunkers on the course, probably as a result of all the practice he got. He was making decent strikes, and he was pleased with his progress. It was easy to determine that his drives were getting longer. He ruefully remembered how short a distance he could hit the ball on his first two visits to the driving range.

Mark had suggested that his next lesson should be in the form of a game of nine holes with Mark coaching. Michael was delighted, and after the session was finished, he felt he was really making progress. He decided to visit the lounge for the first time and see whether he could make some friends.

He walked up the stairs and strode into the lounge. As he stood at the bar, waiting to be served, a hand on his shoulder startled him. He turned around to see William, the club captain, beaming at him. William welcomed him into the clubhouse. Michael offered to buy him a drink as a way of thanking him for his help. After a couple of instances of "Not at all, it's my round," William gave in and carried his pint of lager, towing Michael with him to a table where he recognized some of the faces. Introductions were made. Michael thanked the members of the committee who had helped him to gain membership. Arthur, as he was called, was the club treasurer, and Mark had told him in a moment of indiscretion that

Michael, Waiting

these four practically ran the club, leaving the secretary out in the cold. They were known as the fearsome four.

On being asked about his progress, Michael proudly admitted to being a bit better and that Mark had played nine holes with him, declaring him fit to be on the course. He was certain that the group called the fearsome four were sitting at the table, and he made his mind up not to get involved in golf club politics and certainly keep on the right side of these members. *Keeping my powder dry,* Michael thought.

As he was working later, Michael left the club with its fearsome four earlier than he would have liked and vowed he would return on his day off and maybe get invited to join a game, or at the very least a drink in the lounge.

Thinking about his day off, Michael remembered he was to meet Monica on Thursday to go over the arrangements for the work do. Not for the first time, he wondered how he had been talked into this one. His pessimism showing, he began to list all the things that could go wrong. *This is not helpful,* he scolded himself. He decided to pop into the hire shop and check on his order. Settled on confirming his kilt hire, he got a sudden idea that perhaps Monica would appreciate a corsage, and as he passed by a florist on his way home, he decided to pay a visit and ask their advice. He could pop in on his way to work. It was cold but sunny. Walking would be good.

On arrival at work, he changed from his sweater into his work clothes. When Olivia noticed, she remarked how inconvenient it was to have to carry a change of clothes and offered him space in the hanging wardrobe in her office. Michael was delighted. He could collect his laundered shirts from the launderette and stow them at work. It made running, and possibly cycling, more feasible. He had bought a small rucksack, which worked well carrying spare clothes, but his shirts did not fare well. Olivia had suggested he research a smarter uniform now he was head waiter—a waistcoat and bow tie, perhaps. He would research whilst shopping.

He decided that he needed to shop. His clothes were sadly out of date, and he wanted to cheer up his wardrobe. He had bought a more up-to-date outfit to attend the golf club, but he had little else. So much change in so little time. He still missed his mother dreadfully, but with his busy new life, the pain was diminishing. He was starting to remember the good times more than the loss. He decided to head into town first on Thursday and get to Morningside for their one o'clock meeting. He was feeling very nervous now. The ball was so close.

He wandered through the town wondering about the best place to shop. His last shopping trip had been to a gents' shop in George Street. He couldn't remember the name, but his mother had taken him there for school clothes when he was younger. He felt it to be a little upmarket the last time he had been in. Then he remembered his mother had favoured Jenner's. He walked along Princes Street, arriving at the imposing building on the corner of St Andrew's Street.

Making his way to the gents' department, he passed the shoe department, who were having a sale. Right at the front were a pair of kilt shoes which just happened to be his size. They were less than half price, and such a bargain could not be ignored. He asked to try them on, and they were so comfortable he was delighted. Being unhappy at hiring shoes, and the cost of buying being very reasonable, he bought them there and then.

A delighted Michael went on to shop for sweaters, shirts, and trousers. He even bought his first pair of jeans. Much lighter in the pocket, he headed off to meet Monica. He still had some time, and feeling overburdened with his parcels, he jumped into a taxi and asked the driver to take him to his house, where he stowed his purchases. He then asked the driver to take him to the Canny Man's. He got there with ten minutes to spare. A relieved Michael greeted Monica.

Monica had arrived on time, and laughingly they both chose the same fish smorgasbord and wine. *Just wine*, thought Michael. *Look at the trouble I got into last trip. Highland dress indeed.*

The food arrived, and the comfortable silence as the sandwiches were prepared caused them to eschew conversation. However, plates cleared away, they got down to the purpose of the meeting. Firstly, they exchanged mobile numbers. Monica showed him how to add a phone number, Michael being a bit backward with technology. If Monica was surprised at the lack of numbers in his directory or his lack of expertise, she kept it quiet.

The venue was the assembly rooms in George Street, centre of the city. The meal was to be served at 8.00 p.m. However, Monica wanted to be there for 7.30 to get the meet-and-greet over with. Monica had discussed the dancing and, to spare Michael's blushes, opted for a dislike of dancing.

She was very grateful he was going to escort her to the function; she had no desire to add to his discomfort expecting him to dance. She hadn't even told Michael how important it was. It was decided Michael would be collected by taxi and go to Monica's address to collect Monica, and the taxi would then take them into the assembly rooms.

Michael asked for the address where Monica would be collected, and although Michael had gleaned from conversations overheard in the Dhugall that Monica was in the marital home, her husband living elsewhere, he had no idea where that home was.

Remembering his intent to give her flowers in the guise of a corsage, he asked her what colour her dress was. Monica, straight up on her hind legs, asked sharply, "Why?"

"I don't want my tie to clash."

"Oh," she said, slightly mollified. "It's emerald green." "Sounds lovely," Michael remarked.

He was rememberinging his mother. When given a corsage which did not match her outfit, she had been furious. He had quickly realized how important this was and was determined not to make any social faux pas.

Having finished their food, both having things to do, they parted company, confirming the arrangements for Saturday that Michael would arrive by taxi at 7:00 p.m. to Cluny Gardens, then on to the venue in George Street. As he meandered home, he was thinking that living in Cluny Gardens put her into the upper echelons of society and next to his two-bedroom terrace in Morton Hall, he felt infinitely inferior. Then, taking a shake to himself, he realized he was only accompanying a lady to a social occasion and it was very unlikely she would ever be at his house.

Feeling slightly better, he continued up Morningside Road and popped into the florist and asked for their expert advice on a flower arrangement. After discussion on the type of function, the colour of the dress, and the Highland outfit, it was decided that a wrist corsage would work, and freesia with a single cream rosebud would suit. Times arranged and the corsage paid for, Michael continued up to the hire shop to confirm the arrangements. He was able to tell them shoes were not necessary, as he had bought a pair in the sale in Jenner's,

However, on reaching the hire shop, he was interested to see in the shop window a model dummy wearing the full Highland dress. It did look smart, and he was glad he had chosen to hire it instead of a morning suit. What took his eye was the sale price. It was considerably less money than he had seen previously. He strode boldly into the shop, asking to speak to the young man who had attended to him when ordering the outfit. Michael wisely just asked for confirmation of his booking and the most convenient time to collect the outfit.

At the end of the booking confirmation, Michael pointed out the outfit in the window, remarking on how smart it looked and stating he was looking forward to wearing it. A conversation started up regarding the price of the outfit and the cost of the hire, and the salesman, seeing an opportunity, explained how useful such an outfit would be. Michael demurred and pointed out the lack of social engagements and confessed to the salesman the reason for this particular hire. The salesman was not to be deterred. Financially, he explained, it was the best option.

After a long conversation, instead of hiring the outfit, Michael decided to buy. It was second-hand, having been hired out several times, but in superb condition. He duly tried the outfit on, and the salesman talked him through the dressing stage. It was a perfect fit, and he was very pleased with the way he looked. Adding socks and a cravat plus a wing-collared shirt, he was happy to pay the £500, and the hire was cancelled. Great care was taken packing up the outfit, and as the packing was being dealt with, he looked around at the various wares on display, and his eye caught a waistcoat in black silk. He liked it on sight and began to formulate a plan for his head waiter outfit. The shop called for a taxi to get him home, as he now had far too much to carry. The kilt outfit was going to make it difficult to get home. *Not only is the shopping putting a hole in my pocket, but having to use taxis is proving expensive too*, thought Michael.

As he was exiting the shop to get his taxi, a thought popped into his head. Thanking the staff for their kind attention, he asked them what tartan the kilt was. It wasn't really important to him, but he felt he should know. He liked the deep red and the touch of green on the kilt, but when they replied "MacGregor", he almost burst out laughing at the coincidence. Jumping into the taxi and giving his address, Michael went into a thoughtful mood. Remembering the comment by Mr. MacGregor, he knew he was going to have to talk to him about his mother, which of course sent a pang of grief through him.

Michael, Waiting

When he got home, he hung the suit-carrier, thoughtfully provided by the shop to protect his purchase, in his wardrobe and began examining his purchases. He had very little storage in his small single room. He decided he would sort through his clothes and keep only items which still looked good and fitted him. To be fair, Michael hadn't put on any weight. With running to work and working on his feet all day, he was still trim and fit.

He sat down on his bed—there wasn't much room for a chair—and looked around. For no other reason, he had not moved into his mother's large double room. Then he had simply not accepted the fact she would not be returning. "Am I ready to do this?" he asked himself. With determination, he went next door; and for the first time in a year, he opened the door to his mother's room and stepped in.

An hour or so later, Michael found himself looking out of the lounge window, nursing a glass of Scotch. He was drinking whisky in his house. He decided that emptying the wardrobes of his mother's things could be a step in the right direction. To keep the house the way it was would turn it into a shrine,

and that was not good for the healing process. Also, he needed more space. His mother's friend Angela had made all sorts of offers to help when she died. With his new-found confidence and assertiveness, he decided to enlist her help as offered. It was time to start a new life, and turning the house into his home would be good. After the golf, the book club, his new promotion, and finally a ball, he had to laugh. How had he managed to turn his life around in such a short space of time?

As it was after six in the evening, he was sure his mother's friend would be home, so he decided to phone there and then. He felt rather guilty, as it had been some time since he had made any contact, so wrapped in his grief had he been. He failed to recognize that Angela would be grieving too. After all, she and his mum had been close friends since their school days.

Any doubts he had were quickly swept away, as after identifying himself, the delight at her hearing from him was obvious. He explained his dilemma and asked her for advice. After listening carefully while Michael explained, she started to think as to the best way of dealing with this. She eventually came up with the suggestion that she would come to his house and survey just exactly what needed to be done.

Michael was relieved. It looked as if Angela was going to step up to the plate and give him much-needed assistance. His newly found confidence didn't stretch to this task. Even just looking round the house full of memories left him unable to start the task. With the help of his mother's friend, he felt it could be done.

She suggested Saturday morning for the first reconnoitre, explaining she had a small part-time job during the week and was often called in to childmind her grandchildren after school. Saturday morning was swimming lesson day, and her services would not be required.

Michael woke early on Saturday. There were two important dates with destiny today. Angela was popping round at 10.00 a.m., and tonight he would be going to the ball with Monica. Both tasks put shivers down his back.

He got out of bed knowing sleep had eluded him, showered, and pulled on comfortable clothes. The time for dressing up was much later. He had also decided that after Angela's visit he would go up into the loft and see what was there. This made wearing "scruffs" more suitable. He put on a pot of coffee and popped two slices of bread into the toaster. A couple of eggs on to boil and his breakfast preparations were complete.

At ten on the dot, Angela rang the bell. Michael jumped at the forgotten sound and rushed to the door to find Angela on his doorstep. The tears started to seep from both sets of eyes as they gave each other a hug. Ushering Angela in, Michael offered her tea or coffee, forgetting he had no milk, as he took his coffee black. Angela accepted a cup of Earl Grey, as milk was superfluous.

Sitting opposite each other in the lounge, Angela was trying desperately to hold on to her poise, as her last visit here had been the day of Jean's funeral,

and it was all becoming altogether difficult to bear. However, her best friend's son needed her help, and she pushed her thoughts to one side and concentrated on what Michael needed.

They went up to the bedroom, and although the dust was noticeable, Angela made no comment and looked through the contents of the wardrobes and chests of drawers. It was not as bad as she had feared. Jean liked to wear nice things and was always smart. However, she made an art form out of mixing and matching, so she didn't have a lot of clothes, but those she had were of good quality.

Angela suggested, after a thorough inspection, that over the course of the following week he should rescue any trinkets and jewellery from the room. With a spare key, she would arrange for her son and daughter to come to the house and clear out everything Michael did not want and take it in the big SUV to a charity shop for heart attack and stroke victims. She worked a shift there now and again and was well known to the staff. She was confident, too, that his mother's things would be treated with respect there.

Michael had indicated that he wanted to replace the bed but didn't know how to go about it. Angela offered to help by contacting a shelter for abused women that was always looking for furniture and had a van they could use to come and collect the bed. It would be better still if they could also come on Saturday, as Michael would be at work; arranging it this way would, he hoped, minimize the pain. Looking round the room, Michael expressed a desire that the dressing table and bedside table could go to the refuge too, and he would completely redecorate and reform the room in a more masculine style. The wardrobes were fitted, so they would stay.

Angela was delighted to see how far Michael had come in the year or so since she had seen him. She was delighted to assist him to get his life back, and her pet charity was going to get quite a boost. With the arrangements all made, Angela excused herself, as she needed to shop before the grandchildren arrived for tea.

Michael thanked her profusely, and after yet another hug, they parted, leaving Michael not knowing how he felt. But a sneaky sense of relief was creeping in.

Now to the ball.

Chapter 18

Michael had kept himself busy so as to avoid thinking about the evening in front of him. He constantly rebuked himself for agreeing to the performance. He had promised himself he would stop thinking about it and go into the attic to see what was there.

The time slipped by as he found albums containing old photographs and spent a great deal of time poring over them. He was surprised not to find any likenesses of his father and, in fact, none of any male relatives at all. He stopped to think, and he wondered what had become of his father. After putting the box of photographs to one side, he had a good look around. There wasn't much, really: old toys, empty suitcases and various forms of bric-a-brac. Most of it could go to the rubbish dump, but he felt the suitcases may come in handy. He laughed when he found his old school reports. *Doesn't make for good reading*, he mused, feeling badly about his poor performance.

He checked his watch and saw it was getting late. He had forgotten about lunch. He took the old photographs downstairs and put them in the cupboard under the stairs for a better look another time.

Not having to collect his hired outfit was a good thing until he remembered the flowers. It was already four thirty. He pulled on more respectable clothes and headed round to the lock-up and jumped into his car. It took him nearly an hour, but he got home in time to get ready.

He showered and shaved, as he had been crawling around the attic; and before dressing, he called the taxi company and ordered a taxi to pick him up at 6.45 p.m. He remembered how to add a phone number to his mobile after Monica's tuition, and he added the taxi number for future use. The kilt shop assistants had warned him it would probably take thirty

Michael, Waiting

minutes to get ready, so he started in good time. After fiddling with the straps on the side of the kilt, it wasn't so difficult to finish off the waistcoat and Prince of Wales jacket. As he checked his appearance in the mirror, feeling good about himself, he felt a momentary pang as he thought how proud his mother would have been to see him in his finery.

He checked his sporran for his money and phone when he heard the sound of a car horn. The taxi had arrived on time. Michael locked the door and stowed his door key into the sporran. *I can see why ladies carry handbags*, he thought. Just as he was about to shut the cab door, he remembered he had left the flowers on the hall table. With much embarrassment, he asked for a couple of minutes while he fumbled with his sporran, retrieved the front door key, and rescued the flowers.

Arriving at Cluny Gardens, Michael thought he might hyperventilate with nerves so he took a deep breath before getting out of the cab to collect his date. As he reached the front door, it opened to reveal Monica in a beautiful ballerina-length emerald-green chiffon-and-satin dress. She looked amazing. With a courtly bow, he presented her with the corsage. Her surprise was palpable as she took in the apparition which was Michael in full Highland dress and a corsage. Monica tried very hard not to cry; she was so overcome.

He proffered her his arm and escorted her to the waiting cab, and they sped off into the night to the assembly rooms. Neither could think of anything to say at first, and then Michael remembered his manners, telling Monica how lovely she looked. Monica countered with, "You are looking splendid yourself." A few sentences of small talk and they had arrived at their destination.

The taxi driver opened the door. Michael got out and helped Monica out of the cab. Her high heels had not gone unnoticed, and he really wanted her not to fall, especially in front of her colleagues. Michael knew all about embarrassment. With Michael supporting Monica, they managed the stairs without mishap and were directed to the function room where the event would be held. It was obvious Monica knew her way about, but Michael had not been to this establishment before and was taken aback with the grandeur and splendid decoration. The crystal chandeliers were particularly mesmerizing.

He escorted Monica into the reception room. There were a few people milling about, chatting to each other, but it looked as though most of the guests had still to arrive. Taking a lead from Monica, he took a glass of bubbly from a tray being passed round. Being in the trade, so to speak, it was hard not to make comparisons. He knew he could have filled the tray of bubbly with quite a few more glasses, and he thought the waiters looked a bit inexperienced. Michael smiled to himself at his critical opinion, remembering how difficult it was to find enough experienced staff to make sure a function went with a swing.

The arrival of colleagues Monica seemed to know well brought Michael back to the present. Monica did the introductions, and before long there was quite a group all talking at once, it seemed. Michael's lonely childhood had given him the ability to live in his own world, where there was no conversation. Because of this, he had to work hard just to keep up with the chatter and enjoy a joke. His usual habit was to drift into a daydream. But not this time. He would need to stay alert in order to keep up with the company. Knowing he was the object of their curiosity made it more difficult, and he was relieved when the call to dinner was made. Taking Monica's arm, he steered her into the dining room. Surprisingly, there were no place cards or seating lists. Quietly asking her where her preferred seat was, he got her settled and sat down. Trying not to examine cutlery and napkins, Michael picked up the menu and studied the treats in store.

A wine waiter came to the table offering to pour red or white wine. Accepting the red, Michael had already spotted a beef and mushroom stroganoff on the menu. He was mindful that it was a free bar being provided by Monica's employers but did not want to disgrace himself and embarrass Monica by getting inebriated. He poured a glass of water, and Monica indicated she would like water too.

Feeling obliged to say something, he asked her what she was having to eat, whether she liked the menu, and, more importantly, how she was feeling. With the company getting a bit noisy, he had to lean close to her to be able to hear, and he caught a whiff of her perfume. It was a lovely scent, and he felt the need to tell her how much he liked it. Secretly, Michael thought Monica looked stunning. She had obviously been to the hairdresser, and her rich brown hair had been styled in a very sophisticated way. With all the nonsense she had got up to in his restaurant, he had never before taken any notice of her appearance. Now that he was getting to know her, he saw her in a more favourable light. She seemed to be enjoying herself. Michael was trying his best with the small talk and the fending off of curious co-workers, but Monica rescued him a few times. She had a keen wit and could be quite acerbic at times. Michael thought her colleagues got off lightly.

The banquet went on for some time, and by the time the tables were cleared and the band started up, it was after 10.00 p.m. Monica gave Michael a nod in the direction of the exit, and he followed her to the foyer. He knew the dancing was going on without them. Michael felt she was letting him off the hook by leaving before the dancing started. He was profoundly grateful, but he felt he should address his lack of social skills. *Another time*, he mused.

"Time to go, Michael," she said. He took out his phone, but she said it would be quicker to hail a taxi from the street. Michael stepped out of the door, and as luck would have it, a black cab, resplendent in a lit-up For Hire sign responded to his wave and drew up beside them. They climbed aboard and settled back for the short journey to Cluny Gardens.

They both started talking at once, and the laughter that ensued broke the ice. Responding to the question, she told him that yes, she'd had a good time and enjoyed the dinner, and she thanked Michael for a compliment on her appearance. She felt the need to tell Michael he looked good in a kilt. Monica couldn't thank him enough; Michael was astonished at how comfortable he felt.

All too soon, the journey ended, Michael showing his manners as he escorted Monica to the door. He returned to the taxi and had the driver take him home to his empty house and his thoughts.

Chapter 19

Michael hadn't slept well. A combination of rich food and more wine than his usual intake was making him feel a little off colour. He was glad he'd had the foresight to delay his starting time until 5.00 p.m. that evening. He prowled around the house, feeling unsettled. He had not been looking forward to his escort duties, and to his astonishment, apart from when he had to make small talk to Monica's co-workers, he had enjoyed the occasion hugely. Monica had surprised him with her ready wit and interesting conversation.

He contemplated sitting reading with never-ending cups of tea or coffee. *Perhaps not coffee.* Then he came to a split-second decision. He would go to the golf club and sample one of chef's famous "Fore for Four breakfasts, quickly showered, donned the appropriate golfing gear, and headed to the car and onto the golf club. It was about 10.00 a.m. when he arrived in the lounge and was surprised as to how few people were in the clubhouse.

He went up to the bar, ordered a glass of orange juice, and asked the barman why it was so quiet. "Hang around for an hour or so and this place will be jumping," replied the barman. "They are all out on the course playing in the Monthly Medal," he explained. "New member?"

Michael, after replying in the affirmative, went on to introduce himself, explaining that his golf game was not yet up to medal entry standards. He then ordered his breakfast. The barman gave his name as George Ritchie and told Michael he was the club steward, responsible for the catering, the bar, and general cleaning of the clubhouse. His wife, Moira, did most of the cooking, and George emphasized just how good the food was. Taking in his rotund shape, Michael guessed he was an aficionado and enthusiastic advertisement for his wife's cooking.

He was not disappointed. The food was superb. He had what was affectionately known as "the works", served on a very large plate. It included two sausages, two rashers of bacon, beans, a potato scone, and a slice of black pudding. Replete, Michael ordered a cup of coffee which he took over to the table by the window looking out on the eighteenth green. He was surprised to see three golfers on the green, three more up the fairway, and another threesome cresting the ridge.

It would be mayhem in the clubhouse very soon. He drank his coffee and settled the bill before telling George how much he had enjoyed the food and to be sure and tell his wife as much.

He scuttled to his car and managed to make a clean getaway before the hungry and thirsty hordes turned up in the bar. He did not feel sociable today. He had, however, looked at the menu and seen what type of food was on offer.

He was delighted to notice that apart from the burger-and-bacon roll type of food, Moira was also serving main meals. Fish and chips were one dish, steak pie was another, and as Michael remembered, they also did a Sunday roast. The prices were reasonable. Michael mused as he drove home, thinking it might be a good place to eat from time to time. *Maybe I could invite Monica.* Then he had a word with himself. *The ball was a one-off and a favour.* He thought if he invited Monica to eat at the club, she would be offended. "No," he said out loud, "not a good idea."

He got home around noon, and still full of breakfast, he realized he would not need lunch. So he decided to tidy up and dust and hoover the lounge. He suddenly had a thought. His late mother's friend was coming early in the week to take his mother's clothes and shoes, as well as handbags, to her local charity shop. Michael decided to spend the next couple of hours picking what he wanted to keep. It was a painful two hours, but it had to be done, and Michael was proud of the way he had been able to complete the task. He decided to pack up his mother's clothes to help the ladies coming the following week to collect them. He placed them in neat piles and then finished the job by dusting and hoovering the room.

Michael got to the restaurant early, as usual, and the booking diary was full for Sunday night. A busy night lay ahead. Michael thought inwardly that it was a good job. He felt better than he had this morning as he went to work cleaning, organizing, and checking out the kitchen. He managed to grab a few minutes with Peter and was pleased when he reported that the evening had gone well. He thanked him for stepping into the breach and explained he would be advertising for a part-time member of staff. But for the moment, he and Robert, the other waiter, would both be deputies for Michael.

Later on in the evening, during a lull in the restaurant, Peter asked for a quiet word. Agreeing, Michael headed up to the staffroom with Peter following. Peter explained that a friend of his wife had just lost her job in a restaurant in town, as the business was failing and likely to close. As a widow, she had only her wages to live on and really needed to be employed. He asked whether Michael would consider taking her on.

Smiling to himself and remembering Olivia's request for a female waitress, he thanked Peter and said he would give the matter some thought. In the meantime, he asked whether Peter could provide him with her contact details. Michael had them before the night was out.

Over the next few days, Michael discussed the prospective waitress with Olivia, who was a great believer in employing on recommendation and had arranged for her to come in for an interview. Sylvia Aitken was a lady of a certain age. Her hair, blonde, was swept up in a chignon and fastened with attractive clips. She certainly took great pains with her appearance. However, her air would let you think that she owned the place, or maybe that she thought so. Her credentials were excellent, and the recommendation from her soon-to-be past employer was very encouraging.

After Sylvia, whom they discovered was fifty-three, had been interviewed and left the building, Michael and Olivia discussed the applicant. Michael was not as enthusiastic as Olivia. His attitude towards women stuck fast. They came to an agreement that they would employ Sylvia on a part-time basis temporarily for three months and see whether she was a fit with the other staff. Robert and Peter had already proved they could play the team game. Olivia was very proud of her restaurant, and owing to the memory of the departed Tony, who had failed to meet standards and had conveyed the impression he was in charge, she was afraid of making another mistake, as was Michael. A temporary post allowed them to try her out and see whether she would fit into the team.

Not wasting any time, Olivia telephoned Sylvia and explained their decision. Sylvia was happy to oblige, and tomorrow being a Thursday and a quieter night, she agreed to work and be shown the ropes. She explained that, having been made redundant, no notice was required, and she would be free as and when required.

Michael, still a little uncertain, greeted Sylvia when she arrived in plenty of time to start her shift. He was gratified to see she had adopted the black skirt and white blouse that had been suggested and agreed. She looked very smart, and as they had noticed at the interview, she had a soft, well-spoken voice. He fervently hoped it would work. He looked around, watching briefly at how the work was being carried out. Noticing the white shirts and black trousers, and now a skirt, he was reminded of the conversation he'd had with Olivia about dressing differently to emphasize his elevated status.

He thought about the black silk waistcoat he had noticed when he purchased his kilt and decided to discuss it with Olivia the first chance he got.

As the evening wore on, Michael was delighted to observe that the newbie Sylvia was doing well and was required to learn only the methods peculiar to this particular restaurant. She knew the basics and performed without a hitch. Michael went home feeling relaxed and hopeful that all was going to be well.

It being a Friday night and having the potential to be busy, Michael checked the diary and saw that Mr. MacGregor had booked his usual table for one. Michael thought about how he would tackle this. Should he let the matter drop and pretend nothing was said, or should he quiz Mr. MacGregor to find out where he had gleaned the information?

The old Michael would have let it go, being afraid of confrontation, but the new, improved, more confident Michael thought it was time he found out a little more about his mother and where Mr. MacGregor fitted into the picture.

He waited until the restaurant was emptying and Mr. MacGregor was preparing to leave before approaching him. His reservation was always for 9.00 p.m., so it was closing-up time after he left. Michael asked him how he knew about his mother and how he knew about her death.

Mr. MacGregor hesitated. He had not expected this. He carefully explained that his mother and Angela were best friends at school and he, too, was in their class. He had kept in touch over the years, and Angela had decided to tell him about Jean passing away. There was something in this explanation that didn't ring true. Michael couldn't think what it was. His mother and he had a very close relationship and with the appearance of Angela on a regular basis he couldn't fathom out where Mr. MacGregor figured in the relationship. Not wishing to appear rude, Michael thanked him rather perfunctorily and watched Mr. MacGregor leave the restaurant. Michael's mind was buzzing. He simply couldn't understand how this had come about.

Going home in the bus, Michael thought about the conversation he'd had with Mr. MacGregor and decided he would speak to Angela when she came tomorrow to sort out and deal with the disposal of his mother's things. This time he would not be fobbed off, and eventually he would prise the story out of one of them.

True to her word, Angela turned up in the morning and set off with a determined air. She had hoped that Michael would get around to the task sooner rather than later and was delighted he had finally realized the job needed doing. Also, she was pleased he had asked for her assistance. A couple of hours later, and a coffee break with biscuits too, Angela explained that her son would be arriving shortly to uplift the clothes and take them to the shop as promised. Then he and a couple of friends would arrive later and remove the bed and furniture.

Michael felt a sense of relief. With this job out of the way, he felt the start of closure. He had spotted an advert in the window of his local shop for painting and decorating and had decided to give the house a makeover. After a fishing exercise at the shop to make sure there were no bad reports, he would give the number a call and see what it would cost to redo the wallpaper and paint.

A new carpet was on the agenda too. He was looking forward to the transformation. Now that he was feeling better, he wanted to personalize his home. Not really wanting to think about it, at the back of his mind he knew the whole house needed modernization.

He noticed that Angela was getting ready to leave, so thinking it was now or never, he approached her with the story of Mr. MacGregor. Angela was taken aback. She had no idea that Mike was in touch with Michael. He had not mentioned he had met Michael and regularly ate in the restaurant Michael worked in.

Angela had given a promise she would not break, so her meeting up with Michael need never be mentioned. However, Michael was more curious than expected, and some painful moments were on the cards. She was able to fob Michael off for the time being by agreeing his story to be true. She rounded up her son, and together with his mother's clothes and things they left, to return later for the bed. Meanwhile, Michael had to get ready to work; Angela had a spare key.

Sitting in the passenger seat on the way to her charity shop, Angela was full of pensive thoughts. She knew she had just postponed the inevitable, but now was not the time or the place to let Michael have the whole story. But very soon she was going to have to consider breaking a promise to a very dear friend, someone she cared for and missed so much.

It had been a difficult few hours packing up all the familiar items of clothing and hiding her distress from Michael, who must have been finding this all too much. However, she was pleased to see Michael more cheerful and put together. She hoped his new interests would help him recover, but until she told the truth about the mysterious Mr. MacGregor, she could not be at peace, and Michael deserved to know about his family and his early life.

Saturday night in the restaurant was busy as usual, and it looked very like Sylvia was settling down into the role. She was polite, efficient, and well set into the team concept. Michael dared to hope. He had Peter, his co-deputy; Robert; and the part-time new start Sylvia all working together. Michael remembered the "Tony days" and wondered why his nonsense had been tolerated for as long as it was.

Michael was in his usual vantage point this busy Saturday night. He tried to take as many orders as possible himself and seldom took an order pad to the table. He relied on his very good memory and liked talking to the diners as he discussed their choices. Tonight was no exception. He moved effortlessly into place as the two men sat down, their coats being taken by Robert and hung on a rail in a nook next to the front door. The diners, two men in their late forties, maybe early fifties, were not Michael's favourite clients. They turned up every few weeks, and Michael found their attitudes dismissive and a bit rude. They ordered pretty much the same each time, a well-done steak being the favourite, and, surprisingly, a beer as a drink.

He took the order back to the kitchen, where he input the menu choice into the computer. Gliding around, Michael made sure everything was going well, organizing table clearing and food going out, and the night wore in quickly. The two diners Michael disliked were surprisingly slow with their meals tonight. It was nearly closing, and coincidentally the table next to the two men had also been in no hurry. Hoping to get the staff away home soon, Michael metaphorically rolled up his sleeves and tackled the now empty table of six next to the two men. They had just ordered coffee, so a sharp exit wasn't about to happen. Michael, setting about clearing the table, was aware he could hear their conversation. Normally he would shut out what was being said, but what he could hear began to disturb him. They mentioned a name and then discussed how this person was a nuisance and would have to be got rid of. They mentioned that they "knew just the guy for the job". Various methods were discussed, and Michael began to think he was in the middle of a crime novel. He had been so transfixed he wasn't aware that he had been noticed eavesdropping until they turned to him and demanded their coats and the bill.

Michael rushed to do their bidding, mortified that he might have been found out, and hoped the two would-be thugs hadn't noticed. The bill paid and the coats sorted, with a sigh of relief Michael shut the door behind them. As Michael's heartbeat slowly returned to normal, he reassured himself that they might have been rehearsing for a play. He didn't know how this would turn out.

The days and weeks rolled on with nothing much happening in Michael's life. The weather had not been good, so golf was not an option. The conversation he had overheard preyed on his mind. He had tried to think about other things. *Maybe a plot for a book, maybe a TV script. Who knows?* It was very disturbing.

As he pottered around tidying up his house, he was very pleased with the decorator's work in his mother's room. The new bed organized by Angela was impressively comfortable, and it took Michael a few nights to get used to the larger mattress. The bedroom was big enough for a king-sized bed, and Angela had taken full advantage. He was becoming used to his new quarters and was enjoying them hugely. "Why did it take me so long to sort this out?" he said to himself. He then thought, *When the weather improves, I will sort out the lounge.*

Then he remembered Angela had suggested a firm of plumbers who would do a good job on his bathroom, as he had expressed dislike of the pink suite he was using. Michael grabbed the bull by the horns and made the phone call to the plumber Angela had recommended. After all, the number on the business card had been lying in plain sight for a couple of months now.

Having spoken to the plumber and arranged to meet up the next morning, the plumber offering to bring some brochures, Michael decided to get everything done before redecorating downstairs.

The plumber arrived at the appointed time and day. Michael thought to himself that this was a good start, as he had heard some dreadful accounts of tradesmen falling well below the expected standard. Michael liked the plumber, who announced himself as John on sight. He seemed a cheerful, easy-going man in his forties with a firm handshake. Michael invited John in and showed him into the lounge, where John sat down and produced a handful of coloured brochures. Michael had not really thought about what he wanted and had just presumed it would be a bathroom suite, only not pink.

An hour or so and two or three coffees and biscuits later, a decision had been made. At the plumber's suggestion, the bath was redundant and would not be replaced. Michael had admitted early on that he seldom used the bath as a bath, but it was where he showered, as was his preference. The whole bathroom would be torn out and replaced by a large walk-in shower, a washbasin, and a toilet in white. There would also be a cabinet for his toiletries under the sink, with a mirror above. The entire room would be tiled in grey tiles with chrome fittings. Michael was overwhelmed and just a little bit excited. It would be done the week after next.

He experienced a moment of nostalgia as he considered the memory of how the house had been when he'd lived here with his mother, and Angela's wise words came to mind: "The past is a nice place to visit but not a good place to stay."

After the plumber left, Michael got ready for work. As it was raining, he decided to use public transport. He was so looking forward to the spring, when he would be able to get back to running. Getting off the bus, he walked over to the restaurant, but as he passed the newsagent on the corner his attention was caught by the banner headline for the local paper on the board outside the shop. "Body Found in Canal; Murder Suspected". Michael stopped and looked again. There was no mistake; a murder victim had been found in the canal. With memories of that evening when such a crime was being discussed within earshot, which seemingly had been a long time ago, Michael had to buy the paper. He took his copy, looking around as if he were the guilty party, and practically scuttled into the sanctuary of the restaurant. He then headed up to the staffroom with the newspaper hidden under his coat. Michael couldn't understand his irrational behaviour. There was nothing sinister in buying a newspaper. Thousands do it every day.

Sitting down after making himself a cup of tea, he pulled out the paper and read the front-page news. The body of a man had been pulled out of the canal just a half mile away. Judging by the decomposition and the swelling of the corpse, the man had been in the water for several days. The cause of death was not yet known, nor was his identity, and police were asking for information from the public.

Michael put the paper down and stared into space while his thoughts ran amok in his head. Had he overheard the plotting of the death of this man? He went over the conversation that night in his head and considered the notion of contacting the police. Then, as he brought himself back to the present and got ready for work, he decided to park it for the moment.

The newspaper article had hinted at a gang killing, and the police were treating it as murder. Michael started work and thought to himself that if gangs were involved, perhaps it would be better to let the police do their job.

The evening was busy, and Michael had little time to think unless it was about what task he had to perform next. By the time the evening shift was over and Michael was on his bus home, he had parked the whole thing.

When he reached his front door and attempted to put his key in the lock, an arm came from nowhere and snaked around his throat. Michael froze. Then a familiar voice snarled into his ear, telling him to forget the conversation he'd overheard in the restaurant that evening, which seemed so long ago now. He was told that if he did not do as he was told, his nearest and dearest would have an "accident", and then they would be coming for him. Michael was on the point of correcting their mistake about having any nearest and dearest when he was pushed violently away and banged his forehead off the front door. This left him stunned for a few seconds. He turned around to see a car's tail lights vanishing around the corner, the registration plate a blur.

Shaken, Michael let himself into the house and made sure it was locked and secure. He then checked the back door and all the windows. He was clearly frightened and believed the heavy mob threats. Slowly he felt himself returning to normal, and he ran the conversation through his mind—one sided, that is. He came to the part about his nearest and dearest. Surely they must have known Michael was an orphan with no siblings. They had found out where he lived, so how easy would it be to find out who he was related to? He had no girlfriend, wife, or indeed any relatives whatsoever. The only person he really cared about was his mother's friend Angela, and she was just that—his mother's friend.

He poured himself a nightcap from the whisky bottle which had been in the cupboard from New Year's Eve before his mother died. Michael felt that the events of tonight were a very good reason to open the bottle. One wasn't enough, as it transpired. He was sensible enough to stop at three nips, poured himself into bed feeling a bit giddy, and slept the night through. The next morning, Michael woke with a headache. Nonplussed, he did not understand why he had a headache. It was not a malaise he was used to.

Then, with dreadful clarity, the events of the previous evening flooded into his mind, including the very unusual act of him drinking three glasses of whisky. Headache explained, Michael retired to the bathroom to wash and get the day started. He pushed the thoughts of the previous evening to one side, and as he looked in his mirror over the bathroom sink, he spotted the bruise on his forehead. It was no good. Nothing was going to change or be forgotten. It probably contributed to the headache too.

Although he had little appetite, he made himself tea and toast. Not enough that he had a hangover which had killed his appetite, he also had the very upsetting encounter with the thug threatening him to worry about. He forced the toast down and decided to park the incident for the moment. He would soon have to decide whether he would talk to the police and tell them what he had heard or let them do the sleuthing.

Chapter 20

Michael had already decided he was not going to return to the book club. When he'd spoken to Monica last, she told him the current book was not proving popular and a new book was being chosen. Although Michael would have liked to meet up with Monica again, he felt he had rather a great deal on his plate for the moment. He had seen a notice in the library for beginner's computer lessons, and he rather thought it would be of more use. He left the house to go to work, looking around to make sure he was alone.

Michael thought it would only be courteous to visit Elizabeth to let her know he would not be returning, as he felt he had rather a lot on his plate at the moment. Out of politeness, he remained at the meeting till the end. If truth be told, he wanted another opportunity to speak to Monica again.

As the meeting broke up and the members drifted away, Michael found himself saying hello to Monica and, without thinking, inviting her to lunch at his club. He hurriedly said he would collect her in the car and wondered how it would be received. Had he mistaken their enjoyable evening at the ball as a green light for another date?

As he was thinking about this, he was suddenly aware of Monica agreeing to lunch. Astonished, Michael, having already made sure his day off on Thursday would work for Monica, decided to collect Monica. He told her he would book a table for 1.00 p.m. "Michael," she said, "What happened to your head? "I slipped coming out of the shower and banged my head on the bathroom sink." Lying didn't come easily to him, and he squirmed a bit under her stare. She then recommended a proprietary medication which might help reduce the swelling.

Bidding farewell to both Monica and Elizabeth and thanking Elizabeth for her excellent hospitality, Michael headed off down to the library to find out more about the computer classes.

Strolling down the hill, he decided to walk, as it was a pleasant day. It was still cold, but the watery sun tried its best. He was aware of a pleasant feeling as he contemplated the forthcoming lunch with Monica.

In the meantime, as Monica was driving home, she contemplated the current state. She was a separated woman with a decent job and an impending divorce looming. Before Michael, the thought of spending a life alone frightened her, but she did not want to be in another abusive relationship. She was delighted with the offer of another meal out and was hoping the friendship would continue. She had already made plans to host an at-home to which her school friends and their partners would be invited. Provided the golf club day out went well, she would introduce Michael to her friends.

There were several events coming up, as Christmas would be upon them soon. A new daily menu in the Christmas spirit had been prepared and would be out on display next week, as it was December. Having met with the staff, and bonuses having been agreed on, it had been decided for the first time in Dhugall's history that there would be a one-sitting Christmas Day special with all the usual trimmings.

Michael had also discussed the uniform for himself and the staff. Olivia had liked the tartan trews and black shirt with the silk waistcoat for Michael. She thought it would be very smart. There were to be black aprons with the restaurant logo to protect their clothes, and she also agreed that the staff should wear a tartan waistcoat just to smarten up the whole appearance of the restaurant. The clothes had been ordered and would make their debut on Christmas Day. He decided not to get the bus home and hailed a taxi. He then contacted George at the golf club and arranged to reserve a table in the very pleasant and spacious dining room. George refrained from a gentle teasing regarding Michael's date, knowing full well Michael was not in the habit of squiring ladies about.

He did know about the ball and had been told in no uncertain terms that the ball was a one-off. George reassured him he would give him the best table he had, and at the conclusion of the call, George was smiling to himself as he logged the reservation in the book. *Won't let the guy down*, thought George.

Michael, on the other hand, completely unaware of what George was thinking, mentally stroked the call off his to-do list. He made himself some lunch after spreading a little cream on the rapidly darkening bruise on his forehead.

As he consumed his sandwich, he read through the information he had purloined at the library. It looked like a foreign language, and he was not at all sure he would manage. Looking at his watch, he realized it was time to get ready for work. His lunch time cuppa had gone cold. He made another cup of tea, which he drank on the move as he readied himself to catch the bus. After placing the cup into the sink and checking the doors and windows, he went out and, practically running, got to the bus stop in the nick of time.

The day and the rest of the week went pretty much as normal, and before he knew it, Thursday was upon him. By now he was just a little fed up with the constant questioning regarding his wound. He wished it would go away. As he bathed and shaved, he noticed it was getting a bit better. Monica's cream seemed to be helping. He began to think he was firstly looking forward to the plumber's visit, when the bathroom would be more practical, and, of course, lunch. He really was looking forward to seeing Monica again. His only hope was that she would enjoy the lunch and that the surroundings would not deter her. He had decided he would take the car and not drink. However, if the lunch was going well, he could always get them both a taxi. He had also thought about discussing the dark happenings with her and seeing what advice she would come up with. If he knew anything about Monica, it was that she liked to give advice.

Going through his newly acquired wardrobe, he selected a maroon-and-navy shirt with navy cashmere slacks. Running a comb through his hair, he thought he should visit a barber soon. The outfit was made complete with a pair of black loafers. Feeling good about himself, he strode to the lock-up and collected the car. Monica was ready, dressed casually but elegantly in caramel trousers and a dark brown sweater he was fairly sure was also cashmere. A brightly coloured scarf and a pair of brown wedge-heeled slip-on shoes completed her outfit.

Parking at the club and escorting Monica into the restaurant, he was surprised when it became apparent she knew some of the members as they said hello or smiled in welcome. Sitting down at the table George had picked, Michael was a little put out. The last straw was when George came in with the menu and wine list and greeted Monica with "Hello, Mr.s Stevens, nice to see you back."

Michael nearly choked. *How on earth does George know her?* He was thinking. As he tried to fathom it out, he saw Monica smiling at him, and as the smile became wider, it suddenly dawned on Michael just as she admitted she was also a member and played a little golf herself. She hurriedly explained that she had not been back to the club since she split from her husband and that before, when they were not on good terms, it was not appropriate for her to go places with him.

"So you are Monica Stevens," he said.

"Yes, but I plan to change that status as soon as possible."

Never one to bear a grudge, he finally saw the funny side. He decided to share a bottle of wine with her, and after they had ordered up their food, the chat began. He had already cleared it with her that the taxi was the better option. In fact, it was at her suggestion they left the car at the club.

Before either of them noticed, it was soon 3.00 p.m.; the dining room would soon be closed. Monica was happy to get seated in the lounge, feeling comfortable as members spoke to her and made her feel welcome. It was a big step, she told him, having frequented the place for several years with her soon to be ex-husband. She had always enjoyed the atmosphere in the clubhouse and had made a few friends she was looking forward to being reacquainted with. Her husband had discontinued his membership and apparently was on the waiting list for a membership elsewhere. She happily divulged this little pearl to Michael in a gleeful voice. "Just think; I can come whenever I feel like it."

Michael didn't want to end the day and spontaneously asked whether she would like to go to the cinema, as a much talked about film was showing at the Dominion.

Monica said she would be delighted. It was a film she wanted to see, but she was not yet confident enough to go alone. Celebrating, they ordered another couple of drinks, as the film started at 5.00 p.m. A couple of anecdotes later, after a taxi had been ordered by the ever-helpful George, Monica asked the question that she had been framing for the past hour. "Would you like to come to a small get-together at my house a week on Friday?" He was taken aback. His first thought was *More new people!*

Monica was beginning to understand a little more about this tall, brooding man who kept himself to himself but, when he relaxed, was so interesting and just a lot of fun.

She hastily explained how the evening would be and that he already knew the three ladies, as they were part of the threesome still coming to the restaurant on the last Friday of the month.

After giving it some thought and realizing that he would probably have to work Fridays until after Christmas and this day would be his last opportunity to have a social engagement until the new year, he agreed on the condition that he check the rotas to make sure he was covered. Monica hastily agreed, and as they were waiting for the taxi, both were lost in thought. Michael was beginning to feel he was drifting into some kind of relationship and wasn't quite sure how comfortable he was. For now, he decided to go with the flow. *A get-together may not be so bad*, he thought, and he was grateful to her for helping him climb out of his dark hole.

Meanwhile, Monica was asking the same questions herself, and she, too, was grateful for how he had helped her out of the fug she was in and was ready to approach her boss for a phased return to work.

Settled in the cinema, they both enjoyed the firm and, as the plot unfolded, got quite engrossed. All too soon it was over, and thanking Michael profusely, Monica expressed her gratitude for the escort to the cinema. "Do you fancy a nightcap at the Canny Man's?" asked Michael. "It's still early, and I am enjoying your company." She agreed with enthusiasm. They were lucky, it being Thursday, that it was relatively quiet, and they managed to get the inglenook seat next to the log fire. One silliness after another as the wine went down had them laughing uproariously, and before too long, they poured themselves into a taxi and home, both saying over and over how much fun they'd hod. With "See you next Friday" it was bock to their respective homes to crash out after a fantastic day and evening out.

Chapter 21

When Michael got to work the next day, he checked the rotas and saw to his delight that both Robert and Peter were on duty the Friday of the get-together at Monica's. *Thank heaven for Olivia's insistence that draft rotas be made a month in advance so everyone knows when they are working*, thought Michael. He asked the boss if Sylvia could come in too to make sure the exemplary service they were known for was continued. He felt now was the time to reveal to Olivia the nature of his changing personal status. She knew him well, and with great dignity she remarked to him that it was lovely he had female company and of course the Friday would be absolutely fine.

Gravely he thanked her and went down to start working. In the meantime, as her door closed, she punched the air in a not-so-ladylike fashion and spent the rest of the evening smiling. *A woman in his life, how just amazingly fantastic*, she thought. She had tuned in to Michael's rising mood and newly displayed confidence and suspected a budding romance may be in the offing. For the new partner to be one of the dreaded four Friday-night ladies was even more of a surprise.

True to her nature, Olivia decided to keep her thoughts to herself. Michael would tell her the full story when he was ready, and in the meantime, she would be patient and supportive.

As he got into work mode, he was very thoughtful. "I have just told Olivia I am starting a relationship," he thought to himself. "Is this the path I am looking for?" His other inner self told him to relax and go with the flow. He would know what was right. *One thing*, he mused. *I do not want this to be too obvious for her sake, as it could seriously harm her upcoming legal action.*

He was aware that there was a battle for a stake in the house; although they had lived in the house as a married couple, it had, in fact, been left to her by her parents, who had tragically been killed in a car crash when Monica was still at university, and she had been living in the bungalow since then, as she had before her marriage.

They had been married for only ten years, and although she put up with his verbal abuse, she was glad when he left. She would have preferred he had just left, but for him to move in with his attractive, much younger blonde secretary was a bit hard to swallow. What Monica had not realized was that she, too, was very attractive—slim, with curly brown hair and green eyes. Derek, her ex, was not one to dish out kind words, and she had very little experience in the way of relationships; she did not know she was so attractive.

Monica had figured out that her ex was insecure and had taken his insecurities out on her, putting her down and not allowing her to be herself. He had never complimented her for anything, and criticism was the weapon of choice. Although she had a ready, if sharp, wit, Monica was amusing but her soon-to-be ex had not given her that space to be herself. Already she was starting to feel more relaxed, and she had to give Michael most of the credit.

Hence, the fact that she was very attractive and well-presented was lost on her. Michael had offered a few tentative compliments, but he was sadly out of practice. *Maybe I should talk to Angela and see if she can give me some pointers as to what women like to hear,* he thought to himself. He guessed Olivia would probably make fun of him, so he thought she was not the best person to talk to. His mother had taught him the rudiments of good manners: allowing ladies to go first, walking on the outside of the pavement, holding open a door. Those sorts of things he was well aware of. What he didn't know much about was what to say. His mumbled "You look nice" when he collected Monica for the ball had been well received, so he felt maybe it wasn't so complicated after all.

Chapter 22

Michael answered the restaurant phone, expecting a booking. As he recognized the voice of Mr. MacGregor, he opened the diary and took his pen to mark the date. To Michael's surprise, Mr. MacGregor asked for Michael by his first name. He confirmed he was speaking to Michael and went on to ask whether he would meet him for a drink and a chat. He said he had something he wanted to tell him and would prefer it be done in a more private location. An astounded Michael, silent for a few moments as he processed the request, was interrupted and asked whether he wanted to think about it. Michael agreed that it would be best and asked whether he could call him back. Mr. MacGregor then asked whether there was a table free for that evening, which there was, and Michael booked him in, promising to give an answer then.

The call ended with Michael looking at the receiver as if the answer were there. He slowly put the phone down, rubbing his chin in astonishment. What on earth could a customer have to say that would be so important he couldn't mention it when he was being attended to in the restaurant?

Suddenly he remembered he had not confirmed his party date with Monica. He went upstairs and rescued his mobile from his jacket and tried to send a text—his first, probably. After a fruitless ten minutes, he decided to call instead. That just needed two buttons to be pressed. The ringtone was replaced by Monica saying, "Hello, Michael."

"How did you know it was me?" said the technophobe.

"Your name came up on the screen because you are on my contact list," she explained.

"Oh, I see," he said, not really understanding. "Just to let you know, the rotas will permit me to attend your at-home invitation, so I will see you then."

"Great," she said.

"Looking forward to seeing you!" They both chorused.

Back to Mr. MacGregor—what to do, he thought. First of all, he went upstairs and knocked on Olivia's door. Although she had on numerous occasions told him to knock and come in, his upbringing did not allow this freedom, so he waited for the "come in", which duly happened.

After biting back "Have I not told you?" and the like, and noticing his pallor, Olivia asked him what was wrong. He explained what had happened and the quandary it had put him into.

Chewing the leg of her reading glasses, Olivia went into a thoughtful pose as she mulled over the situation. "Have you got Angela's phone number?" She asked.

"Why, yes, I have. She input it into my mobile when we were clearing the house."

"I have to pop out to the cash and carry," she said, and she motioned to the phone on her desk. "Give her a call here in my office, where you can have some privacy. You can get me on my mobile if necessary." After another plea for help, Olivia showed him how to make the call.

As she climbed into her car, she was seriously tempted to send him to a technical class where he could learn about modern technology. He really didn't have a clue. Little did she know Michael was contemplating a class for beginners and was waiting for Christmas to be done and dusted. He had noticed a class which fell on a Monday morning he could attend without anyone needing to know.

Meanwhile, Michael was connected to Angela and was explaining the reason for the call. Angela's mind was racing. If McGregor wanted to do this, she would be off the hook with her promise to her friend, and Michael would have the information he so richly deserved. *It is going to be a rocky road*, she thought. *This may not go well*. She explained that it would be a good idea to hear what he had to say and left it at that. She was thankful for the direct question of "Do you know what he wants to talk about?" did not get asked, allowing Angela not to have to lie or break a promise. She would need to be there for him to help with the fallout.

On the stroke of nine, Mr. MacGregor turned up, and once the pleasantries were over and the food ordered, Michael went up to him and agreed to meet with him. "Have lunch with me at the Canny Man's?" asked MacGregor. Michael was taken aback. It was his favourite, it was Monica's favourite, and now a customer wanted to eat with him there too.

Agreeing to the meeting place and the date, he left Peter to do the honours with their diner. Michael couldn't face it. However, the meeting day was Monday—not so far ahead that he would have his nails bitten to the quick.

The evening dragged, and with great relief he locked up and headed for home, having brought Olivia up to date. To make the weekend go faster, he popped up to the golf club and had a chat with George, who introduced him to some of the younger members. He was invited to join them.

As he listened to the stories about the legendary hole-in-one and the round where the par score was beaten, Michael began to enjoy himself. The men were fun and didn't take life too seriously, but golf—that was another matter. After a pleasant couple of hours and promising to meet up again, he went home in a more buoyant mood.

He tried to phone Angela a couple of times, but there was no answer. He forgot his number would identify him as the caller. Angela was avoiding him, but with his straightforward naivety, he did not come to that conclusion.

Monday arrived soon enough, and with great trepidation he got ready. Leaving a spare key for the plumber, he headed into town.

He knew one thing, though. He was very glad the restaurant had showering facilities, as when he returned home after his day's work, his pink bathroom would be an empty shell.

Sitting in the pub, having arrived early, he was sipping his customary orange juice. He had selected a table in one of the pub's nooks, affording some privacy. He may not have known what this was about, but his gut told him he wouldn't want an audience. Mr. MacGregor arrived and made a beeline for the table. He hung up his jacket and sat down. Michael was offered a drink which he declined, still having his orange juice. MacGregor went to the bar and ordered a whisky and water. Both of them sensing the need to be clear of the waiter before starting to talk properly, the two men indulged in trivial conversation until the drink arrived.

Mr. MacGregor finally said in a quiet voice, "I expect you are wondering what this is all about?" Michael, caught unawares, nodded. "When you asked me how I knew your mother and I told you we were at school together, it's not the whole story. Your mother, Jean and I, were, as they say nowadays, an item. We were inseparable right through the final year at school and stayed together in college. We made a mistake, and Jean fell pregnant. I insisted we get married and have as normal a life as possible. I really cared for your mother, and it was no big deal we 'had' to get married. It was a quiet registry office wedding with just a few close friends, and we moved into a rented flat. Jean had to give up college, which she was unhappy about, but the day you were born, she was completely smitten. You were her angel, and she loved you more than life itself. I was young and carefree. At first, I was also very pleased with my son. Then, after about a year, things started to go wrong.

"I resented the time she spent with you. I was left out, no longer her partner, and I regretted the day you were born. My life was no fun. I was nineteen; I wanted parties and mostly freedom, not nappies and night feeds. When your mother announced she was pregnant again, I was so immature I couldn't handle it, and I packed my bags and left. I was that awful man who abandoned his son and an unborn child. I will regret that till my dying day."

At this point Michael asked one question. "Are you telling me you are my father?"

"Yes."

Michael sat staring at the man, who until this day had been known to him as a customer. Then, without another word, he stood up, put on his jacket, and walked out the door. He kept walking and walking.

Chapter 23

Olivia was concerned. Her usually punctual and dependable head waiter had not arrived for his shift. He usually arrived about 3.00 p.m., and it was now nearly 3.30 p.m. She tried phoning his mobile, but it just rang out. She noticed he had no voicemail. Trying not to let her agitation show, she went up to her office and called his home number. Again there was no voicemail. By 6.00 p.m. she was seriously concerned. Shortly thereafter, without any warning, Michael walked in, slightly dishevelled, ashen-faced, and wearing an expression that looked as if it had been carved out of granite.

He made his apology through clenched teeth and strode upstairs to get ready for his work. He would deal with Angela later. Downstairs in the restaurant, Michael went about his duties almost robotically, but the professional in him managed to carry it off. His deputies, having had a hurried discussion with Olivia, swept into action and covered his back. The shift was saved, and still, silent Michael went home having offered no explanation.

It was when he arrived home and saw the partially filled skip outside that he remembered the bathroom was being torn apart and replaced. He shuddered. Tonight was not a good night. He went slowly upstairs to survey the damage and nearly burst out laughing in spite of his mood. John the plumber had left the toilet still plumbed in and usable, and there it sat, like a throne, in the otherwise empty bathroom. He had forgotten to mention he had a downstairs toilet with a small washbasin. He would be functional enough to shave, at least, and he would shower at work.

He thought he should be careful, as he poured a rather large whisky, not to become dependent on alcohol to solve his problems. Reaching for the whisky bottle was becoming all too frequent. His mother would have seriously disapproved. His mind then fully engaged on the shocking news he had been handed. There were so many questions to which he rather foolishly threw away the chance to be answered.

Finishing his nightcap and remembering his late arrival for work, he felt ashamed. It was nobody's fault in the team which had warranted the disgraceful behaviour he normally avoided.

He was astonished on remembering how far he had walked in the four hours he was "missing in action". He thought he must have reached the sea at Portobello before he turned and came back after regaining some degree of normality. Going to bed, hoping the whisky would help him to sleep, he decided to deal with the problem in the morning.

His last thought, as he drifted into a troubled sleep, was that he needed to speak to Angela, and if the phone remained unanswered, he would go in person.

The doorbell woke him around 8.00 a.m. After rubbing the sleep from his eyes and donning his dressing gown (while thinking, *Mental note: new dressing gown required*), he allowed John in to start work. He thanked the plumber for his consideration in leaving the rather important piece of porcelain in situ, and they both laughed when Michael showed the workman his downstairs convenience. Immediately sensing a business opportunity here, John offered to redo the wee cloakroom as well for a small extra price, explaining that it would be a port of call for any visitors and that perhaps a more modern look would be just the thing.

Agreeing the price was good and giving John the go-ahead, he decided that if John was going to be clattering and banging, Michael should get washed and dressed and head to the club for breakfast. Then he would visit Angela in person, completely unannounced, and see what she had to say. He was still a bit shell-shocked but was functioning better and in a better frame of mind. A visit to the club might just be the thing. He promised himself he would head for the range on the next decent day and acquire some practice.

A couple of hours later, he found himself standing on Angela's doorstep having plucked up courage to ring the bell. The door opened, and Angela took one look and burst into tears. Opening the door wider, she motioned Michael in as she went in search of some tissues. It wasn't a house he visited

Michael, Waiting

often. He remembered he probably hadn't been there since his mother died, and he felt ashamed. Wound up in his own grief, he had not spared a thought for this woman, who was such a close friend of his mother. His heart softened, and he decided to let her explain the situation rather than accusing her of secrecy.

Manners had him standing in the hall, waiting for Angela to direct him to a chair, which she did whilst blowing her nose. It would seem she was not surprised by the visit. One could imagine that as they seemed to have a relationship, MacGregor would probably have phoned to give her an update.

She vanished into the kitchen, and putting the kettle on and rattling cups made her feel as if she were doing something positive whilst avoiding the forthcoming conversation. Would she launch into an explanation or wait for Michael's questions? She decided on the latter as she took the tea and cake through to the lounge, where Michael waited patiently for his hostess.

Her opening gambit was to ask him what he wanted to know, and she answered quite curtly on his part that he wanted to know everything. That changed how Angela approached the situation, and she launched into the story.

After Michael's father deserted them, Jean was very bitter for a long time, and even when his father begged to come back and Jean miscarried, she would not give him the time of day. "He wanted to be part of your life," Angela explained, "but Jean would not have it. She was a very unforgiving woman and had developed a very possessive streak regarding her small son. It was as if she had traded a father for a son."

"By the time you were due to go to school, she had mellowed a little, but not enough for your father to be allowed into your life. He threatened her with court action to be allowed access, but Jean was adamant that he would not have contact. An arrangement was made. Once a month, they would meet up and Jean would give Mike a progress report and show current photographs, and sometimes she would take you to the park, where he could sit on a bench and watch his son playing. He was under strict instructions not to approach them or he would never see either of them again.

"When your mother died, he felt his promise died too, and he contacted me to let me know of his intention to approach you. I had to agree. After the loss of your mother, I felt it was only fair you had access to your only living relative. I tried on many occasions to talk your mother out of her stubbornness, but to no avail. She was determined. Give him a chance, Michael. He has regretted his actions and tried to put it right, but it was never going to happen. Your mother had sworn me to secrecy, so my telling you of your father's whereabouts was not possible.

"I was already planning to break that promise when Mike contacted me and told me of your lunch meeting. I have to say I heard the news with some relief. It was not my promise that would have to be broken.

"Have I missed anything? Is there anything else you want to know?" Michael stared at the woman he thought he knew and wondered whether he really knew her at all. More importantly, it would appear he didn't know his mother either. Judging by the way the explanation was given, he felt Angela must have put a lot of thought into her "speech". It almost sounded prepared. He felt that she had given enough of the story and that most of the questions he wanted answered should be answered by the man who was his father. He was not ready to see him yet.

Getting up, he thanked her for her honesty, and he then took leave of the woman he would one day soon forgive for her duplicity. At the moment, he didn't like anyone, especially himself.

Not quite ready to explain himself yet, as he started back to work on time, he instructed his staff to refuse Mr. MacGregor a table. The restaurant was full when he called. Then he spotted an envelope on the booking desk with his name on it. He opened the envelope and scanned the contents long enough to establish that it was from MacGregor, and he crumpled it up and threw it in the bin without reading it.

He did not notice Olivia standing as still as a statue at the bottom of the stairs, watching his every move. She had been concerned when he had behaved out of character. Eventually she caught his eye and motioned him upstairs.

Pointing to the chair opposite, she asked him to sit. She looked at him for a minute or two and then uttered the one word "talk".

It took about half an hour for Michael to tell the whole sorry tale, from lunch to the news of his long walk and confrontation with Angela.

By the time he was finished, she knew just about as much as he did.

Michael, Waiting

Going down the sympathy route, she told Michael that if he needed to talk, her door was always open. She also came down in favour of meeting up with his father and getting answers to questions only he could answer. She suggested he make a list and arrange a meeting. As this was coming from a lady who had been a surrogate mother as well as his boss, Michael reluctantly had to agree with her. He knew they would have to meet, but not just yet. Thinking over the whole thing, he realized he was like his father in looks, which is why when they first met Michael thought he recognized him. He recognized him from the mirror.

Now he had two major life-changing happenings. He was aware that the canal murder was still ongoing, and now there was the bombshell of his parentage. It was no wonder his head felt like a sieve. He remembered, with pleasure, he was going to Monica's house on Friday for an at-home, and he was looking forward to it. He decided he would put everything on hold until after Friday, when he would arrange to meet her and ask her advice.

On getting home that evening, being in a better frame of mind, he ran upstairs to check on the progress of his bathroom. He was astonished at the progress. The shower was in, as were the toilet bowl and sink. Not being a plumber, he wasn't sure, but it looked as if it was tiling and the mirror left to do. Impressed, he went downstairs and, to his horror, found himself pouring a whisky. Taking the celebratory route, he raised his glass and said "Slainte!" to the empty room. *Must stop this*, he admonished himself. *It's a bad habit.*

Chapter 24

Monica had warned him in advance that there would be food as well as drink. So he was to leave the car and come with an empty stomach. She assured him there would be plenty to eat, and standing on her steps waiting for the door to be answered, he felt a quiver of nervousness. Michael had taken Olivia into his confidence and had told him all about the forthcoming party. He felt Olivia was an ideal person to be kept in the loop. Sure enough, she suggested to him he should take a bottle of wine as a contribution and that flowers would be a nice touch. Michael breathed a sigh of relief. Olivia was such a good friend, and she had stopped him making some awful clangers with his unfamiliarity in social situations

He was welcomed in, and thanking him for the wine and exclaiming over the flowers, Monica showed Michael into the lounge, where a few people had gathered already. Introductions were made, and with a glass of wine in his hand, he sat down prepared to try to go with the flow. Monica took the flowers through to the kitchen, arranged them artistically in a vase, and put the white wine Michael had brought into the fridge. Secretly she was pleased to see Michael's social skills improving and wondered how much influence his boss, Olivia, was having, or indeed whether she knew of the burgeoning relationship.

A few hours later, Michael found he'd had a really nice time. He enjoyed the company of the ladies he knew from their visits to the restaurant, and he found the husbands rather fun. Whilst waiting for the taxi, he broached the subject of asking advice, and when Monica agreed, he asked whether they could meet up sooner rather than later. She suggested he come over for breakfast. *Certainly good from the privacy angle*, Michael thought, and it was set up. Off he went into the darkness and to the taxi to his house, where he felt better than he had done for a while.

Breakfast was a delight. Monica had arranged it buffet style, with sausages, bacon, croissants, and pastries. The jam looked homemade, and the coffee spluttered through the filter. Compared to his cereal, toast, and marmalade, it was a veritable feast.

Monica was a good listener, and as Michael told his story relating to his overheard conversation and the news of finding a body in the canal, Monica listened intently. He also admitted to lying to her about his facial wound and confessed to the real reason he had a black eye—the assault at his front door—and apologized for the fabrication.

Monica poured more coffee as she bought time, her head full of what she had just heard. Eventually she turned to him and gave advice relating to the canal murders and what he overheard. "It makes sense to report it, Michael," she stated. "I am sure if you explain about the threats, they will afford you some sort of protection. Besides, if the perpetrators are locked up, they won't be able to get to you, will they?"

"No, I suppose not, and yes, you are right," he said. "They need to be caught and put away. I will phone the police station when I get home."

"Phone from here," she countered, bringing the handset and placing it on the table within his reach.

"Do I just dial 999?"

"No, silly, I will get the number. They have been publishing a helpline number for just such an occasion."

With mounting trepidation, Michael dialled the number Monica provided and explained to the policewoman who answered what had occurred. With seemingly much interest, the officer took note. She asked whether he would come into the station and sign a statement. Michael, panicking, emphasized the threat to him if he contacted the police. The officer reassured him it would not happen. "We will increase patrols around your area, and perhaps if you use taxis instead of the bus, it might deter them."

The officer then said she would need to see the booking diary and would come to the restaurant later. After thinking it through, she said she would take Michael's statement there too. "Will save some time," the officer stated.

Michael felt trapped between a rock and a hard place. Now he was having to involve his colleagues and putting them at risk too. Monica was very dismissive. "Nothing bad will happen," she told him. "Take his advice and use taxis for a little while at least."

Moving swiftly on, she advised Michael to meet up with his newly found father and, as Olivia had counselled, go armed with questions. "The first one I should say is why you don't have your father's surname."

Michael blinked a couple of times as the cogs in his head moved round. "Of course," he said. "I should be MacGregor, not Whittaker. Do you suppose they never married?"

"Only your father can answer that," responded Monica a trifle smugly.

"Okay," an exasperated Michael replied. "How come you are always right?" he asked. "Not always," she replied, "just most of the time."

Thanking her profusely, Michael took his leave, and as he had brought the car, it didn't take him long to get back up home to get ready for his next shift. *To say I am not looking forward to telling Olivia her establishment is going to be overrun with police is a bit of an understatement*, he thought, exaggerating a bit.

Chapter 25

He still had a bit of time before he had to go to work, so he decided to go through some paperwork he hadn't been able to face when his mother died. Sorting it into bundles for filing, he came across two documents he really should have taken up. His road tax and MOT were well overdue on the car, and the insurance had run out six months ago. With horror, he realized the car was not road legal and he would have to do something about it immediately. It was also in his mother's name. He cursed himself for his inability to deal with ordinary everyday matters that other people seemed to be able to manage without difficulty. His first thought was to contact Monica and ask her advice again. He called her on her mobile.

After a lengthy conversation during which Monica had specified all the paperwork he needed, and after he had managed to find it all, she offered to buzz up in her car, as Michael's was effectively useless, and collect the paperwork. Most of the work could be done online, and as Michael didn't have a computer, she would help him.

Michael shyly mentioned to Monica that he planned to go to adult education classes soon to learn basic computing. An astonished Monica exclaimed how helpful he would find this in his everyday life and promised to help him as much as she could.

With a sudden thought, Monica asked him whether he had an up-to-date driving licence. Michael thought for a minute and then went to the bits and pieces drawer, where he had thrown a letter from DVLA. He opened the envelope, and his photo ID driving licence was enclosed. He vaguely remembered his mother sending away paperwork to obtain the new photo licence, and the big green paper one was no longer valid.

Relieved, Monica took the paperwork and headed down to the garage to have the MOT done. She had already contacted the insurance company to renew the policy.

With Michael not having driven much and having no claims, the cost was quite modest. "Michael," exclaimed Monica in an admonishing tone, "you are a grown man; why did you allow your mother to do everything for you?"

"Oh, she insisted," returned Michael. "Does that mean she opened your mail?" "Yes," answered Michael meekly.

With a rather unladylike expletive, Monica exited the house and headed home. It took her a while to realize she, too, was treating Michael like a small boy—just as his mother had! "But he brings out the mothering instinct," she said out loud as a means of excusing her treatment of Michael. She vowed then to help in any way she could to bring him into being a more confident and competent grown-up.

Michael, having left Monica with the paperwork, headed off to the restaurant. As promised, during the afternoon, two detectives arrived to take a statement. Completely in the dark regarding police procedures, he was a little nervous about the whole thing. His nerves eased somewhat when he realized they had arrived in plain clothes and had used an unmarked car. There were no flashing lights and sirens to draw the attention of passers-by.

With the police having left with the paperwork they needed, Michael was glad to see them go and settled into his routine. On his way home, in a taxi as suggested, he remembered the dreadful slip-up with the car paperwork and was thankful to Monica for her help. She was coming over with paperwork the next morning, and she had phoned to tell him he had his car booked in at the small garage on the Comiston Road at 9.00 a.m. on Monday morning.

It would appear that the only documents she was able to sort were the change-of-name paperwork and the insurance. The rest would have to wait until the MOT was done. Monica drove them to the club for a light lunch before Michael headed off to work. She offered to drive him to work, which gave them a decent length of time to eat and catch up.

When they phoned him at lunchtime on Monday, the mechanic had bad news. Quite a bit of work was needed, mostly due to the length of

Michael, Waiting

time the car had been sitting idle. The bill would be around £1,500, and that was as long as the parts came free easily. But it was a risk. Michael listened to the litany of disaster and bought some time by saying he would call them back with a decision. Fortunately, Monica was home when he phoned. He told her the bad news. Monica was sympathetic. She knew how much Michael had come to depend on his car, but it was elderly and really not worth spending that amount of money on.

"Could you afford a more modern car?" she asked. She said this after suggesting that the car really wasn't worth spending huge sums of money on because of its age and condition and that he might get a wee bit of money on part exchange. Michael took a few minutes to think, as he had not contemplated this.

One minute he had been driving to the golf club, and the next he was in the unenviable situation of not having the correct paperwork and his car not even being roadworthy. "Yes, I have savings," he admitted. And yes, a newer car might be the answer as he got more confident behind the wheel and started to go places further afield.

"Do you fancy going car shopping on your day off?" she said.

Michael, totally taken aback, was silent as the cogs started again. "Yes," he said, "what a good idea." But what would he do with the car? It couldn't be driven in its current state. He phoned the garage back and gave them his decision not to proceed with the MOT but replace the car instead. "When would it be convenient to take it away," he asked? The mechanic indicated it was still in a dismantled state and it would take a while to rebuild it before asking what he intended to do with the car. On hearing that it was being disposed of, they offered to buy it from him, as it was a popular model and they could use the car for parts.

Pleased as punch, he agreed on the transaction and headed down to collect the modest amount of cash they had offered. Before he set off, he phoned Monica with the news, and she offered to drive him round the car dealerships on Thursday. After thanking her profusely, he terminated the call, donned his jacket, locked the door, and walked to the garage.

Forgetting the police advice regarding his travel arrangements, he became aware of a large four-by-four car driving down the road, keeping pace with him. He broke out in a cold sweat as the memory of the conversation with the detectives came back to mind.

He started to walk faster. He looked down the road and realized he still had approximately a quarter of a mile until the relative safety of the garage. The four-by-four speeded up to stay abreast of its prey.

Suddenly, without warning, the unmistakable sound of blues and twos burst into song as a marked police car came speeding towards them. The large car accelerated, turned into the Braids, and stopped beside Michael. "You all right?" asked the passenger. Trying to keep his voice normal, Michael replied he was "Okay, thanks."

"Take a taxi next time," said the officer, and the patrol car carried on down the road.

He arrived at the garage in a rather nervous state after the altercation. He spoke to the mechanic, without revealing his scary moment, and collected the money. He bade farewell to the elderly Ford Fiesta he had come to use and enjoy. He decided to take the police advice and asked whether someone would phone for a taxi. He was, after all, going to work. He would be a bit early, but that was better than being open to being attacked.

As he headed off down Comiston Road in the taxi to get to work, his mind was racing. He had been shocked at just how easy it had been for the occupants of the large four-by-four to track him down. *The forthcoming purchase might help,* he thought. *A new car ... I wonder what I should buy. A compact car probably, as the streets of the city are quite congested and the lock-up is not large. Monica will keep me right, no doubt.* He thought about his growing relationship and dared to hope.

Alighting from the taxi, he realized he was very early for work. He paid the driver with a generous tip and asked for his number. He was going to have a local taxi number in his phone contacts so he would always be in a position to call for a taxi. Feeling rather pleased with himself, he pottered up Morningside to check out some of the boutiques and nearly new shops.

Spotting a rather snazzy robe which looked remarkably like silk, he thought it might just do the trick, as his old dressing gown was really fit only for the rubbish. No self-respecting charity shop would even touch it. Just as he was about to enter the shop, reflected in the shop window he caught sight of a vehicle remarkably similar to the large four-by-four. He heard the slamming of car doors and turned around. He was horrified to recognize the two thugs from the restaurant. *Oh no,* he thought. How did they know how to find him already? What did they want with him? Did they want to kill him? With sheer terror pumping up his adrenalin, he took off running, hearing from behind once of the men shouting, "Stop! we want to speak to you."

Michael, not believing they did not mean him harm, kept running. He was soon aware of only one set of footsteps, and on cue one of the men said, "I can't go on; I'll go back to the car. You keep on his tail; You're fitter than me." That was the last he heard as he kept going through the streets of Morningside, trying to lose his follower. Michael was seriously worried now. He thought his last moments had come. He remembered that round the next corner was the road leading to a hotel, and he decided to make for it in the hope of getting sanctuary.

Meanwhile, the still running thug was now well out of breath and slowing. Just as Michael reached the hotel, the car that had been following him stopped at the end of the street, collected his partner in crime, and sped off. With a huge sigh of relief, Michael carried on into the hotel.

If he could have seen himself, he would have been mortified. His shirt was undone, and his hair was plastered in sweat.

Going to the reception, Michael explained what had happened and asked whether the receptionist would call the police for him. He said to ask for Detective Winston, who had been one of the officers who took his statement. After a brief phone conversation, the receptionist informed him that the policeman he had asked for was out and about dealing with another matter. However, there was a patrol car in the area looking for the car Michael had described.

A short while later, two uniformed bobbies arrived, and the manager put all three into his office to enable them to talk freely and privately. He returned with a tray bearing coffee and biscuits and then left them to their business.

Meanwhile, back at the police station, Detective Winston was aware of his mobile phone vibrating in his pocket. He pulled out the phone, glancing at the caller display. Seeing a name he really didn't want to see, he quickly silenced the phone and left the building. Calling back, he got the worst possible news. Not only had the hired help failed to apprehend Michael, but right now Michael was safe in the hotel, telling his now lengthy story to a couple of uniforms.

Pacing up and down, his thoughts racing, he tried to find a solution to the mess he was in. Who would have thought a policeman of twenty-eight years and shortly coming up for retirement would have the stupidity to take matters into his own hands regarding the person responsible for killing his son whilst driving well over the limit? The drink-driver had been given probation and a fine.

Detective Sergeant Ian Winston was certain a prison sentence was on the table, but by pleading guilty, this was avoided. Not really in his right mind, from his contacts in gangland he arranged to have the perpetrator disposed of.

Unfortunately for Ian, he now realized he had picked out two of the most inept men, as it seemed the plot had been discussed in a restaurant, with the head waiter overhearing the conversation. Fortunately, the detective had intercepted the report and taken the statement himself and managed to make it disappear. Of course, now the waiter had to be dealt with.

That, too, failed, and the detective was now effectively finished. He would lose his pension and probably go to prison. Life had been difficult after the loss of his son but he still cared enough not to end up in prison. He jumped into his car and drove away at speed. After parking up, he went into a bank he used frequently. He asked for his safety deposit box, producing the necessary paperwork. Once he was in the privacy of the vault, he opened the box and removed a couple of credit cards, a passport in an entirely different name, and an envelope full of euros.

He had managed to avoid being caught as he systematically turned a blind eye to various criminals, earning large amounts of bribe money. He had, over the years, accumulated a sizeable sum and had periodically changed it into European currency. Driving to the airport, he thought about what had happened. He was alone now and would catch the first flight to wherever and hopefully disappear. There was no way he could remain in the country. All the paperwork he had buried was locked in his desk, and it wouldn't take long to break into that.

Back at the hotel, the plot was beginning to unravel. Like pieces of a jigsaw being assembled, the whole story came out. At the police station, frantic efforts were being made to find Detective Winston. His car was found hours later in the airport long-stay car park.

Michael, Waiting

Not being privy to his previous nefarious activities, his colleagues were unable to find out where he had gone. For now he had eluded them, but the two men who had actually committed the murder were still at large, and Michael was at risk.

The bobbies offered to drive Michael home, to which Michael agreed. He would phone Olivia and explain what had happened. He would then shower and get changed, and if he felt more like it, he would have a snack to keep him going. He had just remembered he had not eaten since breakfast. For some reason, though, he did not feel hungry.

Olivia had told him to take the rest of the day off, but Michael demurred, saying he would rather be at work but he would be a bit later than usual. "You know best," said a now disturbed Olivia, thinking to herself she felt there was more to come out of the woodwork.

Always pragmatic, she dismissed her train of thought, deciding to worry only when there was something to worry about—for example, the lump she had found a couple of days ago. Her inner self admonished her and insisted she make an appointment with her doctor. Her outer self said she would get around to it soon.

When Michael arrived at work around 6.00 p.m. he was deluged with questions and words of concern and sympathy. Brushing them aside, he asked for the peace to sort it all out in his head, thanking his co-workers for their good wishes. Then he remembered he hadn't told Monica. She would be furious to have been left out of the loop. He compromised by making a quick call to her, telling her the bare bones and stating that as he was at work at the moment, he would call tomorrow and give her the whole story.

Monica had insisted he tell her the whole story in person, and he was to come to her house, where she would serve him lunch while he recounted his sorry tale. She was a bit shaken, but she was good at covering up. Glad to see him in person, she was able to see he was ok. So after a lovely lunch, the frightening story having been told, they drifted into a nicer topic and started talking about the venture on Thursday, which they hoped would end in the purchase of a car. One important criterion was that he be able to fit his clubs in the boot.

Chapter 26

Thursday dawned bright and clear. Monica drew up in front of Michael's house. She wasn't sure whether to get out of the car and go to his front door or wait in the car until he came out. The quandary was soon solved, as the front door opened and Michael stood on the step motioning her to come to the house. After inviting her in, he took pride in showing off his newly refurbished bathroom and downstairs toilet. Monica was impressed. "I like that you have kept the colours neutral. You can pick any colour of towels that way." Michael looked at her blankly. The colour of towels was not first on the agenda. When he took a towel out of the linen wardrobe, it was just a towel. Monica explained about colour coordinating his bathroom and told him that by keeping his colours neutral he could have any colour he fancied. Michael sighed. There were so many things he had to learn.

Just before they left, he mentioned to her he was contemplating installing a new kitchen and then decorating the rest of the house. That way it would all be new and modern. Monica agreed it would be a good idea and offered to help him arrange his kitchen by adding "a woman's touch". Although rather surprised by her interest, he agreed it would be a good idea to have her opinion and promised to let her know when the decisions were being made.

To himself he thought it would change the house; that would encourage the belief in himself that he didn't need to remain in the past just to be reminded of his mother and how much she had sacrificed for him.

Arriving at one of the many garages situated near Portobello, they got out of the car and approached the second-hand car sales. Naturally they

Michael, Waiting

were pounced on by an overly enthusiastic salesman. It was still early, so Michael had not had a chance to be jaded by the day ahead.

Monica took the lead, explaining what they were looking for with an approximate spend. Naturally, the salesman addressed Michael. Monica was left thinking, *Why do they do that—always assume it's the man?*

After looking at a few vehicles and the prices, Michael was getting a bit fed up with the salesman's inane chatter, and all the cars he had shown them were out of his budget range. He decided to go elsewhere. Parking up in the car lot of the garage next door, they both spotted a shiny black VW Golf sitting on the forecourt. Michael walked up to it and looked it up and down. Monica wisely kept quiet. She recognized a man falling in love with a car.

Michael had a long conversation with the salesman, who incidentally had maintained a discreet silence while Michael examined the vehicle. It was only four years old with a very low mileage, he was told, and although it was a bit above his budget, the difference was not serious, so he accepted the offer of a test drive. Michael was impressed with both the car and the discreet behaviour of the salesman. Compared to the previous experience, he felt he was being given the opportunity to examine the vehicle, and he loved the oyster-coloured leather upholstery. The car was all he had been hoping for. He asked a few questions and hemmed and hawed long enough for the salesman to decide on a discount for cash. A deal was struck, and the salesman explained that certain paperwork required doing, but the car would be completely serviced with a brand-new MOT and ready for collection on the following Monday. He then asked whether Michael would like the car to be delivered. Monica intervened and told the salesman she would happily bring Michael to collect his vehicle on Monday.

When they were driving back, Michael curiously asked why she had stopped the garage from delivering his car, as it put Monica to trouble she didn't need. Monica turned to Michael and said with some asperity, "Do you really want your new car being driven along Seafield Road as if it were Brands Hatch? That's what these young grease monkeys do, you know."

Monica was plotting. Because she only had next week before she would start her phased return to work, Monica wanted to spend more time with Michael, so collecting the car was a bonus and she thought maybe they could go for lunch.

Michael was delighted when Monica had told him the previous week she was negotiating a phased return to work. This meant she was ready to return to work, and that was a good thing. He had noticed an improvement in her general mood, and he rather hoped that he was having a positive effect on her, just as she was on him.

It also indicated she was starting to recover from what had been a tremendous blow. Michael told himself he would support her all he could.

It was a lovely day, and there was plenty of it left. The transaction had been seamless, and the young salesman had been exceptionally adroit. Michael thanked the young man and agreed to see him on Monday. Walking back to Monica's car after Michael had taken a last long look at his new possession, he asked Monica whether she would like to go for some lunch in the way of a thank-you for all her help.

Monica agreed, especially seeing as it was such a lovely day, that she would enjoy it very much. "Where would you like to go?" she asked. However, Michael was not very clued up on nice eating places, not having been around a lot. He tended to use the restaurants in the centre of the city and that was a fair old journey, not to mention trying to find somewhere safe to park her car.

Monica asked whether he had ever been to Culross. He replied in the negative, not even knowing where it was. "Then that's where we will go. It's just across the Forth Road Bridge." He got into Monica's car, and off they went.

Michael couldn't remember the last time he crossed the bridge, and it was possible to see the embryonic stage of the new bridge. They talked about the design, which was not yet apparent but was well publicized, and soon they were entering Culross, and Monica got lucky, finding a parking place outside the Red Lion. It was famous for its good Scottish food, and Michael couldn't help but compare it to Dhugall. He even thought of tips he could pass on to Alfredo.

The food was excellent, and once again there was no shortage of conversation. Sharing a similar sense of humour, they were soon laughing and joking.

Monica excused herself, and in the ladies' she noticed a cardboard cut-out of a kilted athletic-looking figure on the inside of the door. The sporran was moveable, and curiosity got the better of her as she naughtily lifted up the kilt to be greeted by a loud bell ringing, sounding a bit like a doorbell. When she returned to her seat, she was aware the people at the tables close by were smiling and when she looked at Michael, he too was smiling broadly. The barman explained that ladies have a curiosity around what a gentleman wears under his kilt and they can't resist having a sneaky peek. Alas, that's when the bell alerts everyone in the pub that a lady is being curious.

She saw the funny side, fortunately and as it soon would be dark, Michael, insisting it was his treat, settled the bill, and soon they were on their way home. After he was dropped off, it was still relatively early, and thinking about the towel remark from Monica, he went upstairs and checked out his linen closet. Not surprisingly, most of the towels were pink and had seen better days. Then he found, still in the cellophane wrapper, a set of towels in a deep shade of burgundy. They had obviously not been to his mother's taste, but Michael thought they would go well in his new bathroom. Tearing open the package, he distributed half of the packet onto the newly installed towel rails and took a hand towel downstairs.

He poured himself a rather large whisky (which he thought was getting to be a habit) and went back upstairs to view the finished article. He was very pleased and decided then and there the kitchen was next. A call to John was the result. Michael smiled at his impetuousness. *My world is changing,* he thought. John indicated he had been cancelled from a job as a result of illness and was free tomorrow to bring the inevitable brochures, and he added that if the goods were in stock, he could start Monday. When he was told it would probably be finished within the week, Michael gave the go-ahead.

He decided to phone Monica firstly to thank her for the day and secondly to see whether she wanted to put in her tuppenny ha'penny worth. Never one to miss an opportunity to offer advice, she agreed with enthusiasm and arranged to be there. Michael, remembering he had frozen Danish pastries, offered her breakfast. So the date was arranged.

Chapter 27

Monica was very practical, and she was able to advise Michael of what he should have and what he should do without. Michael was grateful for the input. Monica proved to be sensible as well as practical, as she paid close attention to the costs. Had she not agreed to help, he would just have left it to John, the plumber. A quick phone call to the stockist confirmed that what was wanted was available, and to Michel's relief, the work would start on Monday. *I am going to be spending a lot of time at the golf club*, thought Michael. He gave John back the spare key, as he was, of course, collecting his new car on Monday. John left with a cheery whistle, leaving the couple alone.

They sat about chatting for a bit before Michael said, "Do you fancy lunch at the club? I know it's a bit of a cheek having no transport and relying on you, but I want to thank you for this morning."

Monica agreed it would be lovely, but she said, "I will need to be careful or I will put on weight with all this delicious food."

"You look lovely as you are," said Michael, shocked at himself. "Thank you," said Monica simply.

With lunch over, Monica decided the subject had to be broached. "What are you going to do about your father?" she asked, with her fingers crossed under the table. Rather brusquely, Michael retorted, "I don't know yet," and the subject was dropped.

On arriving at work, he was approached by Peter, who gave him the news that the customer MacGregor had twice tried to make a booking and ended up asking to speak to the manager. Fortunately, Olivia had been out at the time. "But he is getting persistent," said Peter. Michael was thoughtful as he went about his work, and by the time he was ready

Michael, Waiting

to go home, he concluded that this was not going away and he had to be proactive before Olivia became involved. He took note of the phone number on the booking diary and caught the bus home, forgetting the advice to use taxis.

Figuring out that MacGregor would probably be retired by now, he made the phone call the next morning. Unexpectedly, a woman answered the phone. Resisting the temptation to slam the phone down, he heard her calling out, "Mike … phone." The remembered voice came on the line, and after announcing himself to the man he had come to realize was his father, he was struck speechless. He had no idea what to say.

His father came to the rescue by asking after his health and well-being. Michael, stuttering, managed to get "Fine, thank you" out reasonably clearly. Another silence was interrupted by Mike asking him whether he wanted to meet up. He was sure that Michael would want more information.

After Michael had agreed to meet at the Canny Man's on his day off, the call was terminated.

In the run-up to Christmas, Michael knew it would be busy. Already the booking diary was filling up. Christmas Day was almost full; however, the decision had been made at the outset that Christmas dinner would be one sitting only, allowing the diners to have a leisurely meal and the staff to get an early night.

He had been that morning, by the good graces of Monica, to collect his new car, and with delight he drove home and parked his new possession in the lock-up. He had taken the route around the city bypass just so he could test the car. He was delighted. It ran very well, and Michael thought it to be very smart. He wouldn't feel ashamed parking outside anyone's door.

However, with trepidation he checked out the kitchen progress. It was surprising how much devastation could occur in such a short time. The noise was deafening. Michael quickly got ready for work and walked to the golf club for some lunch. The kitchen was in no state to prepare food. He had already packed up what little food he had and plugged in the fridge-freezer, which he had moved into the hall.

The thought of the upcoming meeting with MacGregor was very much uppermost in his mind as he walked down the road to his work. Knowing the would-be assassins were safely locked up awaiting court appearances, he felt he could go back to his old habits. He felt he was obsessing on both the upcoming trial and the meeting with the man who had told him he was his son. It was time to put it to one side and deal with the matters when they occurred. He had three days before the meeting with MacGregor, and he thought it wise to write down some of the questions he wanted to ask. He decided that would be tomorrow's task.

As Michael was setting about his work, Olivia surprised him with a telephone message. She handed him a piece of paper with a name and phone number on it. "It's the police station," she explained. "They want you to give them a call. If you pop upstairs to my office, you can call them now," she offered.

Michael wasn't much in the mood and wondered what they wanted. *Nothing else for it; I will have to make the call he thought.* He put the phone down just as Olivia returned to the office.

"Well?" she asked.

"They want me to go to the police station and identify the men who were chasing me," he explained.

"No time like the present," she told him, and she proceeded to phone for a taxi. The station was too far to walk, and he would need two buses.

He called the police back and told them he would be there shortly, explaining his transport arrangements. They offered to give him a lift back.

In the taxi, he began to worry about the impending visit. He did not want to face the men who had nearly killed him and plotted the death of another.

Michael alighted from the taxi and offered money for the fare but was surprised and delighted when the driver told him that the fare was on the restaurant's account. Michael strode into the building with more confidence than he felt. Upon announcing his identity, the officer at the desk made a call, and very soon he was being escorted to an office.

The sweat was gathering on his palms and under his arms. His mouth felt dry at the sheer terror of coming face-to-face with his aggressors. The officer took him into a small office and sat him down. Michael looked about in panic. There would be no escape, and he would be very close to the men he had reported to the police.

The police officer introduced himself as Detective Inspector Peters and said he was leading the enquiry. He was the senior investigating officer—SIO for short. He then began to explain to Michael what was to happen next. They were at this moment finding similar-looking men who would take part in the identity parade. As the explanation carried on, Michael couldn't believe what he was hearing. He would not be facing his attackers. Instead they would be behind a screen with one-way glass; it would be done twice, as the accused would be part of the identity parade individually. It took a good few minutes for Michael's heart rate to settle and his sweat to dry. He was so relieved.

It seemed to be a very long time until the officer came back. In the meantime, he had been offered tea or coffee. It was only just over half an hour before he was escorted down into the basement, where he was shown into a darkened room with a large window. The officer explained, "This is the one-way mirror I was telling you about. You can see everything, but those on the other side only see a mirror."

Five men were led out, each holding a number. Michael was encouraged to study the men and give the number of anyone he recognized. Advised to take his time, Michael gazed at the five men, weighing them up, and without hesitation he picked out one of the men. Yes, he was sure, and the first group were led away. An identical process ensued, and he also swiftly pointed out assailant number two.

Thanking Michael profusely, the detective arranged for a constable to give him a lift back to the restaurant. As he was being driven through the streets, he felt a little conspicuous. It was his first ride in a police car.

The temptation to ask to switch on the blues and twos was overwhelming, but he reverted to his usual decorous self and settled down to finish the ride. He was glad to get back and take up the reins of normality.

The next morning, he had decided to make the list for the meeting with MacGregor. Although Michael knew this man was his biological father, he did not feel any affinity with him and found it difficult to refer to him as anything other than MacGregor.

John, the plumber, was setting new standards of noise, and Michael was finding it hard to concentrate. "Nothing else for it. Back to the golf club and get some breakfast. I can write my list there." Michael set off with a notebook and pen, and after a wonderful breakfast he started on the task he had allocated himself.

The frequency of visits was now beginning to pay off, and he was becoming known as some of the members greeted him. He reluctantly refused their offer to join them for a drink, explaining he had work to do.

They allowed him to work in peace without any meanness. "Another time," one of the parties called, and Michael waved in acknowledgement.

Once the list was finished, he went outside to make a call to Monica. She would want to know what he had picked out for the meeting. She might even point out something he had overlooked. Heading home with his head buzzing both with his own efforts and with Monica's advice, he left the notebook on the table in the lounge and got ready for work.

Curiosity persuaded him to see how his renovations were going, so he made a quick check on John before he headed off to work. He was pleased to notice that the banging seemed to have stopped, and the large stack of cardboard-wrapped flat-packed furniture gave him optimism for a conclusion this side of Christmas.

As Michael struggled awake with the alarm ringing in his ear, he thought the nightly whisky was not doing him any good. It was Thursday.

Michael was not feeling much like breakfast, and John had just arrived, surprisingly this time with another workman. "Just going to get the furniture up and running. It needs two of us," explained John. Michael nodded somewhat absent-mindedly, as his head was full of questions. Nevertheless, he gave John a warm smile and a nod before casting his eye over the list of questions already prepared. Monica had provided other questions he had not thought about. "Let's see how this meeting goes," he said to himself. "If it goes well, we can meet up again to clear up any missing points."

He folded the list carefully, putting it safely in his inside pocket and leaving the workmen to it, and started on the walk down to Morningside. He had decided to walk, against the police advice, thinking it would help clear his head for the upcoming ordeal.

Mr. MacGregor arrived at the pub on time, with Michael already there. Michael greeted him with a handshake and "hello Mr. MacGregor"; this was countered with "call me Mike"—a clumsy icebreaker, but Michael didn't notice. This was almost like a business meeting. Once he had all the facts he could relax and not have to think about him or see him again.

Michael opened the conversation by asking about his name. Why was he Whittaker and not MacGregor? Mike explained that after he divorced

Michael, Waiting

Jean, she wanted nothing more to do with him and adopted her maiden name, which she then passed on to young Michael. "She said she did it by deed poll, but your name on your birth certificate was MacGregor," he explained. "You should have a certificate in your current name, but I had no part in it, so I don't know. I did, however, refuse permission for your mother to change your name by deed poll, but I don't know the outcome of that."

"Where did you go, and where did you live?" asked Michael.

Mike cast his mind back to the time and replied, "Your last surviving grandparent died around the time of the divorce, and your mother inherited the house you now live in. It was a godsend for her, as she didn't have much money and the house was debt free. I carried on at university and lived in a shared flat with other impecunious students. I had given a promise that I would not make any claim on the inheritance, but all offers of child maintenance were determinedly rebuffed. When you were in your teens, she relented and started taking money for you. I guess it was because a teenager is expensive to bring up. However, a couple of years after we finalized the divorce, she began to meet with me, and I was able to hear about your progress."

Michael digested this information and then asked what he had done once he finished university. "I went to medical school and became a doctor. I specialized in oncology, and I still work part time," Mike answered.

"But you don't live alone, do you?" asked Michael, hiding his surprise at the revelation. His father—a doctor. That was a turn-up for the books.

"No, Michael. I met a young lady at university, and we married once I was qualified. You have a half brother and sister. Your half-sister is expecting a baby soon. I am going to be a grandfather—and you an uncle, if you can see a way to let us into your life."

Michael studied the other man in silence as he digested the information. He hadn't known what to expect, and he felt overwhelmed. It was a difficult place he was in. A few weeks ago, he had been alone with no family, only a friend of his mother. Now he had a promotion and a new friend with whom he was happy to let a budding relationship grow. Now he had found out that the father he had no memory of and had never been revealed had a family of his own, and suddenly half-siblings were looming over the horizon. Standing up, completely overwhelmed, Michael said to Mike, "I'm sorry. This has been all too much. I have to leave. I will be in touch; I just don't want to be here." Michael stalked out of the Canny Man's before he broke down, and again he walked and walked. This time he went to Cluny Gardens and the soothing presence of Monica.

Meanwhile, Mike sat disconsolately and accepted the barman's offer of another drink. Eventually he made his way home to his waiting family. Having been aware of Michael's existence from day one, they were curious to find out what had happened.

His son Robert, the elder of the two siblings, had been a lot put out with his father's decision to contact his half-brother. "Why now?" he exclaimed when the news was broken to him. Mike had gently explained that Michael's mother had recently died, leaving him without a living relative that he knew about, and that he felt it was time to reach out. Mike reassured his son that he would hold back until he, Robert, was comfortable with the plan. Mike did not want to subject Michael to any hostility. It would certainly put paid to any relationship, if that were indeed possible, out of the ballpark. Once Robert thought about it, he didn't take long to come around.

Mike arrived home to find his two grown-up children and his wife all in his hallway with expectant looks on their faces. "I'm sorry," he said to his family, "I don't think he is ready for us yet." He then told them what had happened. He explained that Michael had promised to be in touch, so all was not lost, and that there was still a possibility of some sort of reconciliation.

"Did all that work you did in preparation pay off?" asked his wife, Patricia.

"Yes," said Mike, "he pretty much asked the questions I expected, and I have some in the bank when and if we meet again."

"Don't give up," she replied. "Michael needs us, only he doesn't know it yet." Mike looked at his wife fondly. She was always supportive and, in this case, positively encouraging. He loved her dearly, and he told her as much on a daily basis.

Disappointed, the family went to the dining room, where Patricia had prepared a small lunch buffet. She had anticipated that the two Michaels would not get as far as lunch, and Robert had to return to work, having taken the morning off as personal time. Mhairi, the daughter due to give birth in a couple of months, had taken early maternity leave at her husband's insistence. He, also a doctor, was earning enough to support his little family, and Mhairi would be a stay-at-home mum, preferring to look after the little one herself.

The chat round the table was subdued for a while, but the family, enjoying being all together, began animatedly sharing their current news, and the subject of their half-brother was quietly shelved for now.

Chapter 28

Back in Cluny Gardens, Michael, with his head in his hands, had recounted the sorry tale to Monica, who for once sat without speaking, allowing Michael to talk and get the morning's meeting out into the open. She didn't show her exasperation with Michael's hasty exit; rather, she let him come to his own conclusions.

Once he was silent and had exhausted everything he wanted to say, she got up and went into the kitchen to make some sandwiches for lunch. She had established he had not yet eaten that day, and she felt the need to do something practical while she sorted out in her mind what advice, if any, to offer.

She was very sympathetic about Michael's plight and understood the upset he must be going through. However, she did feel that he would one day in the future regret not being part of their lives. Reading between the lines, she also felt that the onus of responsibility for the place he was in was his mother's.

From what he had told her about his mother, she surmised that Jean was a "smother mother" and, although he had not indicated as much, had kept him to herself and refused to allow Michael to get to know his father. He had begged to come back, but Jean had been resolute and unforgiving.

This is going to be an uphill struggle! Monica thought. *But it's one that needs to be addressed.* Taking the snack through, she decided that she would make it her job to show Michael the whole picture. But she would need to tread gently, He had a soft and generous nature with a hint of stubbornness she now believed he had acquired from his mother—unless, of course, MacGregor was being untruthful. She pondered that thought as they ate their sandwiches. Playing devil's advocate, she advised him to think very carefully before making up his mind what he would do next.

With lunch over and Michael in a better frame of mind, he took his leave from Monica, thanking her most fervently for her kindness. He then headed home to see how the kitchen was progressing, hoping that it was still there and not suffering from the ministrations of the gas installer. *Gas can be volatile*, he thought pessimistically.

On arriving home, he was surprised to hear only the murmur of voices and some movement emanating from the kitchen.

John, having heard him arrive, came out to greet him and with relish showed him into the kitchen, which looked positively amazing. All the white goods had arrived and been installed, and the cabinets were almost all in place. John assured him that the work would be finished at close of play tomorrow and the small kitchen table and chairs were being delivered sometime during Friday.

With grateful thanks, Michael adjourned to the lounge and started to complete the application form for the computer course he had decided to join at the start of the new term. The workmen were not making any real noise, and with the door shut he hardly knew they were there. They had indicated they would continue until 5.00 p.m., another couple of hours. Michael picked up his pen and carried on where he left off.

The application was fairly complicated, and he was fully absorbed and got quite a fright when John opened the door and informed Michael he was off for the day and would see him tomorrow at 8.00 a.m. After thanking him while inwardly groaning at yet another early start, he locked the door as they departed. He had some, but not all, of his cabinets, and the new fridge-freezer was running, albeit empty. There was even a digital display where he could see the temperature, but the best things were the ice dispenser on the door and the wine bottle racks.

He was planning to do some entertaining once all the work was done. His painter and decorator having been arranged for the following week, Michael, having a word with himself, thought, "Enough, no more spending. Well, once the house has been brought up to modern standards, no more spending." Michael was enjoying himself.

Although the rather large insurance policy paid out on the death of his mother was intact and safely invested, his not inconsiderable savings had taken a bit of a dent. With a car and the house renovations, Michael felt he had spent enough.

The lunchtime sandwiches had been very tasty, and consequently he was not very hungry. He noticed the display on the door of his super-duper all-singing-and-dancing fridge-freezer was showing temperatures which were correct for storage of food. John had patiently explained this to him.

He decided to transfer his meagre rations into the new fridge. *Shopping tomorrow*, he thought. He also decided to take his new car for a spin and go to the big electrical superstore near Corstorphine and replace the kettle and toaster, as the ones he had were made to look scruffy in the new kitchen. He unplugged his old fridge to let it defrost, ready to go with the skip when it would be taken away tomorrow. He heard his mobile phone ringing. Heading to the lounge, he found it on the coffee table and picked it up and was delighted to see it was Monica calling. He had at first thought it was the restaurant with a staffing crisis, as it was getting to the busy Christmas season.

She cut straight to the chase. One of her friends—actually one from the foursome that used to be—was having a small at-home gathering that evening and had asked her to join them, extending the invitation to include a partner. She asked whether he would want to go with her. Monica kept it to herself that she felt it was very much an afterthought, but an evening out might just be the thing.

Having made a brief examination of his food stocks and found nothing appetizing to eat, he had decided to call for a takeaway. He felt the invitation from Monica might be the answer, and he agreed with more enthusiasm than when previous social engagements had been on offer. *I do believe he is coming out of his shell*, she thought.

Michael, having work the next day, and bearing in mind his increasing whisky habit, decided to take the car and arranged to collect Monica after he had showered and changed. He loved his new shower.

Michael picked her up at the prearranged time of 7.00 p.m., and the couple, tucked up in the new car, headed over to Oxgangs and the home of Dorothy Beattie, who of course was known to Michael, as she and her two friends still frequented the restaurant on the first Friday of the month. He considered he was perhaps finding social occasions more bearable because

Michael, Waiting

he was getting to know more people, and he had to thank Monica for helping with the transition.

Taking their coats and establishing the drink preferences, Dorothy showed the couple into the lounge, where there were other guests milling around and chatting. He spotted the other two ladies from what he used to refer to as the Gang of Four and approached them to say hello. Pamela and Anna had brought their husbands, and he remembered them from Monica's party.

Another couple were shown in, and as they greeted friends, Michael was left to his own devices for a while. Monica had been caught up in conversation, and as he glanced idly around, he spotted nibbles on the table next to his chair. He was particularly intrigued by a grey-and-white-striped seed type of thing. Having not seen them before, not being a party animal, he popped a couple in his mouth, wondering why a small empty dish was placed next to them. As he chewed relentlessly on, he became aware that they were very sharp. He was having trouble chewing, and shards of the outer casing were digging into his cheeks. Monica arrived, and sensing he was distressed, she asked what was wrong. He pointed to the offending nibbles and pointed at his mouth.

Astounded, she asked him whether he had removed the shell. Michael shook his head, as talking was difficult for him at the moment. She took him out to the hall, shoved him into the small cloakroom, and under her breath instructed him to get rid of them down the toilet. Later, on the way home, they were both in gales of laughter at his social gaffe.

The next morning, waking with a clear head as he had ignored the whisky bottle, Michael headed off in the car to buy his new kitchen equipment.

Deciding on black and chrome, as his counter was black, he selected the new retro model. It took him minutes to choose. He then headed for one of the popular big superstores and stocked up on his food supplies. He also bought some wine and another bottle of whisky, promising himself it was for high days and holidays. Michael found himself humming as he drove home in the car. He felt good about the way life was beginning to be fun and was excited at the prospect of filling his new fridge. His old fridge, which had graced the kitchen, was close to twenty years old and very small. It had not had much room for wine, beer, and tasty stuff. He started to plot an evening get-together.

The downside of his chosen profession was that he always had to work at the weekends except for special occasions, such as the ball. He would also be working over the Christmas holidays, which led him to think about Monica. She hadn't mentioned any family members; the only person in her life that he knew about was her husband, and she had confided enough to allow him to know she was not looking forward to the forthcoming divorce. "It is sure to be acrimonious," she said.

As he pondered how to broach the subject, as Monica could still be a little prickly, he thought it was a good idea to invite her to the restaurant on Christmas Day when she wouldn't exactly be alone.

He thought he would tackle that tomorrow, as he had arranged to meet Monica for lunch at the Canny Man's before he started work.

They sat in their favourite spot in the inglenook by the fire, replete after a delicious lunch. Michael sat forward and started to talk earnestly. "Monica," he said, "we have been friends for a good while now, but I don't really know much about you. Oh, I know you are not looking forward to the court case, but you will be pleased to have done it. I have met some of your colleagues and friends at social occasions, but everything else is a blank. For example, I am now feeling very guilty about working on Christmas Day and quite possibly leaving you alone over Christmas."

Monica breathed an inward sigh of relief that Michael was not actually going to stop the relationship. She secretly agreed with Michael and felt it was about time to give him some background. Though she had never been happy talking about herself to anyone, her colleagues especially, she started to give him an outline of her life so far. She started off by thanking him for his concern for her well-being over Christmas and explained that she had an older sister who had chosen to retire to Bournemouth to take advantage of the milder climate and that she would be joining this sister for Christmas. She would be travelling by train the day before Christmas and returning on 2 January. Monica was apologetic and then launched into her life story in as much detail as she was willing to reveal for the time being.

The biggest piece of news took Michael unawares, and he sat silently absorbing the fact that Monica had a son born when she was only twenty-one, having married young the year before. The son had recently been seconded to Toronto in Canada for the next three years, and the plan had been to travel with her husband to visit their son for Christmas. The split had produced an attitude from her son, Jordan, that neither parent would be permitted to fly over to visit until they had "sorted themselves out". He apparently had not taken on board that the split was the result of his father going to live with another woman.

To a still silent Michael, she then proceeded to explain the background to her marriage and career. She had gone to college and completed an HND in business studies. She had an aptitude for administration and organization and had worked her way up to her present position of personal assistant to the CEO of a large multinational banking group. She had been employed by them from graduation and had met her future husband there. He was a trainee bank clerk.

Fortunately, he was now working for a different banking organization, which meant they wouldn't meet up unless by arrangement—something she was grateful for. His abusive personality caused her difficulty in fending him off, but she did acknowledge that her friendship with Michael was proving to be beneficial. As the weeks rolled on and the court date in late January began creeping up, she was beginning to feel stronger and more able to cope. She was still on compassionate leave and was attending the doctor for the stress the split had caused.

She did admit it was probably best that their relationship was kept quiet, as her husband would be malicious if he thought Monica was seeing someone. Oh yes, it was okay for him to form a new relationship, but that was not what he wanted to happen in her life.

She paused while Michael was processing the information. Michael, who always weighed up everything before speaking, seldom said anything before thinking. He was delighted that Monica had somewhere to go for Christmas.

It had been a source of dismay that he would be leaving her on her own, but that particular worry was now eradicated. The son—that was a totally different matter. He felt that the news should have been disclosed much sooner, and for the first time in their budding relationship, he was dismayed by the secrecy. The silence stretched out, and Monica felt the stirrings of fear as she noticed the conflicting emotions flit through Michaels thought processes. She knew she should have told him sooner.

Michael called for the bill, still having not said a word. He had pretty much told her about his life and family and wondered why she had not done the same. He paid the bill and helped her into her coat. He then told her he would need a bit of time to process the information and its repercussions. Apart from the fact he had the existence of a son kept from him, it would make life difficult if her son did not accept the demise of his parents' relationship, far from accepting a new man in her life.

He walked her to the bus stop, still silent, and he turned away, but not before he saw the sadness in her eyes. He told himself he would think this through, and he bade Monica goodbye, making no mention of a next meeting. As he started walking away, Monica had to face the fact that the secrecy had gone too far and disconsolately watched Michael walk away and quite possibly out of her life. "What have I done?" she thought to herself, climbing onto the bus and heading home.

It didn't help much that Michael was so busy with the restaurant and had little opportunity to think, never mind communicating with Monica. He was getting over his fit of pique and was by now missing her greatly. He had not realized just how attached he was becoming. A couple of days before she was due to travel to see her sister, Michael had a rare morning off which he had earmarked to visit the Highland dress shop and arrange for the delivery of the new staff outfits he had ordered. He was very close to Monica's house. He dealt with the restaurant business and then walked quickly towards Cluny Gardens and Monica.

Not sure whether she would be at home, he nevertheless walked up to her front door, noticing her smart RAV4 in the driveway, and rang the bell. A minute or so later, she opened the door. Her eyes lit up as she ushered him in.

She then threw her arms around him, exclaiming how glad she was to see him. Michael completely softened. How could he possibly give up this woman? Before he knew what he was doing, their first kiss was exchanged.

Teacups rattled, scones were buttered, and lots of conversation took place before it was obvious the making-up process had been dealt with. He asked her the question which had been one of the reasons for popping in, although now he realized no excuse would have been necessary. He offered her a lift to the train station, as she was travelling early and it was a bad time for taxis. She accepted gladly and they set a time.

Michael, with a much lighter step, returned to Dhugall wishing he could be going with her.

Arriving at the restaurant, Olivia couldn't help but notice the change in Michael's mood, and after greeting him while heading up the stairs to her office, she was relieved that the "lovers' tiff" seemed to be over. "Thank goodness for that," she said to herself as she shut the office door.

The thought of Monica's train journey and new places to visit gave him an idea. Would she agree to a long weekend away? He would, of course, arrange for two rooms, not yet realizing it was appropriate to share a room.

He broached the subject when he collected her for the train, and to his delight, she thought it a very good idea; after all the festivities were over, they would discuss where and when. He thought it would be best to stay in the UK, as he did not have a passport, never having travelled, as his mother had been a home bird. His next thought was that he should have a passport, and he vowed to deal with that as soon as he could.

He got back to the restaurant after a harrowing drive through the city to the station. He then took the car home. Not having anywhere to leave it, he thought there was a very good reason to use the bus. He hopped onto the bus; the whole drop-off process had taken roughly two hours.

"It's a good job we set off early," he said to Peter. He had taken on Michael's job of polishing cutlery and setting the tables. Michael was very pleased with his decision to promote Peter. He was proving to be an excellent employee, and he and Robert were making an amazing double act. Michael, in his less inhibited state, was even developing a rapport with the two men.

He went upstairs and asked Olivia whether he could take a week off at the end of January, which was immediately granted. *By then*, thought Olivia, *he will need a break, as the festivities will heighten his workload.* There was no point in suggesting he delegate more, as he wouldn't agree to it, so she decided to save her breath. Then he asked her a very unusual question. She knew him more than anyone, she guessed, so when he asked her how to go about getting a passport, she knew instinctively not to tease him. Olivia knew a little about Michael's new family but not enough to form any advice. She, too, was beginning to think that his mother was the guilty party behind the formation of Michael's lack of social awareness. She decided to "adopt" him.

On a sheet of paper, she jotted down all he needed to get a passport. Michael glanced at the list, which on the face of it didn't look too challenging. Then he spotted the "birth certificate", and his heart sank. The first hurdle was that he didn't have the first clue as to where it was, and then it brought back the parent issue.

"What's wrong?" asked Olivia. "It's really not difficult." The whole story came tumbling out. She got up hurriedly and closed her door. This was private. She explained to him that his birth certificate would likely be with his mother's papers but that if he couldn't find it, a copy could be purchased at a registry office or register house at the east end of the city. Then she made a statement so far avoided. "If you don't get in touch and try to develop a relationship, you will regret it for the rest of your life." The hand of peace would be taken back if something wasn't done to affect a reconciliation.

"Besides," she continued. "You have no one. Why would you throw away the chance of a family who obviously cares about you and wants you in their life? That takes some courage. They could have ignored your existence, but they chose not to. I wouldn't lay all the blame on your father either. It would appear your mother is not coming out of this smelling of roses. Live and let live, Michael. None of this is your fault. A few months ago you were alone, without friends and family, deeply grieving for your mother, the only family you knew about. Now you have a father, a stepmother, and half-siblings you knew nothing about. You also have a partner who appears to care for you. Don't throw away this once-in-a-lifetime opportunity."

Pondering all she had said, he felt a little like a son having just been told off. He was grateful for Olivia's support and would certainly admit who his travelling companion for the upcoming holiday was, just so long as she kept it to herself.

The restaurant wasn't too busy. That people were out doing their Christmas shopping was the general consensus. But for the next four days, they were booked solid. Christmas Day was only two days away, but the good thing was it would be an earlier start and an earlier finish. Boxing Day was normal hours, but Olivia had decided to shut the premises on the day after, as festive meals were still going on until January 3, then there was another day off for the staff before it went back to normal. An extra kitchen porter was temporarily hired, for which Alfredo was eternally grateful. The new uniforms had arrived, and everything looked to be on track.

Getting home earlier and still wired to the moon, Michael opened up the attic and let the steps down. At the time of her death, he had sealed up his mother's papers without looking at them. His pain was too raw. Now he was in better fettle to deal with this, and he really would like to be able to travel with Monica. She liked going places, and he had never been anywhere.

He carefully sifted through the assortment of paperwork, letters, and his school reports, not really knowing what to look for, when he found a document signed by the registrar with the details of a son born on 27 June 1974 to Jean and Michael MacGregor, named Michael James McGregor. He stared at it for what seemed like hours. He laid it to one side and came across a similar-looking document, only this time it was a certificate of marriage indicating his parents had been married on 7 February 1973.

He kept searching for the birth certificate—or indeed any paperwork which would indicate that his mother had officially changed his name. He could find nothing to support this until he found a letter from a government agency refusing her permission to change his name without the father's permission. He was thunderstruck. He could fathom his mother's thought process, and he was in a quandary as to how he could proceed. No wonder he and his mother had never gone abroad. He felt let down. His mother, whom he idolized, had handed him a can of worms as a parting gift. After taking the whole box downstairs, he poured a rather large glass of his whisky. Although he had replenished his stock at the supermarket, it would only be one drink, as he emptied the first bottle into his glass.

He was furious. For the first time in his life, he was furious with his mother.

Chapter 29

The restaurant did well on Christmas Eve, and the tips were staggeringly generous. Everyone was full of praise. As well as a kitchen porter, Olivia had taken on another waitress. She did give Michael the courtesy of approving her choice; however, she would be another pair of hands. By now Sylvia had been given a contract, but the latest one was employed over the festive season with no promises. Michael was happy with that. It would be a restaurant first, as they had to produce sixty Christmas dinners all at once.

Filled with trepidation, he welcomed the staff with "Happy Christmas!" and they set to work setting tables and polishing cutlery. A few days before, the waitresses had decorated the dining area and Peter and Robert had arranged for a tree to be delivered and helped decorate that. Dhugall was looking great and ready for Christmas. Crackers lay on the snowy white tablecloths, and small ceramic Christmas candleholders on the table centres gave the restaurant a festive air.

The meal was starting to be served at 1.00 p.m. and would be paced in order that the guests would have a leisurely and relaxing time. It was fortunate most of the tables were set for six or eight. This made it easier, as a maximum of eight would be served all at once.

The rest of the day went in a blur, and the highlight came as the departing guests were handed a wrapped gift consisting of a miniature of whisky for the men and a gold-foil-wrapped chocolate for the ladies.

By seven o'clock, the tables were all back to normal and the staff had eaten and were, for the first time in living memory, all sitting down with a festive drink. Olivia sprang a surprise on her staff as she handed out envelopes looking suspiciously like Christmas cards. To the delight of the

Michael, Waiting

staff, enclosed in each Christmas card was a sum of money commensurate with the experience and rank of the member of staff who received it. Even the small amount presented to the temporary staff was treated with enthusiasm. It was a very successful day all round.

As one by one they all left to spend what was left of Christmas with their respective families, Olivia took the opportunity to quiz Michael about his father. He admitted he had done nothing but was now favouring getting in touch.

"What better a day could you ask for?" she asked as she passed him the phone. All the work was done, and he couldn't think of a good reason not to call. As Olivia finished the locking up, Michael phoned his father.

Mike answered the phone by stating, "Merry Christmas, Mike speaking." "Hello, it's Michael, just to wish you a happy Christmas."

"Merry Christmas to you too. Hold on." A chorus of voices shouting "Merry

Christmas!" echoed in his ear. "You are on speakerphone now." Michael gulped. *This is getting a bit serious.*

Mike asked him what he was doing. He replied he had just finished working and was about to go home but added that he had called now because he didn't want to disturb them too late in the evening. Mike replied that it was wonderful to hear from him on this special day and said, "Why don't you jump into a taxi and come over for a drink and some party games?" Surprising himself, Michael agreed and took a note of the address for the taxi driver.

As the taxi pulled up outside a large house in the Grange, Michael was impressed. Light spilt out onto the path as he was paying the taxi driver. There seemed to be people everywhere, and feeling a bit on edge, he was escorted into the house, where a glass of champagne was pressed into his hand. Made to feel welcome, he began to relax. Nibbles were passed round, and questions came from every corner, with Michael doing his best to supply answers.

Patricia was the first to remark on the likeness between the two men and similarities between Michael and Robert. It was obvious they were related. It was a very enjoyable evening, and all too soon it had to end. Mhairi offered to drive him home, but Michael refused by reason of her expected confinement and didn't want her out driving, although it wasn't far. A taxi was called and whisked Michael away from his new family to his home,

which was by now redecorated, with a new kitchen and bathroom, looking smart and welcoming.

Although he had drunk quite a bit more than usual, he poured his customary whisky and contemplated the day, followed by the evening. He lay back on the chair, ruminating on his new life, and was looking forward to telling Monica all about it. He had called her earlier to wish her a happy Christmas, but that was before the day had really started. It was good to hear her voice and seemed a long wait until she got back.

During the week between Christmas and New Year, Michael had no days off but still had a few mornings when he didn't have to start until about 3.00 p.m. They had hired a waitress, Ann Whyte, for the Christmas festivities, and he and Olivia were in discussions regarding employing her on a more permanent basis.

She, too, like Sylvia, was a team player and had contributed greatly to the Christmas Day success. Michael had expressed a desire to have more time off, but not till the New Year was over. Besides, he had booked a week's holiday so he and Monica could go for a quiet break.

Home after another busy shift, Michael was relaxing on the chair, listening to music, when he noticed his mobile vibrating across the coffee table. It was on silent, and to his amazement the caller ID announced Mike. Michael, surprised, picked up and listened to the man he had now begun to accept as a father. Oh, he wasn't ready for the whole "Dad" bit; however, he did accept he had a father in his life, along with his half-siblings and stepmother. After a very strange call, he disconnected. Being on holiday for the whole of the festive period, Mike had said he was free to come over for a visit and a chat. Rather stunned, Michael had agreed, and once it had sunk in, he quickly tidied up and looked out some biscuits.

Monica had insisted when he was remodelling the kitchen that he purchase a coffee maker which made all types, one cup at a time. She explained it would be much easier, especially in the morning. He was beginning to enjoy sampling different types of coffee and acknowledged that she was right—again.

He showed his father in and settled him on the armchair. He made coffee to his father's likes, offered him a biscuit, and sat down to listen once again to what was on Mike MacGregor's mind. The essence of the conversation was to establish Michael's intentions. Was Christmas Day to be a one-off and no more contact, or would Michael accept his new-found family and be part of their lives? Michael listened intently, and after a silence which stretched out like a piece of elastic, he gave Mike the answer he was delighted to hear.

"It may take a bit of getting used to," said Michael, "but it would give me great pleasure to be included in your lives." They started conversing animatedly, and Michael was overjoyed. Now that he had accepted the facts, he was keen to be involved, slowly at first, until everyone had got used to the idea. Besides, he surprisingly wanted to be on the scene when Mhairi's baby arrived.

The culmination of the conversation was that Michael was to come to theirs on Hogmanay for supper, see the fireworks at the castle, and bring in the New Year with his family. "There is plenty of room," said Mike, "and you can stay over, as taxis will be difficult to find on such a night."

After Mike left, Michael was mesmerized at the turn of events. He had, of course, accepted the offer from his family to spend New Year with them and would drive over after he had finished work and went home to collect his overnight bag and his car. He told them he would be there about 9.00 p.m. It was a happy step he took to work that day.

The midnight hour was approaching, and Michael stood at the large bay window in his father's house watching the fireworks flash and bang until he was almost deaf. It was an awesome sight, one he had never seen before, and with the sheer drama of the fireworks and the happy, welcoming family round him, Michael was moved to tears. Surreptitiously, a tissue was passed to him, and as the bells announcing the New Year sounded out from the castle, Michael was aware of a contentment reaching into his very soul.

New Year's Day dawned, and it took Michael a few minutes to realize where he was. The memories of the evening flooded back, and he was aware of the sound of movement drifting upstairs.

It was a very comfortable room, and taking advantage of the en suite shower, he quickly abluted.

When he went downstairs, he was surprised to see the family all seated around the large kitchen table; only Mhairi was absent. A well-deserved rest was the order of the day. Patricia offered food and placed a large plate on the mats in the middle of the table. There was a lot of food, all of which tempted Michael to fill his plate and sit up to devour the sausages, black pudding, and bacon, just for starters. Chatting about the festivities, it was clear they were a close-knit family and seemed to spend a lot of their spare time together. The biggest topic of conversation was the impending new arrival. To his surprise, Michael was looking forward to seeing the new baby.

It was a very different type of Christmas and New Year than he had envisaged. He was very pleased he was able to embrace his new family, and he looked forward to meeting Monica and telling her all the news. She would be travelling home tomorrow, and Michael had missed her.

Bidding farewell to the family and thanking them profusely, Michael took his leave. He promised to come for dinner on his next day off, and if she was agreeable, he would bring Monica to meet them.

He got home around one in the afternoon, which didn't give him much time to get to his work for 3.00 p.m. Glad he had showered and shaved at his family's home, he decided to drive there. He thought the streets would be quiet and he should be able to park.

He was enjoying his new vehicle hugely, and although he would have liked to drive Monica for their time away, he figured it would be better by train. He was thinking York would be nice. Monica had expressed an interest in the town, and it appeared to be an easy journey by train.

The day passed quickly, and soon he was on his way home at a reasonable hour. Olivia had a good idea when she decided to serve festive food from three to six and allow the staff an early finish. He was picking up Monica from the station the next day. She was travelling on the overnight sleeper, so it would be an early pickup.

It was still holiday time in the capital, and the streets were quiet. He drove into the centre, and as parking was difficult in the station itself, he managed a space on the street behind the station. From memory he knew Monica's luggage was on wheels and not too big. Looking anxiously at the arrival boards, he was relieved to see her train was on time and would pull into the station in about twenty minutes. He decided a coffee was the answer, and when the train finally arrived, he was at the gate to meet her.

After a long hug and a swift peck, they headed off to the car. It was still only 9.00 a.m., and Michael didn't have to be at Dhugall until about two, but Monica was tired. Not having slept much on the train, she wanted to unpack and have a sleep. She was also very hungry. As she did not like what was on offer in the buffet car, Michael suggested taking her to the club for breakfast, and for the second time in two days he found himself tucking into sausages and bacon.

Relaxing over a coffee, having consumed a large plateful of food, Michael asked Monica what she thought about travelling to York for a few days. She was delighted with the idea. Funnily enough, she herself had thought about York. Although she had been before, she was pleased with the idea, having wanted to go back. She explained to Michael she had been born in the town of Harrogate, which was not far from York, and suggested maybe they could spend a day there sightseeing, as she had not been back since she was a baby.

He took Monica home, as she was anxious for a sleep, and took his car to the lock-up and prepared himself for work. The parting shot from Monica was that once she had revived herself and unpacked, she would get her laptop out and source accommodation within their budget. Michael was aware that the hearing for the divorce was getting closer. In his opinion, the trip to Yorkshire would serve to soothe her after the hearing was over.

At the restaurant, he reconfirmed the dates with Olivia and settled down to work. Now that the festivities were over, life was returning to normal, and the prospect of a few days away in congenial company bolstered his mood. His day off was tomorrow, and he was looking forward to spending time with Monica. He had a lot to tell her: firstly, the matter of the passport; secondly,

all the stories from the visits to his new-found family; and thirdly, of course, the matter of selecting accommodation for the trip to York.

They were to meet for lunch, having decided they had not visited the Canny Man's for some time. There was no point in using the car because of the difficulties parking; however, he took his little black VW Golf to meet up with Monica at her home, and they would get a taxi into Morningside.

Enjoying their lunch, they swapped stories of the Christmas break. Monica described the time she had spent with her sister but confessed to having missed Michael's company. She told him how she had walked along the promenade and how the weather had seemed warmer. Her sister's small bungalow was quite close to the sea, and she had made the most of it by walking along the shore most days.

When he realized that she had finished, he quickly launched into the description of how he had made contact with his father and the fantastic events which followed. Secretly she was pleased. She had no intention of trying to talk him into an acceptance of his family, but she did, however, hope it would happen. She was delighted, too, that an open invitation to visit for dinner with Michael was on the table. Desperately curious about the family, Monica was looking forward to that meeting.

A taxi was ordered, and the happy couple, so very glad to see one another, headed to Monica's house and the trip to be planned for. The laptop was brought out and the notebook produced, and bit by bit she showed him various bed and breakfast establishments. Michael was more surprised at the laptop and what it could do. He exclaimed to Monica, "How did all that happen on an electrical appliance?" Having no knowledge about computers, he was mesmerized.

"I think we will need to work on your lack of computer skills," Monica said firmly. "Honestly, you will need to catch up with modern technology. You use a computer at work."

He went on to explain the one at work was a simple computer designed to process orders, and they were in number form, so not much knowledge was required. But he agreed the lack of computer skills was something he needed to address. His intention was to start a course in basic computing, but the application form had moved from the coffee table to the sideboard and was now hiding in the drawer. Michael shuddered at the thought of admitting this to Monica, so he held his own counsel and agreed with her.

Flipping through the pages with a bit of discussion, they selected a small hotel about two miles outside York with a local bus to take passengers into the city. It was described as a boutique hotel and was famous for its good food. The picture on the website was of a pretty hotel on a leafy walkway, and a large beer garden. Monica typed in their request for a four-night stay in twin rooms with breakfast on the date specified. Within minutes, their request being processed and confirmed, they both exclaimed their happiness that their choice was available.

Monica explained about her wanting a wander round Harrogate and the reason behind it. She showed him the timetable for a York–Harrogate train journey, which was incredibly inexpensive. They could both travel to Harrogate and back to York for £13.50. Also, on the Internet she had found a special ticket for a round trip to York for £25 each. The trip was sorted. Just four weeks to go.

The following evening in the restaurant, he noticed in the diary two familiar names. This in itself was not unusual, as the bulk of the customers were repeat diners; the mainstay of the establishment was the regulars. The restaurant not being front line, it required regular customers and recommendation to keep it alive. Olivia worked hard at maintaining a good atmosphere, but these were customers he would rather not remember.

Sure enough, in the appointed time the two men he had overheard plotting to "get rid of a nuisance" walked boldly into the restaurant. Robert took their coats, but their eyes were on Michael. He was frozen to the spot. He thought they had been arrested. He hadn't been called to give evidence. Why were they walking the streets? He quickly recovered and requested that Robert look after their "guests", as Michael felt he should maintain a low profile and retired to his corner to keep an eye on the proceedings.

They finished their meal, with Robert retrieving their coats. Michael thought he had escaped until, to his horror, one of the men beckoned him over. Sick with fear, he complied, and one of the men shocked him by complimenting him on the meal. Offering a hand to shake, the thug then reached forward and whispered, "I would watch your back if I were you!" He squeezed Michael's hand painfully before sweeping out of the restaurant and into the cold and dark of the street.

Terror washed over Michael, who was still standing in the spot as the men left. Anxious, Robert rushed over to him asking what the matter was. Michael quickly described the incident, relating it to the run through the streets, ending up at the hotel. "Go and talk to Olivia," said Robert.

Explanations over, she took a business card out of her drawer, dialled the number and happily got through to the police station. The detective in charge of the investigation was off duty; however, there was someone there she could talk to. After she had explained what had happed, the apologetic detective told her that the two men who were part of the plot had been granted a bail hearing, as neither of them had a criminal record. This did not sit well with Michael, especially considering the veiled threat. He just assumed they would be locked up until the trial and fully expected them to be found guilty and jailed. He had not thought for one moment that this distressing incident was growing legs.

The trial had been fixed for 1 March and in the meantime, there was very little to be done. Michael was advised to be on the lookout, and a patrol car would make more appearances in the streets around his home. He was advised to use taxis more often and to let the police know of any unusual occurrences. Filled with trepidation, he took the detective's advice and left for home in a taxi.

A few days later, he returned home to see his answering machine blinking—a very unusual occurrence. He had been given lessons on the use of it and had almost mastered the function. Pressing the button, he found that the recording was from his father, inviting him and his friend to dinner on his next available day off. Michael, knowing Monica would be thrilled, explained that since New Year, his boss had agreed to extend his days off to Sunday and Thursday. It was much too late to respond at the moment, but he said he would call first thing and set up what was suitable for everyone.

With the mutually agreed Sunday evening, after contacting Mike and Monica, he was surprised when Monica asked him how easy it would be to change his night off from Thursday to Friday. Mystified, Michael didn't think it would be a problem. "Why?" he asked. She launched into an explanation which he understood to be an invitation to go to the annual dinner dance and prize-giving at the golf club. Although he hadn't won any prizes, she thought he would benefit socially if he were to continue to use the clubhouse and, as this weather improved, the course. Monica also played an ace card, reminding him he would have his Highland dress. She knew he felt good in the outfit.

He agreed, asking what she proposed to wear. She responded with the information that she would also be wearing the same dress as at the ball, as it was "different crowd, same dress!" She explained it was two weeks on Friday.

Michael contacted Peter and asked him to swap days off. Michael, usually off on a Thursday, wanted Peter to work Friday to let him go to the dinner dance with Monica. Peter was agreeable, and with all his social engagements sorted, he sat in his favourite chair with his glass in his hand. Contentment washed over him like a warm shower.

He sat back on his chair and went into a daydream, mostly about Monica. He realized he was getting very fond of her and enjoyed being with her. It scared him. Having grown up without a father, and now having experienced the recent death of his mother, he was frightened to get into a relationship, or indeed get married, because he felt sure he could not go through loving another person with the possibility of losing her. He was afraid Monica would leave him alone and lonely.

His feelings had grown more than he could imagine, and during that short time they were estranged through his intolerance, he had realized he could not do without her. The added complication was that because of his mother's attachment to him, he had not been in a relationship, and at the age of forty-five, he acknowledged he had no experience in dealing with the opposite sex. He was a virgin.

Chapter 30

Sunday arrived, and around 11.00 a.m., Michael drove to Cluny Gardens to collect Monica and take her to meet his newly acquired family at the big house in the Grange. Because he had arranged for Sunday, his father suggested he come early in the day, as it would be a traditional Sunday roast, which they would be eating around 2.00 pm. Mike invited him to join them about noon for an aperitif and a getting-to-know-you hour or so. His half-siblings would be there with their partners—and Mhairi too, unless otherwise occupied. Both men laughed as the baby now due was likely to make an appearance within a week or so.

As they drew up to the house and turned into the driveway, Monica could not help being impressed. It was a beautiful stone-built town house with three storeys and a long, sweeping driveway behind a wall about eight feet in height. It was very grand and offered loads of privacy.

Patricia, seeing them pull up, rushed to the door to greet them. "You must be Monica," she said, "please come in." With a kiss on the cheek for Michael, coats were taken, and the couple was escorted into the large drawing room, where drinks and nibbles were laid out.

Introductions complete, they all sat down, and news was exchanged. Having the car, Michael refused alcohol and settled for a soft drink. He was wary of drink-driving, preferring to use taxis or not drink at all. Patricia had vanished to the kitchen with Robert's partner, Mhairi, sitting looking like she had a pumpkin under her top—a very large pumpkin. It was obvious she was uncomfortable, and having no knowledge of childbirth, Michael did not realize what was happening; he knew only that Mhairi looked tense.

On the stroke of two, they were summoned to the dining room.

Michael, Waiting

Michael had never seen such a large mahogany table. It was set for eight and had room for twelve. The food, as on Christmas day, was delicious, and Monica seemed to be getting along well with his family. Michael felt a sense of peace. He still missed his mother, but gradually he was coming to realize that having grown up fatherless, he was now enjoying getting to know him, and he fully realized that it had a lot to do with his mother and her possessiveness.

The meal finished about 4.00 p.m., and Monica offered to help Patricia and Jennifer to clear up. The men adjourned to the drawing room, where Mhairi was seated with her feet up on a footstool. Michael opened the conversation by asking whether he could ask advice.

He explained about the lack of passport and his birth certificate anomalies and wondered what the best course of action would be.

The younger men were silent as Mike thought about the problem.

Mike explained that his official name was MacGregor and that in order to resume to Whittaker, he would need to change it by deed poll. This was not a difficult procedure but if he wanted a passport urgently it may take a bit of time. Michael demurred, explaining he and Monica were going to York for a few days and that he, having never been anywhere, rather liked the thought of going on holiday somewhere more exotic. Michael looked thoughtful. To remain with Whittaker, a name he had used for forty-three years, an official transfer of that name would have to be done by deed poll. He would ask Monica to check out the procedure on her magic machine.

The ladies arrived back with coffee and mints, and the conversation became more casual. It was a lovely atmosphere, and it was clear Monica had fitted in with the other ladies. Out of the corner of his eye, he was aware Mhairi was shifting about in her seat, and eye signals were passing from husband and wife. Then the whole assembled company noticed something was amiss. "What's the matter, sweetheart?" asked Patricia.

"It looks like I may be in labour," Mhairi replied, sounding agitated. Tom, Mhairi's husband, stood up, and with panic in his voice he started jabbering about not driving, giving the consumption of alcohol as the reason for his reluctance to provide transport in the situation. Apart from Michael, everyone had imbibed at least one or two glasses of wine.

Mike asked his daughter to describe her symptoms. Concluding she was, in fact, in labour, albeit in the very early stages, Mike phoned the hospital, it being a good few miles away, to get advice. The conclusion was that it may be some time and that they should wait until contractions were much closer together. A sceptical Mike, with a father-to-be on the point of collapse, thought the better option would be to get his daughter to hospital as soon as possible, as it was not an inconsiderable journey. Mhairi had her travel baby bag, with all the paraphernalia required for going into hospital, with her. Over the last week, with baby due in a week or so, she had not gone anywhere without it. "Right," said Mike, "let's phone a taxi and get you on your way."

Thoughtful, Michael had a quiet conversation with Monica, who quickly agreed to his suggestion. Michael said, "By all means, phone a taxi; but make it for Cluny Gardens, and I will drive Mhairi and Tom to the hospital."

Mike, startled, said, "You will?"

"Yes," said Michael. "I want to help, and this seems the answer."

Taking Michael to one side, he thanked him profusely and told him getting a taxi to take a woman in labour might be tricky and he was grateful for the help. He quickly took Michael through the phases of labour and what might happen. His last instruction was to phone the police for an escort to the hospital if at any time he was concerned.

In the end, Michael left with Mhairi and Tom, as well as Patricia, who was not going to be left out. Monica got her taxi home, and after covering the passenger seat with towels (just in case), they piled into the Golf, and Michel set off on what would be an exciting ride. Half an hour later, as the New Hospital came into view, Mhairi's waters had broken, and her contractions were speeding up to two minutes apart.

Patricia said nothing but silently thanked her husband for getting them on the road when he did and for Michael generously offering to help.

It took a few minutes to find the appropriate department and a parking space. Tom was dispatched to find medical help as Mhairi was starting her breathing exercises as she had been taught at her classes, indicating she was well into labour. Besides, it was necessary to keep Tom busy, as he was slowly coming apart. It had been arranged that Michael would wait until they settled in, Patricia insisting she was going nowhere, then he would drive home, getting the news when it was all over.

It became obvious when they got to the labour suite to book Mhairi in

Michael, Waiting

that Patricia was anticipating this might be a short wait. A fast delivery was looking more likely as Mhairi's face contorted with pain. In the waiting area next to the labour ward, Patricia and Michael were sitting in silence, Tom being with his wife.

Earlier Michael had had a few words with Tom, reminding him that he was very much needed and wanted to help Mhairi through this very special time and that he needed to be strong for her. Tom took the mild chastisement on the chin and quite literally straightened his back as he headed into the labour suite to await the birth of his first child.

Patricia had asked Michael to stay for the time being, thinking that they weren't likely to be there long. Sure enough, two hours later, the sound of a crying infant permeated the waiting room. They looked at each other in wonder and delight and prepared to wait for the good news. It was only a few minutes, but it seemed like an hour had passed when a beaming Tom announced the safe delivery of a girl. Patricia started to cry with happiness, and even Michael became a little tearful. This was a new experience for him.

They were allowed a few minutes to see the infant, and with a happy smile they crept into the darkened labour room, where Mhairi and the new baby were cuddled in, Tom beaming with pride at her side. A little time and they were ushered out, leaving the new family to get to know one another. Michael helped Patricia into the car, where she promptly made several phone calls, spreading the news. It was some dinner party. Michael did not know whether Monica would still be awake, so rather than phone, he brought her up to date with the news by text. With all the excitement calming down, he popped into the house in the Grange after taking Patricia home and after a quick word with the new grandfather, who made it obvious he had been worried and was glad to hear of the safe delivery with both doing well. He was also grateful to Michael for stepping into the breach and getting the family to the hospital safely.

Michael took his leave, and as he drove home, he went over the series of events that had put him where he was today. He knew it would take more time to be completely comfortable as part of this family, but tonight he felt he had crossed another bridge. He was glad Olivia was so firm with him, resulting in his reconciliation, and he promised himself he would tell her so.

While parking his car in its lock-up, he noticed it was getting a trifle dirty. He decided he would wash the car at the local petrol station, perhaps check the oil, and fill up with petrol. Silly mundane acts like that made Michael feel in control of his life, which until recently had been guided by his Mother. He had his trip to York coming up, but in a few days, he would escort Monica to the golf club dinner.

Monica was getting ready for her divorce hearing, and thanks to her boss, she would be getting legal advice. On the Wednesday, Monica called him to let him know that she had met briefly with her new solicitor and had left all the paperwork with him. An appointment to discuss had been arranged for the Monday after they returned. He would see her at her place of work, as he had explained, but there was a note of optimism in his explanations. Before they met, he said he would arrange to have a conversation with the solicitor representing her estranged husband. Just prior to terminating the call, Monica said to Michael that she felt her spirits rising.

It would be like going back to the start of the relationship. Punctually at 7.00 p.m., taxi waiting, Monica opened her door and took delight in the handsome man, resplendent in full Highland dress, on her doorstep. Michael was getting better, as he complimented her on how nice she looked. "Not so bad yourself," countered Monica. He helped her into the car, the two now being very comfortable in each other's company.

The news about the baby was uppermost in Monica's interest, and he was able to tell her the baby was called Katrina; both she and her mum were doing well, and the baby putting on weight.

They drew up to the club, and helping her out, he thought she looked really attractive, with the green dress complimented by her recently styled dark brown hair. Proud to be seen with her on his arm, he walked with her into the lounge. He had never seen the clubhouse so busy and was gratified that casual acquaintances were greeting him with welcoming smiles. The dining area was beautifully dressed with white tablecloths and red runners. Candles were flickering, giving a shimmering appearance. Introducing Monica to those members he had become acquainted with, he really felt he had, at last, joined the human race.

He was suddenly aware that at his side, Monica had stiffened. He turned to see her looking in abject horror, and a man in a suit and bow tie was looking at her in not a pleasant way. Turning to Monica, Michael asked her whether she knew him and, if so, whether she would introduce him to the man staring at Monica. Monica pulled herself together, saying, "Michael, this is Derek Stevens, soon to be my ex-husband. Derek, this is Michael Whittaker, a friend."

"Not an ex-husband yet," he snarled. He then turned his back on the couple and strode away, inasmuch as any striding could be done in the packed room.

A deflated Monica accepted a drink, which was thrown back very quickly, and as she held out the glass for another, Michael gave her an old-fashioned look. Standing waiting to be served at the bar, he resolved to make the evening as pleasant as he could.

That was an unfortunate occurrence, he thought, *especially with the divorce hearing so close.* He knew it would not be pleasant, as it was clear from their conversations that Derek Stevens was not a nice man.

The evening wore on, and dinner was soon finished. He noticed a few unknown faces among those bustling about serving food and drink. *Temporary waiting staff,* he surmised, and he parked an idea that may help him out. He would speak to George, the steward, and see if any of the on-call waiters would serve his purpose when there was a special occasion at Dhugall—the next one being a Burns Supper, which was happening the day before their trip to York.

Somehow Monica got through the evening in one piece. They had managed to avoid Stevens all evening and before Monica got any more to drink, as she was in danger of becoming very worse for wear a taxi was called and she was whisked away.

He helped her into the house and upstairs. He couldn't in all consciousness leave her on the bed still in her gown. With much reluctance, and with his eyes partially closed, he unzipped her dress, helped her out of it, and put her to bed. Fortunately the front door locked when he pulled it shut, and he jumped into the waiting taxi to be taken home and to think.

Michael left Monica to her own devices. He realized she would rather he wasn't around when she came to, and she would be embarrassed if she knew he had undressed her. *Let's see how little I can tell her*, he thought. Monday was the divorce hearing, and much as he would have liked to go, he had to stay away from the court. He dressed casually; with a bit of luck, he would be able to take her to lunch after the hearing.

Monday morning arrived all too quickly, and so far she had not even mentioned the golf club dinner or the aftermath. Michael was not about to put her in the picture. He had offered to take her in the car. She had, however, expressed a preference for Michael to wait at her house, and she would get a taxi there and back. She needed to be alone. Besides, she said her solicitor was meeting her at the sheriff court. Also, she did not want her husband to see them together again until the divorce was finalized. Michael drove to her house. She gave him a spare key.

Her slot apparently was first, and she had to present herself at 9.00 a.m. at the court. Bringing all the documents she was asked to bring, she waited outside of the court in a waiting area, waiting to be called. Unfortunately, her ex was also in the waiting room. His temper had not improved since the Friday-night encounter. Still snarling, he assured her he would take her for every penny and called her a whore. He went on with the abuse until the case was called. The sheriff officer, becoming totally fed up, called the hearing.

Standing at a table in front of the sheriff with Derek and his solicitor, Monica's solicitor stated her claim on the property and reiterated that her husband was allowed to remove any possessions joint or solely his, explaining the circumstances of how she had come to have possession of the house and cash invested. Derek had left her, she emphasized, and he was claiming half the house, half her pension fund, and half her savings, and she thought this unreasonable. Before his solicitor could stop him, Derek jumped up and questioned all that had been said and stated that he felt that now his wife was involved with someone else, she should give him half of everything she owned. Halting the diatribe, the court officer allowed Derek's solicitor to speak on his behalf.

About an hour later, the solicitors had stated the case for both parties, and the sheriff made the judgement.

Hearing all the evidence and becoming heartily sick at the attitude of Derek, the sheriff granted the divorce and awarded Monica the house and capital she had inherited from her parents. Her pension was also safe. Meanwhile, to Derek's chagrin, she was awarded costs and any possessions still in the house. The couple were told that the proceedings would be

Michael, Waiting

granted absolute in six weeks—the length of time Derek had to retrieve his possessions at Monica's convenience. Livid, Derek barged out with his hapless solicitor running to keep up. Monica, on the other hand, stood with her solicitor's arm round her shoulders as the tears coursed down her cheeks.

Meanwhile, Michael, sitting waiting patiently at Monica's house, became aware of a key in the lock. Jumping up eagerly, he went to the hall to meet Monica. To his surprise and horror, instead of Monica he found himself eye to eye with Derek, Monica's husband. Stunned, he said nothing. Derek was not so backward. "Ah, I wondered where you were. I didn't see you skulking round the court. What are you doing here?"

Still shocked into silence, Michael blinked. Then, getting his voice back, he told Derek he was waiting for Monica to return. Derek, his temper rising, told Michael to get out of his house. Michael's heart sank. His first thought was *Did the judgement go against Monica?*

However, Michael picked up some courage—from where, he knew not—and refused, as he was the invited guest of the lady of the house, speaking in a quiet but determined voice. He was completely taken aback when Derek's fist landed in his face and he fell to the floor, blood streaming from his nose. Just then the door opened to reveal Monica standing on the doorstep with her key in her hand. Derek had left the door open.

"What are you doing here?" she asked calmly as she helped Michael up from the floor. Derek said something about it being his house him being able to come and go as he pleased. "I don't think it is right and proper you entertaining men in my home." Without another word, she brushed past this maniac whom she had married ten years ago, and after helping Michael to the kitchen, she sat him on a chair and retrieved the first aid kit. A few minutes later, Derek barged into the kitchen spouting vitriol; then Monica brushed past him again and picked up the phone. She had the number of the local police station on speed dial because of the danger that lurked in their lives.

"What do you think you are doing!" shouted Derek

"Phoning the police," she answered calmly.

"You can't do that," he screamed in her face. "I was defending myself against an intruder!" As it was obvious Monica was fully intending to make the call, he stormed out with the words "You haven't heard the last of this."

As the door slammed, Monica murmured, "You are absolutely right." She finished the call, accusing Derek of assault. She also couldn't understand how he had been able to access her property, as she was unaware he had a key.

Her next call was to the locksmith, and a change of lock was arranged. She did not want Derek to return and let himself in or remove anything, especially since she was going to be away from home for a few days. She checked Michael over. The bleeding had stopped, and the nose did not appear to be broken.

While they waited for the police, Monica told Michael how the hearing had gone. She was delighted that this particular horror story had come to an end, but she was so very sorry Michael had ended up the victim in a fight that was not his. About an hour later, the doorbell rang, and Monica let in a young uniformed policeman who took a statement from Michael and explained they would go to the home of the attacker and give him a verbal warning, suggesting that any more occurrences of this nature would result in arrest.

Satisfied, Monica thanked the young officer and showed him out. Monica then phoned her boss to thank him for help in court. "Not a problem. The solicitor is on a retainer, so he may as well work for it. Besides, your late lamented ex would be picking up the tab." With thanks ringing in his ears, he terminated the call, but not before establishing when Monica would be back amongst them. She explained the York trip, and a date after her return was set.

She offered Michael a snack as they both sat in the comfy lounge discussing the morning's events. Michael was quite hungry in spite of the incident and thanked her as he accepted, but not before offering to take her out as arranged previously. Monica was not in the frame of mind to go out, she explained, and she asked whether a sandwich would be all right. Monica's sandwiches were superb, almost as good as the Canny Man's, so he had no problem in accepting.

After he had eaten, Michael left to get ready for work. Only a few days and they would be off on their trip, and he was looking forward to it immensely. After returning his car to the lock-up, he readied himself and headed to the bus stop and work.

The train was booked for 7.00 a.m. on the Monday. As was their habit,

Michael, Waiting

the taxi came for Michael and then collected Monica before dropping them at the station in time to catch their train. On the way to the platform, they bought a to-go coffee and a doughnut each. *A naughty breakfast*, thought Monica.

Their seats were comfortable, with a table between them. There were four seats, but no one had taken the other two, to their relief.

They would get a chance to walk, read the papers, and generally enjoy the journey, which would take a little over two hours. Michael was enjoying the trip. The East Lothian countryside sped by, and he was seeing this for the first time. The sea appeared, all pewter coloured with small white horses dancing on the top of the waves. Michael was enthralled. He had never seen the sea before. His furthest trip had been to Portobello. As they crossed the border, he asked Monica why she had chosen to visit Harrogate although their main destination was York.

Monica started her story. She had, she explained, been born in Harrogate, as the father had been seconded to another office which was based in Harrogate. "Mother was expecting me, and Father wouldn't hear of her staying in Edinburgh alone. She had her parents still, of course, but Father wanted her with him, as her mother was a trifle domineering. He would be a much gentler companion, and besides, he would miss not having her to come home to each night.

"I was born about six months after they arrived in Yorkshire, about halfway through the secondment. They returned to Edinburgh, and I have wanted to visit for a long time. Derek was never very keen, so I am really excited to be making the journey now."

Michael was thoughtful as he contemplated the few days they would spend exploring York and the very important visit to Harrogate. Bucket lists were important.

Chapter 31

They arrived in York on time, and a taxi took them to their hotel. It was a country inn type of hotel with only a few rooms, but it boasted fabulous food. The reality was that the kitchens were closed, and yes breakfast would be served. Unfortunately, there was no provision for food at either lunch or dinner. The next disappointment came when, after mounting rather precarious outside metal stairs, they found that one of the rooms was so small one could barely turn around in it. With as much gallantry as he could muster, Michael offered to take the small room, which could only be a box room. However, a relieved Michael thought the larger room, which sported a double bed, looked better. At least Monica would be comfortable.

Back at reception, they made a token protest, but to no avail, as expected. It was clear, to their disappointment, that customer service was not top of the inn's list. They asked about food, as by now it was lunchtime and the donut had long worn off. The rather churlish receptionist recommended a bus or taxi into York. The image of strolling through the streets and having a country pub meal faded as they contemplated their options.

One of the barflies perched on a stool wrapped around a beer glass interrupted them and told them about the pub down the road which served decent food and would take only about a ten-minute walk. Cheering up, they headed off in the direction the kindly local had explained, hoping to find this saviour of empty stomachs,

Indeed, some ten minutes later they found the eatery, and it was a lovely afternoon. The sun was shining, and the trees were starting to bud. This far south, spring was starting to make its presence felt. Ordering a couple of gin and tonics, they were delighted to see the pub had a large shelving unit stacked with every type of gin available. They glanced at each other and smiled.

This was just the place to make the day better. The disappointment of their chosen accommodation was palpable. Perusing the snack menu, they decided on a bowl of soup and crunchy bread, having already decided to return for dinner. The soup was delicious, and they felt it would be a safe bet for later. Besides, the pub offered two for one on Mondays and Tuesdays. The chatty barman asked all the usual questions: Where are you from? Where are you staying? When they told him about their accommodation, he sucked his teeth and shook his head more in sorrow than anything else. Taking the bull by the horns, Michael asked about accommodation in the pub they were eating in. Unfortunately, it was only a pub and didn't offer rooms. The barman then offered the information that the inn in which they were staying was up for sale. This went a long way to the explanation of the lack of service and food. However, five minutes in, a sumptuous lunch accompanied by a gin and tonic went a long way to dishing out a decent welcome.

Just as well, thought Monica. They had already paid in advance at their accommodation, and to double that would prove expensive. They had decided to take a taxi into the city after their lunch, not wanting to waste a minute, and they asked the barman if he would be kind enough to arrange for a taxi to collect them and ferry them into the city. "Ah," said the barman, "if you step out and turn left, one hundred yards will bring you to a bus stop much faster and cheaper."

"Let's do it!" said Monica. "Let's keep our spending money for something more exciting than a taxi." The bus arrived within minutes.

Alighting from the bus in York centre, the bus stop being just across from the well-feted street, the Shambles. They had read up about the sights not to be missed, and this was one of them. It was so quirky, with the tops of the houses leaning over almost touching and the various exciting small boutique shops lining the street. The found a pub which had tables and chairs outside, and as they both had warm jackets, they decided to sit at the cafe and have a coffee while watching the world go by.

I've missed such a lot, thought Michael, who was really enjoying himself. They planned their next day, deciding the wall around the city had to be visited; the York Minster, looking splendid on this sunny afternoon, would be done in the afternoon. Wednesday was Harrogate day, and not trusting the buses, they would arrange for a taxi to take them to the station.

Deciding to freshen up for dinner, they managed to find the bus stop, and it was quite a bit longer waiting for the bus back. They were just about to give in and hail a taxi when the bus arrived. Back at the inn, it was discovered that whereas Monica had an en suite room, Michael did not. After a hasty team talk, Michael admitting he had no robe, they decided to share the facilities. Michael went downstairs and ordered a g & t, whilst Monica showered and dressed. After another g & t, this time for Monica, Michael took his turn for a shower, first retrieving his clothes for the evening meal. This was highly inconvenient, and of course the manager was not available and the receptionist was not in a position to offer them a swap. The G and T worked though.

They had booked a table for 8.00 p.m. at the other pub and planned to have a drink in their temporary home. However, not really liking the atmosphere in the inn, they decided to head off after one drink and enjoy the more convivial surroundings of the other pub while they contemplated what they would eat. They were very hungry. The soup was long gone, and their request to bring the time forward was cheerfully attended to.

They had a wonderful night, and with a light kiss on the cheek, they bade goodnight, arranging to meet at eight for breakfast, and went to their respective rooms.

Breakfast was not a disappointment, they were delighted to observe; and once they had eaten their fill, they headed off to catch the bus. It took a little longer this time, and the sun was yet to make an appearance. However, about three quarters of an hour later, they found themselves at the Shambles.

The walk round the wall was fabulous, and as the sun made an appearance and the temperature rose, the visit to the cathedral was very moving. It was a beautiful building, and they walked round taking in the delight of their surroundings. The effect of the inside of the cathedral was breathtaking, and their joy was palpable. They were both glad they had set aside the time to enjoy their surroundings. In between the wall and the cathedral, they found a snug pub. It was full of inglenooks, reminding them of their home favourite, the Canny Man's, and they had a lunch of a ploughman's sandwich, washed down with a glass of wine.

Michael, Waiting

Catching the bus back, they talked animatedly about their day, which they thoroughly enjoyed. The same ritual took place for freshening up, and this time without the gin and tonic they strode to their inn of choice, deciding to try one of the speciality gins. Michael chose rhubarb, and Monica strawberry. Monica declared the dinner of battered fish and chips was delightful, and Michael enjoyed his spiced pork and rice. There was also some live music going on, and a great time was had by both of the by now weary tourists.

An early night was called for, and the happy twosome headed to their accommodation, arranging to meet at eight again. The goodnight kiss had a bit more substance this time, missing the cheeks and finding the lips. Michael flushed at the thought.

Morning arrived with a beautiful sunrise, and the taxi was only a few minutes late. With plenty of time, and coffees bought, they were soon on the train to Harrogate. Bowling along in the train, they were able to see the countryside. It started flat on the outskirts of York, and they went further east until they reached Knaresborough, where the scenery became more dramatic.

On arriving at their destination, they remarked on how pretty the town was, although the hilly streets made walking about a bit of a chore. Michel smiled inwardly as Monica huffed and puffed up the steep slope to the main street. Michael, continually walking round the restaurant while serving customers, clearing plates, did a lot to improve his fitness levels, and although it was an easy trek for him, he tried not to embarrass Monica. Privately he thought more outings to the golf club and other destinations to help improve Monica's fitness were now on the to-do list. However, after walking around the town and enjoying the atmosphere on this lovely spring day, they decided the lunch stop was a reconstructed winter gardens. The people-watching was fun, and several times, on observing something of interest, a comparison of ideas occurred—sometimes accompanied by some naughty giggling.

Michael asked her whether she knew where she had lived whilst in Harrogate. Monica smiled. "Of course," she replied. "It was 41 Park Drive, and I have my birth certificate to prove it." Without saying another word, he took her hand and towed her out to a waiting taxi and gave the driver the address. Monica blinked and stared at Michael in astonishment. She turned to him and started to speak, but he put his finger gently to her lips and asked her what the point of coming all this way and not seeing where she lived would be, especially as they had the confirmation of her address.

It wasn't far from the town centre, and ten minutes later the taxi driver pulled in outside Monica's first home. Staring in awe, she walked to the gate and gazed at the house for a long time. Amazed at how nice the property was and the upmarket feel of the street, Monica was content. A few shots on her phone camera and she climbed back into the waiting taxi. "Thank you, Michael," she whispered, and as the tears rolled down her cheeks, Michael left her to this important moment.

The taxi pulled up to the railway station. They were a good hour too early for the train, and as Monica felt the day had fulfilled its purpose, they decided to go to a glorious pub next to the entrance called the Harrogate Tap. It was fairly obvious that the pub had gone under some renovation, and they decided to sample it until it was time for the train back to York.

Like all the places they had been whilst in Yorkshire, they found food and drink rather expensive, and this pub was no exception. However, it was a special day. "What does a few pounds matter?" said Michael in a matter-of-fact tone of voice. He noticed that snacks on the bar were very competitively priced, and after demolishing a pork pie for Michael and a scotch egg for Monica, they sat sipping their wine and discussing the day.

He asked whether she would like to go anywhere else; after all, it was only just after three o'clock. But she was quite happy to go back to York and maybe have another walk through the Shambles. She had seen a few shops she would like to revisit. Content with the day, Michael agreed and went to sit in a very comfortable waiting room, as the train would be about thirty minutes. They agreed not to stay in the pub, as they still had the evening to come.

What took their eye was a youth of about fourteen in a full school uniform. He sat very quietly, and in spite of the various power points that were free to use, he did not look at any phone or tablet. Instead he demolished a packet of crisps and to their delight, when he finished the snack, he took the empty bag to a litter bin and deposited the bag. It was a bit of a walk too. Why they did not have a litter bin in the waiting room was a mystery. His behaviour was impeccable, and Monica remarked that the future was bright with young people like their travelling companion.

Although Monica had purchased a souvenir from Harrogate in the shape of a fridge magnet and a mug, she was happy wandering about the Shambles but did not buy anything. "I don't need anything else to dust," she said when questioned, and together they walked to the bus stop and their last night in York.

Monica was in a buoyant mood and was full of their day as they walked back from the inn, having said their goodbyes. They decided on a final drink at their residence, but only one, as they would make the trip home on the 9.00 a.m. train. Slowly they wound their way up the stairs, having got used to the outside staircase. Monica was not pleased with this arrangement, as it did not feel secure. But not wishing to spoil what had been one of the best trips she had taken, she would encourage another.

On this this thought, she decided to push Michael into dealing with the issue of his lacking a passport. Outside her door, she stopped and thanked him profusely for the break and how much she had enjoyed it. When he leaned forward to kiss her goodnight, Monica took his face between her hands, preventing him from pulling away, and the peck turned into a full-blown kiss. Stunned, Michael came up for air, and the process was repeated.

Embarrassed, he turned away and walked to his room. The kisses had provoked feelings he didn't know existed, and as he threw himself on the bed, he contemplated where it would go next. Monica forgot about the subject of the passport. Thoughtfully, she went into her room. She was now thinking that the relationship was moving on and wondering how this could be brought about as she slowly closed the door.

A few minutes later, a knock on the door startled Michael. Thankfully he was still dressed as he reached to open the door.

Monica was standing on the doorstep, brandishing two glasses and a bottle of fizzy wine, asking him whether he would like to join her in her room for a celebratory nightcap. A bit unsure as to whether this was proper, he followed her to her room, where an ice bucket sat on the dressing table. Proffering the unopened bottle to him, she remarked this was more his job than hers. Michael laughed out loud—a rare occurrence, him being the serious sort—and the sound of a cork popping resonated around the small room.

Michael sitting on the only chair and Monica on the edge of the bed, they again started to discuss their day, and Monica took the opportunity to broach the subject of his passport. She intimated that their next jaunt should be somewhere like Paris or Rome, or even Barcelona. Michael was taken aback. As he processed this suggestion, he found himself warming to the idea. But the passport. At the moment he would have to change his name to Whittaker or revert to MacGregor as per his birth certificate.

His driving licence was under Whittaker, as were his bank details, and the car was still in his mother's name. Monica chided him for that and offered to help him with the paperwork.

He said he was unsure about reverting to his real name, as he had got used to the name he used. Monica gave him a look which plainly intimated "really". "Michael," she said, "hundreds of women change their name as a matter of course when they marry. Surely it's not that much of a problem."

Michael stared into space as he often did and contemplated what Monica had said. Thinking about Mike and the agonies he had gone through trying to be part of his son's life, he thought that it was time to let him into his life. The welcome he'd had from his newly found family had been fantastic, and he had immediately fallen in love with the tiny Katrina.

"Monica, you are right," he said so suddenly she nearly jumped out of her skin. She threw her arms about him and enthusiastically kissed him and said she would help him with his paperwork, also indicating she approved of his choice. Michael kissed her back, but this time there was no drawing back. As the kisses got deeper and longer, Monica slowly began to help him undress, and he then, in turn, helped her out of her clothes. Not taking their eyes off each other after slowly undressing, Monica lay on the bed, gesturing for Michael to join her. As sensations he had not experienced before coursed through his body, he thought he had died and gone to heaven.

Chapter 32

Michael felt the need to explain that it was his first time. Monica, however, with a rare moment of compassion, told him she would never have guessed. Meanwhile, she was thinking she would enjoy practising and teaching Michael how to love. They drifted off to sleep in each other's arms, and the next thing they knew was the alarm ringing; it was time to get their journey home started.

Sitting down to breakfast, Michael felt the need to apologize, and before he could speak, she put her finger to his lips to silence him, gave him a smile, and blew a kiss. Although Michael felt a bit uncomfortable, Monica's happy chatter brought him back to himself as they waited for their taxi. Michael had lost his appetite, but Monica made up for it. She was trying to normalize the situation and knew she was going to have to tackle the subject sooner rather than later if this relationship, which she was enjoying, was to survive. The train was not the place.

Michael had brought his book and decided to read part of the way home. Monica, on the other hand, was a bit disappointed that he didn't want to chat. She started getting nervous. Their intimacy had to be brought into the open soon or he would fester and get further away. She tried to put herself in his place to see what was making him tick. He was, admittedly, very inexperienced, and he probably thought he had done the wrong thing. His mother had ruled his life when she was alive, and women and sex were neither discussed nor permitted.

He had been brought up to think it was wrong, and Monica was going to have to sort this out if any chance of them being together was possible.

When the taxi dropped Monica off at her home, it took her some persuading to have him get out of the cab at her home. He announced he was going home. "You must be fed up with me by now," he told her. She insisted he stay and sent the taxi on its way. after practically pushing him through the hall into the lounge and onto the big wing-backed chair he found so comfortable, she went into the kitchen and put the kettle on. Coming back into the room, she told him in a no-nonsense voice they needed to talk. "What about?"

stuttered Michael, knowing full well what the topic of conversation was about.

About two hours later, after an intense and serious conversation which left Michael in a much different frame of mind, he now believed that loving someone was a good thing and physically demonstrating that love was normal. Michael had explained that during his late teens his mother would, without knocking, come into his room with morning tea, and spotting his arousal always led to punishment. She had made the whole subject dirty and taboo. Over the years, he did not realize that sharing physical love was all very normal. Monica, thinking with dismay, realized he was very damaged goods and she would need to tread gently. Could she deal with this? She became nervous. She knew, having had other relationships (unlike Michael), that her feelings for him were strong—but were they strong enough?

Feeling a whole lot better about life, Michael pitched in cooking the meal. They opened a bottle of wine and enjoyed a first home-cooked meal in a while. He insisted on helping load the dishwasher and wiping down the surfaces. After all, he said by way of an explanation, his job involved some kitchen activity. "I can cook a little too," he boasted. "You must let me cook for you sometime." Inwardly Monica breathed a sigh of relief. Michael was getting back to normal, but over the next week she would be careful not to push the issue. She would watch this burgeoning relationship very carefully.

Their few days' holiday passed in a blur, and it was soon time to go back to work. Monica had arranged that the first week back would involve Monday, Wednesday, and Friday, which pleased Michael, as he still had a day off on Thursdays, but this would be the first of the Sundays off. He would have a better opportunity to enjoy a social life. He had already arranged to visit his family for Sunday lunch, and at their insistence, he would be accompanied by Monica.

Michael, Waiting

During his shift, he became aware that Olivia had not made any effort to greet him or indeed ask about his trip.

Olivia had been kept up to date with his friendship, so he was slightly discomfited that she had said little to him. Her curiosity was definitely in park mode. He decided to go and speak to her. There was a lull in the service, so now was as good a time as any. Giving Peter the heads-up, he climbed the stairs and knocked on the office door. Waiting to be given the "come in" shout, he wondered why she kept the door shut when she kept banging on about just coming in.

Standing in front of the desk, he was dismayed to hear the curt tone asking him what he wanted. He looked at her and noticed black circles under her eyes, and her pallor was evident. "I just wondered how you were. We usually have a team talk after one of us has been away; is there something wrong?"

Olivia looked at her deputy, who was her right-hand man and a man almost like a son to her—the son she never had. She had known him a long time now and grudgingly admitted to herself that Monica was changing his life for the better. She wondered what stage the relationship was at and wondered how much she should tell Michael about her current situation.

She elected for the truth. She owed him that.

"Michael," she said, "I have been to the doctor about a lump in my breast, and she has sent me to have a scan. The appointment is tomorrow. My doctor is not optimistic, I'm afraid, but at least I don't have much longer to wait. She is getting the scan done very quickly; I only had the appointment on Thursday. I haven't slept since then." She burst into tears, and Michael found himself with another woman in his arms as he sought to comfort her.

Monica being well-known for her stoicism, Michael was not surprised at the speed of her recovery as she wiped her eyes and dismissed him, asking for the door to be shut behind him.

As he walked slowly down the stairs and the door was firmly shut, leaving this proud lady to her living nightmare, he tried to recover himself. He knew he could tell no one, as she herself would have already told anyone who needed to know. He had to put on a brave face, even if it was only to reassure Olivia. That's when it came to him. She had nobody else to share this with. Her husband had died, and there had been no children.

Searching his memory, he tried to think of whether she had a sibling, aunt, uncle, or nephews. Try as he might, he could not remember any mention of relatives. He thought he remembered a conversation had back in the early days. He had been reassured when she told him they could be a pretend family, as they both had no alternative. *This would have been just after Mother died*, he thought.

Anyway, he had to get back to work—and without drawing attention to his shock. He decided he would tell Monica, if only to get some advice. The restaurant was busy but not too bad, which enabled Michael to do a bit of thinking and planning. He would need to have a fall-back position should Olivia be as ill as she expected.

No doubt surgery would be on the cards, and perhaps follow-on treatment. He thought perhaps he should plan after the results of the scan were available and the planning could be done together.

In the meantime, he decided to let the matter drop and get the work done. He did, however, check the rotas to see who was available to cover, as he knew that in a period of absence, he would be responsible for Olivia's workload leaving a gap on the restaurant floor.

Tuesday arrived and, as expected, Olivia did not make an appearance. Michael knew her appointment was around 11.00 a.m., so he half expected to see her in the early afternoon. When she did not make an appearance in the early evening, Michael was concerned. He could hear the upstairs phone ringing, and he made a dash for the stairs. Answering the phone, it was, as he expected, Olivia. The news was not good. A breast cancer diagnosis had been made, and she was to report for surgery the following week.

Michael walked slowly back down the stairs, deep in thought about the happy memories of his few days with the woman he had to admit he was falling in love with and the other woman in his life, who was now facing a battle for survival. She had been like a mother to him since his own mother had died. Always patient, she coached him through his duties, and gave him guidance which brought him to the perfectionist role he employed whilst he worked the restaurant. Just when things look to be set fair, along comes life and pulls the rug out from under your feet.

For a moment, his mind flashed back to the evening, which seemed so long ago, when Monica had behaved so badly, and he compared this to the different person he now was clearly besotted with. Her transformation had helped him to turn into the more confident man he was now.

His thoughts raced through all that happened over the past six months: the new baby; a father he didn't know he had; the threats from the men who had quite probably killed someone and were now a threat to him and Monica, if they ever found out she existed; and, finally, a relationship which was speeding in a direction he was actually starting to be comfortable about.

All these thoughts were had to try to find pleasant things to imagine. There was no getting away from it.

His boss and mentor was starting a battle for her life, and he had to show support. What could he tell the staff? He did not feel it was appropriate to tell them the whole story yet. He decided to let them know enough to satisfy their curiosity without impinging on her privacy.

He told the staff in two meetings that Olivia had to go into hospital for minor surgery and would be back in a few days. Michael did not know just how long Olivia would be absent, but he felt the explanation would give him more time to find out the whole situation.

Discovering the visiting hours would fit into the early afternoon free time he had prior to beginning his shift, he headed to Western General for 2.00 p.m. the day after the operation. He was pleased to see a middle-aged lady sitting by the bed. *Good*, thought Michael, *there is someone in her life*. Olivia introduced her as her next-door neighbour. Establishing that she was feeling okay, if perhaps a trifle sore, Olivia explained everything had gone as well as could be expected. She would be in for a few days as they did blood tests and a bone scan. When the wound had recovered sufficiently, she would have a six-week course of radiotherapy. She'd had lymph nodes removed for inspection, but all in all she should be fine and be back to work the following week.

With a glad heart, he said his goodbyes, and to Olivia's surprise he leaned over and kissed her lightly on the cheek. This new woman in his life was performing miracles. *I need to meet her*; she was thinking as his back disappeared out of the ward door.

Feeling considerably better, Michael headed off to the bus stop and to his workplace.

The following day was his normal day off. He decided to go into the restaurant first thing and complete all the paperwork that had been generated over the last couple of days; then he would check the menus with Alfredo before popping over to the hospital to check on and report to Olivia. He would then spend the afternoon, and perhaps dinner, with Monica. It was strange how Monica came into his thoughts and plans. He felt they really were a couple. His mind wandered as he took in the scene of sharing a home, coming back from work and her being there. It gave him a warm, rosy feeling.

Not so many months prior, he had pictured his life stretching out in front of him with a feeling of being alone. He was glad he had joined the golf club, where he had made some pleasant acquaintances, and the book club, which he had subsequently decided was not for him.

After getting off the bus, he strolled over to the restaurant and gave his staff an update. Olivia was popular with the staff, being fair-minded and understanding. The staff were sorry for this setback and anxious to hear how she was faring. His mobile rang, which surprised him. Checking the screen, he saw it was Mike, his new-found father. He was phoning to invite Monica and Michael to dinner on his day off. The new baby would be in attendance. Michael was sure this would be fine, but out of courtesy he said he would get back to him as soon as possible, as he would have to check on Monica's movements. Of course, Mike agreed, and the conversation ended.

An hour or so later, Michael consulted Monica, who had been shopping. She agreed it would be nice, and yes, she was looking forward to meeting the new arrival after the drama of her last visit. Michael phoned his father back and confirmed they would be there for dinner. After ending the call, he was faced with a pleasant evening ahead.

It was a boisterous household. Yet again there was the whole family plus one new arrival. As Michael gazed at the baby, he was taken aback. She was so small. She was sleeping soundly, and he was afraid all the talking and laughing would wake her. He looked anxious. Monica whispered to him and comforted him with the knowledge that babies sleep through most things. Michael was trying to remember the last time he had been this close to a baby.

They had a lovely meal. Patricia had cooked one of her specials, chilli and rice, and it went down well. Just as the plates were being cleared, young Katrina decided it was her turn and began to cry. Horrified, Michael

Michael, Waiting

looked at the screaming infant and wondered when she would stop. Mhairi picked up her small daughter and slipped out of the room. She preferred to feed her in more peaceful surroundings. Besides, she thought breastfeeding and nappy changing were perhaps not the thing with Michael; she had picked up that he was a shy man who was unaccustomed to family life.

Michael and Monica were sitting in the bosom of this family, and he decided to break the good news he had been saving. "I am changing my name back to MacGregor," he announced. "Monica will help me with any paperwork, and I will hopefully be able to apply for a passport soon. I have the car to sort and the bank, but I have been assured it is not a complicated process. Is this all right with you?"

There was a burst of clapping and cheering as the family voiced their approval just as Mhairi arrived back. "What's all the noise about?" she asked. Her father explained. With a beaming grin, she walked over, kissed him on the cheek, and plonked the wriggling child into his inexpert arms. He lasted about a minute before he handed her back.

Laughing, Mum put her to bed and took the Moses basket through to the other room to give the small person some peace.

Driving back to drop Monica off, Michael told her that he had not been sure whether they would accept the name change and he was very relieved. Monica, telling him he was being silly, explained just what an honour it was for the MacGregor family and that it was a sure sign of his acceptance of his heritage. "I feel very lucky," said Michael humbly. "I have a new family, and I have you, have I not?"

Monica looked at this handsome insecure man she had come to love and said, "Of course. I can't imagine not having you in my life." To her surprise, as they stopped outside the house, Michael told her he loved her, and he kissed her almost with passion. *Not quite*, thought Monica, *but he is getting there*. As she returned the compliment, she told him she loved him too.

Inviting him in for a coffee, which he accepted, she went off to the kitchen whilst he sat in the big winged-back chair which he had come to favour. It was about ten, and he was conscious of an early start, so he would need to make it a short visit. Thinking back to their last night in York, he thought how lovely that time had been. Suddenly, without warning, the front door was being thumped very loudly, and a familiar voice shouted,

"Let me in!" Derek, was at the front door, obviously frustrated that the new lock did not fit his old key.

"Don't answer the door, Monica. He sounds furious and possibly drunk," said an alarmed Michael.

"I need to sort this," said Monica, and after pushing home the safety chain, she answered the door. A shower of vitriol came out of his mouth. It was hard to make out; as Michael had predicted, he was drunk. His car was half in the garden and half on the path. He had, worryingly, stopped very close to the house.

He was so very inebriated Monica was afraid as to what could happen if he were allowed back on the road. She called the police. Derek had come to demand his possessions. Monica calmly told him to go and to telephone when he was sober and make a convenient appointment. He spewed out that it wasn't fair she should get the house and that if she would not let him in this moment, he would come back with his possessions; he planned on moving back in. Monica explained that would not be happening and said to him, "Please leave now or the police will be called."

"You wouldn't dare," retorted Derek.

"Watch me," she said as she slammed the door, leaving the chain on.

Fortunately, a patrol car was close, and as it drew up to the house, a shocked Derek tried to get into his vehicle, without success. The police car had blocked him in, and he was so drunk he couldn't keep his hands from trembling as he unsuccessfully tried to put his key in the ignition. Fortunately, Monica had garaged the car for safety when they had headed off to York, so no damage had been done. A breathalyzer was produced and, as expected, proved positive. Having taken they keys off the drunken Derek, one officer settled him in the patrol car whilst his partner called the local breakdown company to remove Derek's car, as he wouldn't be driving.

Monica insisted that she and Michael give the coffee a miss and poured a rather large glass of brandy. "I can't drink that!" he exclaimed. "I will end up in the back of a police car just like Derek."

"Like you were going home," retorted Monica

Chapter 33

The next couple of weeks were busy for Michael and Monica. True to her word, she helped him as much as possible with the name changes. They would meet up after Michael's shift finished to discuss and instruct on the next phase. Monica was back at full-time work, so their time together was curtailed somewhat.

She was enjoying being back at her position in the company, and to the delight of her colleagues, a much more empathetic boss had emerged. Monica, on the other hand, was pleased to be able to hold her head up, having a new relationship. There was a bit of gossip floating around which caught Monica's attention that the secretary had resigned from Derek's firm and had gone somewhere down south, leaving Derek on his own. *That explains the night-time visit demanding to be admitted and move back in*, thought Monica. She allowed herself a moment of schadenfreude and realized that the embarrassment was all his.

It was getting on for 9.00 p.m. when Monica, sitting in her house, waiting for Michael, took a phone call on the landline. *Strange*, she thought, *it's a bit unusual for the house phone to ring at such a late hour.* Answering, she was surprised to hear her son's voice. It was unusual for him to phone. They usually used Facetime, and his partner and the new baby would participate. It was obvious that he was not in good form. He spoke in a curt voice. "What's this all about?" he asked. "Dad tells me you have thrown him out and now you have a new boyfriend."

Monica's son Jordan was born when she was twenty-one, and he had been an easy-going child. By now Derek's bad temper and controlling ways had made him decide not to have any more children. She had done her best to shield the young Jordan from his father's temper tantrums, and she was delighted when his career took off and he was seconded to the overseas branch in Toronto for three years. Most of that time had passed, and he had found a partner, followed by the birth of her first grandchild. Derek and she had made a trip to visit and meet the new arrival. It hadn't been a successful visit, as Derek had been quarrelsome and belligerent. It was shortly after this visit that he left the family home and moved in with his secretary.

Monica, listening to the tirade from her son, was horrified. She had told Jordan right at the start of the new domestic arrangements, however, that Monica, being Monica, had left out all the horror of the split and had just said they had decided to part company and a divorce would follow.

Not being entirely happy, he sent grumbling messages, trying to establish what was going on. His last communication indicated he and his family would come home for a holiday in the spring, during which he would see whether he couldn't "knock some sense into the pair". Monica replied that it would be lovely to see them but that as for knocking sense, that was not an option, as she and Derek would be divorced by then.

There followed a horrified silence during which Monica started to explain what had really happened, but the phone was slammed down and the call was terminated.

Monica sat with her head in her hands. Still controlling, her ex-husband was now poisoning her only child. For once she was sitting in the dark. How could she explain things to her son without too much criticism of her ex and not feel her child should take sides? What was she to do now? She was now desolate, and as the tears started to roll down her cheeks, the cheery voice of Michael permeated the hall as he used his newly acquired key to let himself in. Hurriedly Monica reached for the tissues and tried to compose herself, but it was too late. He immediately saw the distress she was in and jumped to the conclusion that another visit from Derek had upset her.

A restraining order had been put on Derek, Monica reminded him, and so far, it was working. "He is living in a bed and breakfast now," she explained, "as his new lover is no more." This made her smile through her tears, and she told Michael what had happened on the phone. Michael was sad for her and very angry with Jordan. He wasn't sure whether Monica had told him about their relationship, but it was very unfair that the son should take sides without listening to the whole story.

"I think you should take a few days off and travel to Toronto and visit," he announced. "Go and visit your son and explain face to face what your domestic situation is. Surely he will understand. After all, it's been nearly two years, and you told him at the time, did you not?"

"Yes, we did," she said wearily. "But Derek took the lead on that and explained that we were not happy any more and had decided to go our own ways. Secretaries were not mentioned, and I let it go."

"Why, then," asked Michael, "is he kicking up a fuss now?"

"I don't know," she said sadly. "I never got a chance to explain."

"All the more reason to go to Canada," he said triumphantly. "I'll think about it," she replied.

Neither being in the mood to discuss Michael's slow-moving name change, they sat on their favourite chairs and talked about Jordan and the best way to handle the situation.

Monica had made it clear that being estranged from her only son after giving up on her marriage would be one step too many to bear.

Michael was spending more and more time at Monica's home, but neither was ready for a full-on "living together" scenario, and he would spend the evenings before his day off at home.

A few days later, Monica announced she had taken advice and had booked a return flight to Toronto that would be leaving in a couple of days and returning a week later. The early-morning flight made it easy for Michael to take her to the airport. Although he would miss her, it was the right thing to do. They had debated the subject of Michael accompanying her but staying in a local hotel. They decided it would probably hinder the reconciliation, should there be one, and Monica would go alone. A message had been sent to Jordan, and he agreed she could stay and he would collect her at the airport. "Looks like a conciliatory step," said Monica, feeling a bit more hopeful.

As he waved bye to Monica, heading for Departures, he felt a pang of loss. They, as a couple, had spent a great deal of time together, and she would be sorely missed. It was like Christmas over again, only he did not have the manic business to keep him occupied.

He was busy with the polishing of the brasses in the restaurant—a job he should really have delegated and sometimes did, but he loved seeing the shine come back. He had come in earlier than usual to get the job done. As he happily rubbed the brass lamp, he found himself humming a tune. His life had taken a turn, and he was happy with the consequences. Of course, Monica was missed and she had told him she would text to say she was safe at Jordan's but not to expect any other communication until she confirmed she was getting ready to board on the way home. She would explain everything in person. Michael had concurred.

Suddenly the internal phone buzzed. Olivia, on the other end, asked him to come upstairs. Michael was puzzled as he climbed the stairs to her office. He hadn't noticed she was on the premises. *She must have crept in and gone upstairs without announcing herself.* Michael had opened up that morning.

With a sharp knock, he entered the office. He was getting used to walking in, but he still knocked each time. Motioning to the seat, Olivia gestured for him to sit down. Strangely, the seat wasn't in its usual place across the desk but was side by side with the chair Olivia now occupied.

Chapter 34

"I have some rather unexpected news I need to share with you," said Olivia. "It's time for my radiotherapy, as the operation scar has healed sufficiently to embark on the treatment. However, a few days ago I was summoned to the outpatient oncology department, where I was told that the bone scan results proved at best inconclusive and at worst displaying cancerous cells in my lower back. The radiotherapy is to be postponed, and I'm to attend the X-ray department for a full M.R.I."

Michael was stunned. He had thought her treatment was going well, although he had refrained from asking her for updates, as she was not the confiding type and he was a man, which would make conversation difficult. Eventually he was able to offer his support and express his concern for her well-being. She thanked him and explained in her usual no-nonsense approach that she would get the scan done as soon as possible and that if the results were bad news, well, she would just have to "get on with it".

Full of admiration for this brave lady, of whom he was very fond, he realized she had the fight for life on her hands, and in parting he assured her he would support her every step of the way, starting with an offer to accompany her to the X-ray for the M.R.I. He knew she didn't like small spaces, but her bravery continued when, in thanking him, she explained she wanted to do this alone, for now.

As Michael left her office, Olivia stood and walked over to the window. There wasn't much of a view from this particular window, but Olivia didn't mind. She was just looking, while her mind raced. She had told Michael only the bare details, and she herself knew that the bone scan had indeed shown cancer cells and the M.R.I was just to confirm the whereabouts it had spread to. The removal of the lymph nodes had also proved the cancer was in her bloodstream and could be sitting growing in any one or all of her major organs.

Olivia felt the cold hand of fear run through her. She was a widow of a certain age, turning sixty-eight at her next birthday. She had not anticipated that life would be so short. She had no relatives to speak of. Like Michael, she had been an only child. She had no children of her own, and a sister-in-law she barely spoke to when her husband was alive had not improved in communication terms now that her beloved Dhugal was with her no more.

She was alone and would have to face this battle all by herself. Michael would be her support, as he had proved in the time they had worked together.

Coming back to reality, she sat down at the desk and dialled a number. She asked to speak to Mr. Archibald, giving her name. Almost immediately the masculine voice asked whether Olivia was well. "Funnily enough, Bill, that's why I have called," she replied.

Her request was made, a date to come into the office was put in the diary, and the call was terminated. Olivia allowed herself to dream about the past: the meeting of Dhugal, the courtship, and the wedding. She had been so happy that day. Only young at twenty-three, with a beautiful satin wedding dress and her new husband resplendent in highland dress, she had felt she was the luckiest girl alive. After a short honeymoon on Skye, they returned to the bustle of the city and the restaurant to assist Dhugal senior.

The years passed, and the longed-for children failed to appear. Dhugal senior took ill and developed pneumonia, which silently killed him and left the running of the restaurant to his son. Olivia promptly gave up her part-time job at the florist and moved in to be the administrator. Her husband did not share her expertise in the accounting department, and Olivia was delighted to be of assistance. There were no babies, but she made the restaurant one. Learning on the job, she brought into play various methods which made the premises run smoothly.

When her husband died at the fairly young age of sixty-two, she almost gave up. She would put the restaurant on the market and retire. The restaurant had been closed when Dhugal died, and it remained closed until after the funeral took place. She was not experienced in running the front of house, and the Dhugall remained closed as Olivia went into mourning. She cut herself off to such an extent her friends stopped calling.

Her only remaining friend was her next-door neighbour, who had befriended Olivia when she moved into her home as a new bride. The two ladies become and remained close friends. The neighbour visited Olivia every day and eventually brought her into the world again. Olivia was faced with the facts that she was alone and retiring was not an option. What would she do with herself all day? After a few sleepless but constructive nights, she came to the decision to reopen Dhugall. She just hoped that the staff she had taken so much trouble recruiting and training had not taken alternative employment. It was, after all, now three weeks the establishment had been out of service.

Let joy be uncontained, Michael was available. His mother was a bit poorly, as he explained when Olivia rang, and he had taken the time just to keep her company while she recovered. She had been having chest pains and was on the waiting list for an operation. They had also taken some time on a trip to the Western Isles to escape the noise and fuss of the city. Later Michael was to be glad he had spent that time, as his mother was to have very little time left.

Michael was delighted to be appointed into the new restaurant, as Olivia had indicated there would be some changes and wondered whether he would be on board. Michael agreed, hoping he would be in a position to make some changes himself. He also had designs on the head waiter position and was optimistic when he heard the current head waiter would not be able to return, as he, too, was unwell and attending the hospital for tests. Michael was to return as deputy manager.

Being deputy for the moment was good enough, but Michael hoped that when it was time, he would get the promotion he wanted above all else. Olivia was full of the memories of teaching Michael the way she wanted things done and his malleable personality; they worked alongside each other in near-perfect harmony. Michael was so shy, she remembered. She used to feel sorry for him when he had difficult diners to deal with, and of course, who could forget the appalling behaviour of one of the four ladies who dined on the first Friday of the month? More surprisingly, it would appear that the new-found confidence had involved him in a romantic entanglement with the aforementioned lady from the foursome. *I wonder whether I have time to write my memoirs?* mused Olivia before returning to her paperwork and reality.

Chapter 35

Michael returned to his duties in a dream. One half of him thought that it would all be okay—that they would treat Olivia and she would be back to her old self in no time. The other half was panicking at the thought of losing his surrogate mother and what was ahead for her. He had to admit she was looking pale, her skin having a waxy appearance. But true to himself, he went about his duties as if nothing had happened, and on no account would he share the news with his team. Olivia had not expressly forbidden him to tell, but then she did not need to. Michael was, as always, discreet and would reveal nothing of the events overtaking them until he had to. It was, after all, not his news to tell.

It concerned him also that if Olivia did not do well recovering from her illness—or worse, not recovering—what would befall the restaurant? Would she sell or get a manager to run the show? In any event, it was not the time to think about it. He was sure things would work out. Maybe Olivia would take some time to get up to speed, but he was sure she would, and in the meantime, he would continue to run the restaurant in Olivia's absence and make no more reference to illness and treatments. He would be guided by Olivia and what she wanted to discuss.

A few days later, it was time to head to the airport again to collect Monica. He had missed her in spite of all that was going on, and also he hoped the journey had proved to be a success. Inwardly, he was furious at Jordan, and although he had yet to meet him, he felt he was a bit of his father's son, and he would like to give him a piece of his mind. *However, let's see how the visit went*, thought Michael. It did not seem appropriate to him to criticize Monica's son. *Let's hear, first, all that transpired.*

Michael, Waiting

A beaming Monica came through the doors from customs and straight into the waiting arms of Michael. "How did it go?" he asked anxiously.

"It all went very well in the end," she replied, "but it's a long story. Have you got time to stop when you drop me off?"

"Yes," he replied. "I have taken this as my day off so we can spend some time together."

"Oh, that's lovely," she replied. "The only snag is that I may drop off to sleep—jet lag."

Michael sat in the big, comfy armchair, sipping tea as Monica regaled him with the whole story from the landing at Toronto to the drive to the house and the week playing grandma. It took only a day to bring Jordan round. He had been taken aback when his father reported what seemed like unusual behaviour from his mother. Wisely, as Jordan warmed to the details, she told him the whole story, leaving out nothing. By the time she was ready to go back home, Jordan and his pretty partner Ailsa were on her side, and they thoroughly enjoyed the unexpected bonus of a babysitter on hand for a week.

An invitation to come back soon and bring Michael was the last thing mentioned as she went to board the plane back to Edinburgh.

Mesmerized, Michael listened to the whole story, giving his full attention, and eventually Monica ran out of steam. He expressed his delight at the patching up and silently congratulated himself for packing her off to Canada. Extra bonus getting to spend time with her son and granddaughter. The small person being named Iona indicated that although she was Canadian born, she would be reminded of her Scottish roots.

Michael told Monica about his boss's illness. He felt that the fact Olivia was poorly may have an impact on Monica, and he felt it only fair to warn her of the turbulence coming their way. Monica was shocked and sympathetic. Like Michael, she assumed that things had been straightforward and that all that was required was a course of radiotherapy.

Meanwhile, back at the restaurant, Olivia was taking a call from the X-ray department offering her an empty slot for her MR.I if she could get there in an hour. Firstly she phoned for a taxi, and then she asked Michael to come to the restaurant to cover for her. Michael also phoned for a taxi and left his car at Monica's.

She was secretly pleased to have the house to herself. It had been a busy week and a long flight home. She needed a nap.

Meanwhile, Michael arrived at the restaurant just as Olivia's taxi stopped to collect her. After a hurried handover, Olivia's cab shot off into the darkness, and Michael went inside to see what was in store. He was a bit distracted, and he found it difficult to concentrate as the evening wore on. Olivia's appointment was for 5.00 p.m., and it was now past seven and he hadn't heard anything from her. About 9.00 p.m. she telephoned and explained she had been held up and was going home to bed and would see him the next day.

Michael was seriously worried; Olivia was more than just a little possessive about her restaurant, and it was not normal behaviour for her to abandon ship so easily. *She must have had bad news*, he thought. With a heavy heart, he closed up and headed for Monica's. Opening the door, he realized that Monica was nowhere downstairs, and on going into the bedroom, he found her sound asleep. He covered her up, and as she didn't have to go in to work the next day, he quietly left, after leaving an explanatory note, and went home.

Dreading what was coming next, he arrived at work the next day expecting to see Olivia behind her desk. She was not there; nor was she anywhere to be seen. Michael checked with the staff, and they confirmed they had not seen Olivia since the day before.

A few minutes later, her phone in the office started ringing. Michael answered to hear Olivia on the other end stating baldly that she would not be in, as she had to go back to hospital. Then, it getting too much for her, the bravery she had been displaying crumbled.

Sounding like a scared child, she stammered out the explanation that she was starting chemotherapy that very morning, as the MR.I had shown tumours on her spine, liver, and lungs. There was also a shadow on one of her kidneys, though it was as yet not conclusive.

Michael was horrified. It sounded really bad, and that she was all on her own made it much worse. Not knowing what else to do, he opened the restaurant and got the day ready for the diners. He was sure that was what Olivia wanted.

In the evening, during a lull, he made contact with his father and explained what had happened and that he may have to spend some downtime in the restaurant as his manager was poorly and he may have to cover. Forgetting completely about Mike's profession, he told him what had happened. Mike instantly swung into doctor mode and proceeded to ask Michael questions.

As Michael did not really have much information, he told his father what he could, and Mike tried his best to soften the blow.

Mike explained the general outline of what was happening but not the specifics, as he did not know the patient in question. To himself, he was determined to find out when he next attended the hospital. What he could tell Michael, he would.

Michael took a call from the hospital the next day. It was the ward sister in the chemo suite, and she asked whether he could spare some time to visit. Her patient, Mr.s Black, had expressed a wish to see him. After settling on a mutually suitable time, Michael got the restaurant open and ready for business. He would wait to see Olivia before he made any announcements. Peter had already expressed an interest in what was happening, but Michael had managed to head him off for now. An explanation had to happen soon.

He arrived at the hospital on time. He had taken the bus and discovered the bus stopped at a park-and-ride facility about a mile from the hospital. While he was waiting for the bus to start up, he realized people were parking their cars and boarding the bus. He thought this might be the future. He was impressed. The bus took so long, and parking at the hospital was ill advised.

Arriving at the chemo suite, he found the door locked. He rang a bell and, after identifying himself, was admitted and taken to the sister's office. After he was given leave to sit and offered tea or coffee, the staff nurse he had spoken to informed him that Olivia Black, having no relatives, had extended the courtesy of next of kin on Michael. She asked whether he would be able to visit and discuss her progress with senior staff, inasmuch as she wanted details passed on. The staff nurse then proceeded to give Michael an explanation of the procedures the treatment required

She confirmed the information Olivia had told him the day before yesterday. "The prognosis was not good," she warned. "However, there was a drug trial available to which Olivia had agreed to try once the present course of chemo was complete. It is unlikely she will be able to return to work in the near future, so your support will be invaluable." She then offered to take him to see Olivia, and when he did, he had to work hard at not being shocked at her appearance. They greeted each other with some affection, and Michael opened the conversation with the expected question "How are you?" Olivia, instead of her usual bluff and bluster, replied saying in a very soft voice that she was a little scared.

Michael squeezed her hand lightly and reassured her he would do what he could to make it easier. Starting off the conversation, Michael went over a couple of points and gave her a rough update on the restaurant. Then he explained what would have to be done in the short term to keep the business going. A bookkeeper would need to be found. A part-time person would work, but some administrative experience would be important too. Michael couldn't do both, and it was clear Olivia's absence was going to be of some length.

Michael suggested to Olivia that he have a word with Monica, as she may be in a position to recommend someone reliable; Olivia agreed this was the best way forward. Although Olivia had expressed a desire to keep the news of her illness to a bare minimum of people, she wasn't stupid. She knew he would have shared the information with Monica, as all couples do. She was also delighted Michael had someone like Monica in his life.

After he left to return to the restaurant, Olivia drifted off to sleep feeling less alone. She had Michael in her corner, and she was going to need him. His progress over the last year had been nothing short of astonishing. From the shy, quiet deputy waiter, he had become more assured and was not in the least afraid to deal with any crisis that came his way. Olivia knew that she had contributed only a small part of the transformation. She was anxious to meet Monica.

Chapter 36

Arriving back at the restaurant, Michael wasted no time in calling a staff meeting. All the staff except Robert, who was on a day off, were present. Michael had already explained to Olivia that the staff had to be told, as the constant absences and lack of information would set the gossip going. This way, he explained, they would know the correct story and their sympathy may be of assistance if anything over and above was required.

Michael told them the bare minimum, having some respect for Olivia's dignity. She had also insisted that any attempts to visit would be rebuffed. Michael explained that scenario in the most tactful way, because if he had repeated Olivia's take on visitors, they may have been just a trifle offended. Olivia was not in favour of gilding the lily. She may be weakened by her illness and treatment, but her spirit was not broken.

Michael phoned Monica at her workplace to ask whether she had any knowledge of a bookkeeper or administrator who would be suitable for a temporary part-time post in the restaurant. "It's not very difficult," he explained, "but it would require someone with a bit of experience so they could hit the ground running." In a very businesslike fashion, she asked him to leave it with her and said she would phone him back.

Michael was a little put out at the tone of the conversation. Perhaps he had done the wrong thing speaking to Monica. He went back downstairs and got on with his duties. A short time later, he heard the upstairs phone ring. Taking the stairs two at a time, he got to the phone to be connected to Monica. Her tone was softer this time as she explained she had a small meeting going on and couldn't talk properly.

Michael breathed a sigh of relief, such was his lack of confidence in his relationship, as she went on to explain about a small bank of temporary staff she held on file. There were two candidates she had in mind. "Do you want to interview them?" she asked. Michael thought for a minute and asked whether Monica could send just the most suitable person, and he would conduct a small informal interview to satisfy his managerial need. Also, he thought Olivia might not approve of his hiring a complete stranger. This way, he thought, he would both please Monica and satisfy Olivia he had gone through the correct procedure.

Michael had been somewhat surprised when Olivia asked to meet Monica. He was surprised on two counts: Olivia was by now very thin, and, of course, she had no hair. She was used to seeing Michael, but for her to invite Monica was a big surprise. Monica agreed to accompany Michael to the hospital, having taken an extended lunch. There would not be much time, which was probably best. The effort Olivia would put into the visit would tire her out, so a short visit was arranged.

Monica was very gentle with Olivia. She did not look horrified but just spoke to her as if they were in a lounge at home. As the goodbyes were said, Monica slipped out, leaving Michael alone with Olivia. She was sure they would need to talk business, but no, Olivia just thanked Michael and squeezed his hand. With a tear in his eyes, he joined Monica and the two went back to their respective workplaces.

Conscious of the fact his life had been centred round both Monica and Olivia, he realized it had been a few weeks since he had made contact with his father. He had the perfect excuse to phone—not that it was necessary. He told his father with delight that his passport had arrived. Also, the bank had taken his name change in their stride, and he had a new bank account complete with the name he had adopted.

The conversation ended with the standard invitation to Sunday lunch, which of course included Monica. Mike then asked his son how Olivia was getting on. Michael explained that the cancer had spread and chemo was being administered. She was due to finish the first batch next week, Michael explained, and she was being tested for a drug trial. Mike listened and processed the information, and then he said, "As you know, that is my field of expertise, and patient confidentiality prohibits me from discussing a particular case, but if you have any technical questions, feel free to ask me, and if I can help, I will. Well done on the paperwork, by the way." With that, the call ended.

Michael, Waiting

Michael came off the phone shaking his head. How could he forget his father was connected to oncology and, of course, would be involved in Olivia's care? He would ask about the drug trial when he saw him on Sunday. Now he had to deal with the administration and accounting as the time drew near for Monica's applicant to be seen.

He didn't know why, but having expected a woman, he was surprised to see that a young man of about thirty had arrived asking for him. He introduced himself as Richard Morris and said he had been sent by Mr.s Stevens, who had told him there was a part-time temporary placement available.

Richard was about the same height as Michael but with fair curly hair and blue eyes. Looking younger than his thirty-five years, he was an attractive young man and spoke with an educated voice. Michael liked him on sight. He settled him comfortably in Olivia's office whilst he gathered up a notebook and took his place in Olivia's chair. He had the wit, with Monica's help, to make a list of the duties the position entailed and went through them step by step.

Richard seemed familiar with most of the tasks Michael described and was equally familiar with Olivia's fairly simple accounting. Michael buzzed down and asked one of the waiting staff to bring coffee and biscuits for two as the two men got to know each other.

Later, after the newly appointed administrator had left, Michael took the bus to the hospital for an hour or so. When Michael would describe the day, Olivia seemed to thrive on the contact with her "baby", the restaurant, and was hungry for news. Michael still hadn't figured out a way to get his car into town to speed everything up. He was bemoaning this to Olivia, together with the delight he felt at the appointment of Richard, when Olivia sat up and exclaimed, "How stupid! My car sits in a lock-up during the day. It's just around the corner, and although my car is there at the moment, you could easily take it to my home and use it for your car temporarily—just until we get this nonsense over with."

Michael was delighted. It would make things so much easier having transport in town. He thanked Olivia profusely. Just then the staff nurse Michael had spoken to on several occasions came up to the big hospital bed hosting Olivia and gave her the news that her chemo would be completed tomorrow and asked whether she could arrange to be collected or whether

185

she wanted an ambulance. Delighted, Olivia agreed to be collected, and she turned to Michael. "Perfect. Hand me my bag." She fished out a set of car keys. "You can collect my car from the garage and bring it here to take me home. Can that work?" she asked anxiously. It was arranged that Michael would call for Olivia around 1.00 p.m.

The next morning, Michael headed off to work in his own car. He parked next to the garage and then drove the sleek BMW out of the garage and replaced it with his smart VW Golf.

He left the restaurant at lunchtime and drew up in the hospital car park. It was busy, but there were a few spaces relatively near the door. Visiting at 2.00 p.m. would have meant a full car park, so he was glad of the earlier time. On arrival at the ward, he was surprised to see his boss tucked up in a wheelchair, ready to go. The porter checking where he was parked took off at a pace which had Michael practically trotting alongside. Her weakness was sad, but now she was home she would get a chance to get back on her feet. *Until the next time*, thought Michael, feeling a spasm of affection for this efficient, brusque lady demonstrating so much courage.

Michael was concerned about leaving Olivia to fend for herself. However, she had forestalled him by hiring a housekeeper/nurse to come in for a few hours a day until she felt more able to do the tasks needed to get by. "I am just weak from the chemo," she said. "I am sure I will feel much better in a day or two." Taking his leave after making tea and biscuits, Michael said his goodbyes, making sure her phone was handy, and returned to work, whereupon he brought the staff up to date.

Sunday came, and it was a glorious early-spring day. Michael, remembering his silent pledge to get Monica fit again, mentioned to Monica he thought it was maybe time to get out on the golf course. Monica agreed with enthusiasm. Monica reminded Michael that the course would be very busy and it would be unlikely to get a slot at this short notice.

"We should book for next Sunday," she suggested. "I am sure the weather will hold. We can try for nine holes at first and maybe go to the driving range during the week." They settled on Thursday and decided to take advantage of the weather today. A trip and picnic was the alternative to golf, and they headed off to the botanical gardens.

As they were going to Mike and Patricia's home for Sunday lunch, they decided to forgo the picnic and headed home to change into more dressed-up clothes and headed for his father's house and lunch.

On arriving at their destination, they were welcomed in, and it was lovely to see them all. The small Katrina was gaining weight and was happy to go to Uncle Michael for a cuddle until Aunt Monica got impatient and removed the infant from the inexperienced arms of her uncle and had a cuddle herself.

Lunch, as usual, was delicious, and Monica followed Patricia into the kitchen to attack the dishes. Michael went with his father to the study, where they discussed the treatments Olivia had been receiving. "It is usually the case that conventional treatments outlive their usefulness," explained Mike, "and we use the patient as a sort of guinea pig, with their full knowledge and permission, to see if we can halt the growth. It usually gives the patients approximately three to five years extra."

Michael explained this to Monica on the drive home, and the sadness they felt was palpable. However, Michael said suddenly, making Monica jump, "She is a fighter, and if anyone can beat this, Olivia can." He then continued. "I've got better news. I have my new bank card, and the passport has arrived, and just this morning my new logbook for the car arrived, so now I am officially Michael MacGregor. It's a good job my father has been using the derivative; otherwise, there would be a bit of confusion."

They had decided that when Michael had his passport they would take a week's holiday where the use of the passport was necessary. Michael, never having been out of Scotland before the York trip, was excited, and there were so many places he wanted to visit that he didn't know where to start. Monica had suggested Tenerife, having been herself. She thought it would be a perfect destination for the unseasoned traveller.

She had been looking at holidays on the Internet and showed the details to Michael. He was enchanted with the deep blue skies and white villas he saw on the computer screen and agreed with Monica it would indeed be lovely. Realizing he could see the ocean from his terrace, he understood why the complex was called Atlantic View. He couldn't wait. So many adventures awaited.

Monica had recommended on an apartment in the resort of Costa del Silencio. It was two-bedroomed and had a small swimming pool. A hired car came with the package. The holiday was duly booked.

Chapter 37

Happily, the next day off proved to be sunny with a slight warmth to the day, and together they headed off to the golf club. They used Monica's vehicle to be able to carry both sets of clubs, and they set off on another first for Michael. As they duffed shots, put balls into the trees, putted erratically, and placed shots into more sand bunkers than the seaside, they laughed uproariously. They putted out for a score well into three figures. Still laughing, they regaled George behind the bar about their first round of golf together. Monica intimated, "I've been playing for several years; there is no excuse."

"At least you were playing with someone who didn't make you look bad," said Michael, still grinning. They ate lunch and decided they would have to do it all again. Secretly, Michael decided he would be on the practice ground whenever he got the chance.

"Michael," said Monica as they sat watching a programme on television, "have you any summer clothes?"

"What kind of summer clothes?" he asked. "I have some short-sleeved shirts and a couple of T-shirts."

"Not enough," she retorted. "I'm afraid a shopping trip is in the offing. You will at least need a couple pairs of swim shorts and shorts, maybe sandals and lightweight long trousers for evenings. We must make a list. Next time I am at yours, we will go through your wardrobe. You will need a suitcase too." He gave her a long-suffering look.

Michael had taken to popping in to see Olivia just before he started work. Having the car available was increasing his mobility. He was delighted to see that Olivia was putting on a little weight and the pallor was disappearing from her face. A very fetching wig covered up the baldness,

Michael, Waiting

and she had apparently been on a small shopping trip with her friend next door. The nurse's hours were being reduced as her strength came back. He told her excitedly about the forthcoming trip to the Canary Islands and had her laughing over the game of golf.

The young bookkeeper, Richard, was blending in well, and he was able to follow Olivia's methods without too much difficulty. He had been told that though it must be tempting to make the system his own, he was not to change anything if he could help it. Richard was happy to oblige. The job was suiting him. He would come in around 9.00 a.m. using the keys he had been entrusted with and work until about 1.00 p.m. Alfredo would feed him, and he would head off to his other part-time job in the city centre.

Monica was pleased. Her prodigy was working well for Michael and Olivia. It would take so much pressure off. The restaurant was humming along. The staff were all working well together. Peter was now the permanent and full-time deputy for Michael, and Robert's hours were permanent too. Sylvia, proving to be a conscientious worker who took the same attitude to cleanliness, had also been made permanent. Olivia had agreed Michael should have two days off. However, the restaurant was continuing to prosper, and at a staff meeting, as Sylvia was unable to work more hours, it was decided to hire another part-time waiter. Part-time staff were invaluable in the catering business. If they were able to change hours to suit the diary, it was better still if they were flexible and able to work at the drop of a hat, should the need occur.

The restaurant welcomed the new addition to the staff. She would be flexible, as she was a widow with grown-up children but was not yet a grandmother. She had time on her hands and a wealth of catering experience. The team happily included the new waitress, Ann Whyte, into their midst.

Olivia, while delighted the restaurant was doing well, felt sadness as she slowly realized her presence was not strictly necessary, thanks to her appointment of Michael and his subsequent hiring of staff who were fitting in and contributing to the atmosphere of the place.

More golf was played as the summer months arrived, and Olivia continued to stay on an even keel. The impression was given that she was making a slow recovery. Soon Monica and Michael would be flying out to Tenerife for the week in the sun. Olivia had suggested she pop into the restaurant every day as she felt more able to return to overseeing the premises. Michael made her promise she would only have a look-see to make sure all was well but not to interfere with Richard.

Michael confessed to Monica that he couldn't swim as they were thirty-six thousand feet in the air, heading for Tenerife South Airport. Monica had been chattering on about what they would do to amuse themselves. Monica had mooted a daily swim and perhaps hiring clubs and playing a couple of rounds. Tenerife, Monica explained, was popular with tourists for golf.

Digesting the fact that they had a villa with a pool for a week and Michael couldn't swim gave Monica the giggles. Recovering, she told him in no uncertain terms he would learn and she would teach him. "I used to be in a swimming team when I was a schoolgirl," she told him. "I think I can teach you enough to be able to get from one end to the other."

On arriving at their home for a week, Michael was astounded at the beauty around them. The villa was small but lovely. The pool sparkled like diamonds under the blue sky. There were olive trees and vines. A barbecue around the back was built in, and they decided to use it as often as possible. It wasn't so easy to have a barbecue in Scotland, and certainly not to plan one ahead of time.

The week passed quickly, and Michael did manage a few strokes. He found he rather enjoyed the sensation of swimming; however, he was rather surprised how cold the water was in spite of the thirty-degree heat of the Canarian sun. They had discovered a small family-run restaurant very close to their accommodation. It was a delight. The food was excellent and all cooked to Canarian styles. To Monica's delight, the menu included several fish dishes. The restaurant, Sabor Canario, was well run, and the three waiters worked tirelessly to keep up the standard.

Michael was pleased to observe them working, especially when they carried trays brimming with drinks, holding the round tray with 3 fingers. Michael was impressed, and before they went home, one of the waiters, Nacho, demonstrated how it was done. Then, as they had made frequent use of the restaurant, they bade farewell to Katerina, Nacho, Fabio, and the boss, the most excellent Chef Diego. They would be missed.

All too soon, it was time to go back to the airport and home to reality.

Michael, Waiting

Michael confessed to Monica just how much he had enjoyed the time away and that he hoped they could do it all again another time. Happily, Monica agreed. She had a plan for their next trip, but she decided to keep it secret for now.

Chapter 38

Olivia was pleased to see Michael back. She did not grudge him a moment of his holiday, judging by his demeanour and comments that he had really enjoyed himself. Olivia was content to see her valued employee flourishing in his relationship. She couldn't, for the life of her, understand how they had got together, and they were now, she suspected, very much in love. Looking back, she thought about the way he had been treated when Monica and her friends came to dine and how he had managed to put that to one side. She was still to find out about the collaboration on the business plan.

Michael, a true professional, glided back into his role in the restaurant and picked up the reins at once. He was enjoying his new-found seniority, and his ambition was now a reality. However, he was not too happy with the way Olivia looked. As far as he was aware, all her treatment had been completed and she now should be in a period of recuperation. A spasm of guilt permeated through his body as he realized that she had probably taken responsibility for his duties when maybe she was not fit enough. He decided to speak to her about it and ensure she got plenty of time off. Thinking about his own recent break, he considered that maybe he could persuade Olivia to go for a week in the sun.

On one of his newly awarded days off, Monica unfortunately had to work. He was meeting his father for lunch, this time in the city centre, and it was at this time Michael decided to ask his father advice of a very delicate nature. "What's the best way to propose?" he blurted out. Mike, resisting a smile, looked over at his shy and earnest son, knowing this was one of the hardest things he would have to do. He gave him as much insight into how this would go, even including Monica turning him down, which Mike doubted would happen. He recommended he present her with a fait accompli and choose a ring that was a bit unusual. He offered to show him a shop he had frequented himself and be on hand to give an opinion on the choice.

They finished lunch, and true to his word, Mike towed his son around the corner to one of the several antique jewellers in Rose Street. Entering the shop, Michael was astonished and not a little fearful. There were so many beautiful objects shining in the lights of the shop. Spellbound, he let his father do the talking, and before he knew what was happening, two trays of very impressive rings were placed on the counter in front of him. They were all so beautiful, and Michael was mesmerized. There was a beautiful single diamond with a circle of green stones, and a solitaire he liked too. However, Mike asked him which month she had her birthday. Puzzled, Michael replied,

"Next month, May." The jeweller then explained about birthstones and added that May was represented by emeralds. The jeweller suggested he could base his choice on that.

A half hour later, Mike and Michael were strolling to the bus stop, discussing the purchase Michael had made. True to the workings of the jewellery business, the ring was chosen and a deposit paid. It was arranged that an exchange could be made should the young lady dislike his choice.

It was also suggested that Michael try to find the correct size, and the ring could then be sized to fit. Mike told him the best way would be to try to find a ring she already wore, as it would be unlikely he could wrap a pipe cleaner around her ring finger. The thought of that touched the chuckle muscle, and they were both laughing uproariously, ignoring the stares from passers-by.

Michael was meeting Monica at her house after she finished work, and she was planning to make them a meal. She was a decent cook, and he was not a fussy eater, so he was confident that whatever she planned would be thoroughly enjoyed. However, the major task was to be able to size the ring. He had almost an hour before Monica would be home. He let himself in with his newly acquired door key and bolted upstairs to her bedroom. He felt a little uncomfortable invading her space uninvited, but it was important, so he swallowed his reluctance and opened her jewellery box.

His first thought was that she did not have much in the way of jewellery, and he decided to change this if he got a favourable response to his all-important question. There were only two rings, one of which was a single pearl, and the other, he thought, a large garnet. There were no emeralds. He knew he couldn't possibly remove either of the rings until tomorrow morning, when he had offered to return. He noticed a small tab at the edge of the tray and pulled it, revealing a bottom compartment where her wedding ring and engagement ring lay nestled in the velvet of the box. Obviously reluctant to part with them, she had stowed them where they wouldn't be seen.

Remembering the small plastic stick with the ring sizes showing a marked hole the jeweller had given him earlier, he decided to use the wedding ring and compared it with the ring sizer. He smiled to himself as he realized she had a finger size which to him seemed apposite. Secreting everything away back to how he had found it, he went downstairs and put the kettle on. He noticed in the kitchen a bottle of red wine was standing on the worktop. Realizing that she was planning a red wine dish, he promptly opened the wine to let it breathe.

They had a comfortable evening, still reminiscing about their much enjoyed holiday, and as Michael's car was back in his own lock-up, which was becoming the norm, he stayed the night. The next morning, after Monica had gone to work, he got up, showered and dressed, and walked into town to the jewellers. Finding the same jeweller on duty, he explained his find and gave him the information, which would enable the ring to fit the first time. To everyone's delight, it appeared the previous owner had also been an M and no alterations were necessary. The ring was put into its velvet nest in the ring box, and the remainder of the cost paid. Putting the precious parcel into his inside pocket, Michael thanked the jeweller profusely, remarking that should a wedding ring be necessary, he would be back. "I am sure it will be necessary," answered the jeweller, "and I look forward to seeing you again."

During the choosing, sizing, and anxiety surrounding such a major purchase, Michael had forgotten to be nervous about the forthcoming proposal. It all came rushing back, and he wondered what he would do if she said no. He had already decided to ask her on her forty-fifth birthday, which was in a few days. As the cold sweat ran down his arms, dampening his shirt, he remembered a quote sometimes attributed to Sir Francis Drake:

"Faint heart never won a fair lady." With this in mind, he straightened his back and resolved to face this with courage and determination. A bit of romance would probably not go amiss either.

The days dragged past, and Michael tried not to let his anxiety show. He did, when questioned, admit to Monica that he was worried about Olivia, which was the truth but not the whole truth. He had decided he would pop into Jenner's, the department store, and purchase some perfume, as Mike had explained she would be expecting a gift of some sort.

"Perfume!" said Michael, aghast.

"It's not a problem," Mike said, reassuring his son. "You just go to the perfume section, and they will be only too glad to help you." He added with a laugh, "Take your credit card."

Off he went on his morning time off. He used the bus, as he did not have the time to walk, which would have been his preference. The weather was getting better, and as the Sunday was his day off, he would be attempting golf again. Nervously he sidled up to the perfume counter and was able to catch the eye of a smart middle-aged lady to assist him with his purchase. Unbeknown to Michael, the middle-aged sales lady had sized him up and already decided he was a beginner in the perfume purchasing game, and she decided to go easy on him. Besides, he was very personable, and with his startling blue eyes, he cut a handsome figure.

The lady was easy to talk to, and Michael told her the reason for his visit. Before long, the entire situation was being laid bare, and five bottles of various perfumes were brought out for him to choose. A memory struck way back in his mind. His mother had used a perfume called Tweed. He hadn't been overly keen on the fragrance, but he also remembered his mother laughing with Angela when they were discussing a film they had seen starring Marylyn Monroe. Apparently she had been known to brag that all she wore in bed was Chanel No. 5. He picked up the bottle with the trade name Chanel and looked at it thoroughly. He thought the packaging was smart and not too ostentatious, and he rather liked the thought of Monica in bed with Chanel No. 5.

With the gift chosen and wrapped as only it could be in an upmarket store, he decided a card was appropriate too and headed to the stationery department. He had given a lot of thought to this venture, and now he had a card bought, perfume, and an engagement ring. He had also been into the Canny Man's and booked the best table. He explained his motive, and the staff were only too pleased to help make it special. When the owner got wind of the occasion, he arranged for flowers to be presented at the appropriate time. Everyone had been so kind. *Now we only have to get a positive answer*, Michael thought. He had decided that if marriage was not on the cards, he hoped Monica would choose still to be his friend.

The days passed, and the fateful evening was upon him. He arrived early and placed the pretty gift-wrapped perfume and card at Monica's place setting along with a red rose (a last-minute idea from his stepmum, Patricia). He had a whole new family rooting for him. Patricia had remarked she needed an excuse to go dress and hat shopping. Both Mike and Michael paled at the thought. "What have I started?" Michael asked of himself.

Monica floated into the restaurant complete with a glorious dress and jacket, looking wonderful. As Michael rose to his feet, they kissed, and he pulled out the chair remarking on how beautiful she looked. Spotting the gift, she asked excitedly, "Is this for me?" Michael agreed it was and, wishing her a happy birthday, handed her the gift and card as she admired the rose. Always meticulous, she took time to remove the gift wrap. She had led her life being meticulous and orderly, and she was fond of the words of Confucius, who maintained that one should not be afraid of perfection because one will never reach it. The gift unwrapping ended to reveal the bottle of perfume

Michael had so thoughtfully bought. Her eyes lit up, and she exclaimed, "How wonderful, I have always wanted Chanel No. 5."

With an inward sigh of relief, Michael thought, *Success number one*. He was now in a quandary. Should he go with the original plan of proposing after the meal, or should he get it over with? He was not sure he would actually be able to eat in the former case, as his nervousness was beginning to show. In the end, he chose to eat, as he knew the champagne he had ordered would probably go with dessert.

A beautiful bottle of Châteauneuf du Pape arrived to go with the steak, and they both ate with pleasure. Michael was doing all right and managed to finish the beautifully cooked food. A while later, the dessert menu was offered, and Monica agreed they could wait a few minutes while the red wine was consumed.

Michael, Waiting

He could delay no longer. The last dregs of the red wine were gone, the waiters waiting for their cue. Michael checked his inside pocket for his treasure, almost disappointed he had remembered to bring it. His hands were clammy, and as he looked across the room, he saw the thumbs up from the owner. Nothing else for it, he stood and took the little square box out of his pocket and dropped to one knee.

As Monica's mouth began to form an *O*, Michael asked Monica whether she would do him the honour of becoming his wife. He opened the box and offered it to her. There was a moment of silence, as Monica obviously had not expected this, and various expressions flitted over her face. Michael's heart missed a beat as it dawned on him she was going to say no.

Then, to everyone's delight, especially Michael's, Monica gave him the answer he craved. A loud pop resonated though the establishment as the champagne cork was ejected, and Mark, the owner, presented Monica with flowers. Michael, his heart racing with delight, nerves, and almost everything else, quietly slipped on the ring. Monica, with tears in her eyes, told him she loved him and the ring was perfect. Michael reiterated how much he loved her and hoped they would have a long and happy life together.

It was quite a party atmosphere in the Canny Man's as the word spread and the customers came over and congratulated the happy couple. Michael felt as if he were in a dream, and he knew not how he had achieved this goal. He now had a wife-to-be and had fulfilled his ambition to be a head waiter. Monica was suitably stunned. She'd had no idea he would propose. In her mind, she had hoped one day he would, and she immediately thought that now was good, as it would give them time together. She had already thought she would have a wedding soon, as they were both in their mid-forties and the time they had left was precious.

Michael wanted to call for a taxi, but Monica said no. It was a lovely, warm night, and she wanted to walk and talk while going home. The champagne on top of the beautiful red wine was having a relaxing effect on them both. She wanted to walk arm in arm and discuss their future. Michael would have given her the moon if he could have. She had made him so happy. First of all, Michael thanked her for accepting his proposal. Monica admitted she had been taken aback, but a refusal was not on the cards. She then indicated that a wedding soon would suit her, as they were both in their forties. She wanted a quiet wedding, an exotic honeymoon, and a long and happy life. "When do you propose we can get married?" he asked her.

"Oh, I think we should have the wedding as soon as the festival is over and before the Christmas rush. End of September maybe."

He looked at her in astonishment. This wonderful lady wanted to marry him, and soon. "Where do you want to get married?" asked Michael.

She replied, "Let's ask at the Braid Hills Hotel and see what availability they have. It doesn't have to be a weekend. In fact, it would be better all-round if it was midweek." She turned to him. "Would Olivia let us have the wedding in Dhugall?"

"Oh gosh, I don't know," replied Michael. "I mean, she would have to close the restaurant. We will be filling it with guests, so she won't lose out; we can probably fill the tables. I will need to check it out, but it's a good idea."

As they walked up the hill discussing their plans, Michael was aware of very bright headlights coming their way. Seconds later, he realized a vehicle was travelling towards them very fast.

Spotting they were on the pavement, Michael pushed Monica into the hedge next to the pavement, but the vehicle collided with Michael, who somersaulted through the air over the bonnet of what was obviously a Range Rover and landed on the opposite side of the road. The car coming up the hill managed to swerve round Michael but hit the Range Rover on the side. Trying to avoid being hit, the driver of the Range Rover swerved but ploughed into the lamppost on the pedestrian island. Airbags went off all around, and Monica, screaming Michael's name, ran across the road to be with her fiancé. It was obvious the passenger of the Range Rover was in a bad way. He had gone through the windscreen, having not fastened his seatbelt, and the big marshmallows of the air bags were slowly beginning to deflate.

The emergency vehicles arrived very quickly, and Michael was driven away swiftly, leaving a grief-stricken Monica looking longingly at the departing ambulance. The police arrived, and witness statements were taken. For the first time in her life, Monica felt helpless. As she had consumed so much alcohol, she would not be able to drive. Her car was just around the corner too. A kind young policeman offered her a lift after her statement had been taken, and when she arrived home, she contacted Mike, who was thankfully not on duty. He immediately offered to collect her and take her to the hospital.

It seemed as though a lifetime passed before Mike arrived with a tearful Patricia. By now Monica was frozen with fear. They clambered into the car and headed off. It seemed as if the hospital was a million miles away; fortunately Mike had a parking pass, being senior staff. It would appear his status afforded him with some degree of respect, and his questions were given due deference.

Although it had looked bad at the scene, the alcohol intake had helped Michael as he flew through the air, and although his landing had taken a lot out of him, he was likely to recover. In theatre at present, Michael was having his spleen removed, and his arm and leg were being reset, as compound fractures in both limbs had occurred when he made contact with the vehicle. The police had taken statements and had come to the conclusion that this was a deliberate attack on Michael by the thugs he had reported to the police, who were currently out on bail. Monica groaned. "Is this ever going to end?" she sobbed.

Mike took her hand, spotting the ring he had helped choose. "Don't worry too much," he said gently. "Michael is fit, and although he looks bad at the moment, I am sure his inherent strength will pull him through. He is in the best place, and his surgeon is excellent. I really admire his work. He will get better, and the two of you will have the life you want." He then added, "Congratulations too, by the way," rubbing his finger over the emerald and diamond ring that had been placed on her finger only two hours prior. Monica sobbed quietly, acknowledging Mike's words of encouragement. She was somewhat reassured but elected to stay with him until he was out of danger. The three most important people in Michael's life settled down in the relatives' room and prepared for a long night.

Chapter 39

Around four o'clock in the morning, just as dawn was breaking, a nurse crept into the relatives' room, where she was faced with three sleeping relatives who had finally succumbed to exhaustion. Thinking her news could keep a little longer, she turned and attempted to creep out again. She hadn't reckoned on Mike's long association with irregular hours and light sleeping, as he sat up and asked the nurse what the status was.

Mike's voice disturbed the ladies, who were soon awake. With trepidation they prepared themselves for the news. It was good, the nurse explained. The consultant would be with them in an hour or so to explain the medical facts to them. At this moment, Michael was in the recovery room after a successful operation. Offering them tea, the nurse left the room, and the small group of relatives looked at each other with some relief. Mike looked at his watch and noticed his son had been in theatre for approximately five hours or more, and straight away he surmised the injuries had not been straightforward. Keeping silent on that piece of deduction, he gratefully accepted the tea the young nurse had brought in.

The consultant came into the room just before 6.00 a.m., apologizing profusely for the delay. He explained he had had to deal with an emergency with another patient and was only now free to give them his undivided attention. He knew Mike quite well and asked him to introduce his family. Once everyone knew who was who, the consultant, John, his correct title being Mr. Fellowes, began to explain Michael's condition.

He first explained that there had been a few sticky moments when he had first been brought in and that he'd had to be stabilized before they could operate. That had to be done quickly, as he was bleeding internally from his spleen. Once Michael was in theatre and his spleen had been removed, things started to settle down. His right leg had been fractured in two places, and his right arm also. Monica was the only person there who was able to confirm Michael was, in fact, left-handed. Several ribs had been broken, and at one point his right lung collapsed. However, Dr Fellowes said he was stable for now and in an induced coma to help the healing process and avoid the massive amount of pain he would normally suffer at this time.

The trio fell into a stunned silence, having no questions to ask. John Fellowes had been very thorough in his description of Michael's condition, and Mike stood to shake his hand and thank him for his handiwork during what would have been a very difficult time. Waving away his thanks, John indicated they could go in one at a time and see Michael, very briefly, and return in the evening. However, it was unlikely Michael would be conscious over the next couple of days. His progress would determine when they would attempt to bring him out of the coma.

They went in one by one, and when they had all had a chance to visit, they regrouped and headed for the car. The two ladies were taken aback by his pale, waxy complexion. He was so still. As Mike steered his wife and daughter-in-law-to-be out to the car and settled them as best he could, he explained to them what had happened and described Michael's injuries and what would be happening next. Both ladies were in tears. The shock, the worry, and now a little glimmer of relief had finally hit home, and the dam burst.

Mike took his time driving home. Although he was alert, he did not want to take a chance that his lack of sleep would affect his driving, and he took it slowly. It was daylight, which helped, and he pulled up at Monica's house half an hour later. Discussion in the car resulted in Monica being asked to stay with Mike and Pat. Arriving at her house, she collected a few necessities before going back to Mike and Patricia's spacious home.

Patricia had not enjoyed the situation of Monica being left to her own devices and felt the better option was for her to stay with them. Monica had been given Michael's possessions, as there was no place in intensive care they could be left. Fortunately, amongst the few things he kept in his pockets were his mobile phone and his keys.

He had not got around to getting a key for Monica, and she knew she would need to access his house over the coming days and possibly weeks. It was the phone she wanted most, because Olivia would need to be told. Patricia had made some bacon sandwiches and suggested they all try for a nap, and later in the day they would phone for an update. As it was approaching eight in the morning and breakfast had been consumed, Monica made the call she was dreading.

She ended the call some ten minutes later, having exhausted all Olivia's questions. It was obvious the lady was really fond of Michael and had been very upset when she got the news. She was even more upset when informed of the visiting being restricted to family only for the next two or three days. Monica had patiently explained about the induced coma and assured her she would let her know as soon as she could when Michael was conscious and ready to receive visitors.

Patricia showed Monica to the room she had been preparing whilst the difficult phone call was being made. Mike had volunteered to let Angela know. She had, after all, known Michael since he was born. Duty done, the exhausted family crawled into their respective beds and were soon fast asleep.

Meanwhile, Olivia, having arrived at the restaurant and passed on the bad news, was very upset. She had thought of Michael as a surrogate son, and now he was lying in intensive care and she couldn't get to see him.

The cold hand of fear clutched at her heart as she realized Michael would not be able to work for some length of time, and she was afraid of what would happen to the restaurant in that time, as her own health issues, under wraps for the time being, would put her in the position of not being able to help out.

Her drug trial was over, and for now she was in remission. Only Michael knew about the precarious state of her health. She phoned Robert, as only Peter was due in today and she felt she needed both waiters to keep the place going in the absence of Michael.

During the first shift without Michael, Olivia did some thinking. She was still able to answer the phone, take bookings, and take back some of the ordering. She decided to arrange a staff meeting to ascertain just how much support she could expect from the four staff members still in place.

Mike had taken advantage of the time and had managed four hours' sleep. Being used to call-outs and late shifts, his body shut down when it could and reawakened with equal speed. He crept downstairs and phoned the hospital for an update. He was delighted to hear that Michael was resting quietly. He was still in the coma, but his vital statistics were good, and he displayed all the signs of stability. Mike was warned, however, that the patient was not out of the woods just yet. Mike thought about keeping the last part of the report to himself for now, but he realized it would do the ladies no favours; as intelligent grown-ups, they deserved to be kept in the loop.

Monica woke after a short sleep, and as she came to, the horror of the predicament came rushing back to her. Getting dressed, she glanced at her left hand. The beautiful emerald and diamond ring placed on her finger by Michael the night before was glinting in the light. Tears were not far away, as she realized it was only the previous night that he had proposed and they had excitedly started the planning for their wedding. Those plans would need to be put on hold for now.

She dried her tears, having indulged in her grief for a moment longer, and went downstairs in great need of a coffee. She found her hosts sitting at the kitchen table. The coffee filter had worked its magic, and she was invited to help herself. Mike reported on the current situation, having admitted he had phoned the hospital. There was a definite lightening of the atmosphere.

After the visit to see for themselves that Michael was in fact doing okay, they decided to go and have a bite to eat. The hospital staff had told them they would be attempting to bring the patient out of his coma during the afternoon of the next day, and if anyone of the family wanted to be with him, it would be arranged. They discussed the possibilities, and in the end, it was decided that Mike and Monica would be there, Patricia having committed herself to looking after the small grandchild, Katrina.

Sitting in the relatives' room, Mike explained to Monica what would happen next, and he stressed that it was by no means certain Michael would respond positively on the first attempt. If it failed, they would try again the next day. Continuing with the explanation, Mike also stressed that this procedure was successful only if the body was ready.

The next day dawned, and after checking with Michael's doctor, the family were told the procedure to bring Michael back into consciousness, and they waited in the waiting room until they were called.

To those in the waiting room, the next hour seemed like a lifetime.

Then the door opened and a nurse scooped them up and took them to the intensive care ward, where a very groggy Michael tried a smile. Mike just managed to catch Monica as she tried to hug Michael, which would have probably broken the rest of his ribs. She had to make do with stroking his good hand and telling him how much she loved him.

Michael was a bit disorientated. He wasn't sure where he was or why he was there. Mike gave his son as much information as he felt was appropriate. Mike had already wondered about the possibility of a head injury, but he had been assured there was no evidence of such an occurrence. A CT scan had been done.

They sat by Michael's bed, watching him slip in and out of consciousness. It was hard to watch. They had been assured that this would continue until the healing process was well under way. Michael was to improve greatly over the next few days, and when next they visited, they would bring Michael's toiletries and perhaps his dressing gown. They left after an hour with Michael, which was long enough for the patient. Monica would have been happier if she had been able to converse with her new fiancé, but she would need to be patient, as this was going to be a slow process.

Mike dropped Monica at the large shopping centre on the west side of the city. First of all, she went into a large clothing store and bought a new dressing gown and a couple of pairs of pyjamas. Ever the optimist, Monica purchased new slippers and added them to the bag. She next headed to the chemist to purchase a toilet bag, complete with appropriate toiletries, and then went to the nearest bust stop to head home. Once in her house, she removed all the labels and price tags, but she had the foresight to keep them safe just in case the sizes were wrong. She then put all the items into a travel bag.

She got into her car and drove to Mike and Patricia's house, stopping on the way to purchase a large, very attractive bouquet of flowers. In some small way, it would underline how grateful she was for their support, but now she had to let them get on with their lives. No doubt they would be back and forth to the hospital as the days went on, and Mike would have access by working in the building. The unmistakeable sound of a crying infant assailed her ears as she mounted the three steps to the door. A harassed-looking Patricia, holding the infant, waved Monica into the house.

"Oh dear," said Monica with sympathy. "What can I do to help?"

"Oh, can you take her for a minute, please? I need two hands to fix her feed bottle."

Monica, looking down at the screaming red-faced infant, thought to herself, *I have been left holding the baby.*

Katrina fed lustily. She fell asleep over the dregs and was gently placed in her cot to sleep until the next time. Patricia put the coffee pot on and sat at the kitchen table with Monica, and over coffee and shortbread, she heard all about how Michael woke up and seemed to recognize them but was unsure of what had happened or where he was. Patting her hand gently, Patricia counselled that he would get better and that she needed to be patient. *Patient!* The word screamed in her head. Gritting her teeth, she managed not to say anything contentious and spent the coffee time listening to Patricia's exploits as a grandmother.

With Michael in intensive care, the visiting arrangements were pretty fluid. Monica and the MacGregors could visit anytime, so Monica headed off in her car just after 2.00 p.m. and decided to avail herself of the park-and-ride facilities near the hospital. Parking was so difficult, and she didn't have Mike's staff pass.

Carrying the travel bag containing Michael's necessities, she rang the bell for entry to the ward. After identifying herself, she was allowed in. She thought to herself that by the time Michael was well enough to go to an ordinary ward, she would be on first-name terms with the staff. Trying, for Michael's sake, to be cheerful, she spotted him before he saw her, and she was gratified to see him awake. He certainly looked much better after his sleep, and he did seem to be more aware of his surroundings.

Driving home, she was more optimistic about his chances, and after bringing Mike and Patricia up to date, she cooked herself some pasta and watched a little television before going to bed early. Monica resigned herself to the long haul.

Chapter 40

The days went by in a blur. Sometimes it would be Monica who would update Mike, and sometimes it was the other way around. Her boss had given her unlimited compassionate leave until her fiancé was out of danger and out of intensive care.

Meanwhile, the police had been busy. They had taken statements from all concerned, and the investigation was made easier by having the driver of the car that had knocked Michael down safely under arrest in hospital with non-life-threatening injuries. His passenger had no such luck, having died at the scene. He had rejected the safety of the seatbelt and had been thrown through the windscreen. They also had a clear statement from the driver of the oncoming vehicle that the Range Rover had struck Michael before ploughing into the lamppost. They had called a few times to update Monica but eventually had to leave a message to contact them, as she had been unavailable due to her intensive care vigil.

When they eventually caught up with her, Monica was relieved to hear that the driver would be charged with attempted murder, ensuring a lengthy prison sentence. Conviction would not be difficult. He was found at the scene, behind the wheel of the car that had ploughed into Michael. He was also being charged with the murder of the man found in the canal as one of the henchmen employed by the men, for which the men were serving life sentences. The policeman speaking with Monica announced cheerily, "Well, they will all be together soon."

Monica was pleased but was not convinced that it was over. "What are the chances of another attempt on Michael?" asked Monica, her bottom lip trembling. She really felt they had been through enough, especially Michael. A picture of her flying over a hedge would remain with her

Michael, Waiting

always, and the fact that Michael had effectively saved her life was not lost on her. The policeman somewhat condescendingly told her he had information that there were no more thugs around to cause any trouble and she was not to worry. "Save your worry for that lad of yours," he said over his shoulder as he made to leave. Monica shut the door thoughtfully. Having good manners, she did remember to thank the policeman, but she was not sure he was telling her the truth.

Glancing at the clock on the wall, she ran upstairs to get ready for another vigil at the hospital. Mike had a large operation scheduled for today, so he would not be able to see Michael. Monica had promised she would update him if he would care to phone her mobile when he was free. It had been two weeks now, and Monica was beginning to despair of progress. Happily, he was talking to her and quite lucid, so she had that to be grateful for, but she just wanted to see him more mobile. It would not be good for him to lie in bed all the time. She was being unreasonable, she knew; Michael had severe breaks in his legs, and they had to heal somewhat before they could bear his weight.

Arriving at the intensive care ward, she was stopped in her tracks by a long, rectangular metal box being wheeled out of the ward. Her immediate reaction was shock. She knew that this was the method of removing patients who had not survived. Her heart almost stopped with terror when she realized Michael's bed was empty and freshly made. With icy fingers clutching at her insides, she approached the staff nurse. Her voice quavering, she asked where Michael was. "Oh, hello, Mr.s Stevens, we were just about to phone and tell you to go to ward 24. Michael has made sufficient progress to warrant a move to an ordinary ward.

Monica whirled around and headed out of the door. She was in the corridor before she realized she didn't know where to go. Sheepishly, she rang the bell and, after thanking the staff nurse, asked for directions. It was a post-trauma ward and was easy to find once she had been pointed in the right direction. With a big smile, Michael greeted her as she arrived flushed and a little breathless. Never would she admit to anyone the effect the fright she had just received had on her.

Michael was exuberant. He had been told about his move at very short notice. He pointed to his travel bag and said that it had still to be emptied, but the best news was that the consultant was due any time soon to explain to them what would happen next. As Monica regaled Michael with the news from the outside world, Michael butted in to say that restricted visiting would come into play and he could be visited only from 2.00–5.00 p.m. and 6.00–8.00 p.m. Just then the surgeon arrived and greeted Michael. He was introduced to Monica, who vaguely remembered meeting him on the night of the accident.

Mr. Fellowes started to explain how Michael was progressing. The breaks were healing nicely, and it would appear that he would be largely unaffected by the accident, other than perhaps a limp in damp weather. He had no head injury, and the constant drowsiness he had been experiencing was the body's way of healing.

He was much brighter now, and after a few days they would attempt to let him have the use of a wheelchair to help broaden his horizons. Weightbearing on his leg would take much longer. Three months was the guess, but regular X-rays would keep the team apprised of his progress. After asking whether the couple wanted any more information, he turned and left with their thanks ringing in his ears.

Monica and Michael looked at each other in excitement. Michael felt a sense of optimism and relayed that to Monica. "When do you think you will be well enough to get married?" she asked. "I know we had thought end of September or beginning of October to fit into the necessities of the restaurant, but could I suggest a spring wedding?"

"I want to marry you as soon as possible," Michael declared vehemently, "and as soon as I get a chance to speak to Olivia about it, we can set a date. That is, if you still want to have the wedding at the restaurant."

"Of course I do," replied Monica, "and I am pretty sure that when I phone and tell her you are in an open ward and can receive visitors, she will be here like a shot."

As the only visitors he had seen since he was hospitalized had been Mike and Monica, he was looking forward to seeing some new faces. They carried on with their discussion about the wedding, and it was plain to see the move had cheered Michael up immensely and he was beginning to feel better about the state he found himself in. Monica also reported the policeman's finding, and they were both horrified that one of the perpetrators dying at the scene did not faze them one bit. "Are we awful people?" Monica timidly asked Michael.

"No, I don't think so," replied Michael. "He was trying to kill us. He deserved what happened to him."

Sure enough, as soon as Monica made the calls to Mike and Olivia indicating freedom to visit, there was a steady stream of visitors pleased to be able to see for themselves that Michael was on the mend. That very afternoon, Olivia arrived with a beautiful fruit basket, a book to read, and, for a bit of fun, the current issue of the magazine *Weddings*. As she beamed at Michael, taking a seat, she asked the age-old question "How are you feeling?" Michael answered positively, remarking on how much he had missed her.

Monica had deliberately left late, arriving at the very last minute, to enable Olivia and Michael to have a good catch-up. She wasn't quite ready to give up visiting yet, so she arrived around four thirty, to be told by a happy Michael that yes, the wedding would be able to take place at the restaurant at the date most suitable for the couple, but to give her a week or two's notice. Yes, they would be able to close the restaurant. Olivia had asked about the ceremony. When told they would like a humanist service, Olivia indicated she would have the appropriate permissions done as soon as possible. On hearing they hadn't a celebrant in mind, Olivia told them about an acquaintance who was a humanist celebrant and would ask him what dates he might have. With that settled, Olivia, after kissing Michael on both cheeks, to his complete surprise, swept out of the room a much happier lady.

The days and weeks passed slowly; Michael's recuperation was taking just about as much time as they had been told all these weeks ago. One rather pleasant day in August, when Monica went in to visit, Michael had some news. Monica had been going to work part-time after Michael had been moved to the main ward. He was now in a four-bedded ward and at least had some company. "Monica," he said, smiling hugely, "if you are up for a wander, they have said you can take me out into the gardens in my super-duper electronically driven wheelchair. What do you think?"

Monica was a bit nervous, but not being able to disappoint him, she agreed. Later, as she helped get him settled in the chair he had become accustomed to when not moving around, she thought the wander had been worth it to see the light come back into his eyes.

They were surprised when the surgeon arrived seconds after they had.

"Next phase!" he exclaimed. "Tomorrow will be a big day for you, Michael. We—my team and I—are going to get you up on your feet. Your leg is not quite ready, perhaps another two or three weeks, but it is healing well. Tell me, Michael, do you participate in sport?"

"Yes," replied Michael, "I do a bit of running."

"That will help the healing process. Tomorrow we are going to get you upright and using crutches. Are you up for it?"

Monica couldn't wait until the afternoon visit the next day. Would he be upright, or had it failed?

When she arrived, his bed was empty, but his wheelchair was there. She heard her name called and looked around. There at the window was an upright Michael on crutches, walking towards her. She was ecstatic, and as he swung himself into his chair, he put his arms out to be hugged until he thought he couldn't breathe.

It was another month when the news was the best they had had. He was to have his plaster removed from both arm and leg. He would use the crutches to help take the weight and would go a prolonged physiotherapy programme. He was to be discharged the following day. It had already been arranged that when this magical day arrived, he would go to Mike and Patricia's house and use the downstairs study as a bedroom to avoid stairs. There was a downstairs shower room he could use. Mike had had this mini suite arranged when his children were teenagers and he worked long and antisocial hours. It would surely be useful now.

Chapter 41

The physio had been a great success, and the couple had set the date. Not wanting to wait until the spring, they decided on 1 December. Olivia had discovered that the venue of Dhugall would be suitable, as she had checked with the Humanist Society that as long as the venue was a safe and dignified place, as stated on the Humanist Society website, the wedding could go ahead. Olivia had already given them a phone number, as she had an acquaintance who was a celebrant.

The couple were delighted. The guest list was small but intimate. Some of the staff would be permitted to watch the ceremony and return to their duties when the formalities were over. Michael had spoken to the chef, Alfredo, and they had chosen a fairly simple wedding meal. There was to be a choice of beef Wellington or a fish pie, and Alfredo had on standby a vegetarian option should it be necessary. Michael had asked for his favourite, cranachan, for dessert, and a cheeseboard was provided for those not in possession of a sweet tooth. They still had to decide on a starter; soup was the obvious choice, but Monica was a fan of prawn cocktail. Eventually Olivia decided and requested the chef to make both lentil soup and prawn cocktail, and the food was settled.

Olivia was really touched when they decided to be married in the restaurant. It was to be her wedding gift to the couple. In spite of her bad health, she was feeling particularly good just now. Watching Michael's fight back to health had been difficult, but now she would see him marry the woman of his choice, and together they would be good for each other.

Monica, meanwhile, was searching for "the dress". The shops were getting busier in November. With some of the shops already dressed for Christmas Monica exclaimed to herself, "It's only November" as she battled with the early Christmas shoppers. As she headed through her department store, she gave a wide berth to Santa's Grotto, which was a beautiful display with a winter wonderland feel. But not having much time—her own fault, really—she needed to find something appropriate to wear. She had put a lot of thought into it. Michael, she knew, would be in his highland dress, and she had some years back had her day with her "blancmange moment". She shuddered at the memory of yards of lace and tulle worn the first time round, but she had been very young, and the thought of looking like a princess for the day had influenced her choice.

She headed for the bridal section to see what was on offer. She really didn't know what she wanted, and she asked the sales assistant to help her. Fortunately, the middle-aged assistant was a down-to-earth kind of person and recognized the traits in Monica.

Establishing she was second-time-round bride and did not want fuss, the saleslady went over to a section where it was immediately obvious the dresses, although bridal, were not as fussy. Selecting four dresses the sales assistant hung them on a rail where they could be seen in all their glory.

It didn't take Monica more than about five minutes before she picked a dress in a rich ivory brocade which was ballerina length with a matching bolero. Trying it on, Monica was enchanted with the dress. It fitted to perfection and the length, reaching halfway down her calves, looked amazing.

From behind her back, the saleslady produced a fascinator with feathers and ribbons, which sat on the side of her head, finishing the outfit. Monica, not usually emotional, felt the tears rolling down her cheeks as she saw herself in a wedding outfit. "It's perfect!" she exclaimed. She looked down and took in the sight of her sensible black shoes. Ruefully, she looked at the saleslady and pointed at her feet. "What about shoes?" she asked. "I'm going to need a pair to match. I can't walk through to the shoe department dressed like this!" "Don't worry," the saleslady said in a soothing voice. "My colleague is on her way and will bring a suitable selection for you to try on."

After the size and preferred style were confirmed, it was not long until the young assistant produced a choice of six pairs of ivory shoes. As Monica tried them on one by one, it became clear to her that a pair with two-inch heels and a silk rose on the front was the preferred pair, as she

Michael, Waiting

kept coming back to them. Not being able to resist, Monica gave a twirl, showing she loved her choice.

After Monica had dressed in her street clothes, the saleslady packed up her outfit expertly in a large cardboard box and the shoes in another. Monica took advantage of the delivery option, and after paying the rather hefty bill, she left the store in a very cheerful mood. Somehow the cost was absolutely not an issue.

Fortunately, Monica, being a private person, managed not to spill the beans and tell everyone about her outfit. *They will see it soon enough*, thought Monica. It was unconventional, but then their relationship had started out that way.

Michael had expressed a desire to have his father act as his best man, which had touched and pleased Mike. Monica had managed to persuade her sister to be her maid of honour, and she also agreed to come a few days ahead of the big day to shop for a suitable outfit. Monica was not concerned. Her sister was a petite size twelve, and there was no doubt that their needs would be met by the saleslady who had so beautifully dressed Monica. She took the precaution of telephoning a few days earlier to book a fitting session.

Michael and Monica spent the evening looking at holiday brochures, as the honeymoon needed planning. Although Michael was still not quite fit for resuming restaurant duties yet, it was planned he would return after a month in some sunshine, bringing them home just after New Year. With a bit of persuading, Michael agreed to book a beach villa on the Maldives. Secretly he didn't know where the Maldives were, but he trusted Monica's judgement, and she so wanted to go there. Michael was content enough that the first month of their new life together would be in the sun. She also insisted he accept traveller's assistance so he would be met at every stage with a wheelchair for his use. He made a token gesture of demurring, as it seemed as though only the previous week he had begun to rely solely on crutches. However, when Monica explained what was involved, he realized she was right. He was also back staying with Monica, as he was not too confident about driving.

The wedding day dawned. Michael had spent the night before in his own house and took a taxi with his best man, a very happy Mike, to the restaurant, where he was greeted with applause and cheering from the guests as he and his father appeared. In attendance were his father and Patricia, his half-brother and half-sister, baby Katrina, Angela, and, of course, Olivia. Monica had not invited many either: her three friends from the Friday-night meetings. Her son had telephoned from Canada expressing his sorrow at not being able to be there, but he pressed an invitation on the couple to come and visit as soon as possible.

Michael was able to stand for short periods, and he used his time wisely as he ensconced himself in his usual corner, awaiting the arrival of his bride. Contrary to tradition, Monica arrived on time with her sister, the matron of honour. The shopping trip went well, and Barbara had chosen a cerise-coloured two-piece which blended with her grey hair. They made a bonny couple. Refusing a limousine, she had arrived by taxi, and Peter, the acting head waiter, watching through the glass panels, saw her arrive.

Opening the door, he greeted her with a courtly bow as he escorted her into the restaurant. There was to be no father of the bride. Monica was a bit touchy about being given away.

A small stereo had been set up, and the strains of the Carpenters' "We've Only Just Begun" echoed round the room as Michael, almost paralyzed with fear and shock, stepped out of the shadows to greet his bride. The gasp as he took in the view of Monica in her incredibly beautiful outfit was audible She looked amazing. Michael had to choke back the tears as Monica made her entrance.

Monica and Michael had made the joint decision that it was to be a ceremony and a meal with no dancing, given their abhorrence of such activities. The meal, however, which was delicious, seemed to last forever as the couple talked to their guests, most of whom were interested in Michael's recovery.

To his complete surprise, Michael was enjoying himself, and he found himself fondly looking at his bride and congratulating himself on his good fortune. He had managed to get a few moments, while the register was being signed, to tell her just how beautiful she looked. "Monica," he said, "you look so beautiful. Your outfit is wonderful." Somehow compliments were becoming easier for him to deliver. She was, however, a beautiful bride.

All too soon, the evening ended, and Monica and Michael left their guests to finish up. With profuse thanks to their hostess, Olivia, and a

Michael, Waiting

flurry of confetti, they were off on an adventure which would take them halfway round the world. They were staying at a hotel close to the airport, as the flight out in the morning was leaving quite early. The first flight was a short one taking the couple to London.

Mike had retrieved the couple's luggage early in the day and had checked it in at the hotel to save Michael, who was still a bit unsteady, the trouble. Patricia and Mike would return in the morning to collect their wedding clothes.

The newly-weds checked in and were shown to their room. It was gorgeous. Apparently Mike had upgraded the couple to a suite, and as they looked around at the opulent surroundings, Monica glanced in the mirror and gave a giggle. The fascinator was beginning to slide and was now covering her ear. She pointed this out to Michael, and together they burst into giggles which rapidly developed into a kiss, and before long they were in each other's arms. With loving tenderness, they made love in the large bed provided by the hotel.

They had time for breakfast before leaving for the airport and reminiscing on the day, and with rising excitement they discussed their travel arrangements. Monica, always practical, mentioned over her toast and marmalade that when they got home, a bed like the one they had just slept in was a must!

Laughing, Michael went to reception to check out their taxi, but the hotel had a chauffeur-driven car, and it would be out front directly. Michael went to settle the bill with his brand-new credit card, having been talked into the card by Mike. Mike had also settled the bill beforehand. He had explained all the benefits of having a credit card where it would be safer not to carry large amounts of cash, especially abroad. Michael made a note to call and thank his father when they got settled in the hospitality lounge. Mike had also insisted he avail himself of a new smartphone so he would always be in contact. More technical support. However, Monica had helped him make the selection and would show him how to use the new iPhone.

On their arrival at the airport, Monica searched for the disabled assistance. It seemed like ages before she found it. *Michael will be worrying*, she thought. After a heated discussion which left Monica shaking and traumatized, she eventually arrived back to where Michael was waiting. He was indeed concerned.

The assistance had offered them a wheelchair but no one to push it. Monica patiently explained that she could not push a wheelchair *and* push a luggage trolley. Eventually they asked to speak to the manager. After the conversation with the manager, an airport porter arrived, and the job was done. "That was awful service," Monica complained. I will be writing a letter as soon as we get home."

"Better still, you can email him from the lounge," suggested Michael. Monica slowly turned around to face this technophobe who was now her husband. "Well aren't you learning fast."

With a burst of laughter, they arrived at the lounge. The service there was much better, and having had a large breakfast, they ignored the food, but the champagne could not be resisted. "Cheers," they said as their journey began.

Chapter 42

They boarded the flight which would take them on their first stage of the adventure. The flight lasted an hour, and with help from the wheelchair porters they were soon on the large Boeing Dreamliner. Having only flown once before on a tourist plane, Michael was flabbergasted at the spacious interior of the aircraft and the comfort of the seats. Michael had secretly worried about how well his recovering injuries would perform during the flights. He would, of course take medical advice and get up and move around. He then realized he was in first class. His father had struck again.

It was a smooth take-off, and before too long the cabin crew were getting into their stride, starting with complimentary drinks. A hot lunch followed, and as much as they were enjoying themselves and enjoying each other's company, they both dozed off, having felt the effects of their big day. They slept for a few hours but were awake in time to experience the landing into Dubai some nine hours later.

The view of some of the tallest buildings in the world was awe-inspiring, and as they landed with a gentle thump, the happy couple looked at each other with matching sparkling eyes. Even the pragmatic Monica was impressed. They were to spend a day and a night in Dubai, as it had been decided that all things had to be sampled. Monica found it very hot, and after a trip round the shops, most of them designer, she was content to sit in the cool air-conditioned splendour of their hotel.

Michael, too, was finding the forty-plus-degree outside temperature too much. It was almost dinner time, and they adjourned to their rooms to shower and change. Their suitcases had been kept at the airport for ease of transit, and their on-board luggage held enough for necessities.

Monica had had the foresight to pack a lightweight dress, and Michael had a linen shirt and lightweight trousers, having been warned of the high temperatures. What they were not prepared for was the height of their hotel; somehow the balcony on the twenty-fifth floor did little to encourage the duo to venture out.

The food was wonderful, with many choices. Michael discovered a taste for Indian food, and Monica, who was much better travelled, was able to sample some of her favourites. There was a live performer at the piano singing and playing softly in the corner, and Michael was aglow with excitement.

All too soon, it was time to be collected and taken to the airport for the final leg of their journey. Saying goodbye to Dubai was sad, but the ever practical Monica announced that it was a lovely place but so very hot. "At least," she said, "we will have the ocean to cool down if it gets too hot."

They were ferried to the island, which would be home for two weeks, in a speedboat which was referred to as the water taxi. Michael was so enchanted with what he was seeing: white sandy beaches, lush vegetation, and the sea going from turquoise at the beach to deep azure further out into the ocean. The necessary sunglasses provided a beautiful sight out on the water. Diamond-like spikes were shooting over the sea and sparkling in the sun. The water was flat calm, and there was hardly any movement as the water taxi took them to their destination. As they alighted on the jetty, small fish were darting just below the surface; and as they stepped into the waiting taxi, they looked at each other with delight.

A short distance in the four-by-four taxi took them to the main building, which housed reception and a bar restaurant. At the desk, it was explained to them that food would be served mainly in the restaurant. Breakfast would be delivered at nine each morning unless specified differently by the guest. For a small sum of money, food could be cooked barbecue style at their bungalow. A table and chairs were provided. A few minutes later, they were back on the water taxi, being ferried to their home for the duration. Minutes later, they were surveying their bungalow.

A large bed, as plush as the one in Dubai, took up most of the space in the one bedroom, which had a wardrobe and chest of drawers to accommodate their clothing. There was a lounge area with chairs covered in plump cushions and multicoloured throws. It looked like a Sultan's tent in the Arabian Nights. The ambience was furthered by the aroma of spice-scented candles lit and waving in the light breeze, placed at strategic points throughout the room. On the glass coffee table, situated between the two overstuffed chairs, was a ceramic bowl in vibrant colours containing a variety of fruit, some of which they were unable to identify, not having seen it in the local supermarkets back in Edinburgh. Michael expressed his enthusiasm to try the fruit and wondered how they might find out what was in the bowl. Monica, although equally enthusiastic regarding sampling the fruit, could not take her eyes off the bowl, which she thought was quite magnificent, along with the throws casually draped around the various pieces of furniture.

The guide to their accommodation, after giving them their instructions, pointed to a small drawer in a sideboard which held a list of the wheres and wherefores of the accommodation.

On looking at his watch, Michael suggested dinner and unpacking later. They had had the foresight to change their watches to the correct time when they landed, following the cabin crew's instructions. Monica had other ideas. She wanted to get out of her travelling clothes and put on something more suitable. The bungalow's bedroom was air-conditioned, but the rest was not, relying on the sea breezes sweeping in the open front to cool them down.

The en suite shower room was beautifully decorated with dried flowers. Scented soaps and shower gels took pride of place on a shelf.

The water cascading down her back was warm, a perfect temperature. Resisting the temptation to linger, Monica stepped out, clean and fresh, to allow Michael to avail himself of the delights of the shower.

There was a small concession to modern technology in the shape of a telephone, but upon examining it, Michael found it to be a communicating device only to reception and other bungalows. *Why would you want to talk to other bungalows?* Thought Michael. Shaking his head, bemused, he turned to go into the shower, which had been vacated by a now sweet-smelling Monica, who had tried all the scented stuff. He spotted a green light on one of the units. It was encased by a black box. Michael went over to examine the flashing light, and Monica appeared to let him know the shower was free, catching him looking at the alien box. "Oh good!"

Exclaimed Monica. "I thought there would be Wi-Fi. It did mention it in the brochure."

Shrugging his shoulders at the thought of his lack of knowledge in all things technical, Michael headed for the en suite to shower. For him the scent was sandalwood. He decided he liked the aroma and vowed he would purchase some for home. He was not usually one for "smelly stuff", but as he said, "New life, new habits."

Michael experienced the same feeling as Monica, not wanting to exit the soft, warm water cascading down his body. They had showered in the hotel in Dubai, but that now seemed a long time ago.

Michael, having dried himself after reluctantly leaving the shower, changed into casual trousers and a cool silk shirt, whilst Monica put on a wraparound dress in vibrant colours. *She looks amazing*, thought Michael. Then he thought better of it and actually said to her how wonderful she looked. Off they set to the main building, which took them on a short walk through lush vegetation, shrubs, and flowers. They found the restaurant going in full swing. A waiter scurried over to greet them and, after checking their accommodation key, showed them to a table.

It was a beautiful spot. The tables were centred around a good-sized pond with large koi carp swimming in the clear water. In the centre, a fountain tumbled water into the pond beside the fish. All around were ice sculptures and carved fruit. It was gratifying that the staff seemed to have a good understanding of English, and Monica, undaunted, asked the waiter what the fruits they had seen in the bungalow were. Pointing to each one in turn, they were not able to recognize guava, papaya, or persimmon. They were able, however, to sample pieces after their amazing dinner. They both ordered the swordfish, and they proclaimed it to be absolutely delicious.

It was obvious that the food in the resort was heading to the fish type of culinary offering, and there were plentiful portions with salads and rice. "Not much in the way of tatties and mince," commented Monica.

Michael looked into her glorious brown eyes and couldn't resist telling her how much he loved her. As he was not known for his openness, Monica was a trifle surprised but delighted, and she could not help but return the compliment. Michael then added, "Let's have dinner at the bungalow before we leave. I think it would be a very pleasant thing to do." Monica agreed, and after consuming more food than they could remember, the two headed off for a stroll back to their accommodation. The time change had knocked their body clocks out a bit, and they were both tired.

"Before we go in for the night, let's go and paddle in the water," pleaded Monica. Not wanting to disappoint, Michael rolled up his trouser legs, took Monica by the hand, and waded into the warm, calm water. The little fish were still there, and the occasional white horse was visible in the bright moonlit sky. The light of the moon pierced the darkness and reflected in the dark sea. There was a hint of the sunset on the horizon, and Michael exclaimed he thought everything was upside down. Monica, laughing, explained they were in the Southern Hemisphere and yes, they were upside down. As she laughed at his silliness, the happy couple headed back to their bungalow "to sleep, perchance to dream".

There were strange noises filtering into the bungalow as the newlyweds slowly came to after the best sleep either could remember. Michael wrapped his robe around him and ventured out for a look. To his delight, a chef dressed in his whites was cooking on the barbecue, and the table was set with orange juice, bread, and preserves, with what looked like mackerel and sausages cooking. The pair ate the lot.

It was a beautiful day, and they decided to get covered in sunscreen and lie on the extremely inviting sun loungers. They also had parasols, should the sun be too strong. Monica was looking very fetching in a cerise pink two-piece, and Michael, with his shorts, looked every inch the tourist. They spent the day leisurely reading, chatting, planning, and deciding on their future ventures.

The days went by in a flash, and apart from a couple of trips to the other parts of the resort, they spent most of the time eating and sleeping—and Michael improving his swimming. "How would you not?" he queried. "The water is so warm and inviting, and I do think the salt water is helping me keep afloat." Monica, with her nose in a book, enjoying her reading time, murmured that he was probably right.

Sadly, it came time to leave the island paradise and head off on the next leg of their adventure. They were going to spend a few days in Hong Kong and then go on to Hawaii before finishing up in Los Angeles.

The scariest thing they had experienced was landing in Hong Kong. With all the high-rise buildings, it looked too narrow to get through. However, they landed safely and were whisked away, after security and baggage collection, to their hotel for the three nights they would be staying. Deciding to use the tours specifically designed for a whistle-stop tour, they set out the next morning on the New Territory Heritage tour. They found it very interesting.

Amongst the amazing sights were Tsui SIing Lau Pagoda and a walled village at Shueng Cheung Wai. At the end of the day, they were exhausted, and after a delicious meal they went to bed early to rest for the next day, on which they would be on a boat for most of the day, touring the Island. The following and last day of their trip here involved the tour of Hong Kong, dinner, and a light show.

It seemed no time at all before they boarded the jumbo jet to fly them to Hawaii, where they would enjoy a more leisurely time at a beachside hotel. They took a couple of tours, but mainly they wanted to rest during the week they were there. Michael did try to fit more swimming into his daytime activities. It was good physio for him.

They liked Hawaii but not as much as their time in the Maldives. Hawaii was just a bit too busy and geared towards tourists—which, of course, they were.

Landing in Los Angeles International Airport with the fog rolling in, the weary travellers were beginning to wish they were home. Perhaps it was too much, all the travelling and stopovers. Still, a few days in LA, and then it was home. Of course, they had to visit Santa Monica Pier and try Forrest Gump's running shoes and then take a stroll down Rodeo Drive before ending up driving through Hollywood and seeing the big letters spelling "Hollywood" on the hillside. To their disappointment, they did not spot anyone famous. They soon got ready to board the aircraft which would take them closer to home.

Chapter 43

The newly-weds had had a wonderful honeymoon. As well as enjoying the food and sights of the various places they visited, they had made time to discuss their future plans. It had already been decided that Michael would move into Monica's house, and they had discussed what he would bring and what he would dispose of.

Monica came up with the best suggestion of all and asked Michael how he would feel about renting his house out. Most of the furniture was getting past its best, and he was getting around to replacing most of it. His new bed was a source of anxiety for Michael. He rather liked it and wanted to keep it.

Monica solved the problem by offering to move her bed, since it had been her matrimonial bed, replace it with Michael's brand-new king-size bed, and put the old one in the spare room. The old bed there could go to the dump as far as Monica was concerned.

Michael wanted to take only photographs; his clothes, of course; and a few bits and pieces which would not encroach on Monica's pristine and uncluttered home. She was very clear about one thing: that it was to be their home and that Michael was welcome with his possessions too.

After flying to Atlanta and changing planes, they were finally on the approach to Edinburgh Airport and home. To their delight, Olivia was standing at Arrivals with a beaming grin on her face. Hugging them both enthusiastically, she took them to her car. After fitting the luggage in and paying the exorbitant car parking fee, they drew out into the traffic and home. Not having the clothing to suit the much colder Edinburgh, Michael asked to be dropped at his house, and Monica at hers. With a toot and a parting shot of "See you in a couple of days," Olivia shot off to the restaurant happy in the knowledge Michael would be back soon. She had missed him, and the restaurant had missed him too. His quiet efficiency had been missed.

Sleeping apart for the first time in a month felt strange to both of them, but they had to get organized to start their new life together. There was mail to open and check. Possessions were to be rounded up and removed to his new home with Monica. The next day, Michael arranged for a small van to transport his bed and other possessions to Monica's house.

He had also arranged for the van man to remove Monica's bed to the spare room and remove the older single bed to the dump.

This would happen at the weekend, and Monica would have to oversee the removal, as by the weekend Michael would be back at work, albeit part-time for the foreseeable future.

Michael, having left Monica with his holiday clothes, packed another case with his necessities and drove to Monica's. It was a tight squeeze on her driveway but was manageable, and hugging his bride, Michael felt a sense of peace come over him. His need to tell her how much he loved her rendered him overcome with emotion, and Monica, glad to have her new husband back in her arms, was overjoyed.

He had not been enthusiastic about reading his mail and had not noticed an envelope addressed to him with "Police Scotland" embossed on the rear of the letter, but Monica spotted it straight away. Monica made him open it as Michael stood looking like a startled horse with the whites of his eyes almost rolling in his head. "When is this ever going to end?" he cried plaintively. Sure enough, his fears had some foundation. It was confirmed that the passenger of the car that ran him down was indeed on the payroll of the murderers recently jailed for life. The passenger had died at the scene; not wearing his seatbelt had ensured his injury would be fatal, but after a month or so, a full statement had been gleaned from the driver, whose airbag had taken the brunt of the collision, but who still had some life-threatening injuries from which he was recovering. He was well enough, though, it would appear, and Michael was being invited to the forthcoming trial to give a statement in court. The letter further asked whether they could interview him before the trial date came around.

"Maybe now this awful business will end," said Michael hopefully.

"Well, I hope you are right and that the last of them gets what he deserves," Monica said with anger and frustration in her voice.

"I will telephone them as soon as possible, but not today," Michael promised, and he proceeded to regain some normality by explaining his plans for moving to Monica's spacious home

The rest of the packing up of his bits and pieces would finish on his next day off. He wondered when that might be after his long break. Would he not be expected to work every day?

On that note, he felt joy at returning to his workplace and hoped that not too many changes had been implemented in his absence.

When he went upstairs to what was now their room, he was intending to unpack and get his holiday clothing washed—not that there was any rush, as it would be unlikely that they would be in use for some time. To his surprise, the suitcase was empty. Walking carefully downstairs again, still being a bit unsteady on his leg, he quizzed Monica about his clothes. She took him into the utility room behind the kitchen, and there the washing machine and the tumbler dryer were going around and round, happily doing their job. "It's all in here," said Monica smugly.

"Oh, that wasn't necessary!" exclaimed Michael. "I could have done that."

"No worries," she retorted. "The machine was going on anyway, and it really wasn't worth putting on a small load, so I did yours as well." We can repack our cases and put them above the wardrobe, ready for our next jaunt." She laughed at his stricken face. It was like a bell tinkling as she watched her husband finally come to terms with the end of bachelorhood.

Michael woke to an empty bed. He checked the bedside clock and, to his dismay, saw it was nearly ten o'clock. He quickly pulled on his robe and, remembering the fragile state of his limbs, went slowly downstairs to be greeted with the unmistakable aroma of bacon and coffee. Handing a steaming mug to her new husband, Monica remarked on his drowsy state and stated that the coffee might revive him a bit.

Thanking her profusely and apologizing for his sleeping in, Michael asked how she had managed to get bacon, and then he noticed the bulky white paper bag and rolls.

"Oh, I just popped into the shop around the corner. They have marvellous morning rolls. It's not barbecued mackerel on a beach, but it is the best Edinburgh has to offer," she stated, laughing.

Over breakfast, the couple did a bit of reminiscing and deciding what was the best experience and discussing the downside. They really couldn't think of anything really bad. There was the funny time when Monica tried to get a photo of Michael on their jetty when he stepped back too far and landed in the water. That caused a bit of laughter. And there was the time Monica came out of the shower and a gecko ran over her bare foot. My, how Michael had laughed when investigating the scream, only to discover it had been caused by a little lizard. They had been particularly careful with anti-bug repellent, and the bungalow had mosquito nets everywhere, but a few bites did occur and were really only subsiding now.

"The menace of the tropics," said Michael, "but it was worth it." Finally, it was time for Michael to get ready and head to work. Monica was not required to return to work until the next day. She promised Michael all the holiday clothes would be laundered and stored. Wishing him luck, she waved as he crossed the road and headed the short distance to Dhugall with anticipation. The holiday had done him good, as his walking had been aided only with a smart cane he had purchased in the Maldives. Part of his recovery was to walk as far as he felt comfortable, and as it was just over a mile to the restaurant, he decided to walk, but he promised Monica he would return by taxi for now.

Welcomed back with much enthusiasm, Michael was glad to see everyone, and looking around, he was even more delighted to see that it looked very much the same as he had left it. Olivia, with unaccustomed gentleness, asked him whether he could manage the stairs to her office, as she had a great deal to catch up on with regards to the events that had taken place in his absence.

It was apparent that information about his holiday was far more interesting to Olivia than the events at the restaurant. Gently steering Michael back on course, he gleaned that not much had happened in his absence. The police had come looking for him, she informed him, and she explained they had been told about his extended holiday. Michael told her about the letter and asked to use the phone sometime later that day.

Olivia told Michael she was coming in only three days a week and most of their administration was being dealt with by their part-time administrator. He was proving to be a big success and was helpful to Olivia, who by now was complaining of weakness and a nagging pain in her side. She told all of this to Michael, who was by now listening avidly, trying to see where the conversation was going. Michael asked about what treatment she was having, and Monica confessed to the fact that her treatment was, for the moment, stopped, and she was due another complete blood analysis, an MR.I scan, and another bone scan at the end of the following month.

Not giving his thoughts away, he pondered on what Olivia had told him. He didn't feel very optimistic, as he had been discussing the subject with his father. Obviously, Mike couldn't tell his son anything relating to patients, but he was able to give Michael an idea as to which way this was going. *It doesn't sound good; that is for sure*, thought Michael to himself.

Olivia suddenly changed the subject, as it appeared to be difficult for her to talk about her personal life with anyone. Michael was so very similar. Like Olivia, he was inclined to keep confidences to himself, and with his ability not to disclose any information he was trusted with, Olivia was comfortable sharing her innermost thoughts with him.

She explained she wanted him in the restaurant around three in the afternoon and to leave around seven or eight, depending how tired he was. Peter and Robert would be in every day except on their days off, which they alternated. Michael would always have one of them on duty and would remain until closing time. Olivia hoped that within the month he would be fit enough to manage more hours, but on no account was he to overstretch himself. "Slowly, slowly catchee monkey," she explained. This way, she went on to say, she hoped he would slip into his old ways very soon. Then she suddenly remembered to ask him how he was!

Michael explained that he was still a bit weak but his walking was improving daily and the holiday had helped immensely. "Well, I am going home now and leave you all to get on with it," she announced. "You can make your call to the police before you get stuck in to your chores. You will find not much has changed." She laughed. "Thought you would prefer it that way." She then vanished through the door and downstairs to a waiting taxi.

The police offered to come to the restaurant to take Michael's statement. They had already got the gist of it while Michael was in hospital, but this was to be more thorough. Michael was extremely unhappy at having to relive this all again and couldn't help asking plaintively whether this would ever stop, just as he and Monica had asked each other the same question.

With the statement taken, leaving Michael feeling like a bowl of quivering jelly at the memory of it all, the policeman, fully understanding how Michael must be feeling, was happy to report that there were no more risks to either of them, as the gang had consisted of only five members. One was found in the canal, two were already incarcerated, and of the last two, one was on trial, and the other in Mortonhall Crematorium.

Chapter 44

The days and weeks went on with Michael picking up the reins slowly and surely. He was happy to be there, and as his hours lengthened, he was able to meet and greet the regulars that he had come to know over the years he had been working there. The three ladies he had so dreaded on the first Friday were still coming and still eating from the specials board, not to mention the obligatory bottle pf Prosecco. He had talked Monica into joining them, and for now she tagged along.

The restaurant was full of chatter and laughter, and occasionally Mike and Patricia would book in for a night without children. Oh, they loved their precious Katrina, but a night with just the two of them was quite appealing, especially considering the long hours Mike had to work. Some weeks were particularly busy and they hardly saw each other. There had been some talk of retirement, but nothing had come of it yet.

The two deputies, Robert and Peter, who alternated their shifts, were becoming a great asset, and the little establishment just blossomed with the joy of good food, good wine, and good company. Michael was feeling particularly pleased with himself. He felt no residual pan in his arm, and only when he stood for long periods of time did his leg give out a reminder of the trauma it had been put through. All in all, it was a decent result.

Thinking it could be much worse, he was brought into the present by receiving a letter from the courts asking hm to present himself as a witness in the upcoming trial. It was only two weeks away now, and Michael thought that soon it should all be over. Then he read the small print, which indicated the trial may go on for some days and he had to be in court every day. He gave a big sigh. Just when he thought everything was going well, this had to happen. *I will just have to be resolute and get this thing over,* he thought. He did not quite believe the nice policeman who sought to reassure him regarding the possibility of further occurrences of violence to him—or, worse, Monica—but he had to put his dark thoughts to one side.

Now that he was back to work full-time and his previous shift patterns were now in full flow, he was able to visit his family, with Monica on Sundays. It was astonishing how quickly the baby, Katrina, was growing. With her having a few teeth and a crawl that could rival Lewis Hamilton, it was often difficult to keep up with her. Michael and Monica loved visiting the family.

Spring was just around the corner, and the golf course beckoned. They had discussed the possibility of playing golf when Michael's membership came up for renewal, and Michael was convinced his injury was so well healed he was sure he would manage at least nine holes at first. "We could always hire a buggy," he laughed.

The couple treasured these moments when they would discuss, chat, and make plans. Both were very much in love, and the relationship was going from strength to strength. They were bursting with happiness.

One Sunday morning, Michael had decided to make breakfast for Monica, as she had been rather good to him breakfast wise. He pulled on his tracks and a sweater, as it was not quite warm enough to go without. He planned to go to the small corner shop a few hundred yards away. *It may be small*, thought Michael, *but its stocks everything.*

He planned on buying sausage, bacon, and rolls. There were eggs in the house, and a few mushrooms. He picked up his keys and wallet from the hall table and opened the door. He was greeted by a familiar figure leaning on Monica's car with his legs crossed at the ankles and his arms folded across his chest. His thunderous expression left the observer in little doubt of his mood.

"What do you want?" Michael asked Derek.

"I want to see my wife, and I want to get back into my home!" he replied belligerently.

"Well," said Michael, "that's going to be difficult, because as you well know, you were divorced a year ago, Monica and I are married to each other, just in case there is any misunderstanding, and I live here with Monica."

"Yes, I thought you were sponging off my wife, moving into my home!"

Michael, Waiting

shouted the increasingly bad-tempered Derek.

Michael was bemused. "Is the man mad? He was divorced, and the property was awarded to Monica. Speaking of Monica, she is surely going to hear this ruckus, and I don't want her to come down and out to this." In fact, Monica had not been asleep when Michael had crept downstairs, but she had pretended to be asleep, as she thought she was going to get a cup of coffee in bed. However, she was not prepared for Michael leaving the house, and realizing he was probably going to the shop, she decided to have her shower.

When she came out all pink and scrubbed, dressed in her fluffy pink robe and brushing her wet hair, she was alerted to raised voices remarkably near their home. Knowing Michael had sneaked out the door, she wondered what on earth was going on.

She ran down the stairs, and through the frosted glass at the front door she could see two figures obviously having an argument. She went to open the door when she heard the voice of her ex-husband, Derek, and she froze, icicles round her heart. Thinking for a moment and deciding to stay behind the door, she assured herself she did so not out of cowardice, but as a way of not escalating the situation; and reaching for the phone, she called the police instead.

She grew concerned for Michael as she heard Derek's voice sounding more and more angry. She had taken abuse for all these years, and hearing the calm, reasonable tone of Michael trying to defuse the situation, she was furious. Why did this man continue to harass her? They were divorced. Why was he not moving on? He had a new partner; what was his problem.

Monica flew back upstairs and quickly dressed in her tracksuit. Her hair was wet, but that wouldn't matter. Racing downstairs again, she pulled open the door and asked her ex what on earth he was playing at. His voice held a note of tightly concealed anger as he explained that she was his wife and was living with another man in his home, and he wanted that to stop. Michael would move out and he would move back into his home.

Monica couldn't help herself bursting into laughter at this preposterous statement. In a cold voice, she explained that he could not bully her. They had been divorced for nearly a year, and he had no claim on the house. "Would you kindly stop harassing me and allow me to get on with my life, which will never include you?"

Without warning, Derek lunged forward and grabbed Monica by the throat. This took Michael unawares, and as he tried to free Monica from this madman's clutches, to his and Monica's relief, a police car drew up. The police were quick to size up the situation and managed to allow Monica freedom from this powerful adversary. It was obvious from the scenario that Monica's ex was guilty of assault, and he was put in the car handcuffed and supervised by the young constable while the sergeant went inside to the warm house and took Michael's statement.

The police car drew away with their prisoner in the back, and arm in arm, a shaken Monica and Michael went back into the house, all thoughts of bacon and sausage flying out of the window. Monica went into the kitchen and put the coffee pot on, feeling the need for caffeine. Michael went upstairs and showered while Monica, waiting for the coffee to brew, went upstairs and got dressed in day clothes because Michael had suggested going to the golf club for one of their famous breakfasts.

"It will make us feel better and we can put this aside," said Michael. "Make no mistake; I don't think we have seen the last of Derek. He really seems to be living in another reality."

"I heard on the grapevine," added Monica, "that he is on his own again, as he has been thrown out of yet another bimbo's flat."

"Oh dear," said Michael, not in the least sympathetic, but trying hard. "Do you know what I think? I think he tries it on with you because in his mind he can bully you and bend you to his will!"

"Do you think so?" Monica responded. "Absolutely," answered Michael.

The couple finished up their delicious breakfast and headed home for a quiet day. Monica suddenly suggested going out for a wee run, maybe to the coast. Michael thought this was a great idea. Remembering the holidays and how much the sea and sun had helped his recovery, he said as much to Monica, who couldn't help laughing at the thought of Michael taking a dip in the cold North Sea.

A couple of hours later, the Volkswagen nosed into one of the few parking spaces in North Berwick. Monica and Michael, now much calmer, walked along the seafront at North Berwick, eating ice cream with the prospect of a fish tea in another hour or so.

It certainly took the sting out of their rather fraught morning. "What do you suppose will happen to him now?" asked Monica.

"I'm not sure," replied Michael. "He has broken the terms of his court order, and the courts do take it badly when their wishes are ignored"

"Oh dear," said Monica. "Do you think they will put him in prison?"

"I don't know," he replied. "It is a fairly minor crime compared to some of the others that you read about in the newspapers. I guess we will just have to wait and see."

Secretly they were both anxious, but hiding their feelings from one another, they continued their stroll. To Monica's delight, some of the boutiques were open, and a browse was absolutely necessary. Michael suggested he take time out and went to the nearest cafe for a cup of coffee and gave Monica a chance to do her thing.

Michael was just beginning to get impatient when a flushed and excited Monica arrived breathless from walking quickly from the other end of town. On seeing the number of packages, Michael raised his eyebrows. Monica chattered on about her bargains. Reluctant for a fashion show, he suggested she wait until they got home and he could see her purchases to best advantage. But no, Monica had the bit between her teeth and gently pulled out a pale blue-and-silver silk scarf with rather an attractive peacock motif, followed by a rather pretty top in ivory with pale blue butterflies.

Finally, a dark pair of trousers was pulled out. *This is the last of her purchases*, thought Michael, However, she was not finished yet, as she pulled out a beautiful cashmere sweater which was principally black but had a checkerboard design in charcoal and grey. "Is that not a bit large?" queried Michael.

"It's for you, silly!" she exclaimed.

"It's very smart," he retorted, and he thanked her profusely while querying why she was being so generous.

"It was in a sale at half price. I couldn't resist."

Placing all her purchases carefully into the bags, she suggested they take the purchases back to the boot of the car before going to the restaurant for their fish tea.

Purchases deposited and fish restaurant found, they were sitting in one of the booths, discussing their day; and before long, their food arrived. Looking at the very large fish on the plate in front of her, Monica exclaimed, "I will never eat all of this. It's a whale!"

"Just do your best," Michael advised, looking askance at his own version of Moby Dick.

As it turned out, most of the meal was eaten, and before long, tired, full of food, and feeling very contented, they made their way home for a quiet night and perhaps a glass of wine or two. It always surprised Michael just how much they could talk about. It had come as a pleasant feeling that they had so much in common, and when he thought back to how it all started, he was astounded that two years on they were married and living in the same house—which reminded him he would need to finish removing his possessions from his house and find a suitable agent to look after the property and find a tenant.

It was just after nine thirty, and both were feeling sleepy after the sea air, exercise, and the amount of fish supper they had eaten. Monica was working starting at 10.00 a.m., and Michael not until three. He offered to get some supplies in, to which Monica agreed with alacrity. "Let's do a list over breakfast tomorrow," she said as they tidied up the glasses and popped them into the dishwasher.

They were just about to climb the stairs when there came a loud banging on the front door, and the doorbell rang insistently. They looked at each other in alarm, and with sudden clarity, they knew the suspect was Derek. The front and back door locks had been changed, and as a precaution, a safety chain had been installed.

Michael walked to the door advising Monica to stay out of sight until he established the identity of their late-night caller. Putting the safety chain in place, he opened the door the few inches the chain would allow. They had been correct. It was Derek, back for another round of harassment.

Michael slammed the door shut, and Monica picked up the phone to call the police. Derek could be heard on the other side calling out rude and obscene remarks, and they were getting quite alarmed at the state he was in. What was wrong with the man? Was he so controlling that he had to have his own way in every situation?

It took a while, but a patrol car arrived. Bundling Derek into the back of the patrol car, the police went to the door and asked to be allowed in to take a statement. Undoing the chain, the two frightened occupants first checked that their aggressor could not get into the house before allowing the officer access.

The more senior officer introduced them and, quoting his rank as sergeant, started to write down their statement.

Once all the doings of Derek were confined to the black book, the officers explained they would arrest him and he would remain in the holding cell to be put before the magistrate in the morning. They would be in touch to give them an update when available.

Sleep would elude them now as they watched the police car drive off with Derek in the back, staring out of the window with a look that could strike anyone down. He was a very unhappy man. Monica kept apologizing to her new husband for this appalling turn of events. Michael was quick to reassure her it was not her fault, saying, "We are in this together and for the long haul."

He then went on to explain that the reason he had never married was that when he realized his father had abandoned him, his sense of loss was acute. He hated school because of the continual teasing. But when his mother died, he was glad he had no wife or girlfriend, because he could not go through with loving somebody and then losing her. However, although this was still the case, as he explained, he could not help but be happy with his lifestyle choice, and he would take the chance at life, love, and happiness. The bad times they would weather together.

Monica, looking at Michael, saw the boy, and what had happened tonight just made it worse. She had decided long ago that this particular fly should stick to the wall, but no, she would have to confess.

Looking at Michael's handsome face full of concern, she quietly told him she needed to confess to him something that had happened a long time ago. If Michael was afraid of the outcome of Derek's visit, he was now absolutely terrified. "What can be so bad?" he asked with a distinct tremor in his voice.

"You were bullied at school," announced Monica, deciding not to sugar-coat anything and just get it out there.

"Yes," said Michael.

"Well, I was one of those bullies. I realized it very shortly after we started coming to the restaurant. Pamela was involved too. Apologizing doesn't come near to what should be done, but how can you ever forgive us?"

There was a long silence as Michael stared at her. "Do you have any more news I should know?" Michael asked in a rather flat tone of voice. Monica confirmed that she had no more secrets. Michael asked Monica for a whisky while he thought this through. Sipping quietly on his drink, he processed the information while Monica, sitting across the room, held her breath for the reaction.

Without warning of what was to come, Michael suddenly burst into laughter. Monica was puzzled. This was not what she had expected. Michael crossed the room, sat on the arm of Monica's chair, and took her hand gently. "Okay, you helped cause me a great deal of angst, but look at the plus side. I left school, went to college, and now am the head waiter in a smart establishment. If I had stayed on at school, there is every chance I might be on the unemployment list. No, what you did was not nice, but it's all turned out well. You and I might never have got together otherwise. Besides, I guessed that years ago!" With a twinkle in his eyes, he remarked, "Now, have we any more dark secrets?"

It was a few minutes before Monica realized that he was joking, and the temptation to slap him was overpowering. She kissed him instead. "Let's have some hot chocolate," suggested Monica.

They made hot chocolate with a serious measure of brandy and sat in the big, comfortable chairs in front of the unlit coal fire. It was symbolic of comfort. The central heating was on, so being cold was not an issue. Michael ran upstairs to switch on the electric blanket while retrieving a blanket which he placed round Monica's shoulders. "It's been a difficult evening," he said as she demurred. "You need to be warm."

Eventually, after consuming a second brandy they went to bed, and with their arms around each other, bringing comfort, they eventually fell asleep.

Chapter 45

While at the restaurant, Michael told Olivia all about the visit of Derek. Normally not easily perturbed, she was rather angry at what the newlywed couple were going through. If anyone deserved a peaceful life, they did, and the most annoying part was that she could not help. But she could listen, and she could give advice, both of which she did in spades. Michael, with a grin, also told her about Monica's confession. The two of them laughed uproariously, and Olivia said, "Wait a minute, didn't you know already?" Through the tears of laughter he could not show the night before, he nodded. The two of them burst into more laughter.

Sometime during the afternoon, Michael's phone rang upstairs—in his coat pocket, of course. He never carried it while he was working. But his ears worked well, and he just caught the tail end as he passed the staircase. He walked up to the staffroom, still a little weak on his leg, and retrieved his phone. He was dismayed to notice he had three missed calls, all from Monica. "Oh dear," he thought. "It must be important. Why, I wonder, did she not phone the restaurant?"

Calling her back and apologizing when the call connected, he asked her what the matter was.

"I have had the police on the phone with the update on that idiot I am happily no longer married to."

"Ah," said Michael. "What's happening then?"

"It would appear he caused a bit of a scene when they were processing his arrest, and they had to put him in the cells. Of course, this did not go down well at his bail hearing this morning. He is to be held on remand until his trial date. They are going to charge him with disturbing the peace, contravening a restraining order, ignoring a police warning, and assaulting a police officer."

"Assaulting a police officer?" queried Michael, the shock quite obvious in his voice. "Yes, he hit one of the officers when they tried to put him in a cell. He had been drinking."

Michael went silent, processing the information. *It is like a horror story*, he thought. He asked Monica whether they had given any indication what would happen to him. Monica resumed the story. "He will remain in the remand centre for approximately eight weeks; when he goes before the magistrate, the charges will be read out." Here her voice became doleful. "I am to appear as a witness, as are you. He is likely to get a custodial sentence. He may have gotten away with a fine or community service, but punching a policeman is just not the done thing." She laughed, her humour returning.

"Ah well," said Michael, "at least he is out of harm's way for the moment. Can we talk about it tonight? I need to get back on the house floor."

"Of course," she responded. "Speak later."

Olivia popped her head round the door and asked him whether all was okay. He gave her the outline of what was happening. She was pleased that it was settled for the moment and wished him well as she headed off home for the day.

Michael had noticed that Olivia was looking tired and did not have much energy. She was still coming in every day but for only a couple hours, and those were getting later and later; the young man they had recruited when Olivia was undergoing treatment was still coming in for three hours three times a week to do the books and keep on top of the administration. Olivia was happy with this, and her motive force was to see that her pride and joy was functioning well.

As the days lengthened and spring approached, Michael and Monica were looking forward to playing more golf. Every second Sunday, they were still enjoying a meal at his father's house. The rate of growth in the little one was, to Michael, quite amazing. He was getting more confident with her and would play and make funny faces as he helped her with her first steps. To everyone's delight, especially Michael's, Katrina called him "Mikee".

Fortunately for Michael, he had informed the police of his change

Michael, Waiting

of address. As he picked up the mail from the mat one day, an envelope reading "Police Scotland" caught his eye. It was a request for Michael to attend the court as witness to the accident which had almost killed him. He noticed an identical envelope addressed to Monica. *No prizes for guessing what that says*, thought Michael as he propped up the mail on the hall able and headed to the kitchen to put the coffee pot into action.

They were not looking forward to that ordeal. The upside was they were expected together on the same days; they were warned they may be required for at least a week. They arrived at the appointed day and time and were escorted to the witness room, not being allowed to sit in the courtroom, where they would most certainly have come into contact with the accused.

The trial lasted three days, and as the verdict of guilty of attempted murder was read out, the couple looked at each other with relief. It was all over, or so they hoped, and with a sentence of eight years, they were glad to see an end of the matter. "I hope this is the end and nothing else comes out of the woodwork," said Michael a trifle pessimistically.

"The police assured us they could account for all the gang," Monica interjected.

"Let's go to the Canny Man's for a drink," Michael suggested, and with Michael still having a few problems with his leg, they jumped a taxi outside the courthouse and headed to Morningside to have a well-deserved drink in their favourite watering hole.

"Just Derek to be dealt with now," said Monica when they were on their way home from the pub.

"Oh yes," said Michael, "I almost forgot. It's in two weeks, is it not? This one won't be quite so harrowing, but I am not looking forward to facing him across a courtroom."

In the end, they didn't need to go to court. Derek had been warned he would be most likely to receive a custodial sentence, and to try for a lesser sentence he pled guilty, avoiding a trial completely, to Monica's utter relief. However, taking the assault into account, he was given a six-month sentence with another restraining order of a mile for two years.

With all the legal trouble out of the way, the couple settled into a routine. Michael was still receiving physiotherapy for his leg, and it was improving almost daily. He was walking to work, but with the long hill to climb, he would take the bus home for the time being. Olivia, on the other hand, did not seem to be faring quite so well. She was very pale and starting to lose weight. She seemed very tired, and there was a niggling cough which troubled her from time to time.

Mike was sitting in his office at the Western General Hospital with a pile of case notes on his desk. It was administration day—a job he did not relish, but it had to be done. As he went through the notes, he recorded into a Dictaphone the next course of treatment or the next appointment, and these would be transcribed into letters to patients—with, of course, copies being sent to GPs. He always tried to speak clearly into his little machine, as typists have been known to misinterpret. All the typists had access to a medical dictionary so they could accurately spell the complicated medical jargon the consultants liked to use.

He recognized the name of Michael's employer when her file came across his desk. Previously he had not treated this lady, her consultant being one of his colleagues. The only experience or knowledge of this patient he had was what Michael had been able to tell him over the months. His colleague had now retired, and the case file fell to Mike. He decided he would read the whole file thoroughly and then invite her in to see him.

Olivia was a bit perturbed when she received a letter from the Western General Hospital, as she usually attended the ERI. The appointment was with a new consultant, and she very quickly realized that the new consultant was Michael's father. She did not know how she felt about it, but having only met him at the wedding, she decided to give him a try out. She considered maybe she could get some help with the cough which plagued her at times, and maybe she could be recommended a tonic to give her some energy. She realized the drugs would leave some residual effect, but she felt it would be nice if she could feel more like herself.

After what seemed like hours, feeling thoroughly prodded and poked, Olivia sat across the desk from Mr. MacGregor, her new consultant. So far, she was impressed. He was thorough and definitely knew what he was doing. Mike looked her in the eye and described what was happening. "I am fairly sure the cancer is starting to spread," he said sombrely. "I can't be sure of where at the moment, but it would appear the drug trial you participated in no longer has any efficacy."

Olivia asked the dreaded question: "Am I not going to get better?"

Mike looked at her and decided the truth would probably give this lady a chance to sort out her affairs. But he told her it was not doom and gloom yet. "I would like to run some tests and give you an MR.I scan."

"Seems serious," said Olivia, feeling rather unreal.

The next day, Olivia found herself in a taxi on its way to drop her off at the ERI. She had blanked the proceedings out of her mind so far. The bloodletting reminded her of the famous sketch by one of our talented comics who, when volunteering to give blood, protested at the amount, to be told, "It's only an armful." Olivia smiled at the memory and was surprised that she hadn't felt a thing, as her whole "armful" was placed into a plastic bag, labelled, and sent to the laboratory to be tested.

However, the MR.I was less pleasant. Not being particularly fond of enclosed spaces, she found the machine uncomfortable. It seemed to make a great deal of noise. Disembodied voices gave her instructions on where to move via her headset, and she was very relieved to finally be ejected from the scanner. She had been trapped in the machine for just over thirty minutes, but it had felt like two hours.

Sitting in the not-too-comfortable seats in the waiting area, Olivia tried to put everything out of her mind as she waited to see the consultant, as he had asked her to wait until he could study the scans and get the blood results. Olivia had been a little perplexed, as when she had attended clinics in the past—and there had been many—she had gone home immediately after and the results had come a week or two later. *Perhaps they are hoping for me not to fret too long*, she thought.

The nurse on duty came over to tell her that Mr. MacGregor would be about an hour yet, and perhaps Mr.s Black would care to go down to the ground floor to have a drink and maybe a sandwich if she was hungry. It was, after all, just after one o'clock, and she had been in the hospital since ten o'clock. *A coffee and a scone would be nice*, thought Olivia as she headed for the lifts.

It was not long after she returned to the outpatients' area, which she had been in previously, that the nurse called her name and escorted her to the consulting room. The nurse also came in and closed the door, first sliding the Engaged sign on the outside. Olivia could feel the butterflies in her stomach. This all seemed different to previous appointments, and her concern grew as she studied Michael's father across the desk.

He was still reading a file, presumably hers, when she entered, but he looked up, stood up, and walked round the desk to greet her. He motioned to a chair in front of the desk and sat down beside her, taking her by now cold and clammy hand.

Pretending not to notice, he began softly by explaining that the scan had shown up what he expected and the blood tests had confirmed the presence of secondary tumours in more organs than expected. He went on to explain that more of the main organs were affected, as were the bones in her spine. It was not good news, he told her. It was unlikely that she would survive more than a year, two at most, but he was willing to try a new drug in their armoury which might delay the process for perhaps another year, but there were no guarantees.

The look of horror on her face prompted the young nurse hovering near the door to come over and put her arms around the stricken woman, who promptly burst into tears. Tissues were produced, and not long after the outburst, Olivia composed herself, dried her eyes, and looked once more at the man whom Michael called Dad. "I don't think I will have any more drugs," she said. "They make me feel ill, and if, as you say, I have very little time, I would like to be able to enjoy what's left."

Mike intimated that he could give her strong painkillers and that she should take iron to keep some of the tiredness at bay, but he added that she must rest at least an hour in the morning and an hour in the afternoon to give her reserves if she had anything planned. He then promised her that Michael would not even know that she had been there and that any information regarding her illness would be what she told him. Thanking him, she turned and walked to the door. As the kind nurse opened it for her, she turned around and asked, "What comes next?"

Sitting in the taxi conveying her home, she had indicated it would be an all-day absence. She had already given up all thought of heading for the shops. As she went over in her mind what had transpired, she was quite sad. She had always thought she would live forever. Now what was she to do? "A year!" she shouted out loud, and the taxi driver glanced in his rear-view mirror.

Chapter 46

Olivia had a bad night. She was quite unable to sleep, and every so often the tears would run down her cheeks. Normally she was of a stoic nature, but this news had blown her away. Getting up at her usual time, she phoned Michael on his mobile to let him know she would not be in that day, as she had business to attend to, but would certainly be in the following day, when she would be in early afternoon. She asked whether Michael could come in a little earlier for a meeting. Michael agreed to this, and the call was abruptly terminated. He was sure there was something in the wind which was going to change the restaurant irrevocably, and he had a premonition of bad news.

Olivia showered and dressed. Promptly at 9.00 a.m., she telephoned her solicitor and asked to see him as soon as possible. A time for 11.00 a.m. was set, as the solicitor, having a cancellation and hearing the urgency in her voice, made sure he cleared his diary to see her at her convenience. He had been the family solicitor for a good while, having taken care of the affairs of three generations of Blacks, and was well-versed in their business.

Before she went out to meet her solicitor, she contacted her best friend and asked whether she had time for a coffee or lunch. Her friend, Moira, agreed to lunch, as she had been a bit housebound with a wicked head cold and had not really been out and about for a week or so. So that was set up. Olivia was looking forward to seeing Moira, as they had not met up for some time, what with all the to-and-froing of hospital visits and the time constraints on her friend, who often acted as babysitter to the grandchildren.

Little did Olivia know that the panic in her voice was giving away the urgency of the situation, and her friend quickly rearranged her diary to enable her to meet Olivia. There had been calls between the friends, and Moira was fairly well up to date with Olivia's illness; and now, with this call, she had a feeling there was news she didn't know about, and she was filled with foreboding.

Back at the hospital, Mike was rereading Olivia's case notes. Although nothing was mentioned, he knew that she knew who he was, and he had made assurances that no one would hear of the downturn in her health. He was checking the test results and consulting his textbooks, all the time looking for an alternative. He consulted with his colleagues and tried to see whether the situation could be helped. By six o'clock, having spent about three hours, he had to accept that nothing more could be done. Of course, he would ensure she had adequate painkilling medication and her needs would be attended to.

The following day, Michael arrived at the restaurant around 1.00 p.m. instead of his usual 3.00 p.m. He immediately went upstairs to her office, with the curious stares from his colleagues boring into his back as he mounted the stairs. He knocked and entered without waiting. He was getting better at not waiting to be allowed to enter. Olivia had made such a thing of it; he was doing what she asked.

He pulled up a chair opposite and looked at her grief-raddled face, his heart sank. Olivia went into the reason for the meeting immediately and told Michael the whole story. Mesmerized, he listened without interruption until she was finished. He knew better than to ask any questions, and when she finished, he looked at her and asked the simple question "What can I do to help?"

At that quiet response, Olivia nearly wept, but managing to control herself, she just said in a quiet voice, "Just be here for me, Michael." Before Michael left the room, she asked, "Would you do one thing for me?"

"Of course!" he replied.

"Will you tell the staff for me? I am just a bit fragile, and it would come better from you. You don't need to tell them the whole story, but they should know I am not going to get better and my appearances here will become less. I will rely on you, Michael, to keep all the plates spinning."

"You can depend on me, Olivia. I am so sorry this has come to pass, and if there is anything I can do, you must let me know."

Michael went through to the staffroom, leaving Olivia with her

Michael, Waiting

thoughts. He made himself a cup of tea to give himself time to absorb the information he had just been confronted with and to gird his loins for the meeting he would have and the difficult months ahead.

At around 3.00 p.m., he called the staff to the meeting in the staffroom. It was a Friday, and usually the restaurant was very busy on Fridays. All the staff except Peter were in, preparing for the evening rush. The restaurant was closed, as it was every afternoon, reopening at 5.00 p.m. Holding a meeting would not inconvenience the customers. This gave the staff time to prepare the tables and the kitchen staff to prep the food for the menu. Michael decided to give the news to Peter first before the meeting, thus giving the man his place as deputy.

Peter was visibly shocked but was able to hide his feelings as he went through the restaurant asking the remaining staff to meet in the staffroom in five minutes. It didn't take long to apprise the staff of the situation, and as they filed their way back down to the main restaurant, not a word was spoken, but the sorrow was palpable.

Michael was aware of the atmosphere in the restaurant was a little on the sombre side, and he took the waiting staff to one side during a lull and asked them to try cheering up for the sake of the customers, as they had no part in the sadness they were all feeling. Olivia was a popular employer, and they were taking the news badly.

They did their best, and when it was time to finish, they all pulled together to clear the tables and return the restaurant to its impeccable best. To Michael's delight, Monica was waiting up for him. She had got into the habit of sitting with him while he had a nightcap and listened to the day's news. She was horrified when she heard the update and hugged her husband to comfort him, as she knew how much Olivia meant to him. She would support him all she could.

A sudden thought came to Michael. What would happen to the restaurant? Would he lose his job? He was ashamed at his thoughts. His employer was having the last fight for her life, and all he could think about was his job. He was mortified.

He did, however, still have savings, and should he find himself unemployed, he would have sufficient funds to keep the pot on the boil for some time until he was able to find an alternative.

A couple of nightcaps later, the saddened couple went to bed, as it was getting late and Monica had an early rise. Monica had taken to going into work early most days to catch up with her workload while her colleagues chose a later start time. That way she could take a late start to meet up with Michael. As long as her boss knew when to expect her, it was no problem. He had also jumped into the new technology by leaving her a dictated message with instructions. It was proving a success, and both Monica and her boss were finding life a good deal better than before.

Monica's boss, David, was into his late fifties and had worked his way up in the financial world. More than once lately, he was delighted with the progress Monica had made in the last year since she had met and married Michael. She was softer in nature and more helpful. David was thankful it had not come to the end he had planned.

When Monica went off sick with depression, she was quite difficult to live with, and more than once David threatened her with a written warning.

When she took sick leave, the office was very peaceful, and although he was contemplating disciplinary action, he allowed her to return to her post on a part-time phased return, and now he was glad of her efficiency and new approach.

Michael was up early, finding sleep eluding him. Although his first thoughts were of the dire circumstances his employer found herself in and how sad it made him feel knowing their time together was ebbing away, in the corner of his mind was the knowledge he may well be out of a job—no, *the* job: one he had done for many years and was a job he loved. His mind went back to his accident and how kind everyone had been, especially when his future was uncertain.

He slipped his robe on and softly crept down the stairs. He put the coffee pot on and made some toast with butter and Monica's favourite, a soft-boiled egg. He prepared the tray, poured the coffee, and came back into the bedroom to find Monica struggling to sit up. She was delighted with the surprise and duly ate the breakfast Michael had made for a treat. It wasn't often he delivered such a surprise, Monica being the one who normally rose first. Thanking him profusely, she headed for the shower.

Monica didn't question the early rise and the breakfast on the tray. She was well aware that Michael had been unable to sleep, being concerned for his employer. She didn't mention the fact that he may not have a job the next year. It was too soon and too crass to job hunt at the moment. She would not encourage him to do such a thing. Besides, she had a glimmer of optimism that the restaurant would probably be sold, and she was sure a head waiter the calibre of Michael would be snapped up. However, this was not a subject to be brought out in the open.

Michael left a little later and arrived at the restaurant in plenty of time for the now habitual meeting, as Olivia liked to call it, at 11.00 a.m. The times Olivia wanted Michael in the restaurant were slowly changing. Olivia was looking at Michael now as more of a manager and wanted him in with her, and his shifts were much shorter except on really busy nights. She wanted Michael to have a more normal life after his accident so he would not be completely worn out. Secretly she wanted his company, and she had Michael training the staff to do his duties whenever possible.

It was noticed that Peter was excellent at polishing glasses; they sparkled when he did them. Sylvia was coming in daily from 2.00 p.m. until 8.00 p.m. and polishing the cutlery. With that done and the tables set, she was ready to take the first orders.

While Michael was off recovering, the light bites at lunchtime had gone by the board. Michael felt it was time to resurrect the practice and asked Ann whether she would take the responsibility of serving the soup and sandwiches normally offered at lunchtime.

A new sous trainee chef had joined the team while Michael was out of action and was now deemed capable of making soup and sandwiches. The other members of the team, Peter and Robert, had worked well and were gelling nicely. Michael had started to fervently hope he could impress a new owner, providing the restaurant was sold on, that the team were worth keeping on.

After his meeting with Monica, he went down into the restaurant and supervised the last-minute presentation of the tables. He checked that the coffee pot was clean and ready for use. His mind counted the bottles of spirits, as he did not want anyone going into the cellar during service. He made sure a few of the more popular red wines were placed strategically in a warmish part of the kitchen on a wine rack to ensure they were ready to be served at room temperature.

Michael was feeling much stronger, and with a little smile he thought to himself, "I'm back!" With his new hours, he was due to leave around

8.00 p.m., but it was busy and a few well-kent faces were sitting at reserved tables. He made sure the orders were taken, food delivered, and wine corked before he left. Tonight his deputy was Robert, and he was rather enjoying his new status. Michael noticed how much Robert had improved in the year he had been part of the team

While Olivia was still in reasonable health and able to keep coming into the restaurant, Michael decided to take Monica away for a holiday. He felt it had been too long since their magical honeymoon. He knew it may be some time before this could happen again, and Olivia did seem able to be left. However, he checked with his staff to find out whether they were prepared to take on the duties, bearing in mind Olivia would be in the background. None had any objections, and Michael broached the subject with Monica.

He suggested they make a trip to Toronto to visit her son and his family. At first she was reluctant, feeling that it would be an imposition, but Michael disagreed and suggested they stay in a hotel until Monica and her son were comfortable in each other's company. Derek had not helped the process, as if he ever would, by travelling over to see his son and spending the entire two weeks whining about Monica and how badly he had been treated.

Michael vehemently explained that the bridge had to be crossed sooner rather than later, and as her daughter-in-law was expecting a baby anytime soon, it would be a good reason to visit.

The last time they had spoken, it was not a friendly conversation, all down to the machinations of Derek. But they had a lovely Christmas card and a couple of soft wool sweaters together with the news of the impending arrival. At last, after lengthy conversations, Monica agreed to at least contact her son and try to arrange a visit. "Remember," said Michael, "It's to be a holiday staying in a hotel."

Monica, deciding to get the plans out into the open, picked up the telephone and chose the number to dial through to Toronto. Monica could feel the butterflies in her stomach. She felt this might be the last time she communicated, and it saddened her. The Canadian voice answered, announcing herself, and Monica did likewise.

"How are you keeping?" asked Monica of her pregnant daughter-in-law.

"Oh, I am doing okay," she replied. "Be glad to get this little person

Michael, Waiting

into the world so I can get a sleep," she remarked ruefully. "Anyway, enough about me; how are you doing? Congratulations on the wedding. I am sorry we could not come. His father was kind of definite we not attend. You must have a reason to call; you want to tell me?"

Monica started to explain that she would like to come over and visit once the new baby was born so she could meet her grandchild. However, what would be more important would be to be able to make peace with her only son. She could not understand what had caused the rift. She could not understand why he was holding this against her, and she felt now that perhaps as some time had elapsed and her ex-husband had been behaving in ways that had led him to prison, it would be a good time to visit.

Monica finished her story and, waiting for a response, heard only silence, which unnerved her. "Of course, if this is not a good time, then of course I won't come. I had hoped to bring my new husband to meet you, but I think this is very bad timing … and perhaps you can tell my son I love him and I hope one day he will forgive me."

She gently replaced the receiver, the tears forming in her eyes and slowly running down her cheeks. "I thought it wouldn't work," sobbed Monica. "What can I do?"

"Well, firstly we will find another holiday destination, and secondly you will go and sit in your chair while I pour us a G and T; then I will cook you a meal. How does mince and potatoes sound?"

Lovely, she said, and she wandered over to her chair as instructed.

She lay back in the chair and closed her eyes, thinking how much she loved him and wishing his idea, which was dearly meant, had been more fruitful. The G and T arrived complete with lemon and the clink of the ice. Monica nearly dropped the glass when the phone, quite unexpectedly, started to ring.

Monica reached for the phone, but Michael reached it first. He was going to try to keep Monica calm, and he suspected the caller was in Toronto—most probably her son, and very likely about to pick a fight. He answered, "Michael MacGregor."

"Well hello, Michael, it's Merlene in Toronto. I have a husband who is keen to speak to his mother. Is she around?" Michael asked whether she could reassure him that Jordan would be kind to her, as she was very upset already and he didn't want her to have her any more upset.

"It's okay," said Merlene. "It's fine ... actually better than fine." "Thank you," said Michael. "She is just here."

"Let me speak to her first," said Merlene.

Michael passed the phone to Monica, who answered guardedly. "Monica!" exclaimed Merlene. "Sorry to beat you up with this. You gave me a bit of a shock, and I couldn't think straight. Please take my apology; it's genuine."

"Apology accepted," Monica said graciously, and Merlene passed the phone to her husband, who was waiting on tenterhooks to speak to his mother for the first time since they terminated their last conversation in anger.

A few hasty explanations as to the nature of the break-up left Jordan in a state of shock and confusion as Monica elaborated on the secretary, the walkout, the subsequent recriminations, the court case, and, finally, the violence.

Jordan was flabbergasted as he proceeded to tell his mother the story according to Derek, who had made it all out to be her fault. He's said that she had found someone else and had thrown him out of the house. Well, she had found someone else, but Derek's timeline was a bit out of sync with the events.

Jordan, contrite at not having given his mother the benefit of the doubt and let her explain her side of the story, was full of apologies and added, for good measure, his delight at the prospect of a visit. They discussed the best dates, and since the expectant mother was due around May, the best time for a visit would be mid-June.

Merlene's mother was coming up from her home in Illinois before the baby was born and would take up the reins until Monica could get over and help. Monica had suggested the middle to the end of June to let the other grandparent meet the new arrival before two grandparents fought over possession. The conversation ended on a happy note, and Monica promised to call as soon as a suitable flight could be booked. Merlene insisted they stay with them. Bidding her son goodnight, she made sure he passed their best wishes to Merlene in the last third of her pregnancy.

Monica vowed she would have a better conversation with her daughter-in-law during the next call. She would call as often as she could.

The call finished, with a broad grin Monica threw herself into her

Michael, Waiting

husband's arms, delighted with the outcome of the conversation but quite angry that her ex-husband had tried to make her out to be the guilty party.

Meanwhile, across the Atlantic, a similar conversation was taking place between Merlene and Jordan. "Oh, I forgot to tell your mom we got the result of the gender scan," she said as she reached for the phone. Jordan gently held her hand and asked Merlene to keep it a secret for now, as his mother would love the surprise. "Okay," said Merlene. "It's just that I am so excited I want to tell the world."

"I know," responded Jordan. "Just a few more weeks."

Monica had opened up her computer and searched for flights to Canada and Toronto specifically. First of all, she looked under specific airlines, thinking it would require a scheduled flight, and she was expecting an expensive flight. One of the sites jumped her to a flight for which a ticket, if she shifted her dates slightly, could be purchased for less than £500 return, departing on 15 June and arriving on 28 June. "Michael, that's perfect. Shall we just book it?" said a very excited grandmother.

"Let's do it tomorrow," said Michael. "I would really like to run it past Olivia. I don't think it will be a problem, but I owe her the courtesy."

Monica understood completely. The two of them poured a nightcap and chatted excitedly at the thought of the upcoming trip. Michael was even getting excited at meeting the babies, as he had developed some expertise with his little niece Katrina.

The following day found Michael in Olivia's office, requesting permission to take two weeks off to go with Monica to Canada to visit her son and daughter-in-law. At almost the same time, Monica was doing the same with her employer. Michael, much to his surprise, as well as getting permission, was also offered the aeroplane tickets as a belated wedding present from Olivia. Michael, stunned, was all aflutter. That is extremely generous, he stuttered, and proceeded to tell her about the flights they had sourced. Putting her hand up to stop him in his tracks, said she would take care of it.

She had a friend who owned an airline and specialized in flights to Canada. She would get him to arrange the trip—well, his secretary would—and she wrote down the dates, shooing him away.

Michael decided not to tell Monica until it was nearer the time, but it was only four weeks away. "I bet Monica takes me on another shopping trip," he said ruefully. Sure enough, the next Sunday found them in Jenners.

A couple of days before the flight, a messenger arrived with a flight wallet displaying the tour company, and as he required a signature, he was shown up to Olivia's office. Michael was getting concerned when he talked to Olivia. She was looking very pale and looked as though she had lost weight. A cold shiver ran down his spine, and his reaction was to postpone the trip. However, Olivia declined his offer, saying she was getting over a flu-type bug and would be her old self in a week or so. "Besides," she said, "it's only two weeks, and Monica will be desperate to see her grandchildren."

They had been given the fabulous news the week before that Merlene had produced not only one baby daughter but two. The well-kept secret was out. Jordan and Merlene had produced identical twins, and because of their Scottish roots, they were to be named Iona and Skye.

Monica and Michael were at the security gates and were a bit confused as there were people everywhere. As they were about to join the lengthening queue, a security guard stepped up and asked to see their paperwork. On inspection of the boarding passes and passport, they were asked to follow the guard, and he took them down a side alley where they placed their hand luggage on the belt, and they were escorted through the X-ray machine and out into the crowds to head for their boarding gate.

They were given a free pass to the executive lounge, and they were soon sitting in the comfortable area, sipping champagne and nibbling on a few tempting bites. Crackers and cheese were their favourites, and before long they were heading for the boarding gate, as the flight had been called. It was raining quite heavily at the moment, but to Moira's delight they would board the plane through the tunnel which snaked all the way from the desk to the plane. "Not a drop of rain," Monica enthused, and she held out their tickets to the cabin staff at the end of the tunnel. As they showed the smartly dressed steward their tickets, to their surprise, they found themselves being guided to the front of the plane into first class and shown to their seats.

Olivia had done them proud. They would travel in comfort for the nine hours they would be in the air. The seats were wide and only two to a row. They had risen early, as the take-off time was 8.00 a.m., and the prospect of having a sleep in comfort on the plane was very pleasing. Also, as they discovered, all the food and drinks were complimentary. The white linen napkins and polished cutlery reminded Michael of the standards he strove to achieve in the restaurant.

Thinking of his workplace and the turmoil of a very sick Olivia, he was reminded of their last conversation before travelling to meet Monica's son—a conversation he had not shared with Monica yet. She was all excited about seeing her son, his wife, and their three little grandchildren. Michael was, in fact, a little nervous. However, since being with Monica, he had become less reserved and was finding meeting new people a little easier. Still, he did not understand why Olivia would ask him to promise not to look for another job. She explained there would always be a place for him at Dhugall. "How can you guarantee that?" Michael had asked. He was so afraid of losing his job, but Olivia reassured him he came as part of the package going to the next owner.

Somewhat happier, Michael was still not convinced this could be successful, but he made the promise, and he would keep it, and for the next three weeks he would enjoy the company of Monica's grandchildren and get to know Merlene and Jordan.

Having thoroughly enjoyed their first-class flight, they were delighted to see Jordan waving excitedly as he waited for them to appear in Arrivals. Michael assumed it was Jordan, as he waved frantically to Monica, who was waving frantically back. Michael looked at his wife fondly, and a flashback to how they had met ran through his mind. Just as he had become more self-assured, so had Monica become softer and warmer. He had never felt as happy as he did now, and it would have been perfect if only Olivia would get better.

Arriving at the seven-seater Buick, Michael was astonished at the vehicle. Jordan picked up on Michael's astonishment and explained they had changed the car when they knew the twins were on the way. With this model, they could get a row of car seats and still have room for passengers. "So, Mike, you and Mum will all get in the vehicle with the babies and us when we go off sightseeing." Monica, sensing the sharp intake of breath at the derivative he'd used, explained that he always answered to Michael; Mike was his father, and he was Michael, and it had been so since he was born.

Monica was familiar with the metropolis, having visited Jordan three times now, but Michael gazed in awe as the city came into view. He was captivated with the all the tall buildings. Jordan, sensing the excitement, pointed out the CN Tower, which had a glass floor and a revolving restaurant. He promised to take them both to lunch there during their visit.

The house was a ranch style with a neat front garden and a much larger garden at the back. A swing was already erected for the older daughter, Ailsa, age three—just the right age for the swing set in the garden. It was a beautiful house with wooden floors and large patio doors leading out to the garden. All on one floor, there was a large lounge area with a dining room off to the side. The four bedrooms ensured the house would always be well accommodated. Monica was, like Michael, a stranger to the house, as the young couple had traded their previous accommodation to the larger house when it was confirmed twins were expected.

They were shown to the room they would use, and to Monica's delight, the room was furnished with a large bed and an en suite shower room. Merlene laughed and showed Monica the other three bedrooms, two with shower rooms and the master bedroom sporting a full-sized bathroom.

The couple were extremely impressed with the house, and when Jordan took Michael down to the basement, he was astonished. A very large television and a small bar were the first things Michael spotted. Around the corner was a full-sized pool table. Sofas and a chair were scattered round the room, and a refrigerator was keeping the stocks of beer cool. "This is my playroom," Jordan said with a grin. "We call it a man cave. I expect I may have to change the layout once the girls get bigger." Meanwhile Michael was thinking how well the young couple must have been doing to be able to afford the lifestyle they obviously enjoyed.

Thankful for the first-class seats and the sleep they were able to have on the plane, they quickly unpacked and rushed downstairs to meet the girls. Ailsa was a bit shy at first. She did not remember having met this grandma before, but she soon got braver as the new toys were revealed. Grandma had been shopping. Merlene introduced Michael to the pretty three-year-old as Grandad, explaining that a grandchild could never have enough grandparents. As her own father had died some years ago, that left only Derek, who up till now had not shown any interest. "Being in prison won't help," remarked Jordan. Of course, they had not been aware of Jordan's father's behaviour, which had resulted in him being jailed. Meanwhile, Jordan was furious at his father's behaviour.

Michael entertained his new grandchild, and Merlene took Monica to the nursery, which was close to the kitchen. The small new Iona and Skye were wailing loudly, as it was food time. Jordan asked Michael whether he was happy entertaining the new grandchild, as the young couple had found it much easier to feed them both together. Michael laughed and took small Ailsa out into the garden so he could be shown round and see all the pretty flowers. However, the swing seemed to attract the most attention, and a very tired grandfather and exuberant toddler returned to the house, needing sustenance.

Merlene explained that on such a beautiful day they would most probably fire up the barbecue, but now Ailsa was getting bigger and into everything, Merlene would cook indoors but eat at the picnic table.

It seemed no time at all before the food arrived on the table, complete with a large pitcher of lemonade. "The gin and tonics will come later," said Merlene, smiling and giving a wink. The feast of ribs, burgers, hot dogs, and chicken legs was accompanied by a large bowl of salad and baked potatoes. Monica was impressed with her daughter-in-law's culinary prowess and had a fleeting thought of just how much weight Michael would put on eating like this every night.

Monica helped Merlene to clear up while Jordan prepared Ailsa for bed, the twins being asleep for the moment. Once all the little ones were asleep, the grown-ups could relax. They all sat round in the big plush armchairs, and the story-swapping began. First, abject apologies came from Jordan for having taken his father's explanation as gospel. Had he known the true facts, he could have been a support rather than a hindrance, but he was delighted to have them out for a visit and pleased to meet his new father-in-law.

However, on a more serious note, he did have news which was a mixed blessing, but he knew it would not be popular. The bank he was seconded to had increased its staffing, and they had requested Jordan come on board as a permanent employee. The salary that went with the job was an eyewatering increase, and he had accepted the post.

Trying not to show her disappointment, she congratulated her son.

All at once, the new babies; the large, smart house; and the larger vehicle all came into place, and she couldn't help but be proud of her son and the progress he had made. Besides, it was someplace nice to come and visit, watching the girls grow.

The days in Toronto were really enjoyable. As it was spring, the gardens and parks were full of colour, and the cherry trees were spreading their flowers like pink-and-white snow. Michael, this being his first time in Canada, was entranced, particularly during his visit to the restaurant at the top of the CN Tower. Monica mostly enjoyed the trip to High Park, where they were able to visit the extensive gardens and the many facilities there. They went to a playground at which Ailsa had a lot of fun, followed by a trip to the Zoo.

The highlight was when they all set off early and drove to Niagara Falls and were able to see the magnificent spectacle. They had brought a picnic, as Merlene was uncomfortable taking three small children into a restaurant and six-week-old twins were hard for most places to accommodate. It was nearly dark when they set off back to their home, and happily the girls slept the whole way. Takeaway food was produced at home from the local pizzeria, and fed and happy, the grown-ups reminisced about the day.

All too soon, it was time to pack and get ready for the flight home. Saying goodbye was difficult. They had a marvellous time, and a very special rapport was in place with small Ailsa. The twins were yet too young to enjoy their grandparents, but an invitation was extended, and promises made. The happy Monica and Michael would return next year, and in the meantime, perhaps a few live calls via the Internet would keep the memory flowing.

To their delight, their seats were once again in first class, and although they had left Toronto at lunchtime, it would be early morning in Edinburgh when they landed. They would try to catch up on sleep on the plane.

Later on in the evening, back at the house, Michael groaned with the tiredness, complaining, "Is this what jet lag is all about?"

"Just let's get to bed and get some sleep," Monica said masterfully.

"But it's only eight thirty," whined Michael. "I will be awake before dawn."

"You will soon be back in sync with your body clock," said an unsympathetic

Monica.

Sure enough, as Monica woke way too early and found the other side of the bed empty, she went downstairs to see a woebegone Michael drinking tea and complaining he couldn't sleep. In fact, it took the couple nearly a week to change their body clock rhythm. In the meantime, work had to be dealt with. They had the day after their return, but soon it was time for business as usual. Michael had decided to go into the restaurant early and turned up at 10.00 a.m. to catch up on the news.

Chapter 47

The place was very quiet, and going upstairs, Michael discovered Olivia was not in the building. He approached Peter, who was on duty, asking where he could find her. Peter answered saying that she had been coming in less and less, and that today she'd had an appointment with the clinic. Michael felt the cold hand of fear run down his back, instinctively realizing that time was running out.

He called her on her mobile, as he was mostly certain there was no clinical appointment. As he had guessed, she answered and admitted to being at home. Michael put his coat back on and asked Peter to cover for a while longer. Michael jumped into a cab which took him to Olivia's house, where the door was answered by her friend.

On entering the house, Michael was directed upstairs to Olivia's bedroom. He was shocked at her deterioration in the two short weeks since he'd last seen her. Olivia in a weak voice said, "Michael, you are back. How was the trip?" Michael responded first by saying how wonderful it was and then thanked her profusely for her hand in the travel arrangements.

She replied that it had been a pleasure and that she was glad she had been able to hear about it personally. Michael knew better than to quiz her on her health and just accepted that the deterioration was a result of Olivia's time shortening. It broke his heart. They chatted for about an hour, with Olivia bringing him up to speed.

Olivia informed Michael she would not be back at the restaurant. She was due to go into St Columbus Hospice next week, where she would be looked after with dignity. She did somewhat feebly suggest Michael not visit, but that was not going to be an option. Michael was fully committed

Michael, Waiting

to being there for this lovely lady who had treated him like a son and was leaving this earth far too early.

Michael and Monica discussed the situation and decided that he would get to the restaurant early for opening before visiting Olivia mid-morning and would then turn up for work around two. However, it was a given that he would be with her when the time came.

The ambulance arrived at the appointed time, and Olivia was settled into her new accommodation. She had a view out of the windows, and as the daffodils were dying off, the tulips were starting to bloom. The hospice was clean and comfy. Flowers on the windowsill gave out a lovely perfume. Looking out of the window, she could see shrubs and flowers, and she spent most of her day gazing fondly into the gardens. After a few days, Olivia experienced a sense of peace, and she felt she was ready. The staff realized that Olivia was running out of time, and Michael was sent for.

Holding her hand, he talked a bit about times shared and how well they had worked to make Dhugall a success. He sat with her through the day and into the night, now just holding hands. The doctor came into her room and checked her vital statistics. He turned to Michael and said it would not be long. Olivia by now had lapsed into unconsciousness, and her breathing was very slow.

About an hour later, Michael came out of the room, to be replaced by the nursing staff. It was all over, and Michael was stunned. It had all seemed so quick. A nurse brought him a cup of tea as he sat taking in what had happened. The senior nurse asked him whether he would return to collect her belongings and death certificate so he would be able to arrange the funeral.

It was the middle of the night, and there was nothing left to do but go home and return the next day. Once it was a respectable time, he telephoned the staff to tell them the news and close the restaurant for now. It would remain closed until after the funeral. *Then it will have to be sold*, thought Michael.

He went to the hospice and collected her belongings, which were very few. She had been there for only a couple of days. The death certificate and a letter addressed to Michael was with her possessions. He looked at the white envelope with Olivia's well-known scrawled handwriting, and it filled him with dread. It just didn't seem right to get correspondence from someone who had just died. He put it in his pocket, thinking he would read it later. But then a thought struck him. Maybe it was funeral instructions or even restaurant instructions. Michael did not want to open the envelope in full view of the staff. He was in danger of breaking down, and he needed privacy. He went home. He was disappointed that Monica was not at home or, indeed, able to communicate, as she was in a big budget meeting.

Deciding to return to the restaurant, he thought perhaps he should have a look at the paperwork and hopefully find out where to go next.

Making a cup of coffee back at the restaurant, Michael finally plucked up courage and opened the envelope. He pulled out a sheet of paper covered in Olivia's scrawl.

Dear Michael,

I am sorry we have had to part company so soon. I had great hopes for our team to flourish, but alas, I am to be denied this. I have made provision for Dhugall, and my funeral instructions are with my lawyer down in the New Town. Ask to speak to Allan Bainbridge. He will take care of everything. Good luck for the future.

Love, Olivia

Michael could feel the tears, and for the first time in many years, he let them flow.

Printed and bound by CPI Group (UK) Ltd, Croydon, CR0 4YY